The Broken Fiddle

ISBN 9781534610248

Dedication

For Mary, my soul-mate

Acknowledgements

This novel began its life as a musical drama, a school show which shaped itself around the talents and ideas of the students, their inspirational teacher/producer, Janet Loughery, and the unique talents of their-loved history teacher, George Dallas. Thank you to all those in Limavady High School who believed in the story and gave it early 'legs'.
I have drawn on many sources of information in developing the story; the documentary ones are listed below but the human ones were far more significant. Thanks, therefore, to the many friends and casual acquaintances who have shared personal stories about the era of the hiring fairs, including Gerry Moore, Gearoid Mooney and his mother, Kitty, and Sam Fleming, a gentleman I came across one night in a Bushmills pub who generously shared his mother's story with me. Thanks also to my late father, Bobby Dunlop, a traditional fiddler himself, who would have been two years old in the year this story is set and who would have been delighted with the idea of a fiddle being the central motif in this my second novel.
I wish to acknowledge the assistance provided by the staff of the Newspaper Archives of both the Belfast Central and the Linenhall Libraries.
I am thankful to Canon Harry Trimble and Councillor James Emery from Castlederg who were an immense help, both in terms of providing historical detail about the area and in checking that my version of Ulster Scots dialect was in keeping with that in west Tyrone.
My good friends, Dónall and Máire Mac Ruairí, provided expert advice regarding the use of Irish in the unique Ulster dialect and, indeed, the English idiom of the people of the Rosses which draws so richly from their Gaelic origins; thank-you for that and for the many other insights and pieces of advice and encouragement.
I have invited a number of friends and fellow writers to critique the novel at various times during its development. Thank you to the following; Jim Simpson, Julia Carroll, Mildred Poots, Mervyn Dunlop and former-pupils, Laura Douglas and Connor Richmond. Connor, in particular, has engaged in this project with great interest, seeing its potential for screenplay; I value this input immensely.
Thank you to a wonderful young Gweedore fiddler, Megan McGinley, whose image graces the front of the book and whose tunes adorn the book's promotional video which is available on my Vimeo stream. The

beautiful painting, 'If I stay' is by David McDowell, another former student, now a professional artist; David also played a role as cover design consultant; many thanks to him.

My son Conall has once again been responsible for transferring the novel into eBook format and inserting audio tracks of some wonderful traditional Irish tunes.

Finally, my deepest thanks to Mary, my patient wife, who has not only supported me in the writing and publishing process but has also been my editor, critic, encourager and inspiration...as always.

Documentary Sources

A History of Northern Ireland Thomas Hennessey, St Martin's Press 1999
Castlederg and its Red River Valley James Emery & Harold Trimble, 2005
Hiring Fairs and Market Places May Blair, Appletree Press 2007
Men That God Made Mad; A Journey Through Truth, Myth and Terror in Northern Ireland Derek Lundy, Vintage 2010
That Old Sinner Frank Sweeney, Irish History Press 2006
The 'Auxies', 'Black and Tans' and the RIC and their response to IRA Violence in Ireland 1919-1921 W H Kautt, www.academia.edu 2003
The Outrages 1920-1922 Pearse Lawlor, Mercier History 2011
The Story of the Rosses Ben O'Donnell, Caoran 1999

Newspapers from 1922
The Belfast Telegraph
The Derry Journal
The Irish News and Belfast Morning News
The Northern Constitution
The Northern Whig

The Broken Fiddle

Prologue

1945

Sally Anne Sweeney

I will write to him this night.

It lies heavy on me to do this and I should not put it off any longer. I must write, even after so much time has gone with the tide.

The old ones would always be telling us that time flies. "The older you get, the quicker it goes," they used to say. All too true, but they did not advise us what to be doing with this wisdom or how to be slowing it all up, did they?

I have the urge to write, maybe as much for me as for him. It is as if I need a way of drawing a line at the foot of this chapter of my life, before I turn the page on it and leave it all behind, for leave it behind I must...and with the help of God, I will. It has been a dark passage, although it began so brightly, and it has dragged itself out for too many sour years.

I sometimes think to myself that I was a different person back then; I feel now, on the threshold of this new journey as I am, that I am looking back on a person I read about in a book; a different person, someone else altogether whose story I have heard, heard in wonderment. If I was to tell the story of that night, of those weeks and months, if I was to tell it to a stranger, to anyone, would they be thinking that it is something I made up? My own strange, sad little fantasy? I think some of them would.

Over twenty years! And yet I remember it, every last detail of it, like it was yesterday. Does that seem a contradiction to you, for it does to me? The person I was then, young and fanciful, so long gone. The flowing fair hair now weathered out to a thin covering of greying thatch. The wrinkles that mock me from the mirror where there used to be dimples; (well that is what he used to tell me anyway; he would try to make me laugh just so he could see them, so he said. The white mouth on him!) Aye, and my figure away to pot altogether. Still fairly thin, mind you, but hanging round myself here and there like a sack of rabbits. Ah well, I will just have to make the best of it in whatever time I have left on the upper side of the sod. At the same time I cannot help wishing that I could be seen again as I was that year, the year I turned nineteen, the year I went to work among the bushes in Tyrone, before.... before everything changed.

I sometimes be asking the question, 'Is that how it was meant to be? Was it all written in the great poem of my life, as we say in my tongue? Indeed in all of our lives, the three of us? A road that we just stumbled blindly along until the bitter end?'

I have often wondered about that over the years. Did we have a choice, any of us? What if... what if I had been quicker that night? What if there had been no moon? Could it all have ended so differently, maybe even ended warmly, happily, for the three of us? Did our choices bring it all crashing down into disaster? Is it that we were each in some way responsible?

This is what I would love to have the chance to ask him. Maybe I will, when I write. I will certainly want to know if he can excuse my part in it, if he thinks that way about it. I am dying to know, even after all these years, if he wants to ask me for forgiveness. Is that selfish of me? Maybe I am just simple-minded; too innocent, would you say? Is it too much to ask? Given what happened to him, was my broken heart a pitiful sentence in comparison?

I wonder is he still so high and mighty of himself? How does he think about me? Still the poor wee deluded maid from Donegal... if he remembers me at all? What thoughts does he have about that summer? Does he think of it in the same way as me? The same detail? He will have had his own way of looking at it, and he is entitled to that, but I am just curious to know... if we were to meet again and talk about it, how much would we agree on? Maybe not a lot.

The events of that night changed the path of my life. How does he think it changed his? It did, of-course… changed it drastically I am sure, although I have never heard the detail of it.

The big *'mortasach'* that he was; so big-headed. So stubborn and stuck-up, always thinking so highly of himself and, at the same time, so vulnerable, so changeable. He bent like a reed to whatever way the breeze was blowing. I remember that frailty in him, for all the grand build of him, right from the very first time I set eyes on him. Yes, and I

do remember that exact moment when I first saw him in the hiring fair in Strabane. My eye noticed him and my heart shone for him right from the start. It was like a moth to a flame. No matter what way I tried to look, within seconds I was staring back at him, like as if he had just descended from a picture-book of our great warriors and heroes.
Some hero! Ah, that is not fair now. I have a right sprinkling of grand memories of that six months; over the years I have often returned to them, dusted them down for a good long look, then put them back on the shelf. Joining me on the shelf, I often be thinking.
I wonder did he ever marry. I am supposing that he did. As I recall, there were certainly enough pretty lassies running after him in my time there, so, if he did not, it would not be for the want of options. But then, after what happened, maybe his bronze was tarnished a bit. Or, given the way they seem to think over there, maybe in some people's book it had a brighter sheen off it, you never know. He certainly had drawn himself a reputation.
I wonder did he have any children? Any son to pass the place on to, like his mother was dreaming of? Maybe a whole brood of them are running around Lismore by this stage. Far too late for me of-course, now that I have turned the forty... even if I did have a man.
Isn't it funny how a sudden smell can bring it all back. Smells over there were that bit different from around here. Even simple, every-day things like a whiff of turf-smoke in the air of an autumn morning. Rosses turf burns with a sweeter scent than what they burn in Tyrone. More like the smell of pipe tobacco. Some people would not believe me on this point but I have a decent sense of smell and I know I am right on it. Tyrone turf seemed sharp to the nose, I have always felt; as if it held tight to a bitterness about how it was laid down all those years ago; cruelly, against its will. You get the same smell in parts of the east of Donegal and when I get the scent of it in my nose I am right back in Henderson's street, in Nineteen Twenty Two. Same thing when I smell a field of ripe oats, or especially when the corn is a-cutting. It takes me back. I can still see the shape of him so proud and manly behind his horses and them straining every sinew to pull his shiny, new binder through the tall golden stalks. And the clatter of it, and him shouting at the animals and laughing with Joe at the pleasure of it all on a brassy September evening.
Smells and sounds. For some reason when I hear the sound of doves it takes me back to my attic room in the farmhouse. They used to coo in

the big beech trees along the lane outside my window, mainly in the morning. I always thought it sounded like the muffled conversation you would hear coming from the confessional. When I told Matthew that he was not best pleased.

"Don't be bringing your Roman notions into this house," he said.

I remember wondering what he meant by 'Roman notions', and why at times he seemed to have no sense of humour at him. Other times he would be pulling my leg and as jolly as the next one.

Just the odd time, over the years since, I would have heard an English accent, maybe a fisherman looking for Dunlewy Lough or the Crolly River, and the way he would be pronouncing things would remind me of that Englishman I met back then. Aye, and I wish I had never 'had the pleasure', for he had his own share of the blame for what happened.

Or if I hear a shotgun go off up behind on the hill. Some fellow shooting rabbits, innocent in itself but enough to freeze me to the kitchen floor for a second.

But above all there is 'our tune'! How can such a beautiful piece of music stab such burning pain into my very soul? I seldom hear it played now but when I do, it is as much as I can do not to cover my ears with my hands to block it out. Why? How can a bundle of notes strung together in one particular order raise such hurt in me? I used to love it, used to love that he would always bc asking me to play it.

"Play us a tune," he would say of a quiet evening. That soft Tyrone accent. That strange way of talking he had, with words for things that I had never heard of before. The English I had at me back then was not the best but the language he had itself was far from what I had been taught in *Scoil Náisiúnta Mhullaghdubh*.

"Play us the wan aboot the boul Eleanor woman!"

Now? Now I would break my old fiddle in two rather than contaminate it with that melody. Agh, sure it is not the tune's fault. It is just that I will forever associate it with that time of my disappointment. My disappointment? My humiliation, more like.

Aye, you are right; I should be able to forget about it but I suppose I am the kind of woman who is forever chasing the times that were. That night changed me and chained me for all these years. Well.... not just that night, if the truth be told. The whole summer before it did too. I often wonder if that is the real reason I have hidden away in my mother's house in Ranahuel ever since, never went out to dances, never courted, let alone married. And people thought I was just doing the decent thing, looking after Mammy, being her voice after Daddy passed, God rest him, keeping her safe when she started to lose her wits. Just doing my duty, they thought. That and having the privacy to nurse the festering scars that I cherished as the marks of who I was in the heart of me and where I had been in the wanderings of my little life.

I remember going to one dance after I came home. In Annagary it was. I had to flee the hall half way through. Every fellow I saw was him. Every face that looked at me I would just look back at for a few seconds before it blurred and its features would curdle into those of Mister Matthew Henderson. It nearly put me away in the head till I got out of there and ran all the way home through the fog of my tears. Rejection ran beside me like a moon-shadow. I found it very hard to step away from that darkness.

I find it so strange to think of the circumstances that have freed me from my confinement so that now, at long last, I can make the decision to start a new life in America.

It was the returning of our Mairead from Glasgow last year that gave me the chance, all because her man had taken to the drink and left her, or she him, whatever way round it was. So now she can take her turn at hiding from the parish and nursing her hurt and nursing our Mammy at the same time. And I am free to go and see what Boston has to offer me. You only have the one go at this life and I am determined to try to make the best of the rest of mine. A happy-ever-after ending, I am hoping, but only after I have had to carry the heavy load of life for a good while first.

I should not be complaining. They were tough times in the Twenties, like they are tough times now. A different kind of tough back then. All those burnings and shootings and bombings. Some terrible deeds were committed, on both sides. Irishmen against Irishmen. Irishmen against Irishmen who did not agree that that is what they were, Irishmen, and clung instead to their Britishness, like a child to his drunken father's leg. And now both kinds of Irishmen have been away fighting yet another war against those same Germans like they did thirty years ago. If history was meant to be a lesson, it seems to me that nobody was paying much notice. Our own parish was devastated by the loss of nineteen young men a couple of years ago and they just playing about in the sea. We are Ireland. We are a neutral country. Unfortunately nobody told that to the German mine that those boys pulled up onto the rocks over on the Ballymanus shore. If that is what it was, a German mine. Nobody ever proved that, one way or the other, did they?

I wonder did Matthew go to fight in this last war, like his father before him in the first one? If he did he might even be dead too by now. Maybe there is no point in me writing him a letter. He will probably never get it. And if he does, what will he think of me?

What does it matter what he thinks of me anyway? I am not writing it for him. Just writing it to him. He can think what he likes. He always did.

I have to say what I have to say and let it rest there.

Chapter 1

Sally Anne Sweeney

Why I went to be hired

It was very plain to me. I had to go. Somebody needed to be making a pound or two for us to stay alive, to have food on our table and clothes on our backs.

I was eighteen and eager, just what you would know. I had never been hired, never even been to one of those hiring fairs that everybody else seemed to be so well up on. I thought I had heard everything there was to hear about them, mainly from my uncle Johnny. He had spent his younger days going to fairs, getting himself hired to a lot of different farmers in the Laggan and beyond.

My father was not keen for me to be going though.

"You will not stand in the way of the girls going to the hiring surely?" Johnny had said to him.

"I would not be on for it," was always Daddy's answer.

Then he would rhyme off his usual set of objections.

"It is far harder for girls, far more risks to it. You never know what sort of people they would get in with. Some of the stories that you hear from ones that have been over there would put the hair standing on you. Young ones coming back half starved, after having to live with little more food than the animals they were feeding. Sleeping on a hard floor in a draughty barn with the rats running over them. Getting slapped and punched by some divil of a farmer when he took the notion; money docked off their wage for no reason at all. Having to work on through sickness, six o'clock in the morning until ten at night and them falling off their feet with the tiredness. And no way out of it until the six months were up and they could crawl back home."

Johnny, though, always put a better light on it. He had had some hard times as a hired man but had always seemed to come out of it well.

"Aye, but there be some right decent farmers as well you know. They are not all the cruel type that you hear about. For every rogue of a farmer there's two civil ones."

"Aye, but that is the point. When it came to getting hired you always had luck walking with you. You always seemed to get in with the right man. How could these girls know the decent man from the rogue?"

"They would learn, Sean Ban. We all had to learn the hard way. It made a man outa me, so it did," Johnny would say to him.
"Maybe it did, but you were a man to start with. I don't want either of my girls to be learning the hard way, if you know what I mean."
"Agh, they would be alright. Half the stories you hear are not right at all."
"But if the other half of them are right?" said my father.
We strained to hear him through the bedroom door.
"Far too many girls have come back with a child in them from some bully of a farmer. Their wee lives ruined by it and it not their fault at all."
Mairead and I were young at the time. We looked at each other, the sparks of fear lighting our eyes in the brown gloom. Yes, we had heard such stories from some of the older girls of the parish who had gone to be hired. Mairead would only have been nine or ten at the time and it put the fear of God on her.
Johnny laughed, a short snort of a laugh. "You could always do like that Inishowen woman, a couple o' years back," he said.
"What was that?" my father asked.
"Have you not heard that one? I forget the girl's name; it doesn't matter anyway, but it is a fact from what I am told. Her mother had died and the father got a new woman and married her. Whenever the wee girl got to be fourteen the stepmother marched her down to a hiring fair in the County Derry and got her hired out to some farmer near to a place by the name of Eglinton. They put her out in a hay loft to sleep on a rough bed above the cattle. And as time went on the oul boy took a fancy to her and would visit her at night before going in to his wife. So at the end of the six months, whenever the stepmother comes to collect her, she has a bit of a belly on her. The stepmother says nothing and takes her home without another word. So time passes and the girl has a baby. The stepmother gives it a couple of weeks. Then, early one morning, she wraps it up and puts it in a basket and sets off, and the young mother not knowing a thing about it. She walks all the way to the farm, marches in through the door and sets the basket on the table. "There's your bastard wain!" she says and just walks out and leaves them to it."
That story stayed with me for years. I have never forgotten it, even though I was not meant to be hearing it. I always wondered how the girl reacted when she woke up and discovered that her baby had been

taken from her. She must have been off her head. Although she was not known to me I felt her pain; both the pain of the abuse and the grief of having the child you had borne snatched away from you forever without so much as a warning. I remember saying to myself, "Never let a thing like that befall you, no matter what."

The thing was, if those were my father's objections back then, how much stronger were they to become when the violence in the north began in the early Twenties?

On top of the usual stories of exploitation came even more serious ones. Stories of religious persecution; people being intimidated and beaten up, just ordinary Donegal folk who had gone to work in the new northern state. At hiring fairs there would be name-calling, stoning, gangs of young fellows attacking strangers. We had heard these stories from folk who had returned after not getting hired, so you could say that these accounts were maybe exaggerated. Except that somebody produced a newspaper from Derry and there it was in black and white. Seems that it was particularly bad in that place.

'Migrant workers threatened by Protestant elements within the city'.

My father read it aloud to me but I had not a notion what they meant by 'Protestant elements', I have to say. He read another account about five hundred workers from the Rosses who had arrived at the docks in Derry to get the Glasgow boat. They were too late; the boat had sailed without them. They were mad for they had just had to walk the forty miles.

'And why was that,' the paper asked, 'when there is a railway line running all the way from Burtonport to Letterkenny and to Londonderry?'

They answered the question themselves; because the IRA campaign against the railway, holding up trains and ripping up the track, had closed the thing down.

I got the impression that this paper would not have been much on for the IRA.

So how, in the light of all this, did I persuade my father to let me go to a hiring fair in Strabane?

It is a long story but circumstances changed things. When I quit the National School my father had got me a job in the carpet factory in Annagary. It was not a great job or anything; the hours were long, the work boring and hard on my fingers till I got used to it. The wages were not great either. But I was only thirteen and it was a wee bit of money coming into the house. And it was close enough for me to walk to from our cottage on the mountain. I could still help out a bit around the house, our mother being the way she was; and I could play with Mairead on a Sunday. I used to love those Sunday afternoons with the family on the beach at Carrickfinn. The feel of the fine sand running through your fingers and the chill of the sea-water up to your knees, while Mammy sat up on *Oileán na Márbh;* 'her island', we called it.

I was well pleased when I was sixteen and got a small increase in my wages in the factory. We celebrated well that night. There were a few good tunes and a bit of dancing and the poteen flowed. I knew how to enjoy a party with the best of them.

I was not in the least bit interested in politics and, as far as I could tell then, it was not in the least bit interested in me. We were not connected in any way. I was hearing stories of the local fellows who were joining the volunteers, taking on the British and fighting 'to free us once and for all'. Nobody that I knew disagreed with them, but it was all something that was happening 'out there', somewhere else, over the horizon. It did not really affect me.

Even when I heard that the boys had derailed the Burtonport train at Meenbanad, not far from our house, and that shots had been fired at the soldiers on board....it was still over the horizon; a nearer horizon, three or four mile away, yes, but still not in my world.

I remember a fellow saying in work that it served the railway right, for it was making a load of money out of transporting Black and Tan soldiers into the Rosses. I had not known that, and me living near enough beside it. I knew of-course that it transported wool to our factory and carpets out of it, as well as fish and kelp and knitting and livestock. The railway had done a lot of good for the Rosses, if you think about it.

That was not how the local IRA boys saw it though. I suppose they had a point, when you started to see the crowds of British troops that it brought in. In no time at all the soldiers had swamped our area. It was rumoured that there were five thousand of them brought to put a cordon around the whole of the Rosses and round up all the men between eighteen and seventy, my father included.

"Looking for IRA men," he said afterward, a hot temper on him. "Some of them soldiers were so thick I am surprised they could spell IRA!"

The innocence was soon to be knocked out of me though. I can still remember the terror of them coming into our kitchen on that dreadful day, poking their sharp noses into everything, drawers, pots, our bed. Even the very thatch on the roof was not safe from them, rummaging through it with the point of a bayonet as if they were trying to kill rats. I just sat and cuddled our Mairead on my knee, despite the fact that she had wet herself. The only time I spoke was when they started shouting at Mammy. Shouting and swearing in their strange English tongue. Even I could barely make out what they were saying and I had reasonable understanding of their language. Mammy just stared back at them as if they were khaki cut-outs, a blank stare on her face which they mistook to be some sort of Irish thickness. I could stand it no longer so I just said something like, "Leave Mammy alone. She does not be talking and she has no notion what you are asking her anyway."

I was so angry at them! Especially for taking my father. It did not matter that he was let out in a day or two. Looking back on it later I was surprised at my own boldness and very relieved that I had got away with it. From the stories I have heard there were plenty of ones got shot for less.

After that, more fellows were joining up with the volunteers and the railway became a major target for them, as you can imagine. Trains were held up regular and searched. Track was torn up, boulders pushed down the mountain-sides onto the line, bridges destroyed. Then to top it all, our new government in Dublin put a ban on all trade with Belfast. Carpets included.

I am sure the folk in Belfast really suffered greatly from the loss of our Donegal carpets.

No, I am afraid it was us who suffered. Between the British and the IRA and *'an Dáil'*, it was the end of the railway, for the time being. And it was the end of my job in the factory, like everything else that depended on the railway.

I remember coming home the day I got the news and telling my father. I thought he would be fit to be tied at the injustice of it all but he just looked at me, a far-away stare and a shake of the head.

"It is not your fault, Sally Anne," he said.

"How are we going to manage though?"

"Don't be worrying yourself about that. It is not your responsibility."

"But there are hardly any spuds left in the pit. Where are we going to get the money to buy food?"

"We had it tight before. We will survive."
"I will go to Dungloe and look for another job....there must be something," I said hopefully.
"You can try but I doubt it. The whole area is closing down. This boycott has put an end to so much work. And the hundreds of folk that did not get away to Scotland, they need jobs too. It is going to be a very tough spring. For everybody, *a thaisce.*" This was his 'pet' name for me; I was always 'his treasure'.
Shortly after that I went to Dungloe but I got the shock of my life there. The volunteers had more or less taken over the town and were holding their drills in public, marching up and down the main street, rifles over their shoulders as if they owned the place, which I suppose they did. There were crowds of people, some just standing watching but most folk cheering them on. Not a hint nor hair of the RIC to be seen about the place.
It did not take long to prove to myself that there were no jobs to be had in Dungloe, nor at the fishery place in Burtonport. I made up my mind. This was the year I would have to go to Strabane and look to be hired.
This was late February. I would have to work on my father gently, cleverly, before May. Hiring fairs were generally around the start of that month. I started to get excited about the whole idea and it took the edge off the hunger that often gnawed away at my belly through those grey weeks of March.
I was not alone. It is hard to believe, nearly eighty years after the famine of the hungry forties, but people in our parish were starving in the spring of that year. With the shortages in basic supplies, the price of everything went up. People were very angry at the shopkeepers, thinking that they were making big profits out of the whole mess. They may have been right, I do not know for sure. What I do know is that I was fed up looking at that yellow Indian meal which we ate for weeks on end, and that without even a pinch of sugar to give it a bit more taste. If it had not been for a few fishing boats bringing supplies in from Derry the shops would have had nothing to sell. We never had much milk either; one cow would usually be dry and anyway, my mother would give the last drop of what there was to any neighbour or beggar who happened to ask for it.
The strange thing was that if my mother had not taken ill I do not think my father would ever have consented to me going, so afraid was

he of what might befall me over in the black north. My mother took to her bed in April with some sort of cold, as thin as a rake. She needed nourishment and I made the most out of the situation. I had a fear at me that she would not survive the next winter if there was no decent food in the house; that was my line. It was true too. We argued about it every time I brought the subject up. He had all the same old reasons against it. I had just the one for it....necessity.

In the end I wore him down.

I had to make a few dozen promises, it seemed to me; several times over.

"And you will not be going near no young fellow over there, you hear me girl. Promise me now!" he said again.

"I did already Daddy, but sure if they are as persistent as you how will I ever be able to fight them off?" I laughed.

"I am not joking, Sally Anne," he said and then he threw me a difficult one. "You say you are going to Strabane. How are you going to get there?"

I hesitated. "The train?" I said slowly.

"What train? Sure the train is not running." He thought he had me.

"I was thinking if I could get down to Glenties I could take the train from there. It is still running I am told. Or I could walk to Finntown and catch it there. What do you think, Daddy? What would be best?"

'Always bring him in on the decision; make him feel responsible; distract him from the obstacles; he will rise to it,' I thought. Sure enough.

"I could get the pony and trap from your uncle Johnny and take you the length of Finntown. You could catch the evening train on over to Lifford. A lot of ones do that. You will likely meet up with them. I am told they stay in some woman's barn for the night and walk over the bridge to the fair in the morning."

I had a secret smile to myself. "Would you, Daddy? That would be great."

Of-course he would.

So I was set for the Rabble Fair in the town of Strabane, the Twelfth of May, Nineteen and Twenty Two.

Just a few months short of nineteen and not what you would call shy about it.

Chapter 2

Matthew Henderson

What was I looking for in the fair

It would not be wrong to say that I went to the Rabble Fair that day with a very open mind. I wasn't decided in my head what kind of servant I was looking for, apart from the notion that a woman of some sort would most likely fit the bill.

I would take my time about it, of that I was determined. Look at the field and be patient; make a well-thought-out decision rather than a rushed one; avoid getting caught up in the whole excitement of the carnival. I know it was only a hired hand, and for only a period of six months, but it was important to get these things right. No mistakes this time around.

Three things made me lean towards the idea that a servant woman around the place might be the best plan; the political tensions in the country, the particular circumstances of our family and the state of the farm at that point in time.

Last year, I felt, had been a bit of a mistake. It was not that the fellow couldn't work. The opposite in fact. I had no complaints about Kevin Duggan's abilities, nor about the effort he put into his labour. As good a ploughman as there was in the whole locality; very good with the horses; always did as I bade him. Last year was a big year for draining several of those rushy fields down the back, towards the burn. Duggan stuck at that task like he was born for it, difficult and all as it was.

So what, you might ask, was the problem? Well, there was just something about him. I'd rather not say too much in these difficult times, indeed dangerous times. A body has to be careful. Let's just put it this way; if Duggan had been as circumspect in what he got up to away from my farm as he was when he was here there would be no problem; I would re-hire him tomorrow, even if he was sometimes as twisted as a dog's hind leg. But, given the whispers I had heard and given the nature of his dealings with Mary Kearney, my neighbour's daughter, it might be as well for all of us if he was to get himself hired

at the other end of the county. Or perhaps just stay over there in Donegal, on his own side of the border.
Anyhow, there was less need for a strong man-servant here this year. There were no more drains to be dug. The winter ploughing that Duggan did had made it easier for me to get the land cultivated and sown out this past spring. I could always rely on my good friend, Joe Kearney, to help with the hay and the harvest. We would be grand, as far as the fields were concerned. That was what Joe and his folks said as well when we chatted about it.
Mrs Kearney's point was this.
"It is more your mother who has need of help than yourself, Matthew, if you don't mind me saying so. You seem to me to be well on top of things about the place but Eliza, God love her, she's just not at herself at all these days. You know yourself, son; there's no need for me to be pointing out the obvious to you...."
But she did anyway of-course. Monica Kearney could talk the leg off a stool.
"Whether there is an illness in her somewhere or maybe she has never just got over the shock of losing her father, I don't know. But even before that, she wasn't the best. She had that bad time after the twins were born; never really seemed to come up out of it. And how long ago is that? What are they now?"
"They're eleven," I said.
"Eleven. There you are, you see. God, eleven is it? Well, well! Mind you, if they had a year or two under them they'll be right and useful to you. Jane will anyway; maybe not so much poor wee Millie. But they're too young yet to be doing anything around the farm. Are they any use at all in the kitchen, are they?"
"Not a lot. They..."
"It's just a pity Emily is so far away in Belfast. Brains!" said Mrs Kearney. "The ruination of young girls, that's what I always say."
Anthony got his tongue in edgeways. Well, as her husband, he didn't want for the years of practice which I lacked.
"Don't be hard on the girl because she is smart, Monica," he said. "If she has the wit to get a good job in the city then fair play to her. It's not for everybody, staying around these parts."
"I'm not saying anything to the contrary," argued his wife patiently. "Just that her mother would have more use for her being at home to look after the place."

"I don't think that would ever work now," I said. "Emily is far too important to be getting her hands dirty around here."
It was true. I wasn't being bitter. Four years older than me but a whole world of difference between the pair of us.
"You'll just have to get a woman, Matt!" said my old mate Joe, straight-faced except for the slight curl of his upper lip and the gleam of devilment in his eyes. I knew the look and I glanced away from him quickly, back to his mother.
"Joe is right, Matthew. What you need is to hire a decent wee cutty that can run a good kitchen, keep the house clean and in order, work out in the yard feeding, helping you with the milking and all."
"And snuggling up to you in the cold winter evenings." Joe couldn't resist it, no more than I could resist punching him in the stomach. He gasped and spluttered and giggled at the same time, if that is possible, and so missed his mother's rebuke.
"All that nonsense aside," said Anthony, "it does make a lot of sense. And you'll understand what I mean when I say that you'd be doing our family a right good turn if you didn't bring that ruffian Duggan back to these parts."
I did understand exactly what he meant. Well, as I say, I had picked up some of the rumours.
"He'll not be back, don't you worry," I said.
"If you like, we will be heading to the fair as well, border or no border. I have that mare to try and sell. Monica is going too, with her knitting and the like. She could give you a hand when it comes to hiring a girl."
Anthony was always trying to be helpful. He had always been like that, with me and with my father before me; as civil a neighbour as there was in the country.
"A girl now, is it?" said Joe. "If it's a girl he's after sure I'll be there beside him; I'll look her over for you, Matt; check her teeth; see what shape her legs are and all. You don't be wanting a girl with one leg shorter than the other for sure you have the ploughing all done. I'll do all the advising you will ever need and I'll not take a penny for it."
Full of blether as usual, Joe.
His father laughed hearty at him.
"I'd like to see the girl you would pick for him, son. You'd have far more need to be looking about one for yourself."
"Don't you worry about me, Da. I have them waiting for me in a line," said Joe.

"Not a hope of that happening," I said, seeing my opportunity to get my own back. "You'd have to hide that nose of yours."
Joe took it well enough, I think, even if it was a bit below the belt. His nose had always been a sore point for him, maybe just a couple of sizes too big for the face of him. Apart from that he was a decent enough looking chap. Skinny as a greyhound, a lot shorter than me and as dark as I was fair. And of-course, of the other religion, though that had never been an issue for us, just as it hadn't been for our two fathers before us. Even the rebellion over the past few years, the 'War of Independence' as they were starting to call it, and the setting up of the Free State hadn't come between us. Well, not much anyhow. It was just something we made a point of not talking about.
In the end it was agreed that, come the day, Joe would travel with me to the fair.
Before that though I had to convince my mother of the wisdom of this plan to hire a woman instead of the usual man. Nothing for it but to come right out and say it. She would see the wisdom of it and give me her blessing with no dispute. So I left it for a day or two, then a week or two, until I found myself having to raise the subject the night before the fair. We were in the kitchen after tea which, by coincidence, lent support to my argument. The meal had been a bit of a burnt offering. Jane and Millie between them had managed to boil the potatoes dry and burn the bacon so that it looked like a pile of autumn leaves, crisp and brown.
"Mother," I began, sounding as decisive as I could manage, "I have been talking to Anthony and Monica. They think that I should be hiring a woman this time. Somebody with a bit of experience in the kitchen end of things, as well as being able to work in the yard. I don't really need a man on the land this year."
"A woman?" Our Jane sounded shocked, disgusted.
"Aye," I said, stepping lightly on her toe under the table. "Somebody who could boil praties, maybe even cook bacon without the taste of cinders off it."
Jane began to respond but the pressure of my boot on her bare toes distracted her. So I turned to my mother again.
"What do you think, mother?"
"Think...about what, son?" she said slowly, that vacant look on her face.

I looked at her pale blue eyes, empty as the sky, and it hit me again that what I was seeing was the beginning of her doting stage. She was wasting away in front of our eyes but it had been so slow that, for us living with her, it had been hardly noticed. Yes, of-course she would repeat questions whiles, or forget a person's name. You would see her sitting staring out the back window to the street at times when you might have expected her to be doing something; just staring and sometimes shaking her head sadly. But, for whatever reason, maybe denial on my part, I had always expected that this was a phase that would pass; it was just some sort of delayed grief over my father that she had to go through. She would eventually come out the other side and be the lively woman who had managed everything and everybody around Lismore Farm in my younger days.

"About hiring a woman to work here?" I said.

"Whatever you say, son."

She got up and shuffled back to her armchair.

"Forty nine years of age she is and more or less finished, dear love her," I thought to myself.

"Don't be bringing another woman, Matthew. She'll likely scoul us, maybe even bate us." Jane's pretty wee face had panic all over it.

"Sure that will save me having to do it," I said, getting up to run the dishes under the pump outside. We all had to do our turn. Hopefully that would change for the better, come the day after the fair.

Chapter 3

Sally Anne Sweeney

What I thought of the fair

The Hiring Fair shocked the heart out of me. I would say I was in awe of it all. I had never seen anything like it in my life. Mainly the number of people there, the crowds of them, like flocks of sheep, wandering up and down the streets of Strabane. Half of them, I am sure, had not a notion what they were doing there. Probably just looking at the other ones for a clue. Following the crowd, and such a colourful crowd it was.

Young ones, older ones; some well-dressed and turned out nicely for the day; others more like me in their working clothes, bundles over their backs and wee bunches of twigs in their hand. On the train from Finntown I fell in with a girl from Kincasslagh; Ailish O'Donnell was the name on her and we got on like a house on fire, talking away to each other in our own language. It was her who told me that the handful of twigs was the way you let the employers know that you were for hire, so I picked some from the sally-bushes beside that big river. I never saw a river so wide in all my born days. 'The Foyle', they call it.

There was a crowd of big policemen standing on the bridge over this river. It put the thought in me of a herd of black bullocks waiting at a gate. They were staring into our faces as we crossed from Lifford. It was clear to me that they were searching for somebody but they were very cheeky about it all, stopping some folk, asking them questions and looking through their bundles. They put the fear of God across me, sent shivers running up the back of my neck, whether they meant to or not. They had a couple of fellows up against the rails of the bridge, their arms and legs spread out while they searched them. I could not take my eyes off them, the roughing up they were getting, and them swearing away in Irish at the peelers. Not that they would understand, I imagine. Ailish saw the look on my face and pulled me away towards the fair itself. It was my first taste of this new northern country and it was not a welcoming taste either. I suppose those policemen must have had their reasons but at that stage I could not have told you what they were. Nor could I have told you if they were the old RIC or what. Ailish thought they were from the 'Special Constabulary', whatever that was.

As we walked on into the town I noticed some posters advertising particular newspapers. The slogans were similar to the headlines I had read on the front of a traveller's newspaper opposite me on the train. He was reading the 'Irish News'. I had quaked a bit as I had read,

"BELFAST OUTRAGES
SHOOTING AND LOOTING
ANOTHER SCORE FOR THE NOTORIOUS CUPAR STREET GANG"

And in another column,

"THE ANTRIM CRIME
'B' SPECIAL SERGEANT CHARGED WITH MURDER"

The posters on these hoardings did not help to improve my nerves. This paper was called 'The Northern Constitution' and its headlines read,

"3 CONSTABLES SHOT IN BALLYRONAN
REPRISALS IN DUNGIVEN
BELFAST BURNINGS CONTINUE"

"Sure that is miles away," Ailish consoled me. "There will hardly be any burnings about where we are going."

Little did she know!

I was as guilty as the next one of following the crowd but I did not know what else to be doing. Most of the Donegal ones gathered themselves by a big building that turned out to be the Town-hall and Ailish and me joined them. There we stood and watched. And were watched!

As the morning wore on and the fear of it all wore off me I began to enjoy it more. I wandered around the streets a bit on my own in my curiosity. Never have I seen such entertainment. Children screaming on swing-boats and bobbing up and down on hobby-horses. Magicians and card-trick fellows conning themselves a wee fortune. A woman with the most colourful birds you have ever seen doing tricks and trying to talk through their big curved beaks. Green and blue and pink feathers that you could not imagine, more than likely painted on for the fair, I would think. They could never have been natural, those colours. I wished my mother was here to see them for she loves bright colours like that.

There were men and women shouting and screeching above each other to be selling their wares, all in the English I noticed. Jokers and singers and musicians, all trying to make a penny. I nearly wished I had my own fiddle at me, for I could have played as well as any of them, I thought.

I saw a little man on a cart playing an accordion; he was good too, but I noticed that he had no legs; either that or he had them tucked away under himself for sympathy. There was one old fellow who looked to be from some foreign part by the tawny colour of the skin on him; he had a strange piano of a thing that he turned a handle on and it squeaked out a tune, if you could call it that. But better still, he had a dirty looking monkey that sat on his shoulder, its head jerking this way and that, its fingers poking in places where they should not have been poking. The people were in fits at it but, if they got too close, it would jump at them. It even pinched the cap off the head of some wee lad and that caused a row, for it did not want to give the cap back, no matter what its master shouted at it in that strange foreign tongue. 'Italian', somebody said he was. 'Goodness but he is well-strayed from home,' I thought.

I wandered round by the markets for a while having a look for myself, watching the farmers and the dealers haggling over prices, shouting and swearing, spitting on their hands and slapping them together. There were dozens of horses and ponies and donkeys. I saw more cows that day than there is in the whole of Donegal, I am convinced of it. The hullabaloo of it all, between pigs squealing and roosters crowing and different other animals; it must have been heard for miles around. The smell would have travelled some distance as well, I was thinking.

As I stood there watching those huge horses, twigs in my hand, my bundle on my back and a half smile of curiosity on my face I am sure, a farmer spoke a greeting to me in Irish. This surprised me. I had not been expecting to hear my own language from a Tyrone farmer but the sound of it lifted my heart, even if the accent was very different.

"If you are looking to be hired would you not be better standing at the Town-hall, *mo leanbh*?" he said.

There was a nice gentleness about the way he spoke to me; the words came off his tongue with a soft sweetness. It stood out as a contrast to the roughness of everything else that was going on.

"That's the usual place. Up under that big arch. You don't want to be missing your chance now, after coming all this way from wherever you live."

That was true and I took his advice in a minute.

"Why is it called the 'Rabble Fair'?" I asked him as I left.

"Sure just look around you," he smiled and went back to his horse. I liked him, this stranger. The sort of man would make a very nice father. The public houses were making the big money and I passed them by as quickly as I could on my way back. All the more so when I nearly got caught up in the middle of a row between two gangs of young fellows. I have no notion what started it but, from what they were shouting at each other, it seemed to have turned into a religious dispute. Fierce angry they were. As I got myself slipped away from the gathering crowd, I met the police hurrying towards the fight. I was nearly relieved to see them, thick black sticks in their big, bulging fists. Some skulls were going to feel the weight of them, I thought.

As I took my place back at the Town-hall I noticed that the numbers of people waiting to be hired had thinned out a lot. I had not expected that. There was maybe only half of what there had been before I went on my walk about. There was no sign of Ailish.

'She is likely hired already,' I was thinking. Still, there was plenty of time, I consoled myself. I stood under the arch and waited.

I waited a long time!

Farmers came and went. Mostly they were looking at what fellows and men were left, I could see. They would make the Donegal boys walk up and down the road, grab their arms to feel the muscles on them; one even said to a lad, "Pull up yer breeches and let me see the thickness of your leg."

'God look to me!' I thought, 'If anybody does that to me he would need to be watching his ear for I will give him a right wallop.'

But the fellow showed his legs as he was ordered, without a murmur out of him. Thankfully he did seem to have good sturdy legs and the farmer seemed satisfied.

"And what money did you say you would be needing?" he asked, his words tripping over each other.

"I would be looking six pounds."

"You might be lukin' for it for a quare while," said the farmer, starting to turn away. "Things are tight in Tyrone you know. You will not get that kind o' money the day or the morrow nor anytime soon and you have a right cheek on you to be asking for it."

"What will you give me then?" said the young fellow, with just a little bit too much desperation sounding in his voice.

"I had a guid worker last year and he only got the four pound. Will ye take that?" He held out his hand. I watched all this closely, learning as I went along and hoping that if anybody talked to me they would do it a lot more slowly and not come out with these strange words that I was not used to.

"I will not," said the Donegal chap. "Don't be insulting me. I'm worth more than that."

"Maybe tae yersel' you are, but naw tae me," responded the farmer, stepping away.

"Will you not give me five pounds ten shillings? If I had that itself I would work for you."

The farmer stopped, still looking the other way. He pretended to be giving this deep thought for a minute, then he turned back and stuck out his hand.

"I'll give ye five pound and not a penny more. You would better be worth it, for I hae niver paid that tae any man afore," he said.

They struck hands and the deal was done. I was sorry for the fellow for I thought he had been outwitted by this strange-tongued farmer. When it came my turn I would play harder to get.

If it ever came my turn.

Over the course of the morning not a soul spoke to me, apart from those standing with me. A few women got hired; they were all older than me, bigger and a bit tougher looking. One or two farmers came and stared at me, generally from a distance; they looked me up and down but said nothing. One brown-looking wee woman, probably a farmer's wife, came and threw her eye over me. I felt like some kind of animal for sale in a cage and I did not like it, not one bit. I found myself starting to stare back at her in the same way she was looking at me, head to one side. She did not like it that much either.

"What are ye lukin' at?" she said angrily. "Ye'll never get yourself hired, girl. Ye're far o'er thin and sharp o' yersel'," and she moved on.

I was wondering, 'Do they all speak like that here?'

I wanted to say, "You are one to be talking, Missus!" But I held my tongue. It would never do to be rubbing anybody up the wrong way around here.

By the middle of the afternoon I had only had two enquiries. The brown woman and a greasy old specimen of a character that I did not even think was a farmer anyway, by the look of him. I did not like the way he stared at me. He had the bearing of an undertaker, I thought, the way he was looking me up and down as if he was measuring me for my coffin. He had the cut of a man that there would be no money in his pocket. I turned and walked away from him which he was not pleased about and swore after me. I did not care. I had a terrible thirst on me anyway. I went and bought myself a drink and the finest big red apple you ever saw. It was so long since I'd seen an apple for there had been a want of them around our parts the past year. When I finished my cup of tea I took a scobe out of the apple and the juice of it ran down my chin. I went back to take up my patient stand again.

Soon I noticed the same farmer who had spoken to me in Gaelic at the horse market earlier. He seemed to be going around talking to all the girls and women who were still waiting to be hired. When he saw me he came limping straight over to me. There seemed to be something the matter with his legs or his back, I thought.

"What way are you now? Are you not hired yet?" he said in Irish.

"I am not hired yet," I said.

"Well," he said, "Wait there a minute and don't be going anywhere until I come back."

"I am not going anywhere. Divil the chance of it!"

'What is this about?' I thought to myself.

After a while I noticed him standing on the other side of the road with two younger fellows. By the way they were glancing over at me it was not hard to work out that they were talking about me, weighing me up. The bigger of the two seemed to be shaking his head doubtfully and looking away up the street, while the smaller one was near enough dragging him across the road towards me. I saw too that the older farmer, the one with the Gaelic at him, had a wife and a clatter of children behind him.

"Go sábhála Dia sinn!" I thought. "Lord preserve us! That would be some handling."

Over the road he came, dragging a leg but business-like, the two fellows after him.

"This girl is looking a position," he said to them over his shoulder. He changed into Irish. "Isn't that right, *mo leanbh*?"

"That I am, Mister," I said.

"Well, this fellow is needing a servant girl," he said, indicating the big chap.
I gave the young farmer a sideways glance.
"He is a bit shy of himself so you might have to do all the talking," the older man whispered with a half smile and sidled off to speak with an acquaintance. That left me with the two young men. I looked up at the tall one, standing there with the glare of the late afternoon sun behind his head like a halo. Goodness, he was younger than he looked at a distance. I felt the blood rising up my neck for he had as handsome a face on him as I had ever seen. A strong jaw, sun-browned cheeks that had been closely shaved, well-trimmed fairish hair, dark-blue eyes that seemed to hold onto mine when I looked at them. It was the kind of face you would remember and think about later. My mouth went sort of dry and I know I was blushing like a beetroot but I used the sun behind him to cover my fluster. I put my hand up to shade my eyes.
"The sun is in my eyes," I got out, unnecessarily, "but I am still for the hiring. Is it yourself that would be needing me?"
The younger, shorter fellow laughed out loud at the shape of me squinting up at his giant friend.
"Aye," he said, "it is him that needs you alright."
"Shut up, Joe!" said the big one. "Let me talk to her in peace."
"Go on then, I'm not houlin' you back, am I? You haven't said a word to her yet, as far as I can hear."
There was a bit of a silence while he just looked down at me.
'Lord above,' I was thinking. 'This fellow must be well over the six feet.'
Then his eyes bounced off mine to look at the few other women and girls who were still standing nearby. Some of them had started to wander over towards us. One, a stout lump of a girl from Arranmore Island I believe, tried to intervene in our conversation, such as it was. The Joe chap, to his credit, came to my aid and shooed her away like she was a hen.
"Go on with you," he said to her. "Matthew has his eye on this cutty here and if that doesn't work out he'll be over with you after."
So that was the name he had on him? Matthew. It was a strange name to me. It sounded a bit like a name the priest would be saying when he was reading the gospel during Mass. There were no Matthews in the Rosses, to the best of my knowledge. I could think 'Matthew' but it did not fall easy to my tongue to be saying it.

"I have not got my eye on her," the Matthew fellow said between his teeth. "Stop interfering Joe. Anyway, I think she's far too skinny of herself. There's naw a pick on her. How would she ever...."
I was hearing all this, even though he was whispering, translating it in my head as quickly as I could. 'Naw a pick on her,' is it? Whatever he meant by that, I was not too pleased at his description but I just stood and watched him drown in his own lack of confidence.
"Agh Matt, she's grand."
Matt. That would be easier spoken, I thought. Just the one syllable... like cat.
"She could just do with some good Henderson kitchen, by the look of her. Go on and ask her something afore some ither boadie cuts in on you," the Joe one continued.
Faint chance of that, I thought, but it would not have been the right time to say it. Eventually he came up with something to say to me. Slowly, deliberately, like I was a child.
"So, ah... what can you do?"
Strange question. The fellow called Joe thought so too for he started laughing again; like a braying donkey, he was.
"What can you do?" he mocked. "She can dance a three-handed reel all by herself and sing and peel spuds and all at the same time like."
"Alright, alright Joe." Then to me again, "What I am looking for is somebody who will take on work in the kitchen and the house but be fit for a bit of work aroun' the farm as well."
"I can handle that," I said.
"You don't think it would be o'er much for you? You don't seem very well at yourself."
"Well at myself?" I repeated. I must have looked as if I was not making a lot of sense of his way of speaking because the Joe one came to my aid again.
"He means you don't look very strong," he said.
This was beginning to annoy me.
"You just look a bit thin for farm work," the big one said, turning his side to me as if he should begin to look for somebody of a heavier build.
I have no idea what came over me then but I was suddenly brave, either that or scared of the thought of having to walk all the way back to my father with no offer of work.

"Do you want me to turn around so you can get a good look at me?" I said, spinning around, my skirts whirling out like I was on a dancehall floor. My intention was sort of to help him out and maybe more to take the high ground in this haggle.
"What do you think now?" I asked.
He could not very well say anything negative now, could he? I did not give him the chance anyhow.
"I may be thin but I am as strong as any of these women here," I said, hoping at the same time that none of them would take me up on the matter and challenge me to an arm wrestle. "I am eighteen years of age. I can read and write. I have cooked for my own ones at home. I have had a job in a carpet factory and I have helped my father with his animals. I can milk and I can...."
"Do you have any references?" he interrupted.
References? That had me for a minute.
"I have never been over to be hired before, so no, sorry but I don't have any references." Then an idea came into my head. "But sure you can be the first man to give me a reference when I have done my six months," I said with a smile behind my eyes and, as I said it, I knew I had a position. Just by the look on his face, the small gleam behind his eyes and the way he went a reddish sort of colour around his ears and his neck.
"*Maith thú féin!*" said the Joe fellow quietly. "Well said!"
"So he has Gaelic as well?" I thought. "*Iontach*".
"How much will you be needin'?" asked the tall one turning his body away from me self-consciously.
"Needing?" I said. The money side of things had gone out of my head for the time being.
"Wages," he said. "You'll likely want wages, will you not?"
"I will. As much as you can afford," I answered. "I will not take a penny more."
'Where did that come from?' I thought to myself. I was pleased with it though. My confidence had suddenly lifted itself, ever since I saw how he had been affected when I gave him a wee smile. After listening to that other fellow earlier, I had been thinking about how to deal with the money question and that was the line that had come into my head. Again it seemed to work. He stopped and took a minute to clear his throat.
"What do you think Joe? What is she worth?"

Joe looked at me and then back up at his friend. Again I could sense his embarrassment.
"Wait and I'll go and get my mother," he said. "She'll know how much."
He dived off into the middle of the crowd, leaving me with this Matthew. An awkward moment. He decided to look at the passing people. I looked up at the town clock, as if to study the movement of its two hands. They seemed to have stuck for the time being. No more conversation until...
"Where...?" We both spoke at exactly the same time.
He looked down at me.
"You go first then," he said generously.
"I was going to ask where your farm is," I said.
"It's near enough ten miles south o' here, on the road to Castlederg, if you have ever heard of it. Some o' you Donegal ones call it Garrig. But sure we haven't come to any agreement yet?" he said.
I looked up at him, trying to find some little teasing twinkle in his eyes. I was not sure it was there.
"We have not," I agreed with a wee smile. "I could be walking back to the Rosses before the night is out. Fifty long miles by the light of the moon, for I haven't a penny to my name for the train."
And again I saw that I had come out on top in this strange conversation. He just gave me a look and said, "Aye, that would be a long walk now. So is that where you are from? What sort o' place is it?"
"Agh, it's a grand place, if you like bogs and rocks and loughs and the like," I said, watching Joe lead his mother and a few children across the street.
"What would you both say to four pound and ten shillings?" the woman asked me.
In my case I was delighted with this suggestion, so I just nodded. I had heard other women have to settle for a whole lot less during the course of the afternoon. I hoped the tall farmer would not try to haggle and, to be fair to him, he did not.
"Four pound ten it is then," he said. "I hope you're worth it."
He held out his hand to me. I hesitated.
"Can you tell me where I will sleep and what food...."
Joe could not wait to be making a smart comment.

"Sure Matthew has a big double bed...." But he got no further. Between his mother's tongue and Matthew thumping him in the chest, the wind was knocked out of him entirely and he wheezed to a stop.
"Don't pay any heed to him. We have an attic with a couple of rooms in it. You'll be fine up there," Matthew said. "And the food? Well, if it's poor you will only have yourself to blame, for it will be you will be cooking it."
This time we did agree on it. He raised his big coarse hand and looked at me.
I threw down my bundle of sweaty twigs, wiped the green stain off my hand on my skirt and stuck it out, hoping he would not be too rough as he slapped it.
"What are you called?"
"*Is mise Sally Anne Nic Suibhne*," I said.
He looked blankly at me and then at his friend. Joe smiled at me.
"He didn't understand the '*Is mise*' bit," he said to me in Gaelic. Then to Matthew, "She's called Sally Anne Sweeney."
"Well Sally Anne Sweeney, we will be ready to leave for home by six o'clock," he said, "so meet us at the front of the Post Office, down that street there. Don't be late for we'll not be waiting for you and it's a lang wie hame, as you said yourself."
With that he and his friends were gone. I was still standing there with my bundle on my back and a satisfied smile inside me.
I was hired. Well hired. I had a good feeling about it.
I found Ailish again, waiting by the Post Office as well. She had been hired by a man from some place called Newtownstewart. She said she thought it was not a terrible distance away from this Castlederg so we might meet up again sometime, with the help of God.
I told her about my handsome big farmer and she just said, "You watch yourself girl. Keep him well away at arm's length. You don't want to be bringing any trouble on yourself."
I just laughed at her.
"Trouble? Divil the bit of it. I can look after myself, so I can."
And, the thing was, I really believed myself.

Chapter 4

Matthew Henderson

How I got into a row at the fair

So I got us a maid. I have to say that I was surprised at myself because she was the last thing I had imagined coming home with. If you had told me the night before that I would be hiring such a thin wee waif of a girl, albeit a pretty looking one, I would have said you did not know me very well. As soon as I had shaken her hand I started wondering what my mother would say about her. Maybe not a lot though.

As long as she didn't mix her up with one of the twins!

There was a part of me, just a small part, that kind of resented how I had come to the deal. It was as if I had been railroaded into it, against my better judgement. Partly I blamed Anthony Kearney, and Monica too, for that matter, but all they had done was get me talking to her. To be honest, apart from looking at a few of those women waiting to get hired, she was the only girl I had actually managed to speak to. That was just how circumstances had worked out. She had not been at the Town-hall earlier in the day when Joe and I had first looked. Partly I blame Joe himself for being far too pushy on the matter, for he obviously liked the look of the lass. But of-course he was only being his normal self, making a laugh out of everything. Largely though, I blame her herself. More to the point, I blame her eyes.

Even from across the street, when Anthony had pointed her out to us I could feel those eyes on me as if they were burning into me. In a nice way, all the same. They were the greenest eyes I have ever seen on anyone or anything; green, but with a sort of a light in them, like when you are walking in the dark and you see the flame of a candle flickering behind somebody's window pane. Mind you, apart from the eyes and, I suppose, the shape of her face and the fair hair down to her shoulders, there wasn't all that much attractive about her. Far too thin for a farm girl. No meat on her at all, top or bottom, if you know what I mean. How will she ever cope with carrying bundles of hay to the cattle, bringing them buckets of water, carrying feed to the pigs and hens?

"Lord, I hope I haven't made a dreadful mistake," I thought several times as Joe and me walked through the fair. "Well, if the worst comes to the worst and she's not worth her money I can always send her back to wherever she's from."

It did not help that he wouldn't shut up about her.

"You are going to have some craic with that one, Matt," he kept saying.

"She'll not have time for craic and neither will I," I answered. "She will be too busy working, mark my words. There's a heap o' work to be done around our place."

"But hasn't she the greatest smile on her," he persisted. "And she had the answer for you when you asked her about a reference, didn't she?"

"Joe," I said, "will you ever give my head peace. She is only a servant girl."

"Aye, that's as maybe," he said, "but she will fairly shorten the autumn evenings for you, you have to admit it."

"And what is that supposed to mean, you half-wit?"

"Agh, work it out yourself," he answered and led me into McSwiggan's Public House where we would usually drink a pint.

The place was so crammed full of happy drinking people that we had to force our way through to the bar. Now I would not be a big drinker, you understand, but you couldn't really come home from the Rabble without a celebration of some sort, it just wouldn't be right. So we ordered a couple of stouts and slipped into a little snug which was emptying of a few farmers.

I had bought a newspaper, The Belfast Telegraph. Some of the headlines were enough to take the smile off anyone's face, that's a fact. Nothing but trouble and violence in the country. It was especially bad in Belfast but the border areas were seeing some terrible goings-on as well. Roads being dug up by the IRA to frustrate the police and stop their vehicles. Attacks on Protestant houses here and there.

"Magherafelt Murder; Bereaved Mother's Story; Tracks of Gunmen in the Fields!" I read out loud to Joe. "An eighteen year old Special Constable shot while defending his father's house in Donaghmore."

The more I read the more annoyed I became. It probably showed on my face and in my voice because Joe put his hand over on my arm and said, "Matt, you would be better not to be reading that out loud in here."

"Why not?"

"Because. It's likely all nonsense anyway. It's the Belfast Telegraph, Unionist to the core. Put it away and read it at home."
I looked at him over the paper and I have to admit I got raised at him. He just couldn't help himself having a dig at a Protestant newspaper. For all his friendliness to me, I was thinking, he still kicks with the other foot.
"But it is terrible what is going on in this country. The IRA is going to ruin the place for all of us," I said. "Thugs and criminals. Why don't they just leave us alone and stay over there in the Free State if they don't want to be under Britain any more?"
He looked away, turned around sideways on his seat and stared dully out of the snug.
"What?" I said. "You don't agree with them, do you?"
"Whatever I think is my own business," he came back quick at me, "but this is not the place to be talking about it. Anyway, it is not all as simple as you make out. The IRA aren't the only ones here with blood on their hands."
"What do you mean by that?"
"Your bloody Special Constabulary are even worse. They have been stirring things up all over, so they have. I bet you there's no reports in your paper about Specials going into Catholic houses and shooting people at point blank range, innocent women and children that have nothing to do with the IRA or anything else. They just report what...."
"You tell him, Joe! The B Specials! They're the real thugs around here!"
Joe and I froze in our seats and just looked at one another. The voice came from the other side of the partition. We both recognised that accent, that voice, straight away. My stomach lurched in me.
There was a shuffling of bodies in the snug next door to us and Kevin Duggan slithered around the corner, taking up a stance and blocking the entrance of our compartment with his short wiry frame. He raised the remains of his dark pint to us, as if he was giving us a mock salute, I thought.
"How're you doing, Master Henderson. I just thought it was your voice I was after hearing. Joe, are you alright, oul friend?"
"Hello Kevin," was all I could manage through my porter-dry mouth.
"I was looking for you earlier on up at the Market House but I couldn't see you," he continued, a slight slur dragging its way through his words. I noticed his eyes had that blurry yellow look off them as they often had after a night's drinking when he was working at our place. "But I

am here now. You'll be wanting to hire me again this year, I'm sure. After the grand job I did with those drains. You had no complaints about that anyhow. I'm sure they are all running full of water, are they not?"

"I am sure they are. I haven't looked recently...."

"Ah now, you should look. I did a good job on them. What have you lined up for me this year, Master?"

I did not like his tone at all, nor his bullying familiarity, nor the presumption that he could just talk his way into my employ again. His whole bearing was insolent, all five feet six of it. So I stood up and looked down at the top of his curly black hair from my six feet two vantage point. Joe stood as well and stared him straight in the eye before downing the remains of his pint in one long gulp. Ready for a getaway, I thought.

"As a matter of fact I won't be hiring you again this year, Kevin," I said firmly. "I have no need of a man this year. There's no drains to be dug, no sheughs to be cleaned out. I have the ploughing all done. I wouldn't have the work for you and that's an end to it."

As I spoke I picked up my paper and folded it under my arm, just to have something for my hands to be doing.

"And who is going to do the work for you this year?" said Kevin. "You're not going to tell me you can do it yourself?"

"I am not going to tell you anything, for it is none of your business," I said, the temper rising in me.

"And you're not going to tell me that this here wee chap can manage it," he said, indicating Joe. "Sure he wouldn't have the strength for it. A day's hard work would wear him out in no time. The weight of the shovel would be too much for him."

The smile was one part humour and three parts sarcasm. Joe didn't like it much.

"Nobody wants your opinion, Duggan," Joe took a step forward towards the door, arms bunching by his side and fists clenched.

"Agh Joe, I was just joking, oul friend," said Kevin and he attempted to put his arm around Joe in the manner of a drunken man. "But I'll tell you what. You were just right to be standing up for your country there. These Protestants think they have got their way with this border thing but it won't take long for us to blow it away like the chaff it is, you mark my words."

"Let me go," said Joe, struggling against the labourer's strong arms. "Take your hands off me!"
"Well now," said Kevin with an ignorant grin, "that's not what your sister said last night."
Joe swung his right fist at Kevin's face. Had he connected it would have been a mighty blow but, tipsy and all as he was, Kevin Duggan was the master of the bar-room brawl. He simply swayed back and caught Joe's flailing arm, holding it like it was a flapping hen.
"Easy now, oul friend," he said. "You don't want to be starting anything you can't finish. I am your fellow countryman and we are on the same side. But, just while we are being honest with each other, let me give you a piece of advice. You need to be deciding who your real friends are and not be making enemies of them at a time like this. You hear me now?"
I rose to the bait at once.
"He knows who his friends are, Duggan. He doesn't need the likes of you to be advising him so just take your hands off him."
Duggan looked up at me, a dark, surly stare. Slowly he let go of Joe's arm and pretended to straighten out his ruffled coat. When he spoke the sarcasm was thick in his sing-song Donegal voice.
"I will surely, Master Henderson. I was just trying to stop him from hurting himself unnecess....unnecessarily. There," he said wiping a spill of saliva from his mouth with his sleeve, "we are alright now; maybe Joe or you want to buy me a drink just to show there's no ill feeling like, just for old time's sake. It's a pint of porter for me."
"I doubt if you will be that lucky," I said. "Come on, Joe. We were just leaving."
"Were you now?" said Duggan. "Well, I am sure I will run in to yous some other time."
Neither Joe nor I missed the element of threat under the slur of his words.
I pushed Joe firmly through the pint-holding watchers towards the door. Several of them scowled at me as I walked past but I paid no attention to it. The atmosphere in Strabane had definitely changed this year if McSwiggan's bar was anything to go by. It wasn't any better in the yard where we had left the mare. A half dozen men were arguing loudly. 'Drink was in and wit was out,' as my father would have said. We gave them a wide berth and drove back into the town in search of the new maid.

We found her by the Post Office door an hour later than we had planned and she was relieved to see us looking down at her from the height of the cart.
"Are you alright?" I asked, reaching down a hand to help her up.
"I am, sir," she said as she climbed to join us.
"Did you think we weren't coming?" Joe asked her.
She gave him a funny look.
"I wondered. I have had more than enough of this place and its mad folk. I think I have seen more people today than in my entire life. I am dizzy looking at all their faces going past, trying to recognise if it was you two. It nearly got to the point where I wanted to say to some stranger, 'Agh, you will do instead!'"
I wondered if she'd had a drop o' drink herself, so much silly chat came out of her in a rush.
Joe laughed. "That would have been a big mistake. There's no substitute for me and Matt."
She sat down beside him on a bag of straw while I sat, reigns in hand, on the other side of the cart. The mare jogged along eagerly towards Clady once we got clear of the crowded Strabane streets. Joe kept her in conversation for a few miles. At the start I didn't mind that at all, except that it was all in Irish. They were good chat together but I didn't understand a word of it.
I was minding my own business, wondering what they were talking about, but after a while I could feel her gaze on me from the side.
"Will I be able to go to Mass, sir?" she said in English.
I turned towards her, intending to make a pretence that I would not allow this, just as a bit of a joke, to see how she would react. But the intensity of those green eyes disarmed me at once and I spluttered, "Of-course you will. You can either come to the village with us or Joe and his folk could take you. We are Methodists but our service is around the same time. I don't mind giving you a ride to Mass with us if you like."
"Thank you," she said.
"We don't work on the Sabbath," I told her, "so there will be no need for you to work either, except for the milking and the feeding. And whatever needs doing in the kitchen."
"Sabbath? What's that?" she said.
Joe mumbled something to her in Irish.
"Ah, Sunday," she said.

"So the rest of the day is your own to do whatever you want," I said. "As long as it's dacent."
She seemed puzzled by this but she nodded her head. "Whatever you say," she said.
"And we will always try to have fish on a Friday," I added, at the same time thinking to myself, 'That's a strange thing to be saying to her. We didn't have fish very many times when Kevin Duggan was here last year. He just had to like it or lump it."
Joe said, "Are you going to take up fishing in the Derg then, Matt?"
I didn't answer. Joe was laughing at me behind his hand, I could tell. He was a right fellow, Joe, but there were whiles he would scunner you altogether, trying to be the funny man. Now he was trying to show off to this cutty. That was what the Gaelic talk was all about. He knew right well it would annoy me; that was why he kept talking to her in it, like as if him and her had a special connection and I was on the outside of it.
A blind man on a galloping horse could have seen that Joe had his eye on her already.
'Well, we'll have to see about that,' I thought. 'She's my hired hand, not his. His folk wouldn't be fit to pay one, even if they had the need of one.'
The sun sank towards the blue Donegal hills beyond the Finn River to our right.
After a while I heard her whisper something to Joe that sounded like, "Ka jay Methodist?"

Chapter 5

A Strange Home-coming

He was running for all he was able, like a punch-drunk hare.
Like a hare, wounded, hounded, trying to escape a pursuing greyhound on the side of a heathery hill back home in Inishowen. But he was nowhere near such a hillside, much and all as he might have wished. No airy open slopes here. This run was hemmed in by the mouldering grey-brick walls of a tight alleyway in the arse-end of Strabane. The soles of his boots skittered on dog-dirt and rotting rubbish, the tippings of those who had the bad fortune to dwell in the wee streets near the river.
Heart thumping and head spinning from the drink, he bounced from one wall to the other. Near the end of the narrow passage he skidded to a stop by the yard door of the next-to-last house. A quick look behind him along the grimy half-light of the passage, gagging and gulping for breath at the same time.
No sign of them.
Yet!
Hand through the gap to lift the rusting latch and he was in, shunting the two new bolts into place behind him.
He didn't think he had time to warn Mary inside. Not knowing he was in the coal-shed outside would make it easier for her to plead innocence anyhow. No fearful consternation would be clouding her eyes when they tried to bully her for information.
Swiping the coal-dusty cobwebs away he hunkered down in the darkest corner behind some salvaged planks of wood and drew an old coat over his body. He lay in the darkness and listened.
They came, of-course they came. But not because they had been sprightly enough to follow him and see him run up the back alley. No, they came to the front door.
'How in the hell do they know that I have anything to do with Mary?' he thought. 'How did they know I would make for here?'
He heard the thunder of their knocking and the guttural rasp of their demand.
"Open up! This is the police".
'Jesus, I'm done for,' he breathed into the mustiness of the coat.

He could only guess at what was going on inside. She would be dwarfed by those big black bastards but she would not be intimidated, the same girl. He could just imagine the calm pretence of cooperation, the screen she would shift into place to mask that defiant steel he so often saw in her eyes. She thought about the enemy the same way as he did. She would give nothing away. It was nothing she knew anyway, not even the simple truth that her man was hiding, curled up like a hedgehog, in her coal-bunker at this very moment.

Would they believe her and go about their business? Would they search the house? The tiny back yard, with its stinking latrine and throw-all shed?

He didn't have long to wait.

The rear door of the house busted open. He heard the murmur of unfamiliar voices coming into the backyard; then Mary's calm tones, confident, smarmy almost to the point of bravado.

"Search away. Any place you want!"

Little did she know.

If they found him he would just have to go quietly. He wouldn't be wanting any rumbustiousness, for there was always a chance Mary might get hurt. He would just have to trust that O'Donnell and his other Donegal volunteer mates could get him sprung from wherever he would be held. That's if these black bastards weren't intending to put a couple of quick bullets in him and claim he had refused to stop for them. Worse they were capable of, that he knew. There was no point in trying to run for it or make a fight of it now.

"Take a luk in the privy, Sam. An' that coal-shed forbye!"

'A good Donemana farmer he sounds like,' he thought. 'I would know that accent anywhere. Too often I had to listen to their orders and their cheek.'

The shed door grated open on its corroded hinges and he sensed a ghosting of light enter the gloom of the place. He closed his eyes and held tight to his breath. Nothing he could do about the thump of his heart against the wall of his chest.

Then he heard Mary speak again as the hobnailed boots scrabbled around on the gravelly floor.

"If yous know so much about me and Kevin Duggan yous'll know that him and me broke up six months ago, after he took up with some Donegal woman, the name of Eithné Coyle."

The scuffling of the boots stopped for a split second.

'God, you're a genius, Mary!' he thought.
The name had rung a bell in the heads of the two peelers. Just enough to distract this one from pulling the timber aside to look closer into the corner where he lay. He sensed the man turn around and leave the shed. The door swung closed behind him with a rusty croak that sounded to him like a sigh of relief.
"Whaat did ye say aboot Eithné Coyle?"
Smiling to himself like a man spared from the noose he listened to Mary spin some yarn about a new relationship which he himself was supposed to be engaged in. Eithné Coyle would love it if she ever heard the story; if indeed she survived the struggle.
The voices faded as the backdoor closed again and he allowed himself to relax for a while, a good while, before he dared venture in to his Mary to tell her how close she had been to losing him, maybe for good.

~~~~~

"I knew right well you were somewhere around," Mary argued.
"How on earth did you know?"
"Agh Kevin," she teased. "The two bolts."
"The two bolts? What about the two bolts?"
"They didn't close by themselves, did they now? And I didn't close them. I left the door open as you always be telling me to. So as soon as I let those boys out into the yard I looked and saw the bolts closed and I knew you must have come in."
He looked at her, appreciation and wonderment in his growing smile.
"So that was why you came up with that line about Eithné Coyle?"
"Aye, it was the first thing came into my head. I was just hoping you wouldn't be fool enough to come out from wherever you were hiding to deny it!"
He pulled her down onto his knee on the couch and her arms went around his neck.
"You are some girl, Miss Kearney," he said into the dark mane of her hair, his free hand intimate on the sprawl of her figure.
"Stop it Kevin," she said, pulling herself free of him and rising. "This'll never get the tea made. Tell me about the fair. Any trouble? Any news worth passing up the line?"
"Nothing much. Big crowd of Specials standing guard at the Belfast Bank. As if we'd try to rob it in broad daylight, in the middle of the fair.
~~~~~

Eejits! I got searched and questioned by the police on the bridge. Right and rough they were too but I got away alright. I showed them the fake reference and they fell for it."
She smiled.
"I should be getting paid for all those letters I wrote. Who were you this time?"
"A Mr John Quigley from Creeslough; 'the best ploughman I ever had', according to some farmer from Ardigarvan."
"So, if they believed you, how come they were chasing you?"
"Aye you'd wonder that. A few things happened later on."
Kevin took a cup of tea from her hand and stretched out on the sofa.
"What few things happened? Did you get into bother again?"
"Not at all. There was a bit of a fight by the Market Hall. Mick and one or two others were getting it tight from a gang of hard men; young fellows, farmers, likely orangemen from out the country. I just threw a couple of punches to help out and the next thing the police were running at us from everywhere."
Mary turned from the table, frowning.
"You know you are supposed to keep yourself out of bother. 'Just gather information,' they told you. You are no use to the cause if you are in some British gaol somewhere."
He laughed at her.
"Don't be worrying yourself. Sure didn't I get away no bother. I lay low in McSwiggan's for the rest of the day. Had a pint or two."
"Or three. Or four, by the sound of it. So what happened to put the police on your tail then?" Mary quizzed.
Kevin sat quiet for a bit.
"That's what I don't know," he said.
She lit the first candle and pulled the blind over the net curtain in the one tiny window of the room.
"Could somebody have recognised you and given them the nod?"
He sat thinking, slowly, deeply, then suddenly sat forward.
"Henderson!"
Mary stared at him, waiting for the rest.
"Matthew Henderson! I had words with him and Joe in McSwiggan's. He must have gone straight to the police!"
"You saw Joe? You never said."
"I was coming to it," he said. "They were in having a drink and I heard them arguing. All I was doing was giving Joe some backing."

"I can't think what our Joe would have been saying that you would be giving him backing. What was it about?"
"Agh, you know; the usual."
"And you were stupid enough to get involved arguing with Matthew Henderson in a public house? In the middle of Strabane on the day of the Rabble Fair? You must be mad, mad or drunk!"
"Come on now, Mary; I'm not that daft. All I was arguing with Henderson about was... was that he had been looking for me up and down the street. He would have hired me again this year. I turned him down! That's all! I swear it!"
"And I suppose the reason you gave was that you are working as an intelligence officer for the IRA this year? Kevin Duggan, sometimes I think you are..."
He interrupted in temper.
"Shut up, woman! I know what I said and what I didn't say."
"And what did you say, if you are so sure?"
"I said I had got a position somewhere else. Gortin, I think I said."
Mary gave him a dully disbelieving look.
"Anyway, that's when he stormed out of the place, with Joe behind him like a dog on a lead. And that's when he must have gone to the police, the bastard! That's why they came ploughing into McSwiggan's. If I hadn't been out the back for a piss I'd a been caught."
"But why would he have gone to the police?"
"How would I know that? Out of spite likely."
"You think?"
"I do think! And I won't forget it either. The time will come when I get the chance to strike back at him in his big protestant mansion. Those hay-sheds of his would make a grand fire up on the hill there, wouldn't they?"
Mary held her answer inside her head and they ate in silence. Tea, soda bread and sausage.
"Nice sausages them."
"Devlin's best."
"How was the Post Office today?"
"Same as usual. A bit busier, with the fair and all."
"It would be."
The fire bleached out to an ashy yellow and the small chat gave way to a hush, punctuated by the mellow snoring of Mary Kearney's volunteer lover.

Chapter 6

Sally Anne Sweeney

What I thought about the Henderson farm

I enjoyed the chat with Joe on the journey to the farm of my new employer. He seemed a very friendly fellow, this Joe. Better still was the fact that he had a good bit of Gaelic at him. The first thing he asked me was, *"Caidé do bharúil den aonach inniu?"*

Did I enjoy the fair today? I did but when I started to tell him what I thought of it he stopped me and told me to slow down a bit.

"My Irish is not as good as yours," he said, "so take it easy and I will understand you."

It was good advice and I learned from it.

Joe rambled on about this and that and I helped him out when he got stuck for a word or a phrase. Sometimes he was giving me a bit of information about the area we were going through. When we reached the small village of Clady he told me there had been a gun battle there back in February.

"The Specials were ambushed by our lads," he said. "There was one constable shot dead. Bullets were even fired into the priest's house."

"Are you trying to scare me?" I asked him.

"Not at all."

A while later he told me, "This place is called Tullymoan. They have a ghost here, a very tall man with white hair. He can run like the wind. He doesn't do any harm, just scares the local women out of their wits. They say he can run quicker than a horse."

"Might be worth getting to know," I said. "In case I need to go somewhere in a hurry."

"You are not wise," he laughed.

As we talked I noticed that my new employer said nothing and just ignored us. He seemed to be preoccupied with something, just staring straight ahead, glaring even, I would say. He did not join in the conversation at all but then how could he if he had no notion what we were saying. We drove past a burnt-out house that looked as if it might have been a pub. I happened to notice the tall fellow's face as he looked at it; he shook his head slowly in annoyance, I thought. Then he turned towards Joe and gave him a strange stare that I could not understand except that it was not a look that was full of the joys of friendship. For a second Joe met his eye, then he turned away, a sadness about him, and stared at the hills to the west of us. This all meant something, I thought, but I had no idea what.

I risked a comment to him about my new boss, in a small voice that only Joe could hear, just in case.

"So he does not have Gaelic?"

"Not a word of it," Joe replied. "Hardly a soul about here has any Irish."

"How come you have it then?"

He warmed to this question I could see.

"My folk all have it. My father is a great speaker. He could light a fire with his Gaelic, so he could."

I laughed under my breath at this old expression. I had not heard it in ages.

"It is the truth you are saying," I told him, "if that was him I was talking to at the fair. I am surprised all the same. I did not expect to find many Irish speakers over here."

"You are right too. We are the only ones around."

"How is that?"

"We are not from here originally, the Kearneys I mean. My father's family came down here from Gleneely, up in the Sperrin mountains. In times past that was a Gaeltacht area you see, so they brought the language with them. My father is keen to keep it alive in us, the same way he got it from his father."

"Fair play to him," I said.

"My mother would not be as sharp in it though. Just what she learned from my father."

"He was nice to me anyway."

"Good," he said, "and why wouldn't he be?"

I looked away; this was getting too friendly. He just laughed at me.

"You will have to come over and meet the rest of the Kearneys," he said.

"I will. Are there many of you?"

"Three girls and three boys," he said. "Mary, then me, then Kate and Rosie, then Seamus and wee Hughie."

"Grand," I said.

Later he said to me, "You should be starting to feel at home now. We have just crossed into Donegal."
I looked around me. I was confused.
"How is that?" I said. "I did not see any...."
"You did not see any border, did you? No, and you won't. The boundary between Tyrone and Donegal runs all over the place here. In a minute you will be back in Tyrone and you will not know any difference. We only know because we were born and reared here."
We travelled along a winding road through some fine stone-ditched fields, lovely grass in them. You do not get many fields like that in the Rosses, believe me. Most of the cottages I saw were a lot grander than what you would see around home too. We rounded a bend and saw a fine looking farm ahead of us. The horse slowed to a stop at its driver's bidding.
"This is where I get off," said Joe. "You see that farm? That is Matthew's place. I live away down this lane here. The two farms are sort of side by side. We're in the hollow by the burn, he's on the hill. We are neighbours. You will see plenty of me."
"Whether I want to or not," I said. He seemed to be the kind of fellow who brought out the tease in me. There was no helping it.
"That you will," he said, ignoring my taunt.
Matthew looked as glum as a rain cloud and barely turned to acknowledge him leaving.
"See you later, Matt, and thanks for rescuing me in McSwiggan's."
He skipped off down his lane into the deepening dusk of the evening.
I was curious about this rescue but I was not going to ask. My boss did not seem to be in the mood for conversation anyhow. But suddenly he turned to me as we came into his lane, his chin with an unpleasant set to it.
"I'll thank you to speak in English when you're around my place," he said.
I was taken aback by this but I managed to mumble an apology.
"Tá mé buartha," I said before I realised that I was still thinking in Irish.
He glared again. I was mortified.
"I mean, I am sorry," I said.
He must have seen the fluster on me for he softened his look a bit and spoke in a more consoling tone, "English is a guid an-ugh tongue. Keep your Irish for Donegal."

I said no more. At the same time I wondered what 'Guid an-ugh' meant.
The house was set a field-length back from the road. A row of tall trees lined the side of the lane, all very uniform and organised of themselves. It was a very nice entrance. Very pretty. The dwelling on one side of the lane was balanced by a large, tree-covered hill on the other, an old fort of some sort, I thought. Some distance behind the farmstead the land rose sharply towards the dark of the evening sky.
As we came at the house and I got a clear view of it through a gap in the trees, I was taken aback a bit by its first appearance. It was a big two-storied house, like the parochial house in Annagary. I had not thought that it would be so grand. Imagine me living in such a place. The front wall of it near the door, in fact the whole ground floor, was covered in ivy, thick, green and rich-looking. It made me think of a man's face with a beard on it. A face that seemed to be scowling at us from beneath eyebrows of thatch. If the truth be told though, it was dull old thatch that looked as if it had seen better days. In front of the house was a small garden but, as we passed it, I could see that no one had been bothering with it for a while. There were weeds where once there likely were flowers, overgrown bushes that had probably been nice wee shrubs. We rounded the side of the house and were in a square-shaped street, closed in on all sides by various outhouses. The horse made a spurt towards its stable where yet another horse neighed a welcome over the half-door. Tired after its long journey, it dunked its head into the water trough beside the door.
"Lord above, they have two horses," I thought to myself. I did not know anybody in the Rosses with two horses. Like ourselves, most folk had only a donkey or a wee pony, if they had anything itself.
I was nervous entering this grand farmhouse. I had no idea what it would be like inside or who I would be meeting. Two girls jumped toward me like welcoming collie dogs, curious and friendly. Twins obviously, by the similarity between them; about ten or eleven years of age, I judged them to be. Nice enough looking girls but in need of a bit of a tidy up, especially their long fair hair which would have been better tied back or in plaits or something. They were forever pushing it back from their faces, like they were echoing each other.
They gave me a right good welcome.
"I am Jane. This here is Millie," said one of them.
"I'm Mawey," said the other.

'Twins but very different,' I thought at once. 'God left his hand on this one, *an créatúr bocht.'*
"This is Sally Anne," Matthew said.
"Why you hae two names?" said the Millie one. The muffled way her words came out took me a second to understand what it was she was asking me. Then I saw what she meant and smiled at her honest curiosity.
"Because where I come from most people have two names. Sometimes three or four. Sally is my own name and Annie is my mother's name, do you see?"
"Why you want your mo'er's name too?"
"That is just the way it is, Millie," I said.
"You are going to sleep up above us in the attic," said Jane.
"Fine."
"Dere's mice up dere," said Millie.
I understood that alright but I did not show her any panic.
"I can handle that, with the help of God. I have a bit of the cat in me," I said, and I turned my hands into claws and made as if to pounce on her, like a cat would do; I was feeling at my ease with these children already. She screamed and scampered out of the kitchen to whatever room lay beyond the door.
"Aye," said Matthew in a quietly teasing voice, "I thought there was a bit of the cat about you when I saw those green eyes."
'What?' I thought. I was not quite sure how to react. Here I was, just in through his door and already I was thinking that this fellow's banter was a bit too free and easy.
'Do I just be good mannered and ignore this or do I be myself?' I thought.
My father always taught me to be true to myself but he had also warned me about these types of men. I turned away so he would not see my confusion. I set my bundle on the kitchen table.
"As long as I don't ever have to deal with your claws," he added.
I ignored this too and said nothing. This Matthew seemed to be a different character in his own house, away from Joe. What was he expecting from me? Banter? An argument? I started to take off my coat and looked around the place for the first time.
It was a fine looking kitchen, it has to be said, even if, after a closer look, there were things that could have done with a good cleaning. The four-paned window looking out into the backyard for a start. My eyes

fell on two framed pictures which were placed there on the sill; one was a wedding picture with just the bride and groom, the other was of a family group, the Henderson parents, no doubt, with this Matthew, another girl and two toddlers that I took to be the twins. On the mantle-piece above the hearth stood another photograph, one that seemed to be taking pride of place between two oil-lamps. It showed a man in soldier's uniform standing in a garden, a row of trees behind him.

'Saints preserve us,' I thought as his eyes stared down at me. 'What sort of family have I come into that has a picture of a soldier where there should be a Sacred Heart of Jesus?'

The dresser was a big solid one, made of some dark wood and stacked with all manner of crockery. In the middle of the room the kitchen table took up a lot of space and had six sturdy chairs around it. The thing that most took my attention, though, was the huge grandfather clock, standing soberly against the opposite wall, dominating the whole room as if to keep everybody in order. I had never come across a clock like that before. The first impression it made on me was that I should never think to disagree with it.

"You will be wanting a cup of tea?" I said.

"Aye, but come and meet my mother first. She's through here."

He led the way across the hall, past a staircase and into a parlour sort of room, a good bit smaller than the kitchen. I counted three soft chairs and a sofa in there, all a bit cluttered. A couple of grand paintings of country scenes looked down from the walls with some sort of verses written on them. No religious paintings at all though; not a statue in sight, not a candle nor a holy water font; not even a Saint Brigid's cross.

The woman of the house sat quietly on the sofa with her back to me, seeming to be staring at the turf fire in a small hearth.

"Mother, this is Sally Anne Sweeney."

She turned her head slowly to me and I saw two sad old eyes in a face that was still far from old, a face that had still a faint shadow of the beauty of its youth. Not so much in the skin, which had the greyish texture of spilled candle-grease, but in its firmness and shape and in its features. I could see where Matthew got his looks from straight away.

"Who?" she said.

"Sally Anne," said Matthew. "Remember I told you I was going to hire a maid today at the fair in Strabane. Well, this is her. This is my mother," he said to me.

"Hello Mrs Henderson," I said holding out my hand. My father would have been proud of me.
She took my hand in both of hers, very gently stroking the back of it in a strange and intimate gesture. She stared up into my eyes as if trying to recognise me from before. I could tell she was still a bit puzzled. It took her a while to speak and when she did her voice was flat, like a fiddle string that had not been tuned up in a while.
"Hello dear," she said, studying me without expression. "Lord bless us but there's not much to you; you're just a slip. And have you come far tonight?"
"I have; I am after coming from the far side of Donegal."
"Donegal?" she said with a bit more enthusiasm. "Sure that's not far. That's Donegal you can see out of the kitchen window. Them hills over there is Donegal. On the other side of the burn is Donegal. You're nearly home now."
I looked at Matthew.
"She is right," he said. "Those hills you see rising up behind Joe's place....that is the Free State. So anytime you feel lonely or too far from home just go and take a look over there."
"And is Joe's farm in Donegal?" I asked.
"It is. It's in the town-land of Gortnagappel. This is Lismore. There's only a wee burn and a stone ditch and a bit of a hedge down there on the march between the two farms," he said. "Between the two counties."
"Gortnagappel," I said. "The horse's field."
"What do you mean?" he said.
"That's what it means. It's Gaelic," I said. "*Gort* is field; *capall* means a horse."
He just made a funny expression with his face, eyebrows up and corners of the mouth down; I think it meant, 'Strange. I didn't know that.'
I continued in this line of thinking, being comfortable with it.
"And your place likely takes its name from the fort."
He stared at me, waiting for an explanation.
"*Líos mór*," I said. "It is Gaelic for 'a big fort'...like the one in your field."
I immediately got the impression, just by the look that crossed his eyes, that he resented me knowing something about his place that he did not know himself.

"That's as maybe," he muttered, "but stick with the English and don't be trying to teach any of that stuff to the girls."
I said no more, thinking that I had maybe said too much already. I was thinking that it would take me a while to know what sort of things I could say to this man and what to avoid.
"And what brings you over here to us?" Mrs Henderson was staring at me again.
Matthew answered her with just the smallest bit of disappointment on his face.
"She is going to be working here, mother," he said. "She is our hired hand. She will be helping you in the house and me on the farm. Do you not remember I told you before I went to the fair?"
"Oh right," she said. "That's great now. There's nothing like a bit of extra help. And you'll be able to go home every night to Donegal."
"No, Mammy. She is staying here; sleeping in the attic. Living here all the time," said Jane.
"Oh, I'm sure?"
She sighed, gave Matthew a long thoughtful stare and turned back to the glowing turf.
"Girls, take her up and show Sally Anne her bed. Then come down and I'll show you around the kitchen," he said.
I soon got the layout of the house and the kitchen. There were three bedrooms and a bathroom on the first floor, with another room they called the guest bedroom on the ground floor, behind the parlour. My room was one of two small rooms, up at the top of a steep ladder, under the thatch. The first of these was a sort of storeroom; it had a wee skylight; my room was dark but cosy enough and the bed they had set up for me there was firm and comfortable, better than my own at home. Seven decent rooms, I counted, not including mine in the attic and the wee box-room beside it. At home we thought we were doing well with three; three and an outside toilet. How would I ever get used to the trips outside in the cold of a winter night when I was home again?

Chapter 7

Sally Anne Sweeney

How I got used to life in Tyrone.

I took it in my stride; it was not a bother to me.
The work was straight forward and there was not a bit of it that I minded at all. The blood blisters that rose on my hands in the first few days soon hardened into calluses. Baking bread, churning butter, making the dinner... I was used to this. The lady of the house stayed well out of my way. She sat by the fire for large parts of the day, just watching the flames. She seemed to have little energy for anything and little or no interest in what was going on around her. A nice enough woman but you would never really get very far in a conversation with her. She would just ask the strangest questions, and then ask them again in ten minutes. I was sad for her. You could see that something was wrong....and you could see that she had been a grand mistress of the house in her time. I often looked at her and wondered what sort of a woman she would have been to work for when she was at herself. And, if she suddenly came back into herself, back to the person she had been in earlier years, what would she make of me taking over her domain? What would she think of her son giving orders to a total stranger, and a skinny wee Donegal one at that, in what had been her kitchen? At times I could not help notice some of the similarities with my own mother back at home, except of-course that the causes of her problem were very different from Mrs Henderson's. But it definitely was a big help to me that I had had a lifetime of working around a woman who was content to spend her day ignoring me.
I wondered about the man of the house, her husband, Matthew's father. Where was he or what had happened to him? I did not like to ask if that was him in the picture on the mantle-piece and nobody seemed to want to mention him to me. At least in our house my mother had my father to be looking after her and talking to her. The woman of this house had only her children.
The two girls were the best of company and I enjoyed helping them with their school lessons in the evenings. Jane was smart enough and I

did what I could with wee Millie. We got on well most of the time. I found it hard not to be talking to them in Gaelic; indeed the odd word or sentence did come out when I was not thinking. I wanted them to see the way my mind worked in my own language; I was nearly sorry for them that they were stuck in the English and were lacking the richness of my tongue and the dialect of the Rosses. They did not know what they were missing. I found myself telling them that some of the things they said and the way they said them were coming straight from the Irish language; then I would be scared they would report me to their big brother so I had to cover myself with all the tom-foolery I could think of.

They would sing me some of their wee songs and of-course I would sing them some of mine. I was putting them to bed one night and we were singing to each other. I was singing them an old Irish lullaby that I like; *'Dún do shúil'* it was called....'Close your eyes'. Suddenly I heard Matthew's heavy footsteps coming up the stairs. Never before in its history had that song been translated into the English with such speed. The girls noticed, of-course, but to their credit they did not give me away; they just kept innocent looks on their faces when he put his big head through the door to ask me about some calf I was supposed to have fed.

They had their own way of saying prayers at night and I left them to it. Not a sign of a rosary bead in the whole house. I found it strange too the way Matthew would set a big black bible on the table most mornings after breakfast, read a bit out of it and say the 'Our Father'. All in English of-course, but I have to confess that in my head I was rhyming it off in Gaelic.

Out around the farmyard was a bit tougher. I thought my arms were going to pull away from my shoulders, especially in that first couple of days but, as time went by, I got more used to carrying the heavy buckets of pig feed and water from the yard-pump. There was a lot of poultry on the Henderson farm and it was understood that I would manage all of that work. Matthew never looked near it. He did seem to be disappointed in me about not being able to work with the horses though. Horse work was something I had no experience of at home. When we talked at the fair he had never mentioned horses. Maybe that was a good thing.

He was well organised and, once he got me doing things his way, he seemed to trust me and leave me to it. The only exception was the milking; he would take the lead in that and I would just help where I could. That suited me fine and I liked watching his way with the cows, with all his animals. He was a natural around them and had a whole level of kindness with them I could never have imagined. He had names for them all; when he was listing them off to me he told me that the white one was called 'Sally Anne' but he was only making a joke of me.

The rhythm of the day soon turned into the rhythm of the weeks and before I knew it June had arrived. We seemed to be cut off from the bigger world up there in the hills and the troubles of the country did not reach us very much at all. The weather was great that June. We worked together in the mountain bog, him and me, an hour's walk up behind the farm. The word Matthew put on it was 'footin' the turf; around home people called it *'cróigeadh'*, and back-breaking work it was too, whatever language it was said in. The turf had been cut some weeks before and the strong sun had put a good hard crust of a top-skin on them, so much so that they blistered my hands as we turned their damp sides up to the weather. Very dark turf it was, I would say, black and slimy as a slug on the underside. I made the remark to Matthew that I had noticed that the turf they burned here had a different smell to what we burned in Donegal.

"Not at all," he laughed. "Sure this is Donegal turf. This mountain is across the border you know. We're in the Free State at the minute."

"Is it?" I said. "How come your land is in Donegal?"

"Only a bit of it is," he said. "We have always had rights to this bit of bog. I don't expect that it will change now, border or no border."

"These midges pay no heed to your border anyway, and that is no word of a lie," I told him as clouds of the wee beasts chased us off the hill in the evening. I swiped them off my face.

"Let them be," he said. "You kill one of them and every midge in Ireland comes to its funeral."

I killed more than one of them as we were walking side by side off the hill down the bog rodden towards his place. I had the feeling he was sneaking a look at me out of the corner of his eye. Then he caught me by the arm and sort of pulled me round to face him. The shock of it made the heart jump in me.

"Give us a look at you," he said, staring close at me and then a grin coming on him like what you might see on a donkey, the teeth shining in his mouth.

"What is it?" I said, the blood rising up my neck as usual.
"You are a sight," he laughed. "You have two big smudges of dirt on your cheeks. Here, let me wipe it off."
Maybe he was trying to be kind but I was not going to let him be touching me, dirt or no dirt. I was that embarrassed that I pulled away and ran ahead of him while I tried to wipe my face clean of the peat dust.
"Ah for God's sake lass; I was only trying to help," he called after me, far too happy of himself altogether.
In between working the turf, he had cut his hay crop. This was earlier than usual, he told me, to make the best of the sunshine and the breeze.
One evening we were working out in what they called 'the fort field', the one with *an líos* in it. The strong rays of the sun were slanting in through those huge sycamore trees; you could see *na míoltógai* dancing in the shafts of dusty light, a nuisance, those midges, though they did not seem to trouble us as much as they did when we were up at the turf. The swallows were having a great time, swooping around looking for their supper. I was loving the fresh scent of the drying hay.
Joe was there helping Matthew, as was the custom. Around here they called it 'morrowing'. 'You help me today and I will help you tomorrow or whenever you need it'. At home we have a word for helping each other; *meithael;* I suppose it means something the same. The three of us were raking the hay into low ricks to stop the evening dew from dampening it too much. We were casting very long-legged shadows across the sward. The twins were running around, jumping over these moving shadows, laughing and chasing after Fly, the sheepdog. At one point they came scurrying across the meadow, excited about something.
"There's somebody coming down the loanen," they called. I had heard them use that word before when they were meaning the lane in from the road.
The dog took to frantic barking.
We saw a strange looking head bobbing slowly above the height of the hawthorn hedge.
"It is Tam Glenn," said Joe with surprise as the figure turned in at the gate and trudged towards us.
Matthew and Joe left me to go to meet this strange-looking individual, forks stuck in the ground in the meantime. I followed slowly, just being

my normal curious self. Work could wait, it seemed. The girls ran to the visitor, whooping away like seagulls.
"God bless the work!" I heard him call in a rasp of a voice.
The greetings were warm on both sides. He did not look like a man you would rush to hug though, it has to be said. He had a whole blizzard of hair on top of his head, mostly white but with a few strands of darker colour; below that there was the most comical face I think I had ever seen. Bright, sparky eyes set on either side of a potato of a nose, a nose with a cobweb of thin red veins stretched over it. The face was well browned by constant living outside, I was thinking. He had a patchy grey beard that straight away made you want to scratch your face in sympathy. Trying to escape from the middle of the growth was a grinning slash of a mouth that reminded me of a child's drawing. Several brown and yellow teeth stuck out at different angles but, for all that, it was as happy a mouth as I have seen. There was a smile playing itself around the corners of it, as if this man knew a secret that the rest of us had no notion about. He wore a dark shabby coat which might have been leather at some time in its history and was now tied together at the front with a length of hemp rope. Below the uneven hem of the coat there was a much-darned pair of moleskin trousers that looked even older than the character himself. Well-worn boots on his feet with barely the skin of a sole on them. Under one arm he had a brown-paper parcel; sheets of tin stuck out through the tattered corners. Below the other arm I was delighted to see what looked like an old fiddle case; over his shoulder hung a cloth bag. It would have been hard to say what age he was; somewhere between fifty and the grave.
After I was introduced to him, the visitor stared long and hard at me until the twinkle in his eye and the curl of his lips had me so flustered that I picked up my rake to put myself to work again.
"Agh, I'm right sorry, girl," he said. "I was just lukin' at you to see if I knew any of your kin. I travel a lock aroun' the whole country and I tend to mind faces and families. It's a hobby of mine, you might say. But I can't place you at all now. What art do you hail frae, dear?"
I must have looked puzzled for Joe came to my rescue.
"Where are you from, he wants to know?"
"I am from Donegal, the Rosses," I answered; "a townland called Ranahuel if you know it?"

"I don't," he said. "That is one part of the country that I haven't been much in. I was through it once, going north from Dungloe but it wasn't great for a man in my trade."
I looked back at him, my face asking for an explanation as Matthew turned back to his work.
"You see, I have to depend on the goodness of the people for my daily bread. The west of Donegal wasn't the best of a place."
"Why not?" I said, rising to defend my own people. "We are as good as anybody else."
"Aye, indeed you are," Tam said. "I agree with you. I found that the folk there would give you the bite out of their mouths. But that was the trouble. They would have nothing left for themselves after it. So I just thought it was my duty to keep moving on. They couldn't afford my skills anyhow. It wasn't fair on them. Good folk though."
"And what skills were at you that they could not afford?" I asked, resting on my rake for a minute.
"I am what you call a 'tinker'," he said. "I make all kinds of pots and pans and mugs and things. Whatever you need, I can make it. Or fix it."
Joe joined in. "And he's the best fiddle player in Ireland. You should hear him, Sally Anne."
"That can wait till later," said Matthew. "Here girl, you've quit working so take Tam in and get him a bite to eat. We will redd up here and be in after."
'Could I not ask the man a question itself?' I thought, but I did as I was told anyway.
A fiddler? Now that was interesting. I had left my own fiddle at home of-course; I could not very well carry it with me to the hiring fair. It would be nice to hear this man play; maybe get a tune myself. So I made him a dish of potatoes, bacon and buttermilk and he kept me in chat from the corner. Then he tucked in as if there had not been food across his lips in weeks, which might well have been true.
"Brave praties these," he muttered through a full mouth. "Luk at the big white smiles on them, and them about to be et. I was in plenty o' places where the folk would never so much as ask if you had a mooth on ye, never mind setting me a plate o' vittles the like o' this!"
It took me a second to understand what he said and then what he meant. It was a funny way he had of talking, stranger even than the people round here. He sounded a bit Scottish, to my ears.

"*Na Rossan* is it ye come frae?" he said. "So you speak the Gaelic then?"
"I do," I said. "*Agus tú féin*? Yourself?"
"Just a *cúpla focal* that I picked up on my travels," he said. "There wouldn't be a big lot of Gaelic left where I come frae."
"And where is that?"
"The fair county of Antrim. I am one of the Glenns."
He laughed at himself and slapped his knee, as if this was great humour. I looked at him, not understanding this.
"Agh, you poor child; you're not far travelled, are you? You never heard tell of the Glens of Antrim, did you?"
I had no notion what he was meaning or if it was a joke or what, so I just watched him giggle to himself and wipe the froth of the buttermilk from his beard with the back of his filthy sleeve.
He finished his feast and pushed the plate towards me across the table.
"There's a lot of grand music and great players aroun' the west of Donegal," he said and he told me about some of the well-known fiddlers from Glencolmcille to Gweedore. Most of these were folk I had heard of, some I had even played with but I made him none the wiser.
"I have some of their tunes," he told me, tapping the side of his head. "In here."
"You stole tunes from our fiddlers?" I said with a laugh.
"That is the truth, me girl," he said. "You see, there's a lot of grand tunes that never manage to get out from the parish they were made in. They get tied down there, stuck in some wee valley behin' the hills or hemmed in by some river. And they are great tunes, tunes that the rest of the country needs to hear. So I always think that it falls to me to lift them and carry them wherever I go; share them aroun' wae ither music folk."
"Sure that is grand then," I said, working round him.
He was warming his legs by the fire, deep in thought, when he suddenly turned to me with what I thought was going to be an urgent question.
"So how are you getting on with our Matthew?"
"Fine," I said. "He is a good man to work for."
"The best of a fellow," he agreed. "Just needs to be getting himself a wife."
"He has no need of a wife while I am here," I said. Then, realising what the old fellow might take from this, I added, "I mean, he does not need

one while I am here....to do the work just, I mean....oh I have nothing against him getting a wife. Aye, he needs a wife."
This was the reddest I had been in a while. I prayed to God that Matthew would not come walking back in the door and see the glow on me. Tam Glenn just smiled at me and stroked that ridiculous beard of his; I thought he was looking for bits of bacon or potato that had escaped and taken refuge there.
"So that is the way the wind is blowing, is it?" he said quietly, as if to himself.
"No, it is not the way the wind is blowing. That is not what I meant and you know it is not. I only meant that I am working here at the minute and so he has no need of another woman to be.... he does not need a wife to be working for him," I said.
'*Dún do chlab, girseach*! Just shut your mouth and you won't be putting your foot in it,' I told myself in my head.
"I know rightly what you meant," he said, his eyes working double time at the twinkling mischief. "And I won't be saying a thing to him about it."
I looked at him. "You better not, if you want any more food from my hand," I said.
"That would be too big a price to pay," he said and we both laughed, even if I did not know yet if I could trust him or not.
I kept a close ear to his conversation with Matthew and Joe when they arrived back in the kitchen later but their subjects tended to be more political and I felt safe from any teasing. Joe was asking Tam about his experiences while wandering the roads of this troubled land.
"And you never have any bother with the Specials or anybody?"
"Not at all," he said. "They have stopped me and searched me be times. I don't know what they were looking for but if they find it, they're welcome to it. I'd be as surprised as them. Sure they searched the Cardinal of all Ireland too so I'm in good company. I just play along with them, don't antagonise them. Just pretend I'm lost."
"Which you likely are," said Matthew.
"I take out the fiddle and play them 'The Sash'. That keeps them happy. Then if it's the other boys hold me up, I'll give them a verse of '*Mo Ghile Mear*'. The fiddle knows no boundaries," he said. "No sides. It just turns out whatever tune is needed at the time; sure some of them are the same on both sides anyway."

"Like enough," said Matthew. "What was it like when you were coming up through Fermanagh? Has it settled down again after that IRA invasion?"
"Well now, they had a tough enough time of it. It was terrible they say. Days of gun battles. Seems the soldiers eventually got the better of them and chased them back into Donegal. But there's a lot of very worried folk there, on both sides of the fence," he said.
"The British lost more men than the volunteers did," said Joe quietly, seeming to need to make a point of this. Matthew gave him a dark stare.
"You don't know that for sure," he said. "Anyway, we have the place back in our hands, after the IRA trying to take it over."
I noticed Joe's dour face and I felt for him in this moment. Tam must have done too, for he smiled a lob-sided smile and started talking again.
"Fermanagh is a strange place you know, like as far as this new border is concerned. It goes right through the middle of some places, and people get caught living on the wrong side of it. Take a place like the village of Pettigo. I called in with one woman. She's an old friend who lives there. She told me that the border runs through the middle of her house. When she is in the parlour she is in the north; when she goes to the kitchen she is in the Free State."
"What about her bedroom?" asked Joe.
"Her bedroom? Ah, that's no-man's-land. Believe me, I tried," he laughed. "Nothing doing there."
Matthew and Joe roared at him. I could not help but laugh too but I did feel it my duty to say, "You are a terrible man, Tam! You may be grey on the head but it is not from being wise."
At that he looked at me and winked.
"Matthew," he said, and my heart started to thump. "This girl was telling me that you have no need of a....of a hired man about the place this year for she can work as hard as any man. Is she working hard for you?"
'Oh, the oul divil!' I thought. 'He had me going there.'
"She is, Tam. No complaints yet," said Matthew.
But Tam was not finished yet.
"She'll make somebody a great wee wife," he said.
I turned away sharply and busied myself with the plates.
"She likely will," said Matthew. "Will you want to stay the night Tam?"
'Oh Lord no,' I thought. 'Not up in the attic next to me?"

"That's guid o' you Matthew. I will take you up on that."
"Good," said Matthew, "but we'll have a tune out of you first. If you're not too tired."
"Never too tired to play a tune."
He took his fiddle from its box and launched into a few reels and jigs which he played with amazing speed for a man of his years. Before each tune he had a word or two about its origins, what county he had found it in, who he had first heard play it. I gave him good ear for he was full of knowledge and stories. At the same time my fingers were itching to get hold of that bow, so much so that I had to sit on them to stop them flexing. As he started a tune he would close his eyes tight and only open them again as it came to its end, with a wee half-smile as he glanced around our faces to see if we had enjoyed it. After a bit he looked at me, winking again like the western star on a frosty night.
"Will you dance for us, Miss Sweeney? I never knew the Donegal girl who couldn't dance. Will you dance to a hornpipe?"
"I will not," I answered.
"Ah come on with you now. Show us your steps," he continued. "Matthew, bid her to get up and dance for us."
Joe was nodding away, his eyes gleaming at me. Before my boss could give any orders I spoke up.
"I am no dancer but I will tell you what I could do. I will play your fiddle if you will dance."
They all looked at me.
"You never told us you could play," said Matthew.
"You never asked," I said.
"Are you serious? Are you a fiddler?" Joe's wee face was all surprise.
"You be the judge of that," I said and I took Tam's fiddle from his hand and launched into my favourite reel, *Ríl Dhun Na Ngall.* I have to say I played it with a vengeance on those weeks without music since I left home. Slow at first, I closed my eyes and then let it rip as fast as I have ever played it; I could not help but hear the tapping of hobnail boots on the tiled floor as those men tried to keep time with me. Whenever I finished with the usual flourish and looked at them they were all watching me with their eyes shining and their mouths open; certainly in the case of Joe anyhow. Even Mrs Henderson had arrived into the kitchen from the parlour and her legs were quivering as if she was about to break into dance.

"Lovely; the Donegal Reel; lovely," said Tam into the split second of silence before they all began to clap.
"That was quick," said Joe, still clapping when the others had stopped. "Even Tam would have bother keeping up with you."
"You didn't lick that off the wall, me girl," said Tam. "There's music in your very blood and bones. We can all see that, but who taught you?"
"My mother," I said.
"Your mother taught you...she must be a great fiddler then." Matthew's eyes were beaming at me. I was nearly embarrassed to look at him, so smitten by it was he. I think if I had asked for a rise in pay then and there I would have gotten whatever I asked for.
"No, that is the funny thing about it. My mother never taught me anything. She does not speak, you see. She was born that way. But she is one of the best whistle players you will ever meet. My father bought me a fiddle when I was wee, for he saw me listening to her and humming the tunes. And then I found that I was able to pick it up by myself."
"You never had a lesson?"
I shook my head. "No, but I watch other fiddlers."
"Donegal ones too, by the sound of it," said Tam. "If I didn't know already that that's where you're frae I would know by the wie you han'le the bow; that deep droning sound you get; lovely!"
"And why did you not bring your fiddle with you?" Matthew said.
I looked up at him. "I hardly think you would have hired me if I had been standing there in the fair with a fiddle under my arm. You would have walked away and looked for some girl with a fork over her shoulder and hay sticking out of her hair."
"You might be right," he laughed. "And I will maybe have to go looking for her yet if you start playing around the country."
"How could I? Sure I have no fiddle," I said.
"That's true," he said, and with that he got up from the table and left the kitchen in an abrupt way that made me wonder what he was doing. Had I said something to offend him?
"That's a great story altogether. And your poor mother can't speak? I'm sure you miss her, or maybe she misses you more," said Tam. "Give us another tune there, when you have the thing in your hand. It'll not want to be coming back to me after that anyways."
I resisted the temptation.

"I will not indeed. That will do me for the night. It's your fiddle. You play away," I said, forcing the fiddle into his hands again.

No sooner had Tam launched into another tune than Matthew came back into the kitchen. He stood there in front of me with a fiddle in his hand. He was trying to wipe the dust off it with the tail of his shirt. He had the bow under his arm.

Tam's tune slowed and stopped as he looked up at Matthew.

"Here girl," said my boss. "See if you can get a tune out of this one."

I reached up and took the fiddle.

"Is that your father's oul fiddle?" Tam spoke almost reverently.

"It is. It hasn't been out since.....Can you get it into tune?" Matthew said to me.

I hesitated, staring at its rich, red-brown wood. His father's fiddle? I was still waiting for somebody to talk to me about the man of the house but I had worked out that he had passed away some years before. Although I knew nothing of the circumstances it was clear to me that the death of her husband had had a major effect on Mrs Henderson, on all the family. That was why Matthew was '*fear a' tí*', the man of the house, at the age of twenty or whatever he was. And here I was with his father's fiddle in my hands, about to launch into some wild Irish reel. I could not do that, not for all the tea in China.

I held it out to Matthew.

"I cannot play it," I said into the quietness. "It would not be right."

"What would be wrong with it?"

"If it is your father's fiddle...."

"But I am asking you to play it. It is not right that it has been hidden away on top of a wardrobe these six or seven years," he said.

I looked at Mrs Henderson. I saw she was staring at me too, as was everybody else.

"But your mother?" I whispered to him.

"She will hardly..."

Mrs Henderson interrupted him.

"Go ahead and play it, girl. James would want to hear his fiddle again if he was here."

"She is right," said Tam. "James would be as pleased as punch if you played a tune for him on his fiddle."

I was still hesitant, the instrument almost shaking in my hands. I twanged the strings. They were well out of pitch. I blew some dust from them and started to tune them up.

"What was his favourite tune?" I said to Matthew.
He looked at his mother.
"There was a tune about some cutty called Eleanor that he used to play," she said.
"'Eleanor Plunkett'," said Tam with a wink and a nod of his head.
"Will you play it with me?"
"It will be an honour," he said and he did. It went well, if I say so myself. In my head it was a sort of tribute to the father of the house that I had never met, and I could see that Matthew took it the same way.
It was the last tune we played that evening but there would be many more such evenings.

~~~~~

I could not tell you how glad I was that old 'Tinker Tam', as I started to call him, had arrived at the house that day. It gave me a new lease of life and I think Matthew started to see me in a new light. It was clear to me that he was not one of those people who had no use for music. Joe as well. I heard him speaking to Matthew on the street when he was leaving; he did not know that I was listening from the toilet window above.
"Well, did I not tell you she was more than just a pretty face, Matt?"
"Away you on home and dream about her then," was Matthew's reply.
I climbed up to my attic bedroom. I was dreading finding old Tam perhaps getting ready to bed down in the room next door or, worse still, maybe on my bed but thankfully there was no sign of him. I was safe for the time being anyhow.
I think that was the worst night's sleep I had the whole time I was at Henderson's. It was not just that I was stiff and sore from the day's work; not at all. It was not even the familiar dry *scréach* of the corncrakes from the dusky fields beyond, a sound that often kept me awake. It was the tunes that were flying around inside my head like circling starlings and they seemed to have no notion of roosting. As the cooing of the doves and the crowing of the rooster woke me up around dawn I was still fiddling away in my mind. I put it down to the length of time since I had heard or played any of my music. I had not realised how much I missed it. It was just a pity the distant corncrake could not be keeping time with me!
~~~~~

In the morning I came down to the kitchen to light the fire. Tam was lying there, badly in my way.

'How am I going to work here and he stretched out on the floor before the hearth?" I thought to myself. 'I may waken him.'

As I was about to put my toe to him I noticed that there was a sheet of paper and a stub of a pencil lying beside him. I picked it up and had a look. The handwriting was rough and scratchy.

I could just about read what was written there.

'The Maid from Donegal'

Come listen to my story boys for many things I've seen
And many stories I have heard in the places I have been
But ne'er afore this moment as the evening shadows fall
Have I seen or heard the equal of the maid from Donegal

She was working in the hay field as I turned in the lane
And at first sight I must admit I thought her very plain
As skinny as the rake she held and nearly half as tall
But she could work, I'll grant you that, this maid from Donegal

She cooked me up a dinner that you could have served a prince
And when I played a hornpipe I asked her could she dance
But she took the fiddle from my hand and surprised us one and all
For she played the sweetest music, this maid from Donegal

She has magic in her fingers and mischief in her eyes
And if I'm not mistaken she doesn't realise
That she's cast her spell and both these lads are heading for a fall
For she will bring them trouble, this maid from Donegal.

My eyes nearly jumped out of my head. At the start, as I read it, it was kind of funny; very nice and complimentary and all. A very strange feeling for me to realise I had been the subject, for the first time in my life, of a poem. Albeit a poem written by a crazy old fool who was lying snoring at my feet. But when I read that last verse I felt like giving him a good kick. What right had he to say that I was casting a spell on Matthew and Joe? Worse still, what right did he have to imagine that I would bring them trouble? The cheek of him. It was all I could do to stop myself launching into him as he slept, giving him a piece of my mind, the old fool. But I thought better of it and held myself in control. What I did do was fold the sheet of paper up and stick it deep in the pocket of my apron. I could destroy it later. The last thing I wanted was for it to fall into the hands of Matthew.

I opened the door to the street and went about my morning work as if nothing had happened, but I was more guarded in myself for a good while after it.

When I came back inside Tam gradually woke himself up. He turned over a few times, stretched himself and broke wind with a long, loud rip.

"Tam," I said. "Control yourself. We have to eat in here."

""That's naethin'," he said, getting stiffly upon all fours. "In me prime I coulda farted for Ireland!"

"I do not doubt it," I said, "but this is Northern Ireland now, at least that is what I am told, and they have a law here against that sort of rudeness."

"You could be right, girl," he said, getting up. "They have laws against everything else so why not that too?"

He went out to the pump to give himself a wash. Not that you would have noticed when he returned. He went over to his things where he had been sleeping and seemed to be searching for something.

"You didn't see a wee piece of paper lying around?" he asked, his pencil stub pointing at me.

I turned away, crossed my fingers and lied of-course.

"A wee piece of paper? *Ní fhaca,*" I murmured, "I did not."

"Strange," he said, looking in the hearth. "I could have sworn I wrote a poem last night."

"Do you write poems as well then?" I asked.

"I do. For my sins. People need to write things down for the generations that folly them. How else will the young ones know how we lived?"

"You have a point," I said, setting the breakfast plates on the table. "But not everything is worth writing down surely?"

I could feel him studying me long and hard at that comment but he said nothing.

"I'll be on my way after a bit," he said, "if you have no need of any buckets or mugs or anything."

I thought to myself, 'He knows I took it and I have hurt his feelings somehow.' It was not in me to be doing that.
So I smiled at him and said, "Don't be in any hurry away. There's one or two of those tunes you played last night that I never heard before. Could you teach me them, do you think?"
"Rather than you steal them like?" he said and I glanced at him quickly. The twinkle was back. I smiled inside myself and turned to the porridge.

Chapter 8

Matthew Henderson

What I felt about Sally Anne

I was starting to think that this Sally Anne cutty was taking over my life.

Against my will.

Well, not really against my will, if I'm being honest.

It was just that everything seemed to start to revolve around her. I would find myself taking into consideration how she would feel about something, without even realising I was doing it. Me, wondering how a hired hand would feel? This was very strange country I was travelling in.

I suppose I first caught myself on that Saturday morning when Tam Glenn was taking to the road again. As was his wont, he had stayed with us for a couple of days. He mended a few buckets and things, hardly enough to merit the food he ate but that was just how it was between us. On his last evening we all headed down to Kearney's house and we had a great night of ceili-ing there; music, stories, dancing, the usual. Sally Anne played a few tunes too, to great acclaim. A servant girl, the centre of all attention? It wasn't usual.

Nor was it usual that I walked out the lane a bit with Tam as he was leaving our place the next day. He seemed to find that strange too, for his chat dried up suddenly and he gave me a couple of sideways glances.

"Are you doing alright now, Matthew?" he asked, in a kindly sort of way.

"I am," I told him. "My mother's not the best. I'm sure you noticed that. But Sally Anne is doing a grand job for us in the house; out around the farm too."

"She seems a very nice girl."

"Oh she is that," I said. "The best of a girl."

"And a great wee player into the bargain."

"Aye, she can fairly handle my father's oul fiddle, no denying."

"And a lovely looking lassie she is too," Tam said.

I caught myself on.

"Where are you thinking of travelling to next?" I asked him.
"At the end of your lane I'll turn right....or maybe left, and see where my feet take me son."
That was Tam for you.
The next day being Sunday we went to worship as normal, the four of us in the trap. Sally Anne had left earlier, after her morning work, to go to Mass with Joe Kearney and his folk. The Methodist Church in Castlederg wasn't big, which was just as well for it seemed to have been shoe-horned into too small a gap between houses there in the Diamond. I sympathised with it as I sat squeezed into the tiny pew and tried to force myself to listen to the clergyman, a visiting preacher from Sion Mills. He was in an agitated mood that day as he got stuck into us, and him standing up there in his pulpit, black-suited and six feet above contradiction. Maybe it was the coming season of Orange celebrations or maybe it was the newspaper reports of six young men shot in Armagh during this week but the atmosphere in the church was very strained. It was as if a dark cloud of fear hung over us. We had a lot to be thankful for though, despite the nearness of the border and the rumours of a crowd of the Irish Republican Army assembling over in the Free State, there had been little trouble around here compared to other areas. The minister was praying that this would continue but the very fact that he was praying about it at all made us all the more concerned that his prayers would likely not be answered.
I found bits of his sermon strange. Our own minister would not be a political man and the Methodist Church is not that way inclined. So why this stranger felt the need to try to give an argument from Scripture to underline the importance of the border was beyond me. His sermon was all about how people should submit to the authorities because they have been established by God. So any rebellion against the government of the land is rebellion against God; that was his point as far as I could make out.
We all knew that he was getting at the Irish rebels of-course. Not a soul in the congregation would be for arguing with him on this whole business.
He preached from the book of Acts, that God decides the times, the boundaries of nations and the places that people should inhabit.
'How dare the Boundary Commission think of redrawing the border? God decides these things'. That was the gist of it, if not the exact

words, his clenched fist thumping home the point on his Bible till I thought the pages were going to fly out of it for relief.

'Well,' I thought to myself, 'I just hope God decides to leave things the way they are. The last thing we want is for this part of west Tyrone to be lumped in with Donegal and the Free State. Heaven preserve us from that.'

It was all becoming a bit of a muddle in my head so my eyes went, as they often do when I am bored in church, to the War Memorial tablet on the side wall and to my father's name there among the others who fell.

Cpl James R Henderson, Royal Inniskilling Fusiliers

How many times had I read that since the plaque had been placed there? Read it and remembered his face, distorted through my teary eye. His handsome face, looking proud and strained at the same time, as he left us from Castlederg Station those seven years ago. The last time I saw him of-course. The last time any of us saw his big, wide smile.

No point in dwelling on it though. It doesn't bring him back.

I looked to the choir for inspiration. Well, actually to one particular girl in the choir. Alice Porter, although much younger than me, had begun to develop into a fine looking lassie, in a girly, flirtatious sort of way. The self-confident English accent may have been part of it, I imagine. I couldn't see her; she was huddled down in the seat behind her heavily-built mother and right in front of her father. He was the new bank manager in the town; all three were in the choir; big singers, the whole family of them. So I looked up to the roof beams and I counted them for the umpteenth time in my twenty one years. Except that, by the time I had counted into the thirties I was thinking about Sally Anne yet again, imagining her face and her dimpled smile and her hair and the way she walked when she was working around the farmyard. I found myself wondering how she was getting on at Mass with Joe. He would be enjoying her company, I had no doubt; I could just imagine him kneeling close beside her during the prayers, his mind on higher things. Not likely! Not a chance of that when she was beside him. Here I was, a good half mile away, and she was distracting me.

That Sabbath afternoon was the first time she annoyed me. It was strange how it happened. She did not appear back in our street until nearly six o'clock. I found myself starting to really resent her spending so much time away with Joe. She should have been back with me much earlier, not least for the work. I had started the evening milking by myself when she came out, still tying on her bag apron for the yard. Initially I ignored her; just kept working on with my head down to the task.

"I am sorry, Matthew," she said. "Me and Joe lost track of the time."

"Mister Henderson," I heard myself saying, even as I wondered at the strange way she had of saying my name. It sounded more like 'Mattieu'.

There was a silence and when she spoke her tone had changed.

"Sorry. Mister Henderson."

The glum silence returned. A horrible tension grew in the quietness between us, feeding on my resentments and, no doubt, on her's as well. I hated it.

'Why did I say that?'

Eventually I could stand it no longer.

"So where were you and what kept you?"

"I was on my day off," she said and walked out of the byre. What was that in her tone? Anger? Hurt? Defiance? I wasn't good at reading her yet but her sweetness had disappeared and I wasn't sure I liked what I saw in its place. She had annoyed me but now I was even more annoyed at myself.

When she came back I tried to soften my tone. "Were you over at Kearney's?"

"I was." A harsh snap.

"Are they alright?"

"They are."

"What are they doing today?"

"They are not doing much."

"What about Mass?"

"What about Mass?"

"Was it....was it the same as back at home?"

"Mass is Mass. But it was in the English."

"Why, what is it in at home?"

"Gaelic."

"Aye, of-course. It would be. So you enjoyed your day off?"

"I did."

"You're not too tired after the week's work?" Goodness, what was I saying?

"I am not."
The cow stirred and I moved the metal bucket away from its feet. I looked at her across the byre. She was biting her lower lip in that characteristic way of hers, her two front teeth and the small space between them visible to me in the dimness of the outhouse. She turned her face away from me.
'Well, that's fine then', I thought. 'Play hard and see if I care.'
She took a bucket of milk to the can and poured it in. Far too quickly. Some splashed out on the floor. I said nothing. I could see the tension in her body, the way she walked. On the way back she seemed to stumble on the uneven floor but regained her balance with a skip of her feet. Too late I stood as if to help her. She jerked her figure away and froze, arms raised in defence.
"Let me be," she said brusquely. "I don't need your help."
I let her be and sat down again to my task.
'This girl may be light on her feet,' I thought, 'but she can lay her words down with the thump of a sledge hammer.'
"Sally Anne," I said when I could stand it no longer.
"What?" A blunt grunt after a moment of silence.
"I am sorry."
She worked on without lifting her head.
"Did you hear me?"
"I did.... but it is me who has to be saying sorry."
"You already apologised for being late."
"It won't happen again," she said.
"It's alright."
"And I am sorry for calling you Matthew, Mister Henderson."
I winced. She still wouldn't look at me.
"Matthew is my name," I said. "It's what you should call me."
"No, I will call you Mister Henderson as you wish," she insisted. "Even if it does take me longer to say it."
The spark was coming back in her.
'Good', I thought.
"It was just me being stupid," I said. "Trying to make a point."
"You had every right to make it."
We worked on.
"You get on well with Joe," I said. 'Why do I say these things?' I thought.
"I do," she replied. "Is that alright?"

"Of-course it is. He's the best of a fellow. The Kearneys and us have been friends for ever. Especially since my father didn't come home from the war."
There was a silence.
"Your father was a soldier? I thought that must be him in the picture on the mantle-piece, the man in uniform but...."
"That's him alright."
"And you say he didn't come home from...was he.....?" she asked. She straightened herself up from her task and pushed her hair back behind her ears.
"He was killed at the Battle of the Somme."
"Oh God, I'm sorry. I never guessed. Joe never said.... I just thought he had passed away."
I said nothing. More silence. Then she spoke again.
"That must have been terrible for you, for your mother especially. For all of you."
"It wasn't great now," I said. "Anthony Kearney was there too; same regiment, same platoon. But he survived. Only just. He was sent home wounded."
"Joe's father was wounded in the war?" She sounded very surprised by this, almost as if she didn't believe me. "Is that why he has that limp?"
"It is. He was hit by shrapnel. He still has some of it in his back, he says. They couldn't take it out in case it paralysed him."
"But why was he fighting in the war?"
"You will have to ask him that. Why would he not fight? Sure hundreds of Donegal men fought too. He and my father joined the same day. Went all the way to Omagh to sign up. A lock o' neighbours signed up together, both Catholic and Protestant."
She seemed to be thinking about this for a bit.
"Are you a Protestant then? I thought you said you were something else."
"I'm Methodist. Methodists are Protestant too, but don't hold that against me."
"I have a lot to learn about over here," she said. "You are all so hard to understand."
We worked on in silence for a bit. She was deep in thought. Then she straightened up and spoke.
"I just never thought that Joe's father would have been fighting in the war. He doesn't seem like a soldier type to me."

"Well, like I say, you'll just have to ask him. In my father's case it was a natural thing to do, to fight for King and country, farmer and all as he was. The Germans had to be stopped. That's what he gave his life for."
"Would you have done it if you had been old enough?" she asked.
"I never thought about it but I suppose I would."
"And what about this border war? Would you fight against the Free State?"
'That's a question and a half for a hired girl,' I thought. I answered carefully.
"I don't think it is going to come to that. I hope it doesn't. But if I had to I suppose I would," I said.
"And I would have to fight against you," she said with a smile. "That would be a strange one."
"But you're not political, are you?" I asked, slightly afraid of the answer.
"No I am not," she replied. "Not at all. I have been searched by British troops sitting in my own house minding my own business... and I have lost one job because of the IRA destroying our railway, so I would not be greatly on for either of them."
"Fair enough."
"Nor do I want to lose another job over it," she said.
We had reached the end of the milking several minutes ago and were just standing talking across the entrance to the byre by this stage. It was a still, peaceful evening with the orangey sunlight warming the street and putting a reddish tinge on the feathers of the hens as they dabbed at corn spilled on the stone cobbles.
"Well," I said, "what will we do now?"
"You are the boss, Mr Henderson," she answered.
I allowed a wry smile.
"Do you want to take a walk down the back lane to the burn?" I said.
She looked at me strangely, I thought.
"Do I want to take a walk?" she said. "Not really; I would be lonely down there by myself. Anyway, it is time I was making a bite to eat for the family."
She strode away across the street towards the house leaving me standing wondering why I had made such a stupid suggestion. Then she called back over her shoulder.
"Sure you go for a walk yourself, Mister Henderson."
I watched her, trying to see if there was a smile with that suggestion.
'Goodness, she has me tied in knots', I thought.

Chapter 9

A Belfast Evening

Evening coal-smoke lay like a sagging hammock between the parallel red-brick homes of Cupar Street. Not a breath of wind on this grey July evening. It was very late but one or two lamps still spilled a weak, sulphury splash of light from cramped parlours through lace curtains and grimy four-paned windows onto the cobbles. Most people had already gone to bed, rosary said and fingers crossed against the unseen threats of the night. Little sound, apart from a very rare motor vehicle travelling slowly up the Falls Road, the yelping of some mongrel in a nearby back-yard and the eerie mewling of a couple of invisible cats. They had the place all to themselves. No-one in their right mind would be out walking in the wee streets at this time of night, given the current state of things in the new capital city of Northern Ireland.

But if someone had had the misfortune to stray along the road towards the broken, burnt-out houses at the far end they would not have been alone. Not that they would have realised the fact. Not until it was too late.

His brow, cheeks and eye-sockets were blackened with boot polish. Even his thick black moustache and eyebrows seemed to enhance the camouflage effect. Dark eyes bored through the brick-sized slit into the gloomy fug.

Waiting; the only movement he made was the slightest shifting of his weight from one knee to the other as he knelt in the shelter of a crumbled wall. This had been a home. Before the pogroms and the fire-raising of the past few years a family had called this heap of rubble their home. Many a brew-up of tea was made on that rusting kitchen stove; many a story told to a huddle of wide-eyed children in one of the two upstairs bedrooms; many an argument between father and mother, with the soft caressing of reconciliation and love-making following, like day after night.

'Now where are those families? And what stories are now being told to the youngsters?' he wondered. 'Most likely in some Dublin parochial hall, waiting for this all to be over before they can return to their native city. Or not, as the case may be. They'd be wiser staying where they are, where they are wanted.'

"'Ere Jimmy," he whispered, standing up. "Your turn mate."

To Jimmy's East Belfast ears it sounded more like 'Ua toon mite'.

The man behind the black moustache did not know it but he had just interrupted a march tune that had been stomping around in Jimmy's head, a tune the lad had been practising in the past few weeks in preparation for the big day. Not too long to go now. He could nearly feel the flute, smooth and sleek in his hands, his fingers twitching in his pockets as he imagined them flickering over the instrument's holes. He could not help how he was thinking, nor would he try. It was almost a deliberate mental switch, to be thinking music as a distraction at a time like this; a strategy to lift his mind off the reality of what he was involved in here; an antidote to danger.

Instead of a flute it was the cold barrel of a Browning pistol in his jacket pocket that his fingers fiddled with at this minute.

Jimmy moved silently from the shadows and took over the watch.

If only the other boys in the band could see him now! What would they make of him, in these circumstances? Some would not believe it. He knew that for a certainty, for he did not seem like the normal type to get involved in something like this. His father, a former UVF soldier in the British army, had always told him that he was far too shy, far too quiet. Worse than that, it had always been an inner suspicion of his that he was a natural-born coward. He would never argue back; he always avoided confrontations and would run a mile rather than take somebody on. Inside himself he still carried the memories of his Da's despair when he would come home with a bloody nose from some hiding he had taken at the hands of one of the street's bully-boys.

"If you ever darken my door like that again, I'll bloody it twice as bad for you!"

Even in the band, surrounded by all those other lads from the low streets around their beloved Oval football ground, he could never quite shake off the nervousness he felt when about to go on parade. He would be running to the toilet for hours before, especially on the Twelfth. Thankfully when he was around fourteen he had discovered that a couple of glugs of brandy from his Da's secret supply seemed to settle the nerves of his stomach and put him in the right frame of mind for action.

And the brandy was working well again tonight. That and the march tune. 'The Green Grassy Slopes of the Boyne'.
'Te-do-ray-ray-ray-ray-soh-fah-me'.
It was playing so strongly in his head that he had to deliberately check himself to make sure that it wasn't escaping as a lightly whistled melody.
Nervous sweat was building up around his armpits; his hand stretched around behind his back to ease the irritation of his damp drawers contracting into an aggravating rope, tight in the sheugh of his arse. The night was warm and the air Belfast clammy. Clammy and smokey and not helpful to someone who was doing their best to avoid the urge to cough it back up out of their lungs. Jimmy desperately wanted to clear his throat; as soon as he began to try this, as silently as possible, he instantly heard a sharp "Sshh!" from behind him.
Just as well too, for at that exact moment a huddled figure appeared in the smog at the Falls Road end of the street. Jimmy raised his hand to attract the Englishman's attention; then, realising that in the gloom of the tumbled house this might not be seen, he whispered, "Man!"
But the Englishman was beside him before the word had entered the stale air in their hide-out, shifting him gently to the side, squinting through the slit.
"Is it him?" Jimmy breathed.
The hand of silence went up. Eyes staring into the haze. Head still as a tombstone.
The figure came towards them along the pavement, sticking tight to the walls. Short and spindly, even by the standards of this Belfast ghetto; a greyhound of a man. He moved fairly quickly, slightly side to side, toes pointed outwards in a vaguely Charlie Chaplin type of waddle.
The Englishman's head nodded twice and his revolver came snaking out of his coat pocket.
Twenty yards to come.
Fifteen yards.
The Englishman's head moved slowly back and to the side of the look-out slit. Now he stared at the irregular space where once there had been a door.
Jimmy pressed his back against the wall, head diverted down to his accomplice, pistol angled up against his chest.
Ten yards possibly.

The sound of quick clip-swish of shoes on the flagstones, getting very close.
Jimmy tried to re-swallow whatever organ was trying to make its way up his throat and into his mouth. He was choking here. The sound was urging its way out of him. He opened his mouth...but somehow kept the gag swaddled in silence.
The figure shuffled its way past the opening. A fleeting image in charcoal, hunched and oblivious.
The Englishman stepped cat-like onto the pavement behind it.
Five yards away, maybe less. Revolver up, rigid and aimed.
" 'Allo Martin!"
Soft; teasingly friendly and simultaneously menacing. Manchester in flavour, mocking in tone.
Martin stopped in his tracks, strangely, slowly, almost as though he had just remembered that he had left his cap back in the pub and thought to return for it. In the split second that he had to live he probably thought of very little; if he had had more time he might have thought, 'I don't recognise that voice?'
Or 'What is an English accent doing here at this time of night?'
Or 'How does someone know my name, and it as dark as this?'
Or 'Oh God no; it is an ambush by the Brits!'
The split second freeze melted immediately into action. He did not begin to run. Well trained. He dived to the side, to the cobbles. He hurled himself away from the line that he thought the bullet might travel along. Then he bucked to his feet like a frightened animal and flung himself into a swerving, darting sprint.
It was a brave attempt. But it was a futile one.
Two quick cracks ripped through the stagnant silence. Two bullets entered Martin's lungs from the back and he flopped to the stillness of death on the basalt-black cobbles of Cupar Street.
"That's for Sergeant Millar!"
Then to Jimmy," Let's go mate."
Ears jangling, it occurred to Jimmy that it was a strange thing to still be whispering after the echoing explosions of the two shots.
"Is it definitely him?" he said, stepping towards the prone figure.
"Who cares? It's one less rebel. Let's go!"
"Are you sure he's dead? Should I put another..."
But the Englishman was several steps away up the street in the direction of the mills and the safety of the Shankhill.

Jimmy stumbled into a crouching gait in pursuit as doors began to crack open behind him and single eyes slanted their gaze out through the hanging coal-smoke.

Chapter 10

Sally Anne Sweeney

'As if I could not guess!'

Every month there was a market in Castlederg. I was dying to go to it, as much to get away from the monotony of the farm as anything else. That is not to say that I did not like working at Matthew's....I did, even though it was back-breaking work at times and I was often tired to the bone. But I had been there for six weeks and, apart from going to Mass in the town and getting over to Joe's place occasionally, I had not had the opportunity to meet and talk to anybody other than the Hendersons. Them and Tam Glenn of-course.

Matthew had a few bullocks that had been well fattened up and I knew that he was intending to sell them at the fair. I could sense the excitement building up in him as that week went on and I was waiting for him to ask me to come with him. No such luck; I waited in vain. Eventually I thought I would raise the subject myself.

"Will you be wanting me to come with you on Friday?" I said.

"Why would I be wanting that?"

"No reason. I just thought you might."

"What you really mean to say," he said, "is that it's you yourself wanting to be at the fair."

"And why would I be wanting that?"

"So you don't want to come?" he said.

This battle of words and wills was becoming ridiculous, even if there was a part of me that was enjoying it. Most times I thought I could come out on top but you could not take anything for-granted. Sometimes to get what you wanted you just had to play your cards in a different way. That much I had learned. This was one of those times. So I gave him a little smile, dimples and all.

He buckled.

"Alright," he said, "you can come with us."

"Us? Who is the 'us'?"

"Joe is coming with me."

"Oh," I said. "Joe is coming?"

I must have had some disappointment in my voice.
"What? I thought you would like Joe to be coming?" he said.
'What is he playing at now?' I wondered.
"Of-course," I said, obliging his half-serious taunt. "Bring him too. Sure the pair of you are as big as a horse with two heads."
He just shook his head at me.
"I never heard that one before," he said.
The three of us walked to Castlederg that day; I say walked but in truth a good deal of the journey was done at a run; the three bullocks, just fresh from pasture, were determined to exhaust us. While Matthew drove from behind, both Joe and I were running ahead of them like a pair of wild folk, trying to keep them out of other people's streets and fields. I say 'keep', but the way Matthew pronounced it, it sounded more like 'kep'.
"Kep them bastes oota thon feel o' Bonds!"
Strange expressions they had around Tyrone, but I was getting used to them. The banter was great and I felt like a wee girl again that day, with the fresh summer smells of the countryside in my nostrils and the warm breeze streaming my hair back over my shoulders as I ran down the slope of the road.
The market itself was just a typical fair, with a great fuss going on in the Diamond and the narrow streets of the village. Joe and I left Matthew in the market with his animals. We wandered out of the muck and the din of the cattle into the streets to see what was happening there. We stood and listened for a minute to a very somber-looking preacher on a wooden box who seemed determined to scare us all out of hell with his ranting. This was something entirely new to me and I found myself getting a bit annoyed, both at the tone of his voice and at the things he was saying. It had never crossed my mind that the world was about to end anytime soon but, listening to him, it seemed we were on the brink. Joe shook his head and took it in his stride.
"I've heard all this afore," he said. "Don't be worrying about him. He's just an oul blether. He'll blow himself out in an hour or two and the world will carry on as normal, for all his shouting!"
"But why is he shouting those things? Is that what it says in that big black book he keeps hammering?"
"I wouldn't know, Sally Anne, but if you want to come back in a while and ask him I'm sure he will have an answer for you. He'll maybe even convert you. Now that would please Matthew, wouldn't it?"

"Why did you say that?" I asked. "Is he the same as Matthew?"
"No, I don't think so," he laughed. "I think he is what they call 'Brethren'. The only reason I know is that there's a family up our road who go to that church. The Bonds. They are a very serious sort of a family. Two brothers and a sister."
"'Brethren'?" I said. "Is that another kind of church or is it a Protestant one as well?"
"Agh, don't ask me, Sally Anne," he replied. "I can remember a lot of years ago there was a crowd of our fellows fired stones at them preaching and chased them. The police had to intervene."
"Come on and we'll see what else is happening," I said and slipped my hand in under his elbow. If I had given him a gold sovereign I don't think he could have been half as pleased.
We left them to their shouting and no sooner had we rounded the corner than who should we run into but Ailish O'Donnell, the girl I had met on my way to Strabane. She and I had a great conversation, mainly about the kinds of farms we were working on and about our employers. Her farmer had the strange surname of Spence and seemed to be a very harsh, middle-aged man. The more I talked to her the more pleased I was that I was with Matthew Henderson. I told her all about him while Joe stood back against the wall and pretended not to be listening.
"*Tá sé ina fhear dathúil,*" I think I said. "A handsome man. Nice to work for, nice to look at. Very tall, big broad shoulders on him."
We giggled a bit about that.
"I do believe you have fallen for him," she said.
"Not at all," I replied. "You will not catch me at that. He is just my boss, that is all."
"Well, just you watch yourself now Sally Anne. Don't get too attached and don't encourage him to get too attached. The way things are between them and us at the minute, that could be very dangerous," she said.
I just laughed at her. "You sound like my father," I said.
"I don't mean to be spoiling your fun but, if he is as handsome as you say he is, you could end up getting hurt. You can't afford to forget that he is one of them."
"How do you mean, 'one of them'?" I said.
"I mean that he is your employer, he is a Protestant and likely an Orangeman and it just does not do for us to be getting too tied up with

them," she said. She had stopped smiling. I think Joe must have noticed the tone of this part of the conversation and came to my aid.
"Agh now," he interrupted, "there is no need to be worrying Sally Anne about things like that. Sure am I not her guardian angel? I will be looking out for her, so don't you be fretting about her. You sound like you have enough on your plate to be concerning you, with those people over in Newtownstewart."
Ailish took the hint. "Well at least there is no chance of me falling for Farmer Spence," she said. "He is as sour as a barrel of crab apples, that man. Never saw him smile once since I came. And that wee wife of his! She has a head on her like a cabbage. Not a wrinkle out of place. They never let me out anywhere, not even to Mass. I only got to come to the fair today because he needed me to help him carry a creel of hens that he is selling. I can't wait to see the back of them and this is only June."
"That's a terrible sentence," said Joe. "I'll tell you what, there's always a bit of a barn dance in the autumn, sometime around the end of the harvest. If we get word to you you could always come over for a good night's dancing. They would surely let you out for that?"
"That's very decent of you to ask," said Ailish. "Let me know and I will do my best."
She left us and disappeared towards the market. I was well taken by Joe's kindly attitude towards Ailish for she was a stranger to him. We walked towards 'The Ferguson Arms' where Joe was going to buy me 'a treat', he said.
I could not help noticing that the place was thick with policemen. They looked to me like they were very worried about something, as if they were expecting to be attacked by the volunteers at any minute. They made me nervous just looking at them.
We did not actually make it into the public house because sitting on a wee stool at the door of the place was none other than 'Tinker Tam' and he playing his fiddle. He was in full flow, his bow dancing on the strings of his instrument and a crowd of onlookers clapping along to the rhythm of his tunes. It was a sight to behold. An old felt hat lay at his feet to receive whatever coppers might be thrown there by the listeners; as a result, his whin-bush of hair bounced around on his head like it had a mind of its own. Even though Joe and I were well hidden at the back of the crowd his sharp little eyes picked us out and he grinned and winked a greeting to us.

"Oh dear," I thought, "I hope he does not affront me here by asking me to play in front of all these strangers."
When he finished the tune and the applause had died down he announced, "Now here's a wee song about a place not far from here and it's called 'Killeter Fair'." He made a great fuss of clearing his throat and spat whatever he had found there into the gutter. Away he went into a few verses of this local song which a lot of the crowd seemed to know, judging by the way they joined in. His voice was as gravelly as the street but it seemed to me to suit both the song and the singer. One verse went something like;

For her eyes they shine like diamonds and her cheeks are like the rose
She is my first and only love no matter where she goes
She stole my heart completely boys, the truth I do declare
And the first time that I saw her 'twas in Killeter Fair

'Would you ever stop looking at me and grinning like an eejit when you are singing words like that,' I thought to myself. He was such a character, a born entertainer, and I could tell that he was loving playing to this audience. There was just something about this old fellow; he had such a winning way with him that people found themselves responding to him whether they wanted to or not.
Myself included!
He pointed his fiddle bow out through the crowd at me and closed one eye, like he was sighting me for the kill. "There's a wee Donegal lassie out there and she is just dying to get playing a tune for yous," he said. "Now folks, I warn you, you have not heard anything this good in all your born days; so give her a bit of encouragement there. Come on up here beside me, Sally Anne Sweeney; come on now."
I was mortified. I tried to turn around and pretend he was talking about somebody else behind me. Then I tried to hide behind Joe but he was not cooperating. And anyhow, the people near me were sort of pulling me and pushing me into the middle of everything and towards Tam.
"What will I do, Joe?"
"Nothing for it but to go and play a tune for him!"
Before I knew it I was standing before him like a shy child in front of her school-master.
"What will you play?" I heard him ask.

I was at a loss. This was very embarrassing, standing in front of dozens of fair-goers beside this character. We were a strange pair to the eye.
A hush of expectation fell but it was not something I noticed. Tam's fiddle in my hand was everything at that moment.
I began to play slowly. Another old O'Carolan tune from centuries ago, known as '*Sí beag, Sí mór*'. Perhaps a strange choice but I felt too nervous to go straight into a dance tune.
My eyes were closed for most of the performance; there was a great atmosphere of appreciation from that crowd of country folk. Towards the end, though, I glanced up towards the back of the audience to see if I could see Joe. Yes, there he was behind his toothy grin and standing beside him was Matthew. Matthew and another fellow and a couple of girls, standing far too close to him, the pretty, black-haired '*cailín*' especially. But he smiled across the space at me and I have to say that until that moment I had not missed a note. Now I did, but I made it to the end of the air. The people did not notice the mistake of-course and they clapped until I was nearly tired listening to it.
Matthew came pushing forward through the crowd with the other fellow and girls in tow. I could tell by him he was pleased with me.
"It's a pity you hadn't my father's fiddle with you," he said quietly. "It would have sounded even better."
I noticed that his friends hung back from me and that he made no attempt to introduce me to them. To be honest, the fellow with the red face had a surly look off him and the black-haired girl was a bit of a giggler with far too big a chest on her for a girl her age, so I was not too much in a bother about it.
The three of us made our way home up the hills to Lismore. We walked three abreast along the narrow lanes, me in the middle. Both Joe and Matthew had hessian bags over their shoulders, well-filled with the groceries that they had bought in the village.
I had had a good time of it at the fair but there were a couple of curiosities sitting in my head and refusing to take bidding when I tried to tell them to go away. I wanted to know about the young lassie who had been so free and friendly with him. That, now, was a silly thing to be thinking. It was none of my concern, was it? And he would have every right to be telling me that, even if I was stupid enough to say what was in my head.

'Thon wee dark-haired girl is far too young for you to be carrying on with,' I wanted to say. I could think it but never would it ever come out of my mouth.
'It is none of my business,' I told myself, 'so forget about it, you silly Donegal servant-girl'.
Joe was unusually quiet at the start. The one thing he did say was to point out the Bond farm to me. A tidy, low-set cottage, newly white-washed and freshly thatched; it was wonderfully situated halfway up the side of the hill, with some outhouses and a grove of trees behind it, not half a mile from Henderson's place.
"They have a nice view out across to the hills," I said.
"They have; that's 'Bessy Bell', that mountain they are looking over at," said Joe.
"Aye, and the funny thing is," said Matthew, "the woman of the house is called Bessy as well. We used to joke that her mother was bate for a name for her when she was born, so she just looked out across the valley and said, 'There's Bessy Bell; sure that'll do her!' And it stuck."
"They're a wild religious crowd, so they are," said Joe. "You never see them out anywhere at dances or anything, do you Matt?"
"Naw, they've always been good-living. They just look at the world through the windows of their wee mission hall," said Matthew.
I was not sure what he meant by any of this but I let it pass.
"Do you mind the tricks we used to play on them?" said Joe.
"How could I forget?" laughed Matthew.
"What tricks?" I asked.
"Agh, why would you want to know that?" said Matthew but he had every intention of telling me of-course. "Things like the time we whitewashed one of their black cows."
"You did not?"
"We did; it was Joe's fool notion....he put me up to it. In the middle of the night him and me sneaked over with a tin of his father's paint and gave it a nice bright coat, head to tail. They never knew who did it. I'm sure it scrubbed off alright though."
"We could never stop ourselves laughing every time we saw them in the market with a black cow after that," said Joe.
"You divils," I said. "Did they ever catch you at your tricks?"
"They did once, away at the start when we were just wee nippers; but it was a simple enough crime. All we were doing was raiding their orchard. We didn't even get thrashed for it. Oul Bessy actually gave us

an apple each after she had lectured us for a while. Never even toul our wans," said Matthew.
"'Toul our wans'?" I said.
"Never told on us."
"Ah. And that was how you rewarded her kindness? By painting her cow?" I laughed.
"And that's not the half of it," said Matthew.
This was a side of him I had not seen before; it was hard to imagine Matthew as a child, as a growing boy, getting up to such rascality with Joe. I would have liked to have known him then. I was thinking about how he must have been affected by his father's death. Not just the loss itself and the emotion of all that but also of how it had made him have to grow up too quickly. He was forced to become the man of the house and the boss of the farm itself, and all far too soon, before he had had a chance to enjoy his youth and get to know himself. It was something that I had been thinking about for a day or two.
He had had no father to guide him for the past four or five years, in those important years when he was becoming a man. No father to be advising him about the big decisions, like courtship. No father to be trying to organise a suitable match for him.
There was a shyness about Matthew, an awkwardness at times. I had been wondering was it possible that he had never even had time or inclination to be walking out with a girl. When most other fellows who were going through that age would have been looking around and starting to court whatever girls were available, perhaps Matthew was dealing with matters on the farm and trying to cope with whatever was wrong with his mother. Not to mention being a daddy to the twins. This was a big curiosity to me.
I found myself wishing that I had known him a lot earlier, that I had been with him through the tough times he had had in his life; silly thoughts like that were trickling around in my head without me giving them permission.
As we walked the banter had loosened his tongue and he began to chat about the events of the day. The bullocks had made less than he had expected. From his conversation I could gather that the present uncertainties, the political troubles were to blame for a drop in prices at the markets locally. He mentioned the huge amount of smuggling of cattle and sheep that was going on across the border from Donegal and that this was flooding the market and bringing down prices. He was

more than annoyed about this of-course and I understood. I could also see why Joe was more inclined to blame the northern Unionists. If they had not drawn up this new border there would be no need for smuggling.

"Look at it like this," Joe said. "We have been taking our cattle to Castlederg fair for ages. But now if we do it, we could have them all impounded because they are considered to be Free State cattle. We took a chance when we took that mare to Strabane the day of the Rabble fair. My father could have been arrested. By right, we are supposed to take our cattle to Raphoe market but to get them there we have to march them up the road on the northern side of the border all the way to Clady and then across the bridge over the Finn river and back into the Free State. It is completely daft. The border is a nonsense."

"No, it's not a nonsense," said Matthew defensively. "It is needed. With the trouble between the two sides there needed to be a border. My father used to say, 'Good fences make good neighbours'."

"And what were we before the border? Were we not good neighbours before they put the fence in place?" asked Joe.

"People were good neighbours until your boys started all this trouble. It was them wanted to break from Britain. That's why there had to be a border."

"Not at all! Such a thing should never have been thought of. Just think what our folk in Derry and Armagh and the other counties feel like now," Joe said.

Matthew looked at him for an explanation, so Joe continued.

"It's like they have been cut off from their...their mother. Ireland is their mother," he said. "Now they're stuck here with you boys ruling the roost."

Matthew seemed to laugh at this notion.

"A load o' nonsense," he said. "If that's what they think they can always go back to her. Go and live in their blessed Free State."

Joe just shook his head in disgust at this, as if he could not believe his ears.

There was definitely tension developing, I thought. Not the usual banter. I felt it was my duty to steer the conversation onto something else.

"So you two have been best friends since you were children?" I interrupted, stating the obvious.

Joe gave a twisted half-smile. I think it was a smile of welcome for the deliberate switch of the chat away from politics. He looked up at Matthew across the front of me.
"Aye," he said, "we've had some grand craic together."
Matthew was slower to thaw out. I watched his face and I could nearly see his mind making the decision to let go of whatever dark thoughts had gathered there.
"If he hadn't me looking after him he'd be dead by now," he said, almost glumly.
"Here we go again," said Joe.
"How is that?" I asked.
"We were only wains. Do you mind that time, Joe? We were fishing for sticklebacks in the burn down by the stepping stones. You managed to fall in. You woulda drowned if I hadn't been there to pull you out," Matthew said.
"I was in no danger of drowning. Anyway, it was you that pushed me in, just so you could be the hero and rescue me."
"Nonsense. You were going down for the third time."
"How could I be going down for the third time? Sure the burn is only a foot deep."
"The burn was in flood that day. Anyway, all the size o' you then, a foot of water could have drowned you twice over!"
It was good to see this spirit return between them, I was thinking.
Matthew said, "Aye, those were good days alright."
"If it happened now I'd be drowning in international waters, wouldn't I?" said Joe with just a touch of bitterness in his joke.
After the work around the yard was all cleared up that evening I got the kitchen organised for the morning. Tired and all as I was, I had to wash up a pile of dishes and pots and pans that had been left for me. Seemed Mrs Henderson had not been in the mood for much housework when we were away. Matthew and I ate our evening spuds and bacon to the sound of chirping crickets behind the hearth and the sober tick of the grandfather clock. There was little chat between us for some reason. He was engrossed in reading a Belfast newspaper that he had brought home from the town. What he was reading was not helping his mood either.
"Take a look at this," he said at one point, holding the paper up for me. I squinted at it but the way the oil-lamp was flickering over it I could neither see nor read whatever he was showing me. I got up and moved

around behind him, to read over his shoulder and the manly smell of him rose up strongly into my nostrils.
He pointed to a report and started to read it out to me, as if I could not read for myself, but it gave me time to see a few of the photographs on the page; a lot of burned out mansion houses from what I could see.
"'Raid on Clady Post'," he read. "'Republicans beaten off. Bombs used in the fighting.' That's just up the road, you know."
"I know where Clady is," I said.
"And look at all these houses burned down. Look, Shane's Castle in Antrim, totally gutted. Ruined! How is that going to help anybody? Sheer destruction for the sake of it."
I was not going to argue with him. There would have been no point. No point in trying to tell him that the kind of people who lived in castles like that had been responsible for living off the backs of the poor, ordinary Irish folk for generations and did little or nothing to help them at the time of their greatest need, during the great famine. No point in telling him that his 'Specials' scared the divil out of me and thousands like me. I said nothing, went back to my place and finished off my supper.
Eventually I climbed the ladder to the attic room. I was in for a surprise.
There on my bed was the fiddle case belonging to Matthew's father. I opened it to check that the fiddle was inside.
"Who left that in here?" I thought to myself. "Maybe Jane or Millie, trying to play some sort of trick on me. I should take it back down to Matthew in case he thinks I took it myself."
So I did. He was still in the kitchen on his own, still reading the paper.
"One of the girls left this in my room by mistake", I said, setting the fiddle case on the table in front of him.
"What makes you think that?"
"Either that or they were trying to play a trick on me."
He looked at me for a bit, then he said quietly, "It wasn't them."
I waited, trying to make sense what was happening here.
"It was me," he said.
"Why?"
"Because I wanted to. Am I not allowed to do whatever I want in my own house?"
I was trying to read his expression but not being very successful. There was certainly a hint of anger in his tone but I had the feeling it was put

on. He was trying to sound as he imagined '*an fear an tí*' should sound, the man of the house. This was my boss talking, after all. I just stayed quiet and waited for an explanation.
He broke the gaze first and looked back at his newspaper. After a second he spoke again, with just a shade of self-consciousness about him.
"You can have it."
"I do not understand," I said patiently.
"I am giving it to you. What is there to understand? Now take it and away to your bed!"
In his fluster he was falling back into that grumpy tone that I had heard a few times before. I could and maybe should have just walked out but I needed to make some sense of this.
"But...this is your father's fiddle! I cannot take it, Mister Henderson. You know that....it would not be right."
He sat there, silent, head down to his paper.
I waited for a few seconds, watching the side of his face, the strong line of his jaw and the brown skin of him through the light-coloured bristle on his chin. When I saw that he was not going to say any more I turned away from him, through the door and into the hall, softly as a cat, trying to escape from this intense moment without causing any further annoyance to him. I did not get very far before I heard him.
"Come back here a minute."
I did as I was told but I stopped at the door. I was the servant girl here. Of-course I did what I was told. He met my gaze. There was strength in his eyes, in the set of his mouth.
"I am serious," he said quietly. "My father is not coming back. He will never play it again."
I always thought that the way he said 'father' sounded more like 'feather' to my ears.
"I know that but..."
"I want you to have it; he would say the same. There's no point in the thing lying in its box as if it was in a coffin. You made it live the other night....so....I'm giving it to you."
"No Matthew, it is not fair. What about the girls? What if Jane...?"
He held up his hands, as if he was trying to stop a runaway pony.
"Listen to me," he said more gently. "I am asking you to take it. Play it to the girls while you are here and take it with you when you leave."
"I will certainly play it to the girls but I cannot be taking it...."

"Would you ever stop arguing with me. Just take it with you and go to your bed, for goodness sake. I am trying to read this paper. Now go and give me peace!"

What could I do? I could see that it was not going to be a good idea to go on arguing with him. At the same time I wanted to know why he was doing this...the motives of the man, what was in his head.

As if I could not guess.

A wave of some sort of thankfulness rose up in me. As I picked up the fiddle case from the table I took an involuntary step towards him. I do not know what was in my mind to do. He looked up in surprise. I turned on my heel and near enough ran to the door. Then I managed to stop and compose myself a bit. I did not dare look round at him. I just paused and muttered into the hall in front of me.

*"Go raibh maith....*Sorry, I mean 'thank you'," I stammered.

The fiddle lay beside me as I slept that night.

Chapter 11

Matthew Henderson

How will we handle the 12th of July?

I was swithering a bit about the Twelfth of July; that was something that had never happened before.

I am not a member of the Loyal Orders. I have nothing against the Orange; it is just that I haven't really felt the need to be joining. My father wasn't a member. He was a Methodist first and foremost and he never felt he should become an Orangeman. People tried to persuade him to join, as they have me. John Sproule was always on at me about it. But there is a thrane-ness in the Hendersons. Once you try to push us into something we are more likely to resist it, for no reason other than this independent streak we have in us.

So what was my problem?

Well, although we were not an Orange family, we had always enjoyed the whole occasion of the Twelfth celebrations. The family, so far as I know, had never missed it. The colour, the music, the friends and relatives you meet, the carnival atmosphere. On second thoughts, I tell a lie; of-course we missed it.

Once.

Back in Nineteen Sixteen. We were in no mood to be celebrating anything that year. We had received the telegram from the Army just a few days before. My father was 'Missing in Action; Presumed Dead'. That Twelfth we just stayed at home and thought about what we would have been doing if my father had been here, instead of lying under the clay in some half-dug mass-grave in France. A big number of families in the country were in the same boat that year; we were not alone in our grief.

But back to the present circumstance. This year the girls especially had been looking forward to the day out. My mother hadn't mentioned it, except when Jane and Millie talked about it, but I was sure she would want to go as usual. My sister Emily was to be home from Belfast for the Twelfth-week holiday and she would be looking forward to it as well. I planned to take the pony and trap, have a good picnic packed

and ready and, after the procession, find ourselves a nice spot at the back of the field to watch proceedings.
The trouble was I did not know what to do about Sally Anne.
We had another one of those strange conversations about it when we were hoeing the potato drills in the low field. She was keen to go, she said.
I wanted to know why.
"Just to see what it's like," she said.
"Have you talked to Joe about it?"
"I have. He has been to it in the past. He told me that he stood watching all the bands going past. He said he did not see what all the fuss was about."
"That was likely when he was a good bit younger," I said. "Things were a lot different then. All this bother at the minute changes things. There could be trouble."
"But, if you think that, why are you taking Jane and Millie to it? And your mother? And you say your sister is coming home for it? What if there is trouble?"
She had a point.
"Sally Anne, you don't understand. It's a Protestant thing. It is for the Protestant people....it is our celebration. It's about our religion," I said.
"I do know that. I am not stupid. But does that mean a Catholic can't go along and watch? Am I not allowed to go and enjoy the bands like I do at home?"
"Of-course you are allowed. It's not a matter of not being allowed."
"What is it a matter of then?" she persisted.
"Look," I said. "I would love to take you with me.... with us; but we will be there all day, at the parade, then in the field, listening to the speeches, meeting with old friends and all. You would feel completely out of it. You would be bored in no time."
"What are the speeches about?"
We had stopped working. I was conscious that I was standing there, leaning on my hoe, looking down into those deep emerald eyes of hers and simply enjoying being here, being alive, being with....being with my hired hand.
What was I doing? I caught myself on slowly. I think I sighed and turned back to the work.
"We'd better keep at this," I said. "We're wasting too much time footerin' about."

"Sorry, Mr Henderson," she said. It was that tone again; submissive and apologetic but with some irony, perhaps even slightly mocking. She was a master of tone and I don't just mean when she was playing her tunes.

"Anyway, you don't want to know what the speeches are about," I said.

"Why wouldn't I? I am curious, that's all."

"They would only annoy you. Somebody will be sounding off about politics; the threat of the IRA, all that stuff. And some old clergyman will likely be preaching the gospel. Telling us all how wrong the Papish church is."

"You mean like that man who was ranting on in the Diamond in Castlederg? That would drive me round the bend. Why do you want to hear the like of that?" she said.

Another good question.

"Because.... because it's all part of it. It is part of our religion. It's who I am. Whether or not I agree with all that is being said is not the point. This is the only day in the year when we get to celebrate our heritage."

She paused, puzzled.

"What heritage do you mean?" she asked.

I looked at her again, her back and her slim wee hips to me as she bent over the task. I wasn't sure if it was a genuine question or if it contained a bit of a taunt. I wasn't used to questions like this. It was all so blunt, so innocent. At least, that is what I was trying to figure out when I looked at her. But all I saw was her long, fair hair falling around her face and the bend of her slender body and the girlish shape of her swaying and twisting as she worked the hoe around the young plants and the sweat stains building up under her oxters.

"What heritage do I mean? I mean...you see, the main thing we go to commemorate on the Twelfth is the Battle of the Boyne. You know about that?"

"I have heard of it," she said, "but I would not say I know much about it."

"Do you want to know?"

"Will it help me to understand you?" she said. Then, as if to clarify, "I mean, will it help me to understand why you think I should not be going near the thing?"

"It might, I don't know."

"Go on then," she said, "tell me."

"I didn't employ you to be teaching you history, remember that. I'll have to dock it off your wages. But you did ask, didn't you?"
"I am starting to be sorry for it already," she smiled.
So I gave her a bit of a history lesson about King Billy and King James and the Siege of Derry and the Battle of the Boyne....until I sensed that I was starting to bore her. "And that is why we march on the Twelfth of July. That is why we have King Billy on our banners. That is why we play tunes about him. That is why all the speakers will talk about his victory….the victory of the Protestant faith over the Catholic faith, do you see?"
That stumped her for a while....still working, silently, thinking deeply about something.
"Do you not mean 'The victory of the Protestant army over the Catholic one'?" she said.
"Aye, that's what I said."
"No you didn't," she argued. "You said 'The victory of the Protestant faith over the Catholic faith."
"What's the difference?" I asked.
"Well, surely it was just two armies of soldiers fighting. Fighting for land. It was not two faiths fighting. You and I are of two different faiths," she said. "But we are not fighting, are we?"
Good Lord in heaven, the way she looked at me when she said that. I had a flash of something; I am not going to call it a 'revelation' or a 'vision' but it was a strong response deep inside of me, as strong as the physical arousal I had had watching her working. As if a bell had rung; rung with a lovely new sound. At that moment I wanted to hug her. Not romantically now, don't misunderstand me; just a basic, honest human connection; a physical way of marking a truth, a really important truth that I had just learned from this girl, my hired hand, in the middle of a field of praties on my father's farm in Lismore townland.
"Aye," I said, "you may be right. Armies, not faiths."
We worked on towards the evening. Little more was said. I just enjoyed this new, unspoken warmth between us.
"And what year did you say it all happened?" she said.
"Why?"
"I just want to know."
"I can guess what you are going to say," I said.
"What year?"

"The Battle of the Boyne was fought in Sixteen Ninety."
"What am I going to say?"
"You're going to say that that was a long time ago," I said. "We Prods have long memories."
"I am not," she said. "I don't need to, 'cause you said it yourself."
I thought I would counter this.
"Saint Patrick was even longer ago. Your lot celebrate him every Seventeenth of March, don't you?"
"We do," she said. "He brought Christianity to Ireland. Your King Billy brought an army."
That sort of put an end to the conversation for a bit. I didn't like the feeling that I had been trumped again but I couldn't think of any decent response so I let it go and got stuck into the hoeing.
"Look," I said eventually, "I don't want you to feel that I am against you coming, or that you're not welcome at the Twelfth. The only thing is...I do need you to be around the farm when we are all away. There's all the routine to be done. We will be away the most of the day. So I want you to be here."
"That's alright," she said.
'No rancour there,' I thought. 'Good.'
"If you really want to see what it's like though, you could ask Joe. He could maybe take you down for half an hour to the top of the town. If you stand furnenst the chapel you'll have a decent view of the bands marching past. In the morning only; then he could bring you back up."
"That's grand," she said. "I will ask him and see what he thinks."
Later on she brought up the subject of my sister Emily. Maybe understandably.
"When your sister gets here will she want to take over in the kitchen, do you think? Will you want me to change what I do?"
I laughed at this idea.
"There's very little chance of that," I said. "Emily will hardly lift a finger in the kitchen. She wouldn't be all that domesticated, the same girl. She will likely just boss you around. You'll have to be ready for that."
"I will be ready for it," she said. "Sure you have me well trained. It will just be a change of boss."
"You are are the cheekiest maid I have ever come across, Miss Sweeney. My father woulda put you over his knee and taught you a good lesson. I should do the same myself," I said, trying not to laugh at her.

"Aye, you would just love that, wouldn't you. You would have to catch me first."

I made as if to chase her and she reacted by taking off at a run. Briefly.

"Come on, girl," I said. "Let's keep at this and get it finished. Would you ever stop tormenting me and do a bit of work?"

"I will surely, Mister Henderson," she said. "Whatever you say."

Chapter 12

Sally Anne Sweeney

What happened on the 12th of July

A few things changed on the Twelfth of July, but not for the reasons you might expect.

The Henderson family left for the celebrations shortly after Matthew finished his yard work. He had his mother and three sisters in the trap and himself leading the pony because, for some reason, it was in a very frisky mood and did not seem to be keen to do as it was bid.

While he was trying to get the animal settled, Matthew said to me that it was likely very excited to be going to the Twelfth.

"Maybe not though," I said. "Maybe it is a good Catholic pony and doesn't want to be going near it. Maybe that is why it has the long face on it today."

Away he went, laughing at me.

I have to admit that I was glad to see the back of this Emily for a while. I could not make sense of her at all. She was not like her brother in the least. Where he was generally a warm and interesting person, she was one of the coldest women I think I have ever come across. About the same height as me, she was fairly plump, dark in complexion, with straight brown hair and spectacles. Not in a hundred years would anyone ever have imagined that she was from the same stable as Matthew; the twins either, for that matter. She had arrived from Belfast by train a couple of days ago and I swear I had yet to see her smile. That was the worst part; the lack of humour; there was more craic in the grandfather clock. Ah well, she would be gone in a few more days, I consoled myself. Back to her office in the City Hall where she was a "civil servant in the new government of Northern Ireland", as she kept reminding us.

'Not all that civil,' I thought to myself.

Joe came over around ten o'clock and we rode to the town on a couple of old bicycles. We stood on a raised grass verge at the top of the town, not far from St Patrick's Roman Catholic Church, to watch the parade.

Maybe it was a sub-conscious need to be within sight of the 'mother church', like chickens under the wings of the mammy hen.

Further down the street there seemed to be hordes of policemen, the dark of their uniform very different from the splashes of red, white and blue bunting and the orange streamers hanging across the streets. Several bands marched past behind their colourful banners and flags, each one followed by a group of black-suited men. These men wore sashes around their shoulders and black bowler hats on their heads. Bristling moustaches everywhere; they seemed like a part of the uniform. To a man these Orangemen had a look of determination in their solemn eyes. There was something very orderly and dogged about them, in contrast to the carefree swagger of the marching musicians.

The bands played with great skill and energy, as they do around home, and I found the music entering me and lifting my spirits, almost against my will. I did not recognise any of the tunes but one or two had bits that reminded me of band tunes I had heard in the Rosses. Difficult tunes too, some of them, but those boys were more than able for them. They marched well and were a treat to the eye in their tidy uniforms. Mind you, I have never seen so much colour, especially orange, not in all my born days. Nor so many sword-swinging knights glaring down at me from their great white horses on nearly every banner.

There were accordion bands, some flute ones, a pipe band, (that would have been my favourite, if I had been asked to choose), and one was a drumming band. Those drums rattled the window-panes; they rattled around in my eardrums to the extent that my hands went up to protect my ears. I was not the only one either. Joe told me they were Lambeg drums; just two drummers beating the huge skins with terrible force and amazing rhythms, the sweat pouring off their red faces. I felt kind of sorry for the young fellow who was trying to play some sort of wee flute with these two drummers. He was doing his best but nobody was paying any attention to him, likely because the big Lambegs had totally drowned out the sound of his flute.

I think there were something like nine or ten bands went by, maybe more. They disappeared around the corner into Castlederg village where the crowds along the street waved their Union Jack flags. The atmosphere was enthusiastic and pleasant enough, I thought, while the bands were parading but I could not help noticing that Joe was ill-at-ease.

"What is wrong with you?" I said to him in Gaelic.

"Jesus, Sally Anne! Don't be saying anything to me in Gaelic; not around here on the day that's in it!" he mumbled in English.

It did not help his mood that one or two of the marching men with the sashes on them noticed him and nodded as if they knew him. One of them was the red-faced fellow that I had seen with Matthew in the Castlederg market. Joe seemed to want to shrink down behind the watchers.

"Do you know that man?" I asked.

"I do. John Sproule. He's a farmer from up our way, a friend of Matthew's. He used to run about with us but he wouldn't have a lot of time for me now, nor me for him."

After the bands had passed us a group of young men and girls came walking down the middle of the road, obviously following after the parade to this place that Matthew had called 'the field.' There was a jauntiness about them as they looked into the faces of the crowd that I did not really like. I would say that they put a shadow of fear across me and, if I felt it, Joe certainly did.

"Let's go, Sally Anne," he said, taking me by the arm and leading me away out of sight into the Priest's Lane. "Come on! You never know what that gang of *guilpíns* is looking for. They might recognise me and make things awkward."

We had seen enough. We waited for the crowd to move on, found our bicycles and set off to pedal back up Horse Hill towards Lismore.

"What did you think about all that?" he asked me, back in the Gaelic now that we were alone.

"I don't mind it. It was something different. I have seen plenty of bands in the Rosses but I never saw the like of this before," I said.

"It doesn't make you feel angry?"

"No. Why should it?"

"Because all they are doing is trying to rub it in," he said.

"Rub what in? I did not see anybody rubbing anything in."

"Did you not? Did you not think there was a feeling of 'We're the boys! We won at the Battle of the Boyne and the Siege of Derry and we are still winning. Now we even have our own wee country!'"

"I did not hear that at all," I said. "Maybe if we had gone to the speeches we would have heard it but all I heard was a lot of tunes being played. A lot of good tunes there were too."

"Did you not hear it in the music? Did you not see it in their faces? Ah come on. You must have been watching a different parade to the one I saw."
"Maybe it is different for you," I said. "You are from around here; that is why you feel it more. Especially with you living right on the border."
"On the other side of it," he corrected me.
"Do you ever wonder what Matthew gets out of all this? You and him are the best of friends, yet there he is down there today, enjoying it all?" I said. At the same time I was thinking, 'And him likely cuddling up to his woman with the big chest on her.'
Joe's reaction surprised me.
"Sure he is one of them. Don't you forget it, Sally Anne. He gets himself all het up again, with the faith o' his fathers flowing through his Protestant veins. Just you wait till you see how different he is after today. He'll be as thick as champ for a while, until it wears off. It's always like that. For a week or two after the Twelfth he will be cold to us Kearneys. He'll likely be the same with you."
'Leave that to me,' I was thinking. 'I will just have to work on him with his father's fiddle and warm him up a bit.'
"It is a hard one," he was saying. "The Hendersons have always been good friends to us. It goes away back. If you were to say anything wrong about them in front of my Da he would have a fit. He would throw you out of the house. Our Mary and him have had words about it. He was furious at her."
"What was that about? I never met your sister Mary yet."
"She works in the Post Office in Strabane. Since they fell out she is very seldom home. She has taken a wee house up there."
"That is terrible," I said. "It must have been a bad fall-out."
"It was. It was only last year too, about this time of the summer."
"Do you know what it was over? Or should I not be asking?"
"No, it's alright. I don't talk much about it, being a family thing, but I know you will keep it to yourself."
"I will, but don't tell me if you don't think you should. It is alright."
"It was over a fellow. A fellow who is no good. She met him when he was working at Henderson's last year. He is a Donegal man too, but he's not like you. I wouldn't trust him as far as I would throw him. He was a bad influence on our Mary. She started to get very bitter against the British, even against people like the Hendersons. Then my father

caught him and her...having a roll in our hay barn. That put an end to it, sort of. My father chased him with a pitch-fork."
"Good for him," I said.
"Aye, he did right but our Mary couldn't forgive him for it. That's when all her anger came out against my Da. She was mis-calling him for being a British soldier in the war; then she had a go at the Hendersons. She blamed Matthew's father for persuading our Da to join up, for having a better farm than us, for everything short of the price of sugar. My father grabbed her by the shoulders; I have never seen him like that before; so angry he was purple in the face. He shouted at her, right into her face. He told her she did not know what she was talking about. He said that the Kearneys owed Matthew's father a lot and if she ever spoke like that again she could take to the road."
I was shocked by this. I said, "I'm sorry Joe. That sounds like a fierce row. Is that when she left?"
"Not long after. She packed her stuff and said 'Goodbye' to all of us except my father. It was a very sad day in our house. My mother cried for hours. Maybe him too but he would never show it. We seldom see her now."
I did not know what to say. We rode into Henderson's street in silence.
"Can I walk you down home?" I said to him as I left the bike against the shed door. I was feeling a sense of responsibility for the dullness that had come over him since he shared his family secrets with me.
"Aye, come on; I will leave the bike here until later," he said.
We walked down the back lane, taking the short-cut across the fields towards Kearney's farmyard just beyond the burn.
"Joe, there's one thing I don't understand," I said at one point.
"What's that?" he said.
"Why did your father go and fight for Britain in the war?"
"That I don't really know myself," he said. "I suppose things were different back then. He likely wouldn't be on for doing it now, after the way they have persecuted us in the last couple of years."
"Aye, that is what I meant," I said. "It puts him in a bad light now and yet to me he seems to be a really decent man."
"He is. He can't turn the clock back, that's all."
We had reached the boundary of the field, a boundary which didn't seem to know whether it was a hedge or a stone wall. To me it looked as if it had begun its life, many moons ago, as a wall built from the rocks and stones thrown up when the natural rough landscape was

being turned into a proper field. Then, as time passed and bits of the wall crumbled or were carted away to build outhouses, someone had planted a line of scrawny hawthorn bushes along it.
"Did Matthew tell you that this is where his land ends? Ours begins on the other side of this gap and this burn," Joe said, pulling a couple of loose bushes from where they were acting as a makeshift barrier in a hole in this hedge-wall between two fields.
"So this is what all the fuss is about?" I said, looking at the shallow burn through the gap.
"What fuss are you talking about?"
"This is the Border," I said.
He laughed.
"I never thought of it like that before," he said. "I suppose it is."
There was very little water flowing between Tyrone and Donegal that Twelfth of July, it being after a dry spell of weather.
"Not much chance of you drowning in this wee burn today, Joe," I joked.
He laughed as he skipped across the stepping stones to the other side, almost missing his footing in his clumsiness, then reached out and took my hand by way of helping me over and I followed him.
The trouble was that he did not seem to be wanting to let go of me after. I looked at his face, so earnest and devoted it was almost comical.
"Sally Anne," he started, "if ever you ...."
"Joe," I said, pulling my hand away from him, "you are a good friend and I would not have it any other way."
"That's alright then," he said with a bit of a rueful look in his eyes, "but will you not come in and say 'Hello' to Mammy? What's the hurry on you?"
"I can’t, not this time" I said and turned back across the burn. "Matthew wanted me to be about the place when I came back from the town. There are things I want to be doing for him."
It was not the way to put it, not at that particular moment, and I regretted it straight away. I could see in the sag of his eyes that, once again, I had wounded him without meaning to.
"Thanks for taking me all the same," I said with too glib a tone to my voice.
Far too off-hand of-course; more unintended slighting of him. I wanted to run back across the stepping stones and give him a hug of consolation but I knew it would not be the thing. It would probably

only twist the knife. I could sense his eyes on me as I pulled the bushes back into the gap in the wall.

Back at Henderson's I had a plan in my head to surprise and please Matthew; hopefully Mrs Henderson as well. The mess of the garden at the front of the house had annoyed me ever since I had arrived. That was a strange thing in itself, for we don't really be having gardens where I come from. Outside our front doors you would be more likely to be tripping over a midden! The only proper gardens I have ever seen about home would have been when passing by that mansion of a house beside Dunlewy Lough, Lord Hill's place. But if you are going to have a garden in front of your house you might as well try to keep it in order. So this was the chance I had been waiting for to give it a bit of a tidy up. I got a spade, a grape, a scythe, a pair of hedge-shears and a wheelbarrow and got started. The grass was long and took a deal of scythe-swinging. I was having some exercise that day, between bicycle riding and now this swinging. I raked it up as I went along, working as quickly as I could. I dumped it all in the stack-yard behind the byre.

I was wondering again about the girl with the black hair. Was he seeing her today? Is that why he was so determined that I should not go with him? Was I just being a stupid wee Donegal servant girl to be even letting thoughts like this run so wildly through my foolish head?

I was halfway through digging the weeds out of the first of the flowerbeds when I heard the barking of our old sheepdog. At the beginning I ignored it, thinking it might be barking at a bird or something in the yard. Then, as it continued, I thought I had better go and have a look.

As I arrived around the corner of the dwelling house into the street I got a shock that took the heart out of me.

There was a man standing by the back door which was open, a rifle of some sort in his hands. He neither heard me nor saw me until Fly ran barking towards me. Then he turned, saw me and sort of jumped. His first reaction was to turn back to the door and shout something, obviously to someone inside. His second was to pull a scarf up over his mouth and nose and pull his hat down over his forehead.

My heart was pounding in my chest as I stood there watching him. I was tempted to run but my legs felt like frog-spawn. Something gave me the courage to stand my ground, my hand holding the top of the yard-pump for support.

A second man arrived from inside the farm-house, a shorter fellow; he had a smaller gun in one hand. He was pulling a handkerchief over his mouth and a cap over his eyes. He made straight towards me, aggressively, confidently. For a minute I was terrified that he was going to do something to me.
"What do you want?" I said.
"None o' your business. Stay where you are if you don't want to get hurt. You say nothing about this or you'll be shot."
"I will say nothing," I said, disgusted with the fear in my voice.
Thankfully he and the other fellow kept well out from me as they went past and headed quickly for the back lane.
"Who were you looking for?" I called after them.
He swore at me. "Shut the hell up, you wee bitch. Who are you anyway? Likely Henderson's wee hoor. You keep your mouth shut or else!"
They took off running towards the back lane. I was not about to run after them, believe me. A whole feeling of weakness suddenly came over me and I felt myself sinking to the ground. Maybe it was the shock, I don't know. I finished up lying against the pump for a bit. I reached up and splashed some water round my face from the trough there and that brought me to my senses.
I had a sudden thought that those two seemed to know where they were going. And they knew that this was Henderson's. Might they be going to Joe's place? Either way, I had a strong urge to run to Kearney's, just to be in the comfort of human company. So that is what I did. I took a quick look into the kitchen to see if anything was disturbed, then locked the back door and ran out the front lane and along the road; there was no grass growing under my feet with the rate of me, I can tell you. I did not want to be going near the back lane, just in case those men were hiding in the woods above it. I kept an eye out for them though, in case they would appear and take after me. No more sign of them and I reached Kearney's and poured out my story to them. Monica made me strong, sweet tea to settle my nerves. Joe and his father kept asking me to describe the men but I was not very good at that.
After a bit I felt well enough to say that I thought I should be getting back up to Henderson's; I was supposed to be looking after things and I was still afraid of a return visit from those fellows. Joe of-course, being my guardian angel, volunteered to come with me.

We returned by the road again and we were standing in the yard talking about the whole affair when we both became aware of a very strange sound. It was a high pitched squealing noise and it seemed to be coming from a distance away. Neither of us could work out what it was.

Joe said, "Come out to the fort field and we'll climb up and see if we can see anything."

We raced across the hayfield to the fort. What he was hoping to see that would explain that noise I could not imagine but we climbed up the steep side of the old mound and scanned the surrounding countryside, difficult and all as it was to see through the thick sycamore leaves.

Then we saw it. A column of dark smoke rising more of less straight into the air, there being not a breath of a breeze that day. It seemed to be coming from somewhere in the direction of Castlederg but much closer than the village, not far away at all.

"Where is that?" I asked, "and what does it have to do with the squealing?"

Joe took off down the hill with a suddenness that left me far behind him.

"It's coming from Bond's place. There must be a fire in the pig-house. That's what the squealing is. I'll run. You get the bicycle and bring a couple of buckets."

Joe could run, I will say that for him. He disappeared down the lane like a greyhound. I did as he said and followed him as quickly as I could. When I reached Bond's lane I was smelling the most horrible stench that has ever entered my nose. The smell of the roasting flesh of pigs! Burning pork! I knew we were too late. The smoke was belching up above the trees behind, black as the devil. The squealing had died down.

I reached the yard and Joe was there with another couple of local farmers, carrying water and throwing it over the pig-house. There was no sign of the Bond folk, as far as I could make out. Somebody had managed to open a side door on the building but it had been too little and too late. A couple of sows had made it out through the door onto the street before the whole roof of burning thatch had fallen in on them but they were lying in the yard, obviously badly burned. Their squeals would have made you cry. One of them tried to get up but the

rear end of it was burst open to the air like a roll of bacon in a butcher's window.
"Can we not do something for these two sows?" I asked.
"What can we do?" said one of the farmers hurrying past. "We need a gun to put them out of their misery. Either that or cut their throats."
'*Máthair Dé*!', I thought, 'I hope they do not be asking me to do that.'
"Would you not throw some water over them?" I said. "See if it eases them?"
"Aye, we could try that," he said, "but they're goners all the same."
I started filling buckets of water from the pump for the men. It was going to take a long time to put this fire out. It was likely feeding itself on pig-fat behind those stone walls. There was nothing we could do. The animals were probably all dead or, if they were not, they were suffering terribly. The smell was sickening and my stomach was retching before long. I felt so helpless. I was crying.
It was in this state that I saw, through my tears, Matthew arriving into the yard at full tilt on the pony and trap. It was all I could do to stop running to him and throwing myself at him, so distressed was I by the events of the day. I am glad that I did not though, for riding into the yard behind him was that man again, John Sproule, still wearing his orange sash and looking very wound up.
"What happened, Joe?" Matthew shouted, taking a bucket of water from me.
"No idea Matt; we were too late to do much. There's likely half a dozen dead pigs in there. These two got out but they're in bad shape."
"They're not for livin', that's for sure," said Sproule.
"Matthew," I called after him as he ran for water, "Could you not find some way of putting them out of their misery?"
"Go and get your shotgun. There's not much more we can do 'til the Bonds get back," said Sproule.
Matthew threw his bucketful onto the flaming roof and ran back to us.
"Maybe you're right", he said. "Yous work on here and I'll be back in a minute."
"Where are the girls?" I wanted to know. "And your mother?"
"I let them off to walk home with Emily. They're alright. I didn't want them seeing this."
He turned towards the pony but Joe stopped him.
"Matt, wait a minute. Sally Anne got a brave shock at your place. Go on and tell him, Sally Anne."

He turned to me, impatient.

"Tell me what?"

I was hesitant but I could see that my delay was annoying him.

"There were two strange men," I said. "They were in the yard. They scared the life out of me."

"Two men? At our house? Were you not around the place like I told you? You were likely down with Joe, were you?"

Joe reacted angrily to this. "No she wasn't! Would you listen to her, for God's sake."

"I was with myself, working in the garden," I continued. "The dog started barking. I went round and there they were."

"What were they doing? Did you know them?"

"Never set eyes on either of them before. One was just standing there. He shouted to the one inside the house."

"Inside the house? Did you not ask them what they wanted?"

Joe jumped to my defence.

"They had guns, Matthew. What did you expect her to do?"

"They had guns? My God! You should've said! Did they say anything?"

"Aye. One of them told me not to tell or I would be shot."

I was trembling telling him. The memory of it!

"You see?" said Joe. "She did the best she could....and she has told us. So she is in danger now."

"What were they like? Did they say anything else?"

"One tall, one small. They had things over their faces....I could not see much of them. The big one said nothing but the other one seemed to know you, or at least he knew it was your farm."

"Why, what did he say?"

I was suddenly embarrassed about this part of the affair. I stuttered out, "He said...I don't know exactly what he said but he mentioned your name."

"My name? Go on, tell me! What did he say?" Matthew was right up close to me. I could not judge how he was reacting to this. Was it anger? Was it concern...for his farm? Or for me?

I looked at Joe, and I am sure he could see the blood rising in my neck. I certainly felt it myself.

"He asked me who I was?"

"Is that all? What are you getting het up about?" said Matthew. "And did you tell him?"

I was annoyed at him for making light of me.

"No, I did not tell him who I was or what I was."
It must have showed in my face that I was annoyed at him. I felt I had done a good job with those men but here I was being made to feel I was somehow to blame. I could not tell him that the fellow had called me a 'hoor', 'Henderson's hoor', not in front of Joe. So I suppose I just glared at him in frustration. Everything now felt very uncomfortable between the three of us.
Matthew made a sudden decision.
"I'd better go and get the gun," he said, turning away to his trap again.
"Do you not think you owe her some thanks?" said Joe, catching him by the coat sleeve.
Matthew paused, thinking about this, his back to me.
"Aye, but she was only doing her job," he said.
As he climbed up into his trap he spoke back quietly in my direction.
"I'll get the gun and be back in a minute. You work away there and help all you can."
He drove away out of the yard. Joe looked at me for a second, then shook his head and went back to work. I stood alone by those two suffering sows, feeling very helpless and forlorn.
John Sproule came past with a bucket of water. He had worked himself up into a fury. He stopped and more or less shouted into my face.
"If this was deliberate there will have to be something done about the bastards that did it. They think they can come sneaking over the border and terrorise us out of our homes that we've had for generations! Well, they have another think coming to them for we will not budge one inch, not an inch! We are going nowhere."
There was something about the turkey face of him and the fury in this outburst that really scared me. I did not know how to react so all I could think to do was to grab a bucket and go to the yard pump again. I left Sproule standing staring at my back. Even above the commotion in the street I was able to hear what he hissed after me.
"Aye, and you're likely one of them, ye wee Fenian bitch!"

~~~~~

It was probably about two hours later that we had the fire well-enough doused to stop it re-kindling. We gathered in Bond's yard; Joe, Matthew, myself, the two farmers who had been there from the beginning and a few other local men who had been returning from the
~~~~~

celebrations and had seen the smoke. Sproule had disappeared thankfully. There was still no sign of the Bonds. What on earth were they going to think when they came home? Every sow they had was dead, burnt or shot.
"And none of you have any idea how it started or who started it?" asked Matthew.
"Not a notion," said one man. "I heard the noise from down across the road. I couldn't believe it when I saw the reek. I was the first one here and the thatch was well lit by that stage. Then Joe and Seamus arrived, and your girl, but there was little we could do."
"You were right Joe," said Matthew. "It has to have been started deliberately. How else would a fire start in the thatch, with nobody else around? The Bonds don't smoke. And the sun today isn't exactly splitting the stones. It must have been arson."
"But who in their right mind would be doing that?" said the farmer.
"We will have to leave it to the police," said Matthew. "Some of us should maybe go down to the town and report this. Somebody will need to go and try and meet the Bonds so they don't get the shock of their lives when they arrive home."
"I suppose they are still away at the Twelfth somewhere," I said innocently.
"Not at all. That is the thing about this," said Matthew. "They never go to the Twelfth. Their church wouldn't hold with all that."
"But they must be somewhere, the three of them? All day too," said Joe.
"They are likely away to one of their Brethern mission-meetings. Whiles they have some sort of convention in the Gospel Hall in Omagh," said Matthew. "I only know because they tried to get me to come with them last year."
"That'll be it."
"The people that did this came to do damage. They picked a day when they thought these folk would be away at the Twelfth. They were just in luck, I suppose," said Matthew.
"What would they have against the Bonds though? Dacent good-livin' people," said one man.
"It coulda been any of us."
'*Íosa agus Máire*!' I thought. The connection between the men I had encountered in Henderson's street and this fire suddenly became clear to me.

I was thinking, 'You don't realise it yet, Matthew, but it is you who is the lucky one. It was meant to have been your farm, if I had not been there. I knew that those two men were up to no good. I am sure in my bones that it was them who did this. Thanks be to God I came home from Joe's when I did.'

And, as I thought it, I saw Joe looking at me with his mouth open and his hands up at the sides of his face. He must have read my mind for he was nodding his head at me. He had put two and two together and was reaching the same conclusion.

"Matt, listen to me," he said. "Those two men that Sally Anne scared off from your house....it was likely them. When they couldn't torch one of your barns they came here instead. Do you not think I'm right?"

Matthew looked at me and I saw the truth of it dawning in his eyes.

"Lord above," he said quietly. "You could be right Joe! That is likely what happened. I never thought of it."

"You are one lucky orangeman," Joe said.

"Very lucky, aye," he said. "And if this is true then I am much obliged to you, Sally Anne. You did a grand job and I thank you for it."

The look he gave me would have melted butter.

I turned away from it and hid my embarrassment behind Joe's shoulder.

Chapter 13

Matthew Henderson

What I thought about the fire.

Like everybody else, I was very annoyed. For the Bonds especially, for they are right folk; they keep themselves to themselves; they do all the work on their wee farm by themselves and are never a bother to anyone. Of-course people do like to talk about them, with their religious views that seem to separate them from the rest of the community....and I am no better, but you could get a lot worse as neighbours.

They were going to get a quare gunk when they arrived home to this disaster.

The thing was too that the Bonds have never been political. It's not as if they were mad Orange people, or even Unionists. To the best of my knowledge they don't even vote.

They eventually returned from their services later that night. There was no consoling them. Bessy cried like a child and the two brothers weren't far off it, by the look of them, as they stepped their way over the debris of roasted pigs. Myself and a few neighbours who had been there helping talked to them as best we could.

When I offered to go down to Castlederg to fetch the police the older of the brothers, Samuel, told me not to. I found this strange.

"You will surely want to report it," I said. "It is clear what happened. Somebody set fire to the place."

"That's as maybe," he replied, "but I don't want to be reporting it to the police or anybody else. 'The Lord giveth and The Lord taketh away'."

"I'm sorry, Samuel," I said, "but that isn't the way to be looking at this. If a crime has been committed you need to tell the authorities so they can investigate it. Somebody needs to be held to account for it."

He took me by the shoulder and led me to the side.

"The thing is this, Matthew. I don't want any retaliation for this."

"What are you talking about?" I said.

"Do you not follow what is happening in this country?" he said. "Do you not read the papers? It's all tit-for-tat, eye-for-an-eye. Sometimes

three eyes for an eye. That flour mill that was burned down over in Desertmartin in May? The next night four young Catholic men shot dead in front of their mothers."
"Likely they were the guilty party."
"Maybe they were; more than likely they weren't, but either way they didn't deserve to be shot. At the very least they deserved a court case rather than that sort of rough justice. If word of this gets out to the wrong people some innocent Catholic will suffer by way of reprisal. That is what we do not want to happen. So don't be telling the Police, you or anybody else. Just let it pass, son. The Bonds are not that kind of people, never have been. We will survive. The Lord will provide."
"But what about justice?" I argued. "Somebody needs to be brought to book for this kind of thing surely?"
"'Vengeance is mine. I will repay, saith The Lord'. Just leave it to Him."
"I think you should be telling the Police," I said.
"Well, you let us be the judge of that," he said, turning back towards the yard. Then he stopped and looked at the group of men still standing there. "You see these people? They came to our help when we needed them to. They didn't wait to be asked. Good honest, helpful folk, Catholic and Protestant. Now Matthew, how would we feel if we reported this and tomorrow night one of their barns gets burned down? Or worse still, if somebody gets shot?"
To me this was a very strange attitude. It stood to his credit that Samuel Bond did not want any innocent people to suffer as he had, of-course it did. I would respect his wishes but it sat hard with me. Not to want to find out who was responsible was the part I couldn't accept. Some lucky buggers were getting off with this.
What those two men did to Bond's pig-house was more than likely intended for mine, I knew that. The only thing that puzzled me for a while was why one of them would have the nerve on him to enter our dwelling house. I couldn't work that out. With Sally Anne being there the door was open of-course. Maybe they just pushed it to see if it was locked and then, when they found it open, couldn't resist the temptation to go in.
We were sitting at the kitchen table, my mother, Emily, Sally Anne and myself. The twins were in bed. I was still quizzing her about the events of the day and the order of things.
"You were working in the front garden?" I said. "What took you in there?"

"I was tidying it up," said Sally Anne.
"That was good of you," said my mother. "It needed it but I just haven't the energy for it any more. It could do with a few flowers planted."
"And is that all they said? 'None of your business.' What about their accents?" I asked.
She suddenly looked a bit nervous; a glance at my mother; a blush spreading up from around her neck; a stare down at the dishes in front of her.
"There was only one of them spoke. He didn't really have any particular accent," she said.
"Was he speaking in Gaelic? Or did he sound like he was from around here?" Emily asked her.
"No Gaelic. I honestly couldn't say where he was from. Maybe Derry or Donegal. It was all that quick. I was scared out of my wits. He didn't say much."
"But he did say something else, didn't he?" I was guessing but I remembered her face when I was asking her about this in the Bond's street earlier. She was certainly hesitant about something. Was she protecting somebody? It was a fleeting thought and I dismissed it immediately, but it had been there.
"He did," she said, her head down, "but I would rather not say what it was."
"Come on girl," I said, my voice raising itself more than I had intended. "Tell us. What did he say?"
She looked very uncomfortable and I nearly regretted my insistence. It could be important though. I tried again, in a more gentle tone this time.
"You have to tell me. You did a great job standing up to them and scaring them off but you need to tell me everything they said."
She got up from the table and walked around behind mother and Emily towards the door to the passage. When she reached it she turned and gave me the tiniest wee nod of the head to follow her, which I did. I found her in the parlour. She stood with her head down, her back to me and her shoulders shuddering.
"What is it?"
"He called me a name," she said.
"What name?"
"A bad name. I don't want it crossing my lips."

"Come on Sally Anne. You have to tell me."
She waited for a bit, seeming to swallow something sticking in her throat.
"He called me your hoor!" she said, voice quivering and she crossed herself quickly.
"What?" I said. "What did he call you?"
"You heard me."
"What did he actually say?"
"I told you. He said, 'Who are you anyway? You are likely Henderson's wee hoor!' That is what he said to me. I couldn't say that in front of your mother and your sister. Nor in front of Joe. It's bad enough saying it to you."
"My God," I said, trying to process the shock of this. So they knew whose farm they were at.
"Is that what people think I am?" she said, her eyes down, a wee sob hiding behind her voice.
I couldn't answer for a bit.
"No, people don't think that. Not normal people anyway."
"How do you know?"
"Agh girl, don't be asking me that. You can't stop birds flying but you can stop them building a nest in your hair. Some people..."
"What does that mean?" she said. "I would leave here if I thought that people were saying that."
"Well, they're not and you are not going anywhere. Just because this fellow has a filthy imagination doesn't mean anyone else thinks the same."
"I hope to God you are right," she said and we stood in quietness for a while until the obvious question forced its way into my consciousness.
"So how did he know this was my place?"
"That is what I was wondering too."
"He must be a local," I said. "Somebody who has had an eye on me for a while."
"Likely."
Emily appeared in the doorway briefly. I didn't hear her coming; maybe she had been standing there listening to us for a while. It was an awkward moment for Sally Anne but it didn't really bother me.
"I am going to bed," she said and disappeared towards the guest bedroom at the back.

"And you say they ran out the back lane?" I said to Sally Anne. "Making their escape towards the border?"
"That one seemed to know his way around anyway," she said. "The one that came out of the house."
"What was he looking for in the house? You didn't see anything disturbed? You couldn't work out what rooms he had been into?"
She shook her head.
We stood quietly for a bit.
"So it was meant to be us." I spoke my thoughts aloud.
"That's what I think too."
"And if I had let you go to the Twelfth with us the place could have been burned to the ground."
"I was at the Twelfth," she said.
"Aye, but you were home in time."
"I was."
"What did you think about it?"
"It was alright."
"Did you not like the bands, you being musical?"
"I did. They were good. The drums were a bit loud."
"Aye....the Lambegs."
"Never heard the like of them before."
"Were they too loud for you?"
"I had to cover my ears. There were people buried in that graveyard had to cover theirs as well!" she said.
I smiled at her. We stood there, quiet for a second. I suddenly thought how much I enjoyed talking to this girl. And how much I owed her for how she had handled the events of the day. I looked at her and noticed how tired she appeared to be, half-perched on the back of a sofa, her hair shading her eyes.
I'm not sure why but I moved toward her. It may have been with the half-intention of giving her a friendly hug of appreciation for ....but it didn't happen. She took a step to the side and sort of dodged around me and out the door to the kitchen as quick as a light.
"There's things to be done," she said as she fled.
I followed her, disappointed but more annoyed at myself, at my own weakness. My mother had gone off to bed, I think. We had the kitchen to ourselves. Sally Anne was at the sink. She worked in silence and I sat at the table, watching her in the amber light of the oil-lamp.
"I never knew you had a gun," she said after a while.

"Aye, I do."
"What do you have a gun for?"
"It's only an old shotgun," I said.
"Why do you need a gun?"
"For shooting rats and scaring the crows off the corn. Mind you," I said, "since you came around I haven't needed it much."
"What?" she said, turning around.
"Well, when the rats see those green eyes of yours they think I've got the biggest cat in Ireland."
It was just my clumsy attempt at an old joke. Whatever it did to her, she let the cooking tray that she was holding slip from her wet hands and it clattered to the stone tiles with a crash, spilling soapy water on the floor.
Perhaps that sound jolted me into a realisation, I don't know. A shapeless thought had been trying to make its way up to the surface of my consciousness during the past few hours. Now it jumped out at me like a trout leaping for a fly on the river.
'The gun! I wonder is that what they were after! That is maybe why they came into the house, to see if I had any weapons. Why did I not think of that sooner?'
I had heard of other farmers in Tyrone having their guns stolen by these IRA gangs.
I didn't say anymore to Sally Anne though. She had enough to be thinking about after the day she had put in. Instead I pretended to make an issue of the dropped pan.
"You are far too quick tempered. I was only making a joke. Look at the mess you made."
"I am sorry. I will clean it up."
"That's the least you can do; you're the maid."
"I will clean it up, Mister Henderson," she said.
The 'Mister' again.
"And will you do something else for me?"
"I might," she said. "It depends what it is."
"Don't go away," I said and I ran up the stairs, two at a time, up the ladder, all the way to her room to get the fiddle.
"Here you are," I said, back in the kitchen. "Will you play me the tune you played that first night, Eleanor?"
"Is that all it is?" she said. "I was getting worried."
"What else would it have been?" I asked.

"But the noise will waken the girls."
"Noise?" I said. "If anybody ever says that your fiddle playing is a 'noise' send them to me. I'll put them right and they won't forget it."
"Thank you, kind sir," she said with a sort of mock sweetness.
That smile again; those eyes, with the lamplight reflected in them like a couple of shining coins lying on the bottom of a shallow stream. I watched her as she played; a gentle set of notes that sounded as if they had been meant to be arranged in that particular order since the beginning of time. It was like a medicine of music that would have soothed any worried mind. I had listened to more than my fair share of music on that Twelfth but this was the best of it all. The feeling of dread, the threat that was hanging over me after what had happened today seemed to be washed away by the gentle sound of that ancient tune. A tune that had been passed on from person to person for more generations than could be counted. A melody that had lived and survived through many decades of trouble in this land. It would have been played in other times of rebellion, like the United Irishmen, Daniel O'Connell's time, the Famine, and these are only the ones I can recall from my schooling....and here it is, getting another sweet airing in my house on the northern side of our new border on the Twelfth of July, Nineteen Twenty Two. It was comforting me, reminding me of the hardiness of the folk of this country. It was speaking to me of a beauty in this land that no amount of political bother will ever be able to wipe out. I felt like I was bathing in a river of the clearest music. I closed my eyes and gave thanks in the secret soul of myself, thanks for protection, thanks for survival, thanks for the beauty of this tune and for this girl.
Emily broke the spell though. She appeared in the kitchen door like some sort of jack-in-the-box that you'd see in the Rabble Fair. An angry one too.
"Would you stop that screeching," she said to Sally Anne. "The rest of us are trying to sleep. Have you no sense?"
Sally Anne stopped abruptly, mid-line, bow poised in mid-kitchen, her mouth open in surprise.
"Sorry," she said.
"It's my fault, Emily," I said. "I asked her to play it. I thought you'd be asleep."
"And I was asleep until this dirge started," said Emily.

"Well," I said, "by the time you get back to your bed, Sally Anne will have finished the tune. So away you go quick. I want to hear the rest of it."

Emily turned on her heel and stormed out of the kitchen.

"Go on," I said to Sally Anne. "Finish it off. Never worry about her. I want to hear the end of it."

"I have a feeling," she said, "that this is one tune that you may never hear the end of."

She played again, the bow feathering the strings so lightly, the fiddle whispering its way home through those final few notes.

Chapter 14

A Belfast Proposal

He waited in a doorway, studying the building opposite. An impressive, four-storied edifice, the top tier having a line of beautifully symmetrical arched windows which at this moment were infused with the evening's copper sunlight. Apparently its red sandstone had been imported from Scotland some forty years ago, or so he had read. No surprise in that, he was thinking. So much of this place had its origins over there, not least the majority of its crusty residents, imported settlers from the Scottish borders and lowlands. And, as an Englishman, this city seemed so northern to him that he felt at home here in a way that he did not experience when he had been in the rural environs of the south. The Belfast Telegraph building he was examining could easily have taken its place in King Street or the London Road in his native Manchester.

He pulled his silver timepiece from his waistcoat pocket. Coming up to six, he saw. Another five or ten minutes to wait, unless she was struggling to complete some report for a deadline. That had happened before and his patience, questionable at the best of times, had been pushed to the limits on one of those occasions. Eight thirty it had been before she emerged. Some story had just come in concerning a fire at a hotel on the Lisburn Road; she had had no choice but to type up the report as it was read to her, or so she had told him. It had so maddened him that he had almost allowed his veneer of phlegmatic indifference to slip. Today would not be a good day for that occurrence to 'be repeated.

That dealer in Pottinger's Entry had been so utterly stubborn in his refusal to budge on price, despite his best efforts. He seemed to be a real 'not-an-inch' type, a 'hard-wee-man', so typical of Belfast's shopkeeper classes. Willie Manson had stood behind his little counter, all four foot six inches of him, staring up through ridiculously thick spectacles at his client.

"Ye can take it or leave it, mister! That's my price and until you pay it you'll be walking outa here with nothing but your moustache to impress your lady friend," his Sandy Row sing-song accent grating on his client's aural sensibilities.

Then, shortly after buying a small bunch of red roses on his way down North Street, he had been forced to take cover as a burst of shooting broke out somewhere up ahead. It had not lasted too long on this occasion; the Special Constabulary seemed to get on top of it fairly quickly this time and, whoever the gunmen were, they disappeared towards the safety of west Belfast so as to live to fight another day. It had crossed his mind, ever so briefly, to get involved and he had instinctively felt for the revolver strapped under his left arm. But this was his day off, he consoled himself. Those good Ulster boys could take the heat this time. He had other fish to fry on this particular day and he was not going to be distracted by the matter of itchy-fingered republicans.

What had struck him once again was the image of tramcars and horse-drawn carts continuing about their business as if the sound of gunfire was a mere normality. So strange to see a pair of sturdy dray horses pulling a half-empty grain wagon along the cobbled street towards the sound of the shots with no apparent driver to guide or control them. The wise fellow had presumably taken shelter on the floor of his cart; perhaps he had taken a bout of cold feet and abandoned his charge completely. A tram passed him, scattering the swarming pigeons as it clattered along in the other direction; there was not a passenger to be seen, not until one brave soul gave the game away by popping his head up at a rear window to stare along the street at the scurrying constables. Several shoppers ducked into nearby stores, head's shaking and tongues wagging in disgust as they bemoaned what had become Belfast's daily dose of violence. They were quickly out and about their business again at the first sign of a lull in the altercation. Life would go on in the current 'normal' of this tough, new capital city, even if 'normal' was simply an accommodation of the appallingly 'abnormal' for the time being.

Two minutes after six and she emerged from the side door of the building on to Little Donegal Street. He watched her from the shadow of the doorway as she paused to button up her jacket. Under her arm she held a newspaper which seemed to make it awkward for her to put on her bonnet, so she held it between her knees momentarily. She was oblivious to his presence of-course. He was not meant to be anywhere near here.

His eyes followed her along the pavement as she began to swing into that long-legged stride of hers before he crossed the road in exaggeratedly stealthy steps and took up a position following her a few yards behind. And 'behind' was the operative word. His entire focus was on her behind, that fascinating wiggle of her wonderful hips that she seemed to create so unconsciously and that had mesmerised him since the first time he had watched her dance in the Ulster Hall. She had the longest legs he had ever encountered on any member of the female species and, from early on in his sightings of her, he had developed an absolute fascination with the idea of getting more intimately acquainted with them. The urge had never been stronger than it was at this moment.

He could not shift from his mind an image of her from the one occasion he had persuaded her to accompany him for a swim at Helen's Bay, near his barracks in Hollywood. He had bought a brand new bathing costume for her, the very latest in fashion. Actually he had purchased three of them, in different sizes, just so she would have no excuse. Somewhat to his surprise she had chosen one of them, had welcomed his gift and had worn it, so displaying her perfect curves in a way that would have graced any advertising poster. What a vision she was on that beach that June afternoon; every male head turned to watch her; quite a few females too, jealously so. And now she was his! Almost!

"Victoria," he called in a playful bass tone, "aren't you gonna wait for me?"

She turned mid-stride and came into his arms, surprised delight in her smile.

"You scared me Stanley," she kissed into his ear. "I didn't know you were going to be around today. Why are you not at work?"

"More important things to be doing, honey. So I have a day off."

"More important things? Like what?" she teased.

"Like taking the most beautiful girl in Belfast for tea in the Grand Central," he said.

"Lovely," she smiled, "but what if that girl needs to be going home to her mummy and daddy because they will be expecting her? Her daddy will be wanting his evening paper."

"Forget about them just for once. They will just think you have had to work late again," he said.

"I don't know, Stanley," she argued through the teasing twinkle in her sea-blue eyes. "They haven't met you yet and..."

"Actually, that is no longer true, my dear. We had a very pleasant meeting this afternoon."
"What?" Victoria was genuinely shocked and it showed in how she pulled back from him to stare. "How did you meet my parents? You are playing some sort of trick on me."
"No trick; I happened to be in the Oldpark area and I happened to call with Mr and Mrs Wilson, just to make their acquaintance. Don't you believe me?"
She shook her luxurious blonde curls in doubt and confusion.
"I don't know what to believe," she said.
"Ok, your house has a plum-coloured door," he said. "And the hall has a blue carpet. It's a lovely home you have, Vic."
"You really were there," she said. "But why? Why not wait and let me introduce you? What is going on here?"
He took her arm and guided her from the evening rush of pedestrians on Royal Avenue and into the lobby of the Grand Central Hotel.
"All in good time, my dear. Just wait until we have eaten," he said. "I am famished and, tonight of all nights, I do not want my tummy to be rumbling."
Victoria could no longer control the half-smile of expectation which played around her mouth. She pursed her lips in mock resignation as he took her hand and pulled her along behind the maître-d'hôtel to a small table in a candlelit corner of the dining hall between a substantial oak dresser and the green velvet drapes which hung by the window.
Three-quarters of an hour later he had scanned the Telegraph's headlines a few times but read no further. The news held little interest for him this evening.
'Why read the news when you were so closely associated with making it?' he often thought.
'Dublin's Four Courts Ablaze,' he had read.
'So their glorious struggle for so-called freedom has fallen down around their ears and they are now killing each other,' he thought. 'Typical!'
'Belfast Gunmen Busy.'
'Of-course they are! Haven't I just experienced it.'
'Woodstock Road Tragedy. Young Woman Dies Of Wounds.'
'Just think, if that had been Victoria....'
But it wasn't, and anyhow, tonight was no time to be spoiling things with a course of the stark realities of Ulster's conflicts. Tonight was the

night, if only she would hurry up. His patience was again wearing down to a fray as she savoured the final spoonfuls of her crème brûlée. He reached across the table and took her left hand. Settling himself down in his chair he leaned back and feasted his eyes on her face. Someone should have painted this face, he was thinking. It is pure perfection. High cheekbones, nose and mouth in the most delightful proportions, lips full and inviting, a complexion like the softest lily-white petal you could ever imagine. It was the kind of face that made you think 'wholesome-country-girl-turned-sophisticated-city-professional', an irresistibly tantalising combination. But while he had found it impossible to resist her charms, he had also discovered that, try as he might, the level of intimacy that every sinew of his mind and body craved for was firmly resisted by her. She wore her Presbyterian principles around her gorgeous figure like the impregnable walls of Carrickfergus Castle.

He shifted his hips forward on the cushioned seat so that his knee came into contact with hers below the tablecloth. Instinctively her knees came together in something of a defensive retreat but he held his ground and pushed ever so gently so that he separated them and wedged his knee there against the front edge of her chair. Her eyes looked up from her final bite and he sensed just a shade of surprise and apprehension. No point in beating about the bush here, he was thinking and he stroked her hand between both of his as his knee played side to side, ever so gently, between hers. Her internal struggles gradually eased and he sensed a tender swaying of her legs with his in a seductively secret, under-the-tablecloth dance.

"Victoria," he began, "I know we have only known each other for a matter of a few months but..."

"Three months actually," she interrupted, nervous and excited beyond her ability to disguise.

"Three months, yes; three months which have been the most wonderful three months of my entire life, my dear. Victoria, I cannot contain myself any longer. I want you more than life itself. I adore you more than I can ever hope to explain to you. I love the very air you breathe, the very ground you walk on .... and my heart is bursting to ask you this."

He slipped from his seat to kneel on the carpet beside her. Fumbling in his pocket, he produced a small black box and opened it for her to look at. A line of tiny diamonds sparkled up from the black velvet cloth.

"Well my dear? What do you say? Can I begin to call you my fiancée?"
"Oh Stanley," she said. "I would love to be your fiancée! But have you asked my parents? Is that why...?"
"Of-course I have asked your father. That's why I took the trouble to go to see them today. I couldn't possibly be so bold as to..."
"And what did my father say?"
"He was all in favour of it," said Stanley. "Completely in favour."
No point in telling the truth at such a crucial juncture as this, he reasoned.
"And my mother?"
"Yes of-course, your mother too! So what do you say, Vic? Please don't break my heart on this one."
"My father didn't think it was too soon? After all we have only known each other for ... for such a short time. And what about .... if you are posted back to England sometime soon?"
"I know it's a comparatively short time but, in times like these Vic, matters become so much clearer in one's mind. I have faced many seriously threatening circumstances over the past few months and, believe me, I now know my own mind much better as a result. And I know what I want and what I must have.....and that, my dear, is you. You, Miss Victoria Wilson, as my...my fiancée!"
The warmth of Victoria's smile froze on her lips momentarily. She adjusted a strand of hair which seemed to be intent on intruding into the middle of this conversation. Disappointment for a split second in her voice, she spoke softly into the dark of his hair.
"I thought you might say 'wife' there," she said. "Not just fiancée. Do you want to marry me, Stan?"
"Of-course I want to marry you. That's what I am asking you!"
"And when do you think we might get married?" she persisted softly, his head resting on her shoulder, her hands around his neck.
Stanley's face raised itself reluctantly from its sanctuary on her breast and his hand slipped intimately across her stomach.
"I would marry you within the hour if it was possible, Vic. Let's just say though, that as soon as we possibly can we will get married. Is that enough for you my love?"
She smiled into his eyes, her hand cupped against his face. "That is enough for me," she said.
"So your answer is...?"

"My answer is ...'Yes'!" she finished and kissed him on his forehead just as the maître d'hôtel began his approach to the table, making strenuous effort to shift some sort of imagined frog in his throat.
"Will there be anything else, Sir?" he asked.
Stanley's eyes did not leave Victoria's face for a second.
"I certainly hope so," he said. "I certainly hope so. What do you say, Vic? Are you ready for something else?"

Chapter 15

Sally Anne Sweeney

What happened on my birthday

I had my nineteenth birthday on the Twenty Third of August and it was ruined by Michael Collins. Well, not that it was his fault, God rest him. It just so happened that he was shot the day before and it soon was the talk of the whole countryside.

A couple of days before the birthday I had my first letter from home. My father wrote a few lines to thank me for my own wee note. He would not be the best at knitting words together but I was delighted to be reading them all the same. He wanted to tell me that everything in Ranahuel was fine and to say, '*Go maire tú an lá*', wishing me a happy birthday. He was always good at remembering our birthdays, which made up for my poor mother who did not really have the wit to be remembering very much. According to his letter, she is well mended up from the 'flu or whatever had come over her before I left, thanks be to God. Granny Brid is still in good health, he told me, but there was news of a fishing boat lost off Kincasslagh, with four local fishermen drowned. I wondered if my friend Ailish was kin to any of them; she likely knew them, that was for sure. My sister Mairead wrote a few lines at the bottom, not that I made a lot of sense of her. She says she can hardly remember what I look like and to send a picture before I go home in November, so she will recognise me when I arrive. I hope to God she is joking but you never know with that one.

For some reason, maybe because of being away from my folk for the first time on my birthday, I had started to think a lot more about home. Maybe even missing it, I would have to admit. This seemed to start after I went with Joe and his family on Cemetery Sunday, a week or two before the birthday. There in St. Patrick's graveyard I watched the Kearneys as they cut grass and tidied up the plot where Anthony's parents and a few earlier ancestors on Monica's side of the family were buried. Dalys going back for generations seemed to be laid to rest there, snuggling down into the earth between a low hedge of wizened conifers and the sturdy stone wall at the back of the burial ground.

It was the first time I had met Mary Kearney, Joe's sister who lodged in Strabane. I found her pleasant enough, quiet and a good deal prettier than I had expected. I would never have guessed that she was related to Joe; there was little similarity that I could see anyhow. Her face was more like young Kate but she had the greatest head of hair on her, shiny black like the colour of a crow. I watched her with her father and mother and maybe it was because I knew a little bit about the fall-out between them but she was definitely on her guard with them. You would not have needed to be depending on the three of them for conversation, certainly not for warmth anyhow. Kin can be funny, can't they.

On the other hand, there was a great deal of chat with the other relatives, Joe's cousins and his uncles and aunts on his mother's side, who had travelled from far and near for this occasion. That was the custom in Donegal as well as here. I got introduced to a few of these people but I started to get fed up with sly nudges being made to Joe in my presence, and comments such as, "You've got yourself a fine lassie there, Joe!" He was loving it, protesting his innocence in a half-hearted sort of way but all delighted to be the centre of attention. I was not so delighted myself and soon I escaped and managed to put a clump of sturdy-looking bushes between me and him. It was there that Anthony Kearney found me a bit later, just before the Mass began.

"Sally Anne. What are you hiding round here for?"

How sweet to my ears to be in my own language again after so many days of the English.

"I am not hiding," I replied. "Just watching everything."

He looked at me quietly, kindly.

"Would you be missing your own folk?" he asked.

Goodness but did I not let a tear escape and run down my face a bit before I had it captured. I turned away, side on to him.

"It is not that," I said. "It is just...." Then to change the subject I said, "So there is just the one Kearney grave here? Your parents?"

"That's right," he said. "The Kearneys wouldn't be from here you see. So it is just my parents."

"I remember Joe telling me that."

"It's mainly Monica's side."

"There seems to be a right crowd of them buried here. They must go back a good long way in this parish?"

"They do," he said. "Generations. But Monica's father always used to say that before they settled here they were in Leinster. Somehow they got pushed out of there, sent to the west. Maybe it was Cromwell; I can't rightly remember what he said. If it wasn't Cromwell, it was somebody else. A landlord or something."

"Aye, we were always getting pushed around by somebody," I said.

"Still are," he said. "In this part of the country anyway. This is the only place where we can get away from it."

I was puzzled. "What do you mean?" I asked.

"The graveyard," he said. "They can't be touching you once you're under the sod."

"God but you are very morbid today," I said.

"It's the place for it, *mo leanbh*."

He was turning to rejoin his family.

"Anthony," I said and he stopped. I wanted to ask him about the war and why he joined up. This was the first time I had had the chance to speak to him alone but somehow it just did not seem right to be talking about it in a churchyard.

"No, it's alright," I said. "I will talk to you another time."

"Are things going alright for you at Henderson's?" he asked. "You don't feel you are being pushed around there, do you?"

'Such a kindly man,' I thought.

"No, not at all," I said. "I am enjoying it. Maybe just missing being at home on the day that is in it, that is all."

"Well, it's not forever. You are nearly half way through, aren't you?" he said.

"I suppose so. And nearly through another year of my life for it will be my birthday next week."

"Is that so?" he said. "We will have to have a party for you. Will you come over that night and bring the fiddle and we'll have a bit of a celebration? I'm sure Matthew would be all on for that."

"I am sure he would. That would be great, thanks."

With that the priest's booming voice pealed out across the cemetery like a solemn church bell, calling us to prayer for the souls of these departed, the Dalys and Kearneys included. I have to admit though that I put a few Donegal names into the prayers as we went along; names like Maggie Dan and Bartley O'Donnell, my mother's parents, and Frank Sweeney, my grandfather who passed away when I was little. At times like this you fairly get struck by the realisation of time passing,

passing far too quickly and taking the older ones with it, leaving the rest of us to make the best of things while we can.

The Kearneys had me home from the ceremony in good time to be starting the evening milking. The cows had gathered at the gate of the field and were making patient moans when I arrived down the back lane for them. How did they know to be waiting for me, their big vacant eyes like purple plums? I always thought that they must have their own way of telling the time; maybe it was the height of the sun in the sky; more likely it was just the pressure of the milk swelling in their udders.

'I am becoming quite attached to these lovely animals of Matthew's,' I thought as they followed me up between the banks of hedge parsley that lined the lane like lace curtains on a window; each one found its own familiar stall in the dark byre.

I was not long started when Matthew arrived in beside me, all attention and full of questions. He was quick to sense that I was not in my usual mood of banter and carry-on. To be fair to him, he adjusted well and we had a good serious conversation, partly about his own family....even though he started it off by asking what Cemetery Sunday was all about. I explained as best I could, from my own experience of it in Donegal and from the ceremony in Castlederg that day.

"It is strange to me," I said to him, "that you know nothing about it and yet it happens every year, not three miles away from you."

"Why would I know anything about it?" he said with a hint of grumpiness in his voice. "I was never interested in it before."

"So why now?"

"Because... I suppose because you were there, doing whatever you do at it. I'm just curious, that's all," he said.

"You would never have thought of asking Joe about it?"

"No, it never came up. I wouldn't be asking him about the likes of that."

"Why not?"

"He'd wonder why I was asking."

"But you don't mind asking me," I laughed. "So why do you want to know all about it now but you could not be bothered asking Joe any time before?"

"What's wrong with asking you? Don't tell me if you don't want to, like if it is some big Catholic secret or something," he said.

These conversations! We always managed to turn things into a wrangle. It was like we could not look at each other without having a barney of words. And I loved it. So did he, I believe.

"No, there is no big Catholic secret about it. You could have come if you had wanted to. It was not like the Twelfth where I wasn't welcome, if you remember."

"Ah ha," he said turning away from my challenge. "But the difference is that I would not have wanted to go to some Catholic mumbo-jumbo of a thing....but you were dying to get coming to the Twelfth. I'm right, am I not?"

"Catholic mumbo-jumbo? God forgive you! There was no mumbo-jumbo; just a few prayers for the dead; fixing up the graveyard.... and the priest said Mass. The only time I have heard any mumbo-jumbo around here was when those two fellows went past me on the Twelfth beating the hell out of those big drums. And thon wee snake charmer with his flute of a thing, likely calling up the spirits of King Billy and his dead soldiers."

Matthew looked at me and for a second or two he did not know how to react. I thought I had pushed it too far. I thought for a minute that he was going to yell at me. I was nearly about to apologise, but then he had started it with that comment about mumbo-jumbo. What was that I was seeing in his eyes? I could not take a chance here.

"Sorry," I said, trying to sound more submissive.

It worked.

He shook his head, smiling.

"Where did that all come from?" he said. "I was only asking what went on at a Cemetery Sunday. And I'm still none the wiser."

So I tried to explain the day as best I could to this *Protastúnach*. I concentrated on the aspect of respect for the dead, for the ancestors gone before and how they needed our prayers to get them out of Purgatory and so on. Then, when I thought he was becoming bored, I told him about what Anthony had said regarding the Kearney and the Daly family histories. Now that he did find interesting.

"So he came from the Sperrins and he thinks her people came to these parts from Leinster?" he said. "Now that is news to me. And there I was thinking that I was the planter here."

I was a bit lost at this comment. It probably showed in my face.

"I don't understand," I said.

"You see," he explained, "we are always being told that we came here with the plantation, hundreds of years ago; the Protestants, I mean; we were brought over from England or Scotland and took land that had belonged to the Irish after they abandoned it."
I thought about this statement for a minute. 'The Irish abandoned their land, did they? Just walked away from it of their own accord, no muskets involved or anything?'
I did not think I should say this to him though. Instead I asked about his family.
"Ah, I see. And when did your ancestors get here? Do you know who they were, where they came from?"
Matthew seemed to be turning this over in his head. I could sense a change rising in him, resentment and a sort of steeliness.
"I have no idea," he said a bit sharply, "nor do I much care."
To be truthful, I did not know how to respond to this. It left me feeling that a gulf had opened between us again. This coldness I saw in him, this arrogance, was something new to me. With some ancient instinct stirring in me, I knew not to go any further with the conversation. I had strayed unto some sort of sacred ground, some sort of raw nerve, and I needed to stray back off it again. And stay off it.
I changed the subject.
"Anthony has invited me over to his place for my birthday. You as well. And the girls."
"Your birthday? You never told me you were having a birthday. When is it?"
"Next week. The Twenty Third."
"Aye well," he said, "that'll be a good night."

~~~~~

When it came to the night it did start off as a good night.
It was an overcast evening, there had been a downpour earlier and now a drizzle of summer rain had Matthew and I hurrying across the fields, through the gap in the tumbled-down stone ditch and over the burn to Joe's place. I had his father's fiddle under my arm for a bit of music and dancing later on.
Kearney's cottage hunkered down behind the hill as if it was taking shelter from the wind blowing off the Donegal bogs above. There was something odd about its appearance. It looked to me as if it had begun
~~~~~

its life as a small, two-roomed thatched cottage, just like the ones I was used to around the Rosses. At some stage more recently the family had built an extra part onto the lower side of the cottage, this time two-storied and with a slate roof. They had also added a small porch at the original front door. So, seen from the front, the house looked to have very little balance to it. Inside the kitchen itself was neat and tidy but lacking some of the finer furniture that the Hendersons would have had. A faded Sacred Heart of Jesus picture looked down at us from above the hearth and a well-made St Brigid's cross hung by the door, reminding me of home.

There were not many of us in the room that evening, just the family, Matthew and myself. I had wanted the twins to come but Matthew would not hear tell of it, claiming that it would be far too late for them to be up. It being a Wednesday, they would be going to school in the morning as usual. How would they ever be able to get up and walk the two miles down to school in time in the morning? That and the fact that his mother 'needed the company'. Those were his reasons, it seemed at the time.

As it turned out, I wondered later if he perhaps had other motives altogether.

Joe's four younger brothers and sisters were there of-course and they were all very excited. Kate, the fifteen year old, had made up a bundle so we could play 'Pass-the-Parcel' and that gave us all a laugh. I had to play the music, blindfolded so as not to see who was holding the package at any stage. As the parcel was unwrapped each time I stopped and the 'dares' were read out, I was more than relieved to be playing the fiddle rather than the game. Some of the challenges were grand but one or two would have had me in a predicament. As it happened, the final 'dare' fell to wee Hughie. The boy was too young to read it but Joe took great delight in helping him. The challenge was to 'Kiss the Birthday girl' and I was relieved that it had not fallen to Matthew or, worse still, to Joe himself. Hughie was too shy to be following that instruction so I made a bit of a play of chasing him around the kitchen and grabbing him under the table for a cuddle and a tickle.

There were a few more silly kitchen games and I had to play a couple of jigs for Kate to show off her dance steps. She made a right clatter, her brogues hammering on the stone flags in front of the hearth. Joe joined in towards the end, his feet fighting with the beat of the tune and his arms flailing like branches in a breeze to help him keep his balance. His mother moved protectively between him and the table where she had laid out a spread of food, mainly sweet biscuits and buns which she had baked.

We were halfway through the meal when there was a noise in the porch; the door opened and in walked Mary Kearney. This was the last thing the family had expected and the surprise showed on her parents' faces. The children were delighted and a chorus of excited welcomes rose from them. Mary responded to them with hugs but said nothing to her father or mother.

Anthony spoke first.

"What brings you home at this time of the night, *Máire*?"

"Is anything the matter?" asked Monica. "Why are you not in Strabane?"

"How did you get here?" said Joe.

Mary ignored them and took off her coat without a word. From her bag she pulled out a folded newspaper.

"I thought you'd be interested in this," she said to her father. "Your hero has bitten the dust."

She slapped the Irish News down beside him on the table. I could not help but notice a sense of triumph in how she did it but I had no idea why at the time.

Anthony took the paper in his hands, staring silently at the headline for a few seconds.

"'Mr Michael Collins killed'!" he read out. "Oh my God. What have they done now?"

Monica's hand went to her mouth. "Oh no," she said with a wee gasp. "Don't be telling us that."

I felt the shock of it myself, like a turning in my stomach.

"That's what it says," said Anthony with a shake of his head.

Joe joined him, reading over his shoulder.

"'Shot Dead in an Ambush. Great National Loss. Killed in his own native county. Collins' death a veritable blow to the Irish people'," he read.

"Shot by the soldiers he used to lead," said Anthony. "What sort of a mad country do we live in? What a terrible thing!"

There was a hush in the kitchen. A lull before the storm, I could sense. Monica Kearney's two hands now cradled her face, her eyes staring. Matthew's eyes were blank and he said not a word. I could think of nothing to say either. We were all just in complete shock. All except

Mary that is. She had had time to form her opinions about the thing and now we were going to hear them, like it or not.
"I heard about it today in work. The Post Office was buzzing with the news. I knew it wouldn't have reached you up here in the sticks so I thought I'd buy a paper and bring it home to you."
Anthony was still looking hard at the report. I'm not sure if he was reading it or just staring, dumbfounded.
"That was thoughtful of you," he said dryly.
Mary half-smiled.
"I couldn't wait to see your reaction," she taunted.
"Well, now you've seen it and I'm sure you are the happier for it. Are you staying here to gloat or are you going back to Strabane?"
"No, stop there Daddy," interrupted his wife. "She can't be leaving now. She can't be going back to Strabane at this time of night. Sit down, Mary, and have a bite to eat."
I had not seen Anthony this annoyed before. He always had such a soft face on him but there was a hardness in his eyes now; a shadow of hurt with a fair bit of anger there too.
"How did you get here anyway? Who brought you at this time of night?" he said.
"That is my business," she said. "I got left off at the end of the lane. I have no way back tonight."
"I hope it wasn't Duggan who brought you. You are not still running around with that scoundrel, are you?" said Anthony.
"As I said, that is my business. And he's not a scoundrel. He is a patriot."
"Some patriot!" said Anthony bitterly.
"At least he stands up for his country!" Mary's temper flared like a blacksmith's fire under bellows. "For his own country! For Ireland! He isn't fighting for some foreign power that has no right to be here."
"That's enough of that, Mary," said Monica. "You shouldn't speak to your father like that. When you come into this house, show a bit of respect, you hear me?"
"I hear you, mother," she said, "but he is the one that started it."
Anthony looked sadly at her. "And what about tomorrow morning?" he said. "I suppose you expect me to take you back?"
"No, I don't expect nothing from you. I have a lift in the morning," she said.

Anthony sat down again, a defeated air about him. He picked up the newspaper.
"So you just came up to bring us this? And no doubt to rub it in?"
"He had it coming to him," she said. "He'll be no great loss to the people of Ireland. He betrayed everything that Pearse and all the other Easter heroes sacrificed their lives for."
Matthew joined in. Not the wisest thing to be doing, I thought.
"Well, you know what they say. 'Those who live by the sword die by the sword'," he said. "He had it coming to him. You are right in that, Mary. He deserved it, after the number of people he was responsible for killing in Dublin and all around the country."
Not an eye looked at him in the hard silence that stood in the kitchen. Not an eye except mine. I tried willing him to be quiet but he seemed to be determined to put his big foot in it right up to the knee.
"Sure isn't he supposed to have sent weapons to the IRA in Donegal lately?" he continued.
Mary turned on him and the look she gave him was pure poison. I wanted to stand in between him and her to protect him, such was the bitter rage in that look.
"You can shut up, Matthew Henderson. You know nothing about it. This is our argument. We have nothing to hear from a Unionist!" she spat.
"Hush now Mary. Matthew is our guest and that is no way to be talking to him. Keep a civil tongue in your head," said Monica.
Mary gave her mother another icy stare and turned back to her father.
"Collins was a traitor to the Irish people. He should never have signed the Treaty."
"He had to sign the Treaty," replied Anthony. "The IRA was finished. Beat. It was the best he could get from the British. If he hadn't signed the deal his forces would have been totally wiped out."
"So you agree with the Border then? You agree with giving these Protestants their own wee sectarian state?" she said, sneering at Matthew.
"No, I don't agree with the Border but it is only a temporary thing. Once the Boundary Commission looks at the issue the line will be redrawn anyway. It will be moved."
"The Boundary Commission!" she mocked. "How can you agree to dividing the country like that? This is our country. It has always been

our country. You can't cut off a piece of a living, breathing nation like it was a soda scone or something!"
As she spoke she viciously pulled one of her mother's scones into two halves and held them up to her father's face. The children were looking from one to the other, the darkness of bewilderment in their eyes.
"But that is exactly what has happened," said Matthew, getting to his feet. "The Border is real and yous just have to get used to it. Anyway, it's time we weren't here. Come on, Sally Anne. We will go home."
I did not know what to do. This was supposed to be a party for my birthday. I had an inkling that Mrs Kearney had baked some sort of cake. I could not be leaving now. It would insult her.
"Not just yet," I whispered to Matthew as he made for the door.
Monica came to the rescue. She followed him and spoke in a soft tone to him.
"Stay another half hour," she said. "We haven't had any of the cake yet. I made it specially for Sally Anne. And we'll have no more chat about politics tonight. Sit yourself down again, Matthew."
He was persuaded and joined us at the table again. Anthony was still reading the detail of the killing, saying nothing, apart from making little groans of sadness and despair. In fact there was very little said at all after that. To her credit, Mary dropped the subject and just sat by herself, drying out her clothes at the warmth of the hearth. The children's chatter soon filled up the silence as they stuffed handfuls of raisin cake into their mouths.
I had not eaten as well in years, maybe never I think. But it still was not an enjoyable atmosphere. Whatever bitterness there was in Mary's relationship with her folks, it seemed to seep into the very air of the kitchen and I was almost glad when it came time to leave.
The children were put to bed around ten o'clock. I was thanking Monica for what she had done to make my birthday a bit special. Behind me at the door I could hear Matthew and Joe disagreeing about something.
"No honestly Joe, there is no need. There is light enough in the sky still. Sure I know my way back up that lane with my eyes shut," Matthew was saying.
"Not at all. It's no bother. I have this lamp lit now anyway," insisted Joe.
I turned to see Joe with a Tilley lamp in his hand, its light flaring up and down in time with the waves of hissing sounds it was making.

Matthew stood at the door, the bulk of his body more or less blocking Joe's way.
"What's wrong?" I asked innocently.
"Nothing," said Joe.
"Joe lit this lamp to show us the way home," said Matthew, "but I'm telling him there is no need. We can manage."
"Sure just lend us the lamp, Joe. I'll bring it back down tomorrow. There is no cause for you to be coming out tonight into that rain," I said.
"We might need the lamp in the night if anything happened the pigs," said Joe. "Look, come on. It's no bother."
Matthew looked frustrated by Joe's stubborn insistence and I wondered about this. Joe had obviously annoyed him somehow. For the life of me I could not see why or what it was that was going on here between the two of them.
"Right," I said. "Come on then Joe. Show us the way home."
Matthew gave up and moved out through the porch to the yard. I turned back into the kitchen to say 'Goodnight' to the parents and, as I did, I caught the strangest little look flitting between father and mother. A sort of knowing smile and a raising of Anthony's eyes which said something like, "These young ones!"
There was little conversation on the way home. Joe led the way, Matthew and I a bit behind him. At one point Joe spoke over his shoulder to us.
"That is shocking news about Michael Collins," he said. "What on earth is going to happen next in this country?"
"You can never tell that," said Matthew, his tone dry and wary.
The grass was soaking wet and the surface of the rodden had turned to slippery *glar*. A couple of times I caught Matthew's arm to stop myself falling when I slipped; the second time I felt his big strong arm around me, his hand low on my hip, pulling me up tightly, close against his side. I gave a small gasp, partly of surprise and partly because he had squeezed the breath out of me for an instant. I wanted him to let go of me immediately....and yet, I suppose, a small bit of me did not mind his touch, but why could he not be more gentle; why this rough grab at me like I as one of his ewes? Either way it did not matter because my gasp was heard by Joe who spun around at once and just about caught the tail end of Matthew setting me back on my feet again. The split-second

look in Joe's eyes in the lamp-light reminded me of the look in the eyes of the cows, except for the added sadness I saw there.
"She slipped on the clabber," Matthew said, almost as an apology.
"Aye," said Joe, turning back to lead again.
"You are very bold," I whispered looking up at him, the glow from the Tilley lamp glistening in the mizzle of rain sticking to the thin whiskers by his ear. His mouth twisted up at the side into the half-smile of a tease. He bent down to me, his lips touching my ear.
"Would you rather I had let you fall?" he breathed.
Now I understood why the twins were back at home in bed. Now I understood the stupid row about the guiding lamp. How naive I felt. This was the first time he and I had ever been away from the house in the darkness of an evening on our own. Except that we were not on our own, of-course. Joe had seen to that. I was not sure how I felt about the situation.
'"She slipped on the '*clábar*'",' I thought to myself. 'If Joe hadn't been here how would we have ended up?'
It was a very strange journey back to Henderson's that night. I was thinking about the atmosphere of the Kearney home, about this new tension between my two men; I was wondering at the awkwardness of Matthew's physical touch and, at the same time, trying to understand the awful news about the shooting of poor Michael Collins.
By the time Joe had left us right to the back door the rain was teeming down. He quickly said his 'Goodnights' in a strained little voice. Matthew did not even say 'Thanks'. Poor Joe. I felt sorry for him, watching the hunch of his back as he sloped off up the yard in the centre of a fuzzy circle of lamp-light, the raindrops bouncing off him like sparks from a fire. I wanted to hug him, bring him some comfort, but I could not. Instead I just shouted from the shelter of the back door, something like, "I will maybe see you tomorrow," and I waited until the aura of light faded as he disappeared around the corner of the barn.
In the kitchen Matthew had already pulled off his damp *geansaí* and hung it on the rail by the hearth. He was working down the buttons on his shirt as I came in, the belt of his trousers already hanging open.
"Take off your wet things and put them here to dry for tomorrow," he said, bending his long back to unlace his brogues, his eyes down to his task. His words had a tension in them, somewhere just below the normal tone of voice he was trying his best to maintain.

"I will not," I said. "They can dry out above."
I was not going to be taking off any clothes in his presence, not with him in this kind of roused condition. I had been close enough to his maleness for one night when he picked me up like a doll down the lane. To do as he was asking now would be pushing chance too far. I made for the door.
"Sally Anne," he said, more gentleness, more sincerity in the plea of his voice.
"What?" I said on the hallway side of the door.
"Don't be taking me the wrong way," he said. "You never even said......Go on up and change your clothes and bring those wet ones down to hang beside mine till the morning. They'll not dry in the attic. There's no heat."
I stood there, hesitating but determined not to be looking back at the face of him.
"No, it's alright," I said. "They will be fine. I am tired. Goodnight."
I left him alone in the kitchen.

Chapter 16

Matthew Henderson

What to make of her

The girl had me baffled by this stage. Confused and bewildered.
To be fair to her though, and to be fair to myself, I have to admit that I had not had a great deal of experience in dealing with the female kind, despite the fact that I had been reared in a family with three sisters. That had not helped at all.
The twins were still wains, despite Jane's protests to the contrary. You cannot take account of them in the argument. Emily? Emily was my older sister and that was a different kind of relationship. I say 'relationship' but in all honesty there had never been much closeness between the two of us. Emily had always had a wee strangeness about her. She wouldn't have been what you might call a 'normal' girl. As they say around here, 'She was as odd as two left feet'! There was a distance in her make-up. I am not blaming her; it was something that she could not help; it was just the way she had been put together. The thing about Emily was that, for the life of me, I could not have imagined any fellow ever being attracted to her. I suppose she had her own form of prettiness about her but it was more to do with a lack of....probably of womanly charm. If she smiled a bit more it maybe would have helped but that was just not in her to do. So, you see what I mean? There was very little in my own family to be giving me any notion of a plan for handling this whole business of my feelings for a girl.
Joe's sister Mary? A nice enough girl, I always thought, when we were growing up together. She was a couple of years older than me of-course. I can remember things that happened when she was maybe thirteen or fourteen and changing from her childhood. That was when I first noticed the shape of what a young woman could look like.... the breasts and all. I had never been aware of this with Emily. I remember Mary chasing me in a cornfield once. It must have been some sort of game we were playing during the harvest. I would have been maybe ten or eleven. She was quicker than me and she tripped me up from behind, sending me headfirst into a stook of corn which was knocked

over, much to my father's annoyance. That didn't stop Mary from landing on top of me, sitting astride me, her hair falling on either side of her grinning face as she pinned me down by the two wrists.
"You can't do anything now," she had said.
"I can so."
"What can you do now?"
"I can fart!"
"For that," she said, "I am going to kiss you, Matthew Henderson," and, before I had a chance to defend myself, she did, her wet lips all over my mouth like a slug. I was disgusted, so much so that I nearly cried. When my father cuffed my ears and told me to fix up the stook again and to stop acting the eejit I think I probably did cry.
Ah well, how times had changed. Mary had turned into a hard case, with her 'volunteer' man. It was such a shame. She had been a nice girl. Not for me, of-course; not in that way. She kicked with the other foot after all.
I was fifteen when my father met his fate at the Somme. The grief in our house sort of pruned the notion of girls out of my head at a time when they were just beginning to bud and grow there. After that there was a good long time when I wouldn't be going out anywhere, apart from the market, or attending church in Castlederg. I saw nobody, well...very few anyhow.
The one girl who was a great comfort to me at that time was my cousin Victoria, albeit that I only saw her very occasionally. She was my mother's sister's daughter. Aunt Evelyn had left home in Drumquin to study in Belfast, years ago. She met a man there and married him. Victoria was her only child. I used to love to hear of her coming to spend a few weeks here on the farm with us, during her summer holidays. She would have been a year younger than me and the nicest natured girl you could ever hope to meet. Innocent as the day is long, I always thought, though maybe a bit spoiled. She had a way of always getting what she wanted. After my father's death, she and her mother would make a real effort to be down to see us every few weeks, taking the train all the way from Belfast to Omagh and then to Victoria Bridge, the tram to Castlederg Station where we would be waiting with the pony and trap to bring them up home to Lismore.
Those were great days; I have the best of memories of them. Many of these memories have to do with Victoria's innocent questions about all sorts of farming matters which we, as sons and daughters of the soil,

would just have taken for-granted. Being a city girl, she had so much to learn and Joe and I loved playing on her naivety and 'taking the mickey' out of her when we could. I can't recall all the examples but one which was frequently raised in our kitchen for years afterwards was an occasion involving one of Kearney's heifers. Joe and Victoria and I were sitting on the grassy slope of the fort, looking over into the field across the 'march ditch' which separated the two farms. I would say she was about fourteen or fifteen at the time. The Kearney cattle were a bit disturbed, as happens when one of the heifers is in heat. This animal was being driven mad by it and was jumping on the backs of any of the other cattle that would stand still long enough and, in turn, being jumped upon by a succession of them. Fortunately our bull was in the shed at the time, eagerly awaiting this heifer's arrival no doubt. Joe and I were watching all this from behind our hidden smiles at Victoria's comments. She did not have a notion what was going on and we were not the boys to be explaining it to her. So we giggled secretly into our sleeves. But, me being me, I couldn't resist the temptation to embarrass her later on.

We were sitting around the kitchen table for the evening feed. Both her father and mother were present, as I recall, so it must have been around the Twelfth holidays. When I saw my chance I brought up the subject of the cattle activities across the ditch.

"Tell the twins what you were watching in the field with me and Joe," I said to her.

"Oh yes," she said with typical enthusiasm, "I forgot about that, Matthew. All these cows and bulls were jumping on each other's backs. I had no idea that animals liked to play piggy-back. They looked like they were really enjoying it."

There was a strange little silence of awkwardness. Her parents glanced at each other and at my mother. They glared at me. Her father gave a wee shake of his head. Nobody spoke.

"What?" asked Victoria, looking from one to the other.

Then our Jane decided to show off her six-year-old knowledge of such matters.

"It was likely a heifer a-bullin'," she said between bites, with all the calmness of a country girl.

"We will talk about it later," said Aunt Evelyn firmly. "Matthew, have you nothing better to be doing than watching cattle being cattle?"

All the fool-nonsense aside, I would probably have to admit that Victoria was the first girl I ever had feelings for, in a romantic-love sort of way. She was my first cousin of-course, so it was a safe kind of adoration that I had for her. It was never going to go anywhere. But she was the first girl who ever made me feel special, who made me think that we had a close kind of bond. I would think of her often at night, lying listening to a storm roaring in the beech trees outside and a wind that would have cleaned corn, coming whistling in through the gaps in the window-sashes. Those were the nights I seemed to miss my father the most, whether it was the emotional hurt of losing him or the fear of my responsibility for the farm during such weather I can't tell; what I do know is that I would hug my pillow and imagine it was Victoria. She was the comforter of my imagination.

Now, according to her last letter, she was walking out with an Englishman that she met in Belfast, another civil servant of some kind. So I had mixed feelings about her promised visit here in September. She would generally always come for the harvest ceili.

'Fair enough. I will have to get used to her affections being shifted over to this Englishman but it won't be easy to give up my nostalgia,' I was thinking.

Which brings me to the next young lady who had been exercising my curiosity this past twelve months. Another one from good oul England; we can't seem to be doing without them! Agh, that is hardly fair; Alice Porter could not help being in Castlederg at that time, her father's work being the reason. But surely she could have helped the very obvious way that she flirted with me every chance she got.

She was probably fifteen when she arrived in our church last year. Five years younger than me, in terms of how long we have both lived, but maybe a few years older if you were to go by the air of experience and self-confidence she gave off right from the start. I had noticed her more or less straight away; you couldn't help it; everybody noticed Alice Porter. I swear that there wasn't a head that didn't turn in her direction when she walked up the aisle that first morning. She was only in the place three or four weeks when she landed up in the choir. Perfect hat, perfect clothes, picture-perfect face looking down through the congregation....it was almost as if she was advertising. And, for the moment anyhow, I was the chosen client. She seemed to have set her perfect hat at me, certainly more than I had set any cap of mine at her.

If I sound reluctant about Alice there was only one real reason, particularly in recent times. It was not that she wasn't pretty. She had everything going for her in that department and I mean everything. For a sixteen-year-old she had the whole works. If I am being honest....of-course I enjoyed her attentions. She had a way of making herself hard to resist; that warm smile that you felt was just for you; her white hand, like a dove, so delicately lighting on your arm until, that is, you wanted to move on. At that point it became the claw of a hawk. She used all her attributes to their best advantage and I was not one to be complaining about that. On top of all that, she seemed to be intelligent and was, from what I had heard, a bit of a star in her school in Strabane. I had nothing against that either; education is easy carried and our Emily was the proof of its value.

My reluctance had nothing to do with Alice herself. I still found her as interesting as I did when she first came into my life. It was just that now things had changed; they had changed since Sally Anne Sweeney arrived in Lismore.

My maid had me increasingly bewitched. Bewitched and bewildered, especially after the way that the night of her birthday had ended. I could not begin to understand why those events had unfolded as they had. Nor could I work out why it had all annoyed me so much. Was it a case of me mis-reading her, of me presuming too much? Was this where my inexperience of women was putting me at a disadvantage, unbeknownst to myself?

I tried to think over the past couple of months, just to reassure myself that I had not been imagining Sally Anne's response to me. All that conversation we had had. The warmth of our chats, the honesty between us....surely I had not imagined that? Surely I had not misjudged it all? She had seemed keen to get to know me. She seemed to sense that this relationship should not be simply your normal 'hired hand to farmer' relationship. Of that I was quite convinced. Had I imagined too much? Had I read too much into the banter we always seemed to be drawn into? To me it was a much deeper thing than mere fun or simple flirting. Perhaps to her that was all it was. Perhaps she was just a natural tease, an unconscious flirt, the kind of girl who cannot help herself engaging with fellows in that way, without necessarily realising the kind of effect she is having on them.

And yet, when I retold the stories of all our word battles to myself, I could not convince myself that this cutty did not have some feelings for me. I was convinced that she was as attracted to me as I was to her. Which was quite a lot, to understate the case.

If that was true, what had happened that night to make her act so coldly?

It ran through my head that maybe she was a staunch supporter of Michael Collins and that the shock news of his death had produced this difference in her attitude to me as a Protestant. Then again, I had never had any chat with her which would have led to the suspicion that she was a big supporter of the nationalist cause. She never seemed to be too bothered about such matters. Had Mary Kearney's attitudes triggered something deep inside her? No, I could not really accept this.

I hadn't made much of her birthday; I hadn't given her any present, hadn't said much apart from a brief comment at the table in the morning. My plan was to make her night special but that had all back-fired. Maybe she resented this underplaying of her special day, especially so far away from her mother and father? Maybe she expected me to give her something, flowers or something? That could be it.

Or was it Joe? She hadn't seemed to mind him coming back with us to show us the way. She had even welcomed him coming, I believe. She had stayed in the yard to wish him 'Goodnight', after I had come on into the house. Yes, that might be it. It was the Kearneys, after all, who had planned the wee party for her, not the Hendersons as she might have expected. Joe had always had a fancy for her, right from the start; I knew that. Maybe now she was returning his affections, him being Catholic and an Irish speaker and all that. That was why he had insisted on bringing that stupid lamp and coming with us. Joe!

What was it she had said on the lane, after I picked her up to steady her? She told me that I was 'bold'. That was it. Bold, was I? I was only being decent. Yes, I know, it was a fairly intimate way that I lifted her, probably surprising the life out of her, but it shouldn't have shocked her....not after how frank her conversations with me have been these past few weeks. She had felt so good in my arms; she actually felt a lot more substantial than I had imagined. The Henderson feeding was beginning to fill her out a bit where it mattered, I thought. Why was she annoyed by it though? I had so looked forward to bringing her home on my own, protecting her from the rain, putting my arm around her to help her through the mud, holding her hand....all in a completely natural way. But she wasn't seeing it that way for some reason. I

thought she would have. There would have been no threat in it. All I wanted to do was care for her, be her protector.
Then in the kitchen she totally mis-read me again when I suggested that she take off her things and hang them up to dry, as I was doing. That was the most natural thing in the world but she misconstrued it. Going off to her bedroom as if I had turned into the devil incarnate. Would not even look at me! I don't think I deserved that. I certainly hadn't done or said anything to merit that, so far as I could work out.
So what was I to do about it all now? What did I feel about her?
My feelings had not changed but I was disappointed in her. Girls? I just did not understand them sometimes. I would have loved to talk to her about it, to try to see what she was feeling, try to resolve the thing and apologise if I needed to. But I could not very well approach the subject, especially if she had been concealing feelings for Joe from me while still carrying on with me and leading me up the garden path. I could not raise the subject with her.
Instead I made the decision to act coldly with her for a while, just to see how she responded. That was my intended tactic anyhow. Say nothing. If she was not bothered by my coldness then I would know that I had been wrong all along. I would have my fears confirmed that Joe was the fellow she had a fancy for and that would be that. I would have to deal with that if it was true. If she had any feelings for me, this coldness would annoy her and I would notice her annoyance and we could talk.
I needed space to think anyhow. What on earth was I doing with this girl? I could not pretend to myself that I had not fallen for her....and I mean fallen… hook, line and sinker. She was the most fascinating girl I had ever come across, out of the half-dozen or so who had crossed my path. Yes I know, it was a limited experience that I had had; I have admitted that. Nevertheless there was something very special about Sally Anne. One dimply smile, one flicker of those eyelashes or a toss of her hair, one long look from those laughing eyes of hers.....
What on earth would I do when the six months was up and she would leave? Maybe she would agree to staying on over the winter. Probably not though, given her devotion to her mother and father. She would leave, of-course she would. I hated even to think about it. Well, I was determined to enjoy her company in the meantime and leave those decisions up ahead to be worked on later, when the time came.

I started to wonder about the life she would be returning to in Donegal. What sort of people did she come from? What was her mother like, this mysterious woman who could play music but could not talk, apparently? What about Sally Anne herself when she was around her home community? Was she popular with the fellows? Did she have a young man waiting for her maybe? I realised that this was a possibility I had blocked out of my mind and had never made any attempt to find out about her previous love life. Maybe I was just a substitute in the meantime, a 'fill-in' to keep her flirting skills honed for later when she went back to her own people, her own fellow. Perhaps she had had manys a fellow going about with her?
The more I thought about it, the more convinced I became that I was right. This girl could buy and sell me in the whole area of courtship and that was all down to her experience. She was a practiced hand at capturing the attentions of whatever young fellow she happened to be angling for at the time, getting him to take the bait, playing with his emotions when he was on the hook and then likely dumping him back in the river when the thing began to get too serious. She had probably left a string of broken hearts behind her, with all that experience of such affairs. That is where she had the advantage over me, with my limited knowledge and practice.
I decided that I would love to find out about this; I would do my own investigations, find out what sort of girl she was when she was back in that Rosses place. The problem was that she herself was the only source of information that I had. I couldn't ask anybody else; I didn't know anybody who knew her back there. I couldn't think of any way of establishing her character, short of going all the way over there and....and what? Even if I did go, I couldn't very well ride up to her house and ask her father for a testimonial. That was out of the question. There was only one thing to do.
Ask her myself!
Not in a brash, obvious sort of way, of-course not. I would have to be subtle; get her talking about herself, her background, her interests, her friends, her young men and so on. Act like some sort of a poultice and see if I could, without her noticing, draw from her any clues about what kind of girl she was around home. I thought I would be able to manage that; I had always been good at picking up the signs from people's unspoken clues in the past. It wouldn't take too much

discretion to be able to work out if I was just the latest in a long line of 'flies' to be tangled up in her web, her latest conquest.

So now I had two schemes to be working on. The first was to be deliberately cold to her; freeze her out and see how she reacts. The second was to get close enough to her to be able to tease from her, in as delicate and devious a way as I could manage, what sort of experience she had had in the past with young men.

I was pleased with myself.

'Yes, these plans should work well,' I thought, without really wondering how I was going to be able to manage the two opposite courses at the same time.

Chapter 17

Sally Anne Sweeney

What game is he playing?

If there was one thing I could not abide in a fellow it was this contrariness. I hated it when you never knew where you were with them, when one day you might as well be working with a turnip-snedder, all hard metal and business-like and the next day all sweet talk and flattery. One day, the dull clunking of the machine; the next, him piping away like the sweet song of a thrush.

I would be at the boiler, boiling up spuds for feeding the pigs. He would be in and out past me without a word or a look, as if I was not there. We would be milking the cows together as usual but there would be barely a word, other than what needed to be said. "Do this" or "Do that". There were days around then when he would not even answer me if I asked him a question at the kitchen table. I would look at him, long and hard, almost begging him to look me back in the eye; he would just continue to glare into his dinner.

He was so changed toward me.

Even the twins noticed it. Jane was a sharp child for the age of her. Millie too, and she was more blunt when it came to asking awkward questions.

I was trying to help her with her reading of an evening.

"Sawey Anne," she whispered, "is you and our Ma'hew fawen out?"

"What makes you say that?"

"'Cause he never smiles no more at you."

A smart girl, for all her simple-mindedness.

I wanted to understand him. I wanted to know if I had annoyed him or offended him. I wanted to know if he wasn't satisfied with my work. I wanted him to talk to me again. I wanted things to be as they had been before....before what? That I did not know. I wanted to shake him and say, "What the devil is wrong with you? What are you huffing about? Whatever is wrong with you, would you get over it and be normal again."

I remembered back to that night a week or two ago when he had grabbed me so roughly on the way over the back lane. I know that I had reacted badly to him then, especially afterwards in the kitchen. I can still feel the way my heart was racing in me that night, how it seemed to be fluttering and running away with itself, leaving me with a light head.

What was I meant to have done? This man was my boss. He was taking advantage of me, holding me like that, his hands being so intimate with my body as if he had no sense of what was right, no control of his urges, no patience to know how a girl likes to be treated. If he had been slow and gentle it might have been different. But the rush of him! The awkward way he held me...and the embarrassment of his male strength against me; I was too shocked to be thinking of how to respond as I might have wanted to.

Was that how he behaved when he was with that town girl with the big chest on her? Maybe she had been leading him on and behaving badly with him and he was thinking that that was the normal way girls want you to be with them. The Matthew I thought I knew, the fellow that I thought I liked and respected had been corrupted by someone else. Where did that leave me for the next three months of working and living with him?

I started to thank my guardian angel that, although he was sleeping in his bedroom just down the stairs from mine, he had never been so rash that he had come anywhere near me at night... *Buíochas le Dia!*

My father's words were in my ears around that time.

"Watch out for fellows like that. They are after the one thing only."

And yet there had been so much about Matthew that I found very...very attractive, if I am honest. I think I can judge a person fairly well and I was sure in my bones that he was not the type of man who would take advantage of me. He had a deep down decency in him, of that I was certain. He just seemed to be very abrupt, very jumpy. For a fellow who came across as being so sure of himself, running his own farm and being the head of his family at such a young age, he had this side to him that I could not figure out. That and the wavering of him, the changing of his moods. It was as if he had made up his mind that night that he and I were going to be a courting couple; it was going to happen that night on the way home and he would not be put off from his plan, not by Joe's presence with the lamp nor by my resistance to him.

Was he now trying to make me suffer for my modesty? Is that what this coldness was about?

If so, that was not very fair of him.

As it happened, it took another surprise visit from Tam Glenn to bring things back around to normal.
I had been in the habit of going out to the garden at the front of the house at times when I had a spare half hour, generally after the yard chores were finished and before I went inside to get the meal ready. I did not really want Matthew to know about this so I would wait until he was not around, usually when he was delivering milk to the creamery. Then I would see what I could do to try to improve the look of it. I had made a bit of a hole in it too. The bushes were tidier and the weeds more or less discouraged, although no-one had actually noticed or mentioned it. Anyhow, the very day that I was finally trimming the top of the hedge by the lane, didn't Matthew arrive back long before I had expected him. He had told me earlier that he was going to see the bank manager for a loan; I had no notion what that was all about; I could not imagine why he wanted a loan. Now I found myself staring into his face across the newly-cut privet hedge and him staring back over at me with a strange expression in his eyes.
"What on earth are you doing?" he asked.
"Trimming this hedge," I said. "Is that alright?"
"Aye, of-course it's alright," he said, looking over into the garden with the advantage of his height. "You have made a brave redd up in there too, by the looks of it."
"I hope it is alright," I said, "I have the back of it broken but I need a saw or something to shift that branch that is half broken down. I am not able for it."
"I'll be back in a minute," he said, and he was, bow-saw in hand.
The branch was quickly dealt with and he cut it into lengths for the fire. We stood surveying my handiwork and, although not much was being said, I had the feeling of a bit of a thaw in how he was towards me.
"We don't be worrying about gardens back at home," I said to try to make conversation. "Maybe it's because the soil is not good enough for gardens. It is mostly just peat bog. Rushes and rocks. Maybe we are just lazy."
He turned over a spadeful of lovely dark mouldy soil, light and airy of itself.
"Well, this soil is good enough; we can't use that as an excuse. I suppose we have just got out of the habit of keeping the garden in the

last few years. It used to be my mother's pride and joy but then....all that has changed now."
"I am sorry," I said.
"Naw, don't be saying that. There's nothing we can do to change what has happened in the past," he said. "But, fair play to you; you have done a good job of making it a bit more Protestant looking."
At that he laughed...for the first time in several days, I thought. I smiled in a watery sort of a way, for I was not sure what was funny. I was not sure either that I understood what he meant.
"What?" I asked. "I don't understand. Protestant looking?"
"Aye," he said. "It's just what we say around here. When something is all neat and tidy and organised in its proper way people say it's more Protestant looking."
"That is a bit of an insult to me," I said. "I am the Catholic and I am the one tidying up the Protestant garden for the first time in years. I think I am making it a bit more Catholic looking."
"Not at all," he said, still laughing. "Anyway, it's only an expression. It's a joke, sort of. Don't be taking any offence at it."
I saw my opportunity. He was in a good mood and I wanted to know the answer to the question that had been bothering me for days. The question of his silence.
"And what do you take offence at?" I said.
"What? Me? Take offence? I don't take offence," he said, reddening slightly.
I was about to continue with these questions I had been storing up to ask him when we were interrupted by a croaking voice from the lane behind us.
"Hello wains!"
We turned to see Tinker Tam grinning over the hedge at us through his piebald teeth. He had come up the lane so silently that neither Matthew nor I had seen or heard him approach. How long he had been listening I could not guess. He looked as untidy as ever; his hair frizzed out from his head like he had been hit by lightning and his eyes shining with their usual mischief.
"Adam and Eve in the garden of Eden," he said in that teasing way of his.
"Aye, but you know how the story goes. We were doing alright until some old serpent arrived!"
I was proud of that one.

Tam roared with laughter.
"Lord above, Matt, but you have fairly sharpened up that tongue on her," he said.
"Not me, Tam. I can't claim the credit for that. She does that all by herself. What brings you back to this neck of the woods?"
"Why? Am I not welcome?"
"Of-course you are. Whenever was Tam Glenn not welcome in this house?"
"Are you staying long?" I asked.
"Naw this time," said Tam. "I am passing through. I'll be back for the Harvest Dance in a week or two though. I was going south through Newtownstewart and, with being so near han', I thought I should drap in and see you two. Just to make sure Matt isn't working you o'er hard and giving you plenty of time to be playing that fiddle."
I felt a bit embarrassed by this comment, considering how things were between Matthew and me at that particular time. I had the feeling that he was too, for he turned away from Tam as if to return to work.
"Go on in and she'll get you a bite to eat," Matthew said. "Go on, Sally Anne; I'll finish what you started here."
We were sipping tea together in the kitchen, just Tam and me.
"So everything is going rightly?"
"It is."
"You are not tired after a day's work?"
"Not at all."
"And Matthew is treating you well?"
"He is."
"And you are still getting on well enough with him?"
"Why would I not be?"
"But...I mean..."
"What do you mean?"
"Yous are still good friends?"
"Of-course we are...I am his servant girl. What else would I be?"
"Aye, that's what I was wondering too," he said.
I was completely puzzled by this line of questions, so much so that I could think of nothing more to say to him. I just stood and looked out the window to the yard. Matthew was wandering about out there, putting the garden tools away. For a minute Tam said nothing. Then out of the blue and just before Matthew came in by the back door he spoke.

"He's wild fond of you, you know that, don't you?"
In some ways it was a blessing that Matthew arrived in the kitchen at that minute because I do not know what I would have said to Tam. In another way it was a disaster because, as usual for me, my face flamed with confusion. I just dived for the door and ran upstairs to the bathroom where I poured water from the bucket, threw it over me and waited for my head to clear.
Later that evening we played a few tunes together in the parlour. Matthew and the girls sat listening and smiling. Even Mrs Henderson was more livened up than I had seen in a good long time.
"I heard a lovely new song when I was coming through your village, Eliza," Tam said. "A man by the name of Felix Kearney put it together. Wait to we see; I could maybe mind wan verse o' it."
And he did, singing in a high warble of a voice but lovely and true to pitch, I thought.

'God bless the hills of Donegal, I've heard their praises sung
In days long gone beyond recall when I was very young
Then I would pray to see a day before life's course is run
When I could sing the praises of the hills above Drumquin'.

Mrs Henderson loved it. "Aye, good oul Drumquin," she said and I believe I saw a tear in her eye.
Tam slept in front of the hearth again that night.
I was dreading another poem in the morning but thankfully he seemed to have been lacking inspiration for there was no sign of one, just a strange wee smile before he took his leave after breakfast.
I let all this soup of muddled thoughts simmer around inside me for the rest of the morning. I tried to play it very cool with Matthew at breakfast. I did not engage his eyes once, curious and all as I was to see if I could read anything there, although in one sidelong glance from the sink I was aware that he was looking at my back. His eyes bounced away as I turned around into the middle of the floor again.
'How long are we going to be like this?' I thought.
"Do you want more tea?" I asked him.
"No, I'm grand," he said, draining the last dregs from his tin mug.
'Matthew,' I said in my mind, 'why are you being like this with me? There is so much I want to talk to you about. Before too long I will be leaving here and going home.'

"Will you come with me to the field behind the fort today?" he said. "We need to make a start on those potato drills along the head rig. I'll dig and you gather."
"It is all the one to me," I said from the sink.
"After we do the cows."
"Aye, after that," I said.
"Mother," he said, "Did you see the good job Sally Anne has made of the front garden? It's starting to look more like itself."
Mrs Henderson looked over at us from her armchair by the hearth.
"Is that so?" she said with a feigned interest.
"You'll have to take a walk out and see it," said Matthew.
"I will that," she said, turning her expressionless face back to the fire.
I looked at Matthew and saw the flicker of regret in his eyes. What it is to be slowly losing your mother. I knew all about it. On some deep instinct in the heart of me I moved towards him and so nearly put my hand on his shoulder. What would he have made of me if I had? What would he have thought of me if he had been able to read my mind that morning? How did I keep myself under control and not give away anything of that mix of emotions churning around under the surface?
We got through the milking without any need for chat.
'How will we fare at the potatoes all day?' I was wondering.
The day was rising by the time we arrived out in the field behind the fort, lovely and sunny now but with a light breeze in it. We worked together for half an hour, a stone wall of quietness between us. I just could not get the words to say anything about anything. I do not know what he was thinking but he seemed very far away. How long could I let this go on? Would we be still as distant from any real, honest conversation when it came time for me to leave here in eight or nine weeks? I could not bear the thought of that. Was it only in me, this notion, or was it right what Tam had said about Matthew being very fond of me? What if we both went through life never having owned up to what we were feeling about each other? After a good while of putting it off I found the courage to speak. I held a handful of the fine, dry mould up to my nose and sniffed at it.
"It has a great smell to it, this," I said.
The crows in the trees above the fort were making so much noise with their rude crawing that I had to speak again in a louder voice for him to hear me.

"The soil has a lovely smell," I repeated, not raising my head to look at him.
"It has, aye," he mumbled down the length of his spade. He continued working on the drill, turning the soil over and scattering it so I could gather the potatoes. I watched the tightness of his legs and the swing of his lower body as he delved into the drills but I could not get my eyes to lift above his waist.
"They are fine praties," I continued.
"That they are."
'Great!' I congratulated myself. 'We are talking.'
"Quare spuds. The best of pinks," said Matthew.
"Pinks?" I said. "Is that the name on them?"
I knew full well what they were called.
"Aye; pinks," he said. "That's the breed of them, 'Kerr's Pinks'. It's just what they are called....on account of the pinky colour of the skin I suppose."
He rubbed the dirt off a fist-sized potato and held it up for me to see. The earthy smell of it was sweetly wholesome to my nose, the kind of scent that immediately brought back good memories of home. I took the potato from his hand and studied it.
"Galánta," I said.
'Oh dear,' I thought. 'That was a mistake. He is going to tell me off for going into the Gaelic again.'
But I was wrong, wonderfully wrong.
"What does that mean?" he said. "*Galánta*?"
"It means 'lovely'", I answered.
"*Galánta,"* he said again. "That's a nice sounding word...to be Irish, like."
The tease was back in him.
"Where would us Irish folk be without our spuds?" I said.
"Aye, you're right there."
Silence again, for a good five minutes. Silence apart from those rasping crows in the trees behind us and the chirping of the sparrows in the hedgerows; silence apart from the rhythmic scrape of his spade as he thrust it into the earth and the dragging of my creel over the soil; silence apart from the pleading thoughts clamouring around in my mind without my permission.

'Matthew, please help me to understand what is happening here; are you having the same kind of thoughts that I am having? Will these feelings of ours ever find a way of breaking out into the open?'
I kept quiet of-course.
"The leaves have a wee turn of autumn in them already," he said, leaning on his spade as I scrabbled around on the ground lifting the 'pinks' into the creel.
I was glad of the chance to stand up and I followed his gaze to the fort in the next field.
"Just a bit," I said.
Out of the blue he said, "Come with me. Leave this for a bit. Have you ever been up in the fort?"
"What?" I said.
"Come on! Have you ever been up in the fort?"
"I have. That day of the bands. I had Joe at me," I said.
He gave me a strange stare.
"Hmm! You had Joe at you, had you?" he grunted, stuck his spade into the earth with an angry lunge and took off ahead of me.
I followed him. Across the head-rig of the potato field, along the hedge and through a wooden gate into the front field. A couple of his cows paused in their grazing, lifting their heads to watch as I tried to keep up; the long legs of him over the field had me feeling like a child again, following my father across Ranahuel bog.
A magpie rose from the grass ahead of us and flew off in its fussy way, with a dry, clacking song of protest.
'A single magpie!' was the first thought in my head. My eyes wandered around the field to see if I could find a mate to make a couple of them but it was by itself, alone.
"'One for sorrow' it has to be then," I said to myself and it put a darkness across my heart as we started to climb the steep side of the mound, through the shadows of those huge old trees, right to the summit. And steep it was alright; he might have taken my hand to help me up but he was already away ahead of me.
He stood there in the dappled light, waiting for me. I was without breath from the climb, mostly from the climb I think, but it would not be a lie to say that I was flustered by the situation as well. I leaned against a tree to get my wind back.
"What are we doing?" I said, whispering, although I do not know why I was whispering. It was just that my lips felt really dry and my tongue

heavy in my mouth. I suppose I was nervous in some way, nervous or afraid or excited, maybe a mixture of all three. The crows were creating such pandemonium rising from their nests above that Matthew did not hear a word I said.

"What are we doing up here?" I shouted at him as he stared above into the waving branches and the scattering birds.

"Just taking a break," he said. "There's always time for a wee rest surely?"

That answer did not really satisfy me but I wandered around among the trees on the flat surface of the mound and it was not hard to imagine the stares of him following my movement. I turned round on him quickly and saw his eyes rise to my face.

"What was this place?" I asked, simply for something to say.

"It's a fairy-fort," he said. "You of all people should know that. Do you not have them around home?"

"Not to my knowing," I said. "Not in the west anyway."

"There's a lock of them around Tyrone," he said. "People used to think that the fairies lived in them; some still do. There's a pile of oul stories about them. When I was at school the Master told us they were called 'raths'. They've been here for centuries."

"What were they for?"

"That I don't remember," he said. "I suppose people lived on them. That way they could be on the look-out for enemies or people coming to steal their cattle."

"Oh right," I said.

'Enough about history,' I thought to myself. 'What about the future, not to mention the present? What is he really bringing me up here for?'

"You say Joe had you up here?" he said, coming towards me. The breeze was freshening through the trees, blowing his fair hair back from his face and teasing with my skirt. Too late I held it down at the sides as it ballooned out and rose up over my knees and thighs. I only just managed to save myself severe embarrassment. His eyes followed my hands with a strange intensity.

"Aye. The day of the fire. We came up here to see if we could work out where the noise was coming from. Then we saw the smoke at Bond's."

"Ah, right,' he said. "I wondered."

"You wondered what?"

"Nothing," he said.

Another silence. He bent down and plucked a blade of grass, stretched it between his thumbs and blew a long, high-pitched screech into the air. I did not like the feeling of it in my ears, so I put my hands over them for a second. He caught one of my arms in his rough, dirty hand and pulled it down none too gently.

"What are you doing?" I said.

"The two of you; you and him. You said he was 'at you'. What do you mean by that... 'at you'?"

"'At me'. I meant 'with me'. It is the same word in Irish. That is all."

He let my arm go and looked away from my eyes.

"What did you think I meant?" I said.

He stared up at the waving branches. Thin beams of autumn light were dancing down on us, playing irregular patterns on the tawny skin of his face. We were talking; after all this time of silence we were talking...great.

"You and Joe," he said. "I know Joe likes you. He likes you a lot."

"So?"

"So, what about you? Do you like him?"

Ah, so that was what had been bothering him. I could not believe it. The silly fellow. What on earth had given him that idea? I decided, on a whim, to make him suffer a bit for his stupidity.

"Aye, I like Joe," I said simply.

"I thought so."

Unbelievably I saw the wind going out of his sails right in front of my eyes. I watched him turn his back on me and wander away through the trees and towards the rim of the fort again.

'Oh no,' I thought. 'Why am I determined to torment him?'

I called after him, "I like Joe the same way that you like him. He is your friend and he is my friend. Nothing else, if that is what you mean."

He stopped and turned around.

"Are you sure?" he said. "Mind you it is none of my business if you and him..."

"Agh Matthew! I do not like him in that way. Joe would not be my type at all."

He thought about this for a bit. I looked closely at him. The half-smile around his eyes decayed into something else. I felt he was doubting me again.

"And what type is your type?" he said.

"I don't know," I said. I did not like this question. I could not very well say, "Tall, broad-shouldered, fair and brown and handsome, sort of not unlike yourself, Matthew," but that is what I was thinking.
"Well, have you many of your type licking roun' you back there in Donegal?"
I was a bit stunned by the tone of this. It just about knocked the words out of me. I could think of no answer to this question, nor to the meaning behind it, so I just let it sit. I turned my back on him in a manner that he could not misunderstand. Now it was my turn to think about returning to the field to our work.
"Ah come on, girl. I didn't mean it like that," he said, watching my reaction.
"What did you mean then? It is hard to take a question like that any way other than be insulted by it."
"I did not mean to insult you. That's the last thing I meant to do," he said. "I only meant to ask if you have any boyfriends back at home. How would I know the answer to that if I didn't ask you?"
"And you think that is the kind of girl I am, do you?" I said. "You have watched me and got to know me and you think that, because I get on well with you and with Joe....I am some sort of easy woman who has lots of men running after her? Can you not see how that offends me?"
He did his look-up-to-the-sky again and I set my back against the sturdy trunk of a massive tree, taking whatever support and comfort from it that I could. I could hear my heart beating in my ears, whether with annoyance at him or pleasure that we were finally talking in a serious way I am not sure.
"No," I said with a hard edge in my voice that shocked me. "If you think that it is any of your business, if it is of any comfort to your good, Protestant, moral standards....listen to me....I have no string of lovers behind me. I have no boyfriend waiting for me at home."
"Right," he said.
I may have imagined it but he seemed to breathe a sigh of relief. He came to my tree and leaned his back on it as well, sort of at right-angles to me. I looked up at him, his head back against the grey bark and his eyes closed.
"It is very little you have to be worrying about," I said.
"I am sorry," he said. "I owe you an apology. I am a clumsy eejit when it comes to this kind of thing, talking to girls I mean. Talking to you. I don't know why I said that. It is none of my business, of-course it's

not. You can have as many fellows as you want to. I had no right to be asking you stuff like that."
I said nothing. That was not exactly what I wanted to hear him saying. He was drifting away from me again. 'Do I let him go or do I try to resolve this thing once and for all?' I thought. I so wanted the thing to be clear between us but now it was me who was scared of saying something wrong.
"It is alright," I said quietly. "I understand. You were just trying to see what kind of girl I am when I am at home. Believe me, I am just the same as you see me here. Honestly. And Joe means nothing to me compared...."
"So you admit you are a bit of a flirt at home as well then?" he said with a shifty sideways glance at me.
'Oh no,' I thought. 'What a tormentor he is. Why is he deliberately twisting what I say?'
"I am not a flirt," I protested.
"Yes you are," he said. "That's what you are doing now, isn't it? Flirting with your employer. Trying to lead me astray."
"Oh Matthew," I said. I was almost in pain but I was pleased with myself that I had had the courage to call him by his first name in this conversation, given the circumstances. "Why do you have to make friendship so difficult? Why do you have to chew over everything I say? Why not just be normal with me?"
He slid his back down the tree until he was sitting among the mushrooms and leaf mould. I looked down at him, almost pleading for an end to this.
"So that is what we are then?" he said. "Friends? This is all about friendship, is it?"
"Of-course we are friends, are we not?" I said.
He reached up and took my hand, so gently this time.
This was a watershed moment; no going back now. Matthew Henderson was holding my hand! The touch was such a surprise that my instinct was to pull back as if I had been stung by a nettle, but he held on. He pulled it firmly to his face and then he did a strange thing. He brought my fingers up to his nose and sniffed them, sniffed them deeply.
"I love the smell of the potato earth on you. Here, Sit down beside me," he said, not letting go and pulling me down firmly to sit beside him. I sat, noticing a host of little ants scurrying around us.

"Let go of me for a minute," I said and I tried to pull my hand away from his.
"Why would I do that?" he said.
"These ants," I said. "Let me fix myself."
He let go of my hand. I adjusted my long skirt to cover my knees and, at the same time, to give me something to sit on. I hoped not too many ants would want to investigate inside it. We were still facing different directions. I was looking south towards the house and he was facing sort of east towards Bessy Bell.
"Aye," he said with a sort of sigh, "we are friends. So far anyhow."
"Can I ask you something? Something personal."
"Go on," he said, taking my hand again. "It couldn't be any more personal than what I have been asking you."
"Alright," I said, turning to look at his side-on profile. "It is just that lately you have not been as ...as friendly to me, not as chatty as you had been. Did I do something wrong or was I not working well enough to please you or what has been wrong with you?"
He did not answer. I watched the wince around his mouth and thought, 'I have gone too far too quickly again.'
"I am sorry if that is too bold of me. You do not have to answer it."
"No I don't. But you are right though. And I don't know the answer myself. I have had a lot on my mind. You know what I mean," he said.
"Like wondering if I was courting with Joe Kearney?"
"Aye, maybe that. And a bit more besides."
"What else?" I said. "Am I allowed to ask?"
"Sally Anne," he said after a moment of thinking, "I have something to tell you."
"Go on then," I said, a sudden dark cloud of dread coming over me. I pulled my hand away from him instinctively. 'What is this going to be about?' I was thinking.
"You see, there is this girl. I have known her for a good long time. We go back for years and we have been very close. In a couple of weeks she is coming to stay at the farm with us."
If you had pushed that sycamore tree over on top of me I could not have been dealt a bigger blow at that moment. I could say nothing. There was nothing to say.
"She is only going to be staying for a day or two and then it will be back to just the two of us," he said.

I could not believe it. The cruelty of this man. He had a girlfriend. He had led me a merry dance and all the time he had a girlfriend and she was coming to stay in the same house as me. What sort of fellow was he that he would do this to me? He must have known what he had been doing to me, playing with my feelings, prodding and pulling me as if I was just one of his animals. In fact worse than that, for he would not have treated his dog so cruelly. I felt like someone had stuck a knife into me around my ribs, such was the pain running in me. I began to struggle to get up to my feet.
"It is time to go back to work," I said.
I wondered had that little sob made it out into the open when I spoke.
Matthew grabbed my hand again, trying to pull me back down. Goodness, why was he smiling at me like that?
"Leave me alone," I said. "Why did you bring me up here in the first place?"
He let go of my hand and stood up himself.
"Why, do you not like it up here? Sure it is nice and private. Nobody can see us when we are up here among these trees," he said, and that smile he had on him seemed to have turned into a smirk, like as if he was enjoying doing this to me. The heartless man that he was.
"And is that why you brought me here?" I asked. "So you can play with my feelings and insult me and humiliate me where nobody can see you?"
By this stage I was losing all control of myself. My inside had wormed its way through to the outer skin of me. I am sure it was not a pretty sight. The big tears were stinging my eyes; my neck must have been red with annoyance; my mouth was all twisted up and my lower lip seemed to be quivering as if it had a mind of its own. My hands did not know what to be doing. I badly wanted to go to the toilet and if he had not been there I would have used the privacy of the trees to do just that, that and to discover if the strange sensation down there was due to a few nosy ants having found a way through. Instead I simply wanted to get off this fort and get back to the safety of gathering potatoes. You knew where you were with potatoes.
"Please can we go back to work now?"
"Alright, but I have just one more thing to tell you."
"No, do not say another word. You have told me enough. I never want to hear another one of your secrets," I said, surprised at the strength of what was coming out of me.

"Sally Anne, look at me," he said. "Stop and come back here and listen just for ten seconds and I promise you won't regret it."
I ignored him and ran down the slope of the mound, bouncing from tree to tree to break the speed of my descent. As I was getting near the bottom I heard him above the clamour of the swirling crows, roaring at the top of his voice.
"Listen, would you; she is my cousin, for God's sake!"
His cousin?
I was going too fast. I tried to slow down, to stop and turn around at the same time. I missed the tree that I had been aiming for next and instead my foot caught on a root that was sticking up from the ground. I fell headlong over it and a rip of pain went through my ankle as I did. I yelled, a scream of agony; the dread that I might have broken the ankle filled my head and yet, in the middle of it all, there was this grand feeling of sweet relief that the girl, whoever she was, was his cousin. She was not a rival; she was a relation.
Matthew came slithering down the slope and dropped to his knees beside me.
"Oh Lord, what have you done to yourself? Where does it hurt?" he said.
"Right here," I said, my hand on my heart.
He caught my meaning and a smile crossed his eyes for a second.
"I am so sorry. That was all my fault; I couldn't help it. I wanted to see how you would react," he said.
"Well, you saw and now you see me lying in a hopeless heap at your feet. Are you satisfied?" I groaned, holding my ankle.
"It was just me trying to play a joke on you. I'm stupid. Here, let me see that," he said taking my foot in his rough hands.
"She is your cousin," I said.
"She is. And she has a man. I'm sorry."
"Well, I am not sorry that she is your cousin, nor that she has a man. I am just sorry that you know how to torture me," I said, wincing in my pain.
"Do you think it is broken?"
"I did not hear any cracking noise, if that is what you mean. I just twisted it. I think it is probably just sprained."
When he lifted me to my feet, however, and when I tried to mark it to the ground it was suddenly a very different story. The pain shooting

through it was unbearable and the sweat stood out in beads on my forehead.
"I'll have to carry you back to the house; we may have to take you down to Doctor Leary in the town," he said.
"Don't be doing that," I said. "I can't afford it for a start. It will get better by itself. It is likely only a sprain."
"Listen, you will not be paying anything. It was my fault entirely. I shouldn't have been making fun of you like that, so I will be paying."
This while he was lifting me up as if I was a child, but with even more care.
I nestled in his arms like a baby. He carried me down the last few yards of the slope to the field. My face was close to his, inches from the dusty stubble on the side of his face. Even though he probably had not shaved for a few days the fair bristle there felt soft when I leaned my forehead against it. I could smell the breath from his mouth and the manly scent of him, his sweat mixed with the potato soil. They were all good smells to my nose and I cherished the intimacy of them. My arms were around the thick of his neck....as you do when you are being carried that way. The ankle was throbbing so sore I could hardly bear it but it was worth every jab of pain. My heart was racing away and I could do nothing about it, nor about the reddening of my cheeks. For all that, I felt that I was in some sort of heaven.
"I am sorry about this, Sally Anne," he said.
"It could be worse," I whispered into the closeness of his ear. "I could be having to walk."
He laughed at that.
"The last time I picked you up I don't think you liked it. You called me bold," he said.
"Well, you were bold that night, you would have to admit it yourself."
"No I wasn't; I was just trying to help you, after you nearly fell."
"It was not the kind of help I expected from you then."
"But you don't mind it now?"
"Times change."
"You mean you have changed? You're not scared of me anymore?"
"It is not that," I said.
"What is it then?"
"It is just this ankle," I said, "and the only reason I am letting you carry me is that it is your fault, remember?"

He looked at me, trying to judge if I was joking or what. We had reached the gate out of the field.
"Sure you can walk the rest then," he said, pretending to put me down on the gravel of the lane.
I clung on tightly to his neck.
"No, don't," I said. "You are not getting rid of me that easily."
"You see," he said. "You are enjoying this too much. Admit it!"
"I admit it," I said. "It is lovely."
"*Galánta,*" he said...slowly, with a wee grin.

Chapter 18

A Postman at Work

Driving his new mail-van towards Castlederg, Isaac Adams whistled an old psalm tune and thought family thoughts. He was completely delighted with yesterday's news that his wife was in the family way, yet again. This would be his fifth child and probably not his last. He was from a family of thirteen himself and loved it, the continuing bond between virtually all of his siblings, not to mention the ageing parents. He had every intention of maintaining the tradition himself and, from what he sensed of his wife's view on the matter, he had every reason to believe that she would be on for it as well. Martha was a fine woman and as he looked up at the flickering daylight through the passing forest branches he uttered a little prayer of thanksgiving.

"For all Thy many blessings Lord I give Thee thanks."

Life in the country as a whole may be on the edge of disaster but he had so much to be thankful for in his own modest cottage and all that it contained. His children and their mother were the joy of his life. Being a father was the greatest gift any man could have; it was a way of life that came easy to him and he could imagine no other. The laughter of his children was the birdsong of his existence. And now another one was to be joining them.

'Cub or cutty?' It did not matter a hoot to him, for either way there would now be an odd number of one or other.

He smiled to himself as he recalled his dream of the previous night. The smile became an outright belly-laugh as he went over the vivid details in his mind. Martha had been in the process of giving birth. The mid-wife was there. Her mother was there. It was all great joy, no sense of pain or panic....not to him anyhow. He watched through the door as the baby arrived, slimy and squiggly in his mother-in-law's arms. He had not time to ask what it was, however, for suddenly there was another baby there as well, miraculously and mysteriously. The child had turned into two.

Twins!

God be praised!

Except that it didn't stop there.

The two somehow turned into three in that woolly way that dreams have in their unfolding.
Three....and then four. Panic began to set in.
"Merciful God above, let that be an end to it", he heard himself praying.
But the whole thing was getting out of control and babies began to pile up as if from a sausage machine in Brown's butchers shop.
He wanted to go into the room and see Martha. She had lost the run of herself altogether.
"Will ye stap this Martha," he shouted. "Stap these baabies, for the love o' God, STAP!"
Then he felt the sharp elbow of his wife dig him firmly in the ribs.
"Waken up Isaac. You're having another of your nightmares."
He had sat up in the bed, looked around, looked at his wife's slightly fearful face and burst into a fit of laughter, the laughter of relief. And when he told her the dream she joined in, heartily.
"What 'n un'er God were we going to call them all? That was my biggest worry," he said, and their merriment became one of those uncontrollable things that had tears streaming down their early morning faces.
"Ye were more worried about running out of names for them than what way we were going to feed them?" Martha observed. "Ye must be for getting promotion to postmaster or something."
Little chance of that. A lowly postman was what he was destined to stay, he was thinking, as he slowed his van to avoid some branches strewn across the narrow mountain road. He did not have the education to be going any higher up the ladder. Very few folk from around Killeter did. The wee school in the village did its best for them but unless you were coming from money that was all the education you were going to get. The big schools of Omagh and Strabane and Enniskillen were far away and only the professional classes could afford to send their offspring to board there.
'The rest of us just have to stay low, be content with what we have and mind our place in the order of things.'
It had crossed Isaac's mind several times of late that it might be a good idea to join the 'B Specials', just on a part-time basis. The extra money would be more than useful. On top of that he would have the satisfaction that he would be doing his bit for his country, saving it from the threat of the rebels who were intent on swallowing up these

six counties into their new Free State. But whenever he raised it with Martha she was horrified that he would even think of such a thing.
"Ye hae four wains tae think o'!" she said.
Think of them he did, and so he gave in to her doubts. Better to be safe than sorry. Some of the fellows with no dependants could continue to do the job of protecting their beleaguered community. For all the fear and frustration in the local community he himself would stay a calm and contented family man.
What were all these branches doing lying on the road up ahead? This road ran through the forest that straddled the Donegal-Tyrone border for a fair distance and he travelled it often in his line of duty, but seldom had he seen big sturdy branches like this blocking his way. Maybe the odd time in the winter, but this was August and it was not as if there had been any storms of late.
He slowed to a halt and stared through the windscreen of his mail-van. Nothing for it but get out and shift this. Engine still running he opened the door, stepped out and was approaching the obstacle when a sudden fear knifed through him.
What if this was an IRA raid?
Too late he turned back to his vehicle only to see three dark-clad figures run toward him from the trees, rifles in hand, pointed in his direction. He slowed to a stop and automatically put his clasped hands up behind his head. Some instinct in him told him not to stare at the men and his eyes fell to the road as if in submission. Before they did, however, he was able to form the impression that two of his attackers were short fellows and one was tall and sturdy; all three wore cloth caps and handkerchief masks over their lower faces. So this was what the IRA looked like, he thought.
"Down on the ground!" commanded Kevin Duggan.
Isaac obeyed with a strong sense of cooperative resignation, not to mention relief. His legs seemed to have suddenly turned into jelly and lying was far preferable to standing.
"Keep your head down and your mouth shut!"
No problem with that. He even closed his eyes. He always closed his eyes when he was praying.
He sensed one of the men approach. He presumed that the hard point of pressure in the middle of his back was the muzzle of the fellow's rifle. What would it feel like, a bullet entering his spine, he wondered.
"Just lie there and you'll be alright ....for the time being."

As Isaac went through an easy mental visualisation of his children's faces, Kevin and his fellow volunteer opened the rear door of the van and studied the two large mailbags that were supposed to be heading for Castlederg and Clady post-offices. This was one of the roles of the intelligence officer in the Volunteers, the gathering of all sorts of information which could be useful to their campaign. Robbing a mail-van was among the easiest of these operations; it was seldom anything went wrong. Get the bags, tie up the driver and disappear through the trees and across the border again with no need for a shot to be fired. Later he would go through all the mail, examining every potentially interesting letter for contents of value. It was seldom he found anything but you had to keep trying. You never knew when you were going to be landed with a gem.

Kevin pulled the first bag out and gave it to Mick. As he was pulling the second bag from the van he failed to notice that it was partially open at the top. Whatever way he grabbed the bag he inadvertently spilled some of the contents onto the road.

He knelt to pick up the spill of letters and his eye fell to the address on the very top letter of the scattered pile. He read,

'Matthew Henderson
Lismore
Castlederg
Co Tyrone'

"Good God!" he said quietly. "Now there's a coincidence."

Put it back in the sack or have a quick early look at what was being written to his former employer, the man who had not thought to be employing him again this year? The man whose house he had raided back on the Twelfth of July in an exercise that so nearly came to grief. His head came up as he listened very briefly for the sound of any vehicle, motorised or horse-drawn, coming along the road. Silent but for the blackbirds and the thin whistling of the breeze in the pine leaves above.

He ripped open the envelope and took out the letter.

'Dear Matthew,' he read quickly to himself, 'I cannot wait to see you for I have the greatest piece of news you have ever heard. I am engaged. Stanley proposed to me and I accepted of-course. My parents were a bit surprised because they had asked him to wait for a year so we could get to know each other better. You should have seen their faces. Here I was coming home flashing my diamond ring and they thought Stanley

had heeded them. He is some catch, though I say so myself. He is so handsome. And he has a great job in the Civil Service. You will love him. He is all I could ever want in a man and I cannot wait to show him off to you when we arrive on Thursday week. You are picking me up at the station as I have already mentioned in my last letter, I hope. I am just presuming that it will be alright for Stanley to come and stay at yours as well. Oh Matthew, I am so excited for him to see all of you and the farm and the harvest ceili of-course.
Until then, dear cousin, take good care of yourself in these troubled times.
Your loving cous, Victoria."
Kevin folded the letter roughly and stuffed it into his trouser pocket.
'Thon dame!' he thought as he stuffed the remaining letters back in the mailbag. 'Her with the legs up to her oxters and a tongue on her like a saw! She's got herself a man, has she? Master Henderson will not be best pleased with that now, will he? I wonder what sort of a man he is? A Civil Servant? Might be worth checking him out at the harvest dance.'
"Mick," he said to his mate, "How are you at ceili dancing?"
"I'm hopeless. Why?"
"'Cause you'll be going to one next weekend."
"I can't wait."
"Right. Are you ready to go here?"
"I'm ready."
"We'll tie your man up," he said, pulling a length of rope from his jacket pocket and moving toward the prostrate figure with his motionless guard.
"Will I shoot him?" asked the guard.
Kevin looked at him as if he was crazy and shook his head.
"No, you won't shoot him. He's a postman, not a B-man, for God's sake."
"He might be a B-man though," came the response.
'What idiots I have to work with,' thought Kevin. 'Trigger-happy idiots.'
And yet he had a point, the guard. Just maybe he had a point.
"Are you in the Specials?" Kevin asked the prone postman, thinking at the same time, 'He's hardly going to tell me if he is, now is he?'
Isaac shook his head.
"I'm just a postman," he said softly.

"What's your name then?"
"Isaac Adams."
"And where are you from, Isaac Adams?"
"Out be Killeter."
"Right, we are going to tie you up and leave you here for somebody to find," said Kevin. "Put your hands behind your back."
Isaac obliged and in a short time Kevin had him securely bound. He stood to his feet. The guard maintained his position, rifle against Isaac's ribcage. Kevin looked at him.
"Right," he said. "we'll go."
The guard stayed put.
"Does it matter that he heard you call Mick 'Mick'?" said the guard.
Kevin and Mick looked at him. Looked at each other.
"I did not!" said Kevin, a dark mixture of fear and anger in his eyes.
"Aye, you did, didn't he Mick?"
Mick's lips were pursed. He shook his head slowly at the guard in disgust.
"You are a blood-thirsty bastard, Sean," said Kevin turning away. "Do what you have to do!"
The echo of the gunshot rattled around in the trees and Isaac Adams' body bounced and flopped to stillness on the mossy gravel by the roadside.

Chapter 19

Matthew Henderson

How I looked after my invalid

Sally Anne had sprained her ankle as I thought; the doctor took one look at the amount of swelling around it and the black and blue bruising down the side of her foot and just shook his head at it, almost like he was annoyed at the girl for being clumsy. Old Doctor Leary had a great name for fixing broken bones and the like. He was also famous for his stuttering and for certain favourite expressions which came out when he was anxious.

"Wh-wha-what on earth have you done to yourself, my girl?" he said, running his fingers over the skin, pressing in places and twisting the foot gently. "I mean, I mean....it seems to me you have torn the ligaments down the outside. I can find no sign of a break but we will have to wait until the swelling goes down a bit to be sure."

He bandaged it up tightly and told her to rest it completely.

"I...I...I mean, you're not to be doing any work for the next week or two," he scolded, "otherwise this is only going to get worse. Keep this bandage on and lie with your foot up above the level of your body to help the fluid drain away. I...I mean Matthew, you make sure she does this. Then, whenever she is able to mark it to the ground again, cut her a couple of branches for crutches. Can you do that for me? Well... for her, I mean? Bring her back if it doesn't start to improve within the next ten days to two weeks."

I had to carry her back out to where I'd left the pony and trap in the street in front of his surgery. She was as light as a child in my arms. How I loved the feel of her against me. I got one or two inquisitive looks from folk that knew me, this strange, fair-haired lass hanging around my neck like a scarf. She just kept looking up at me with a wee smile on her face.

'Look who's got me in his arms now,' it said.

I wondered how far and how fast that particular item of gossip would travel around the village. For some reason it came into my head to hope that it would bypass Alice Porter.

It was indeed a full ten days before her ankle mended. Ten days without her help around the farm was difficult, especially as the harvest was just getting started. I could have, maybe I should have, been very annoyed by the circumstance but, if I am being totally honest, I wasn't too bothered at all. In fact I was secretly delighted. You see, Sally Anne became so dependent on me, sort of like a pet lamb that I had to take care of....and take care of her I did.

I carried her up the stairs; the ladder was a problem but she clung to my back as I climbed it, giggling so much she nearly let go and slid off. I laid her on the bed.

"Content yourself now. You are staying here until you are better," I told her, putting a cushion under her foot.

"It's not right," she said. "I have my chores to be doing as usual. How will you manage the milking and all? What about the pratie gathering? I need to be out...."

I put my finger to her lips to interrupt her flow.

"Whisht," I told her. "You have to do as the doctor told you and I have to make you do it. You have to stay here on this bed with your ankle raised up."

"No Matthew, I can't be lying here doing nothing. What about food and all?"

I lifted the fiddle and gave it to her.

"If you want something to do play away at this," I said. "And don't be worrying about food. I'll bring you up whatever you want to eat."

"Why are you doing this? I am your hired hand. I need to be earning my keep," she said. "I have to be out working."

"No, you don't. You can't, for a start. Sure you can't thole the pain when you put your weight on it. What good would you be to me around the yard?"

"This is not right. It's not fair. I am nothing but a burden to you."

"You are not a burden. You have been great around the place. You're the best thing to happen to us in years. It is all my fault that you got yourself hurt," I told her. "So just learn to rest and let me look after you."

She leaned on one elbow and stretched herself up towards my face. Then the shock of my life; she landed the quickest wee kiss on my cheek and I heard her breathe, "Thank you."

It wasn't the last one either during that time of her resting. Every time I brought her food I would be hoping for another one and I wasn't often disappointed. I wouldn't let the twins take her a bite. It had to be me. I think I made more cups of tea during that ten days than I did in the whole of my life up to then. I gave her books that I thought she might like; I even borrowed a couple of stories in Irish from Anthony Kearney for her but the candlelight wasn't great for reading the small print. She played her tunes, more tunes than anybody would ever have realised existed in the world. She got Jane to find her sewing to do and clothes to mend.

One afternoon not long after she got hurt I was sitting on the side of her bed. I was telling her about the sad news I had just heard. A postman from Killeter had been robbed and shot by the IRA not half a dozen miles from here. It was a terrible crime and I felt the tragedy of it deep in my very heart. He was a man with a young family. What was to become of them now?

Sally Anne was completely sympathetic about it. I could sense no holding back in her attitude as I told her about it. Things like this were happening all over the country, much of it in her name, you could have said, but she was not on for it, not in the least.

"The poor children," she said.

"Aye, the poor children, and the poor mother too. What good is something like that supposed to do, would you tell me? How does killing an innocent postman help any cause?"

She did not speak for a long time. I could tell she was concerned about the situation. It had put a black cloud over both of us for the time being. There was a lot of stuff that was not being said in the silence that day in her bedroom.

Eventually she took my hand and looked long at me.

"So you and me? Does this affect us?" she said.

This threw me a bit.

"What do you mean?" I asked.

"Well...are we...are you and me...you know...are we walking out together?" she asked me, shy of the question as it left her lips, by the look in her eyes. It was something she had been lying there thinking about, by the sound of how it came out of her. It took me by surprise and I could think of no way to answer it other than to laugh about it, even in the circumstances.

"That is a rare question girl. You lying up here on the broad of your back.... and you're asking me if we are walking out! Not much chance of that, is there?"

She pulled her hand away at that so I had to humour her a bit.
"Why do you want to ask a daft question like that?" I said. "Am I not looking after you well enough?"
"You are, but... all this trouble?"
She left it there. I understood what was behind her question. I had been trying myself to come up with the answer.
After a few days I would come in from the yard and find her limping around the kitchen, trying to clean or wash or cook. I always made a big play of telling her off for this and grabbing her to carry her back upstairs.
"What are you doing, herpling about like that? You are supposed to be lying up there waiting for me....waiting to get better."
"'Herpling', did you say? What is that? You come out with the oddest words," she laughed and kept working.
One afternoon I happened to come into the kitchen from the street sort of quick, I suppose. It seemed to surprise her and I noticed that she was trying to hide whatever it was she was doing at the table. It only made me curious, of-course, so I had to see what she was at. It became a bit of a tease between us, me trying to see over her shoulder and her grasping whatever it was close in to her so I couldn't see.
"Don't Matthew," she was saying, "leave me be."
"What's the big secret?" I said, putting my arms around her and lifting her up.
Wasn't my mother sitting quietly by the hearth and I hadn't even noticed her. The first I knew of her being there was when she spoke.
"Leave the girl alone, Matthew. She's been knitting and now she's making herself a dress; it's for the harvest dance; leave her be, son."
"Is that what you're at?" I said.
"It is. Is that alright? It was meant to be a surprise," she said, still clasping the material to her and turning her back on me.
"Let me see it," I said.
My mother, God bless her, couldn't stay out of it. "Let the girl alone, son. You'll likely see it on the night."
"Where did you get the material?" I asked, noticing the oatmeal colour of it sticking out from under her oxter.
"I found it," she said. "Upstairs, stuffed in the back of a cupboard. Your mother said I could have it, and Monica got me thread of the same colour."

"Good for her," I said, "but she'll likely have to come and stitch it together for you. What would you know about making a dress?"
"God forgive you," she said, "Didn't I spend the last four years stitching carpets in the factory and making clothes for my mother and my sister and myself since I was no size?"
"Is that right?" I joked. "So, if folk start walking all over you at the dance, you'll only have yourself to blame."
This puzzled her; I could see it in her face.
"What do you mean?"
"Carpet," I laughed. To be fair to her, she caught the joke for she had a wee smile on her as she hurried away out of the kitchen clutching this new dress.
To be honest I wasn't bothered too much about her being downstairs; at the start it was just an excuse to hold her, carry her up those narrow stairs, cuddle her slim wee figure without her being able to object. It was always a bit of fun and I believe we both enjoyed it. My mother, if she noticed anything, never said a word about it and I was never too free with her in front of the girls.
We got right and close during that time. The physical attraction seemed to grow by the day. Whiles as I sat courting her on her bed she would have to take hold of my hand and remove it from the places it had strayed to. She never said anything but she was very firm in that, especially early on in her convalescence. I didn't mind at all. I just loved having her so vulnerable, so needing me and so very, very pretty as she lay there. She was my captive butterfly and I enjoyed every last second of the beauty she brought me.
Sad to say though, the butterfly had an instinct to fly freely again in her own independent air. She began to flex her wings.
"Will you ask Joe if he can maybe come and get me for Mass and Confession tomorrow morning," she said. "His father might let him bring the pony and trap."
"You can't be doing that," I said. "You have a bad ankle. You are not going anywhere tomorrow."
"Indeed I am. I have to."
"Why do you have to?" I said. "They won't miss you for one week."
"What do you mean, 'they won't miss me'? It is not a case of them missing me. It is a case of me needing to go to confession and wanting to take Mass."

"You need to go to confession?" I said, amazed at her. "What do you need to be confessing?"
"That would be my own business," she said and looked away from me. Actually that was the first time she had averted her eyes from mine in days; that week, while in the sanctuary of her bedroom, we had stared so much into each other's eyes that I thought I had caught a glimpse of the very soul of her. That glimpse now seemed to have been a bit of a useless daydream.
"Seriously," I said, "you have been lying up here all week... and rightly so. It's not as if you have had any occasion for any great sin or anything. What could you possibly have to be telling some priest? I would see the sense if you had been out ...."
"Maybe that is why I need to be seeing my priest," she said.
"What?" I said. "I don't understand."
"You wouldn't. You are a Protestant. And you are a man. Men seem to be able to handle these kind of thoughts as if they were no great problem. I can never understand how it is in your religion that you don't have to answer to anybody for the things you think or for the things you do wrong. You never have to confess anything. You just sail along as if everything is always alright. You don't seem to have any sense of guilt."
Now we were really talking in two different languages, I thought, and I don't mean English and Irish. I felt out of my depth. What on earth did she have to feel guilty about? I was completely confused and, as often happens when I am that way, I thought I could joke my way around it.
"Sure I will be your priest," I said. I made the sign of the cross, jokily, perhaps even mockingly. "Tell me, my child, in what way have you sinned against God and your fellow man since your last confession?"
"Don't Matthew," she said. "That is not funny. You have no right to be taunting me like this. You promised me whenever you hired me that I would be allowed to go to Mass. Now, all I am asking is for you to get Joe to take me there tomorrow as usual, except that he will have to come and get me first."
"Alright," I said, "we'll make a deal. I will take you to Mass myself, in the morning before our church, but you have to tell me what you are going to confess to the priest."
"Oh don't be so ridiculous. You know that confession is a secret thing; it is private between me and him and God. I can't be telling you. It is not fair of you to keep going on about it either."

"Alright," I said, "I'll still take you but I am just dying to know if my name will feature in this confession."
"Listen to yourself," she said, a twinkle shooting like a stickleback across the green pool of her eyes, the first break in her seriousness. "Of-course you feature. I will have to tell the priest that my greatest sin is my impatience in having to listen to your constant conceit."
"My conceit?" I said. "I have every reason to be conceited. Sure don't I have the best looking maid in the county of Tyrone?"
"That's as maybe," she said, "but she is still a maid at the end of the day and a Catholic one at that."
This was a very stark statement I thought. It set me back a bit from my banter. It was altogether too honest, too painful a truth for me to deal with at that minute. All I could think to say was, "We could always change that."
"What do you mean?" she said.
"Well, why don't you come with me to our church for once? See what you make of it. Come with us tomorrow morning. I'd love to see their faces when I carry you up the aisle. One face in particular."
"You are joking," she said, a hint of panic in her voice. "I could never do that."
"Why not?" I said. "You'd love it; it would be a change for you."
"I can't do that. You know I can't. I have nothing against your 'method' church or whatever it is called but I am a Catholic. I have to take Mass tomorrow. And before I take Mass I have to make my confession."
"Could it not wait another week?" I said. "What is the worst that can happen to you? You are hardly going to be condemned to eternal punishment in Hell for missing Mass on one occasion, are you? Especially when you are laid up."
She hung her head so I couldn't see her eyes.
"You don't understand," she said. "It is my duty. After the week I have had I cannot afford to be missing out on the grace I get in Holy Communion. It would be a double sin not to go."
Now I was really bemused.
"Agh Sally Anne," I said, "why are you so determined to be dreaming up sins for yourself to be guilty of? Why not just enjoy life, enjoy things, without having to be always needing forgiveness for it?"
"You have no right to be talking to me like this," she said. "Especially when it is yourself that is to be blamed."

"So I am the cause of you sinning, am I? And what will you do next week, after you have been to confession and after you have had your Mass? You'll be forgiven for....for whatever you think we are doing wrong but you will come straight back to me for more, won't you?"
"Don't mock me," she said, an element of scolding in her voice.
"And what's more," I went on, "if I thought you wouldn't, if I thought that going to Mass and talking to your priest would persuade you to change how we have been, I would tie you down to this bed. You wouldn't be going to any priest, do you hear me?"
That put an end to the conversation for a while. We had reached some sort of a tipping point and we both realised it. I could sense a real tension in Sally Anne, a dilemma, not so much of her own making but certainly one that had its roots in this blind devotion to her faith. Strange though it may seem, up until that point I had actually had a real respect for her loyalty to her church and her whole moral code. Now I saw some of the contradictions in it and some of the ways that it put too tight a fence around her freedom, her as an individual. Still, I wasn't going to let these contradictions become any more of a barrier between us than they already were.
"If you really want me to," I said, "I will go over and ask Joe to come and get you tomorrow, alright?"
"Thank you," she said, her head still diverted from me. I was getting a lot of 'Thank yous' but how much ground had I lost over all this Mass thing?
Joe took the invalid to fulfil her spiritual duties on that Sunday morning. He wanted to know all about how she had come by the sprained ankle. I have to say that he didn't seem entirely satisfied by our joint explanations as we lifted Sally Anne up into his cart.
I had cut two branches from the ash hedge down along the back burn and fashioned them into makeshift crutches for her. Joe said they were far too thin but with all the weight of her they didn't need to be very sturdy of themselves.
Her second week of recovery saw her hobbling after me around the yard. It was as if she was missing me and couldn't let me out of her sight for too long. Even my mother observed it and raised her concerns.
"That girl should not be out there trying to work yet, until that foot of hers gets better," she said. "Can you not tell her to be staying in the house and resting it?"

"She'll not listen to me," I said.
Secretly though, I was delighted that she was wanting to be by my side. The egg collecting, the milking, the feeding of the horses and the pigs, the dunging out of the stalls....everything was taking far longer than normal and not just because she wasn't helping either. It was more a case of her being there to distract me. I found her physical closeness well nigh impossible to resist. At times we had to keep a watchful eye and a listening ear for the twins who were off school and around the yard quite often. I had kept them at home to help with gathering spuds. At the start they had been delighted by this; the joy wore off them after a day or two as their wee backs began to stiffen and the muscles of their legs cramped up from all the bending over.
I was seldom away from Sally Anne those days, except at night-time of-course, although there was manys a night when I might as well have been with her, given the length of time I lay awake thinking about her into the wee, small hours. There were even a couple of nights when the temptation to go up to her nearly got the better of me; one night I climbed the ladder and stood in the box room at her door a full ten minutes before I caught myself on.
In the middle of that week I took delivery of the new corn-binder. We were one of the first farms in the countryside to invest in such a machine. I had managed to get a loan off Alice Porter's father in the bank and had put in an order for an Albion binder with a crowd in Omagh that brought them in from Scotland. It arrived in our yard on the back of a noisy lorry to great excitement all round.
Sally Anne's eyes were nearly as wide as the twins. It was all I could do to stop myself giving her a hug in front of everybody, I was so pleased that she was here to see this little triumph of mine. I could hardly wait to get it yoked up to the two Clydesdales and get stuck into harvesting our three fields of oats, but I knew that they could do with another couple of good sunny days to get the corn really ripe. I would probably end up cutting for a few of the local farmers too, Kearneys included. The thing was that this machine would save so much time and effort, cutting the corn and binding the sheaves with twine, where before it took many man-hours of sweat; woman-hours too, of-course. The days of using lengths of straw to bind the sheaves were over. We would still have to set them up into stooks for drying but that was a far simpler job.

I had not heard any more from cousin Victoria but I just presumed she would be arriving at the station in Castlederg on the afternoon tram on the Thursday as she had written earlier. I was looking forward to seeing her, of-course I was, but I did find myself wondering how this would all work out. It would be the first time I would be in her company when my affections were now somewhere else entirely. I couldn't help wondering if she would notice and, if she did, what would she make of Sally Anne. Now that she had her own man back in Belfast I was fairly content that she would be happy for me as well. Still, I would tread carefully. I had no intention of giving her any cause to suspect that Sally Anne was more to me than the servant girl. Safer that way, for our Victoria was a very sharp lady when she wanted to be.

Chapter 20

Sally Anne Sweeney

What I thought of the new arrivals.

Victoria was to arrive into Castlederg on the Thursday afternoon. Matthew was to collect her from the station. He left me to do the evening milking by myself for once. I did not mind this. My ankle was a good bit better of itself but I still had the bandage on it for support.

I was near enough finished when I heard the footsteps at the byre door and then the chirp of Joe's familiar voice.

"An bhfuil tú ann, Sally Anne?" he half-sang, looking past me to be sure Matthew was not hidden somewhere at the far end of the byre. "Are you there?"

"Where else would I be?" I said, the Gaelic running off my tongue in sweet relief. "You are far too late to be giving me a hand with this."

"Agh sure," he said, "you can manage the best. What about the foot?"

"Back to the usual," I said.

"Not your usual yet, by the look of you," he said, as I limped over the uneven floor to empty a brimful bucket of warm, frothing milk into the metal can. "Here, give me that."

"Content yourself," I said. "I have done the rest by myself; I can manage this last one."

"You're a wile independent girl," said Joe. "Where is Matthew anyway?"

"He is away to the town to get his visitor," I said. "He should be back soon. You may just wait for him."

"It wasn't him I came to see," he said.

'Oh, oh," I thought. 'What is coming now?'

I said nothing.

"It was you yourself," he said.

"What was that about?"

"Well......" he said.

I watched him as he stood, thinking too hard about how he was going to say what he had come to say, no doubt what he had practised saying all the way up across the fields.

"The Harvest Ceili is on Saturday night coming," he began again.

"So?"
"You will be going won't you?"
"I will."
"Will you be up for dancing?"
"I will, if this ankle is not against me, but Tam Glenn wants me playing tunes as well."
"I just wanted to ask you if you will keep me a dance?" he said.
"Is that all?" I laughed. "I thought it was something exciting."
No sooner said than I regretted it; why did I always seem to be putting Joe down in the off-hand way I spoke to him? Matthew would have laughed back at me for a comment like that but poor Joe took everything to heart, as if I was deliberately trying to cut him.
"That's alright then," he said, punctured, and started to wander towards the door, the stoop of his shoulders following that nose of his.
"Joe, for goodness sake," I said, hobbling after him and catching his arm. "I did not mean anything by that. Of-course I will dance with you... if I can."
"You're such a torture," he said, far too much earnestness in his eyes.
"What do you mean by that?" I said.
"Nothing. Nothing at all. I was thinking as well, wouldn't it be a nice idea if somebody was able to go and get your friend Ailish from the place where she is working?" he said, deliberately brightening up.
"It would be a lovely idea," I said, surprised at him remembering her, if not by the kindness of him. It was so like him. "How would we get her though? We don't even know where she works. How would we let her know?"
"I think I could find out alright," he said. "Newtownstewart isn't exactly Dublin City. Somebody about there will know where she is. I'll take a run over on the bicycle tomorrow if Matt doesn't need me here. I'll find her, trust me. What was the name on that old farmer that she is with? Wasn't he somebody Spence?"
"I believe you are right," I said. "That is very good of you, Joe."
"Not at all. She is a nice enough girl."
I gave him a curious look but he seemed innocent enough on it.
"What makes you think that Matthew might need you here tomorrow?" I asked him.
"Just if he wanted to start into the corn. It takes two to work that new binder thing."

"Ah right," I said. I did not want to say that Matthew had already asked me to help him work the machine. I was not yet sure myself what would be involved.
"So he is away for Victoria?" said Joe.
"He is."
"Him and her were always very close, for cousins like. More than close, I would say."
I allowed myself a secret smile inside.
'Oh dear Joe,' I thought, 'would you ever stop trying to thwart me? You are so obvious.'
"Not any longer," I said. "I think he is well over her."
"What makes you say that?" he said with a long sideways glance at me.
"I think I know him well enough by now," I said.
There was a break then in our conversation. I was thinking, 'Here I am presuming to know Matthew better than his friend since childhood. Here I am again, celebrating my closeness to him, lording it over Joe, boasting about something which is supposed to be a secret between me and Matthew.'
I went to the door and looked back at Joe. He broke the silence, a strange brittle tone in the quaver of his voice.
"Sally Anne," he said, "you may not want me to be telling you this but....you say you know Matthew? Maybe you don't know him as well as you make out. It takes time to really know somebody. Give yourself more time. A lot more time."
I walked away from him.
"Thanks for the homily, Father Kearney," I said as I went. I did not know if he heard me or not.
Joe had disappeared before Matthew's horse and cart came rumbling into the yard. I studied Victoria's grinning face from the shadow of the barn for a little moment. Suddenly I saw that there was another face there, behind Matthew; a man's face.
'Who is this?' I wondered. 'Whoever he is, these are faces that don't fit around here.' That was my first thought. 'They are far too smooth of themselves."
"Just houl the horse's head," Matthew told me. He had a bossy tone of voice on him.
So I held the reins close up at the bit and stroked the white flash of hair on the front of Peggy's face while Matthew jumped down and helped the guests. Neither of the two of them bothered to look the way

I was on. The way they were getting on with each other, it did not take me long to work out that this stranger was her man.
They made straight for the house to greet 'Auntie Eliza' and the twins. The girls were dancing with excitement at the back door. I stood there by the horse watching it all, the flat space of the yard separating us like a swollen river. Matthew had followed them at the start, warming himself in the glow of the family reunion. I could not blame him, mind you, but I did feel very much the servant girl at that point in time. I wanted to go over to this Victoria and say, "I am Sally Anne Sweeney; I may not be as pretty as you but Matthew likes me now, so leave him be."
She had her own man now, so she would probably have just laughed at me, after she got over the shock of it. Anyhow, I did not say a thing, of-course I didn't. I just stood and counted the minutes until Matthew would return to me from his family bonding duties.
Return he did, sort of.
"Sally Anne," he called across to me after a while, still in the master's voice tone. "Come and meet Victoria and Stanley."
I still had Peggy by the reins in the middle of the yard. She was already straining towards the watering trough, tugging me with her despite my resistance.
"What will I do with Peggy?" I said.
They all giggled at that. I could not see what was funny about it. I had no idea why they had all burst out laughing at me, still there in the middle of the street, the huge Clydesdale sort of half dragging me across the cobbles in the other direction, all eight stone of me, as shabby as a rag doll in my working clothes, my bandaged foot slithering in the mud as I fought in vain with the beast.
"Let her go for a drink," said Matthew, laughing with the others. "Come on over here."
I felt only a little bit higher than the sheepdog as I stumbled towards them. It seemed to take me an age. I wiped my hands down my front as I went but when I took a look down at them I discovered they were still filthy from the day's work.
"Who is this then?" asked Victoria, a faint smile of amusement at her.
Straight away I resented the gerning drone of her way of talking. She could not help being from Belfast but surely to God she could have tried to rid herself, even a little bit, of that ridiculous way of speaking.
"This is Sally Anne," said Matthew.

I almost felt that I should have been curtsying or something, so grand did she look in her light blue dress.
"Well hello, Sally Anne," she said, like it was another joke and she was not sure whether to giggle now or wait to laugh at me later. "And you are the new maid?"
I am not easily intimidated but at that moment I could not have moved my tongue, not if you had offered me money for it. Matthew said nothing. To her credit Mrs Henderson spoke up for me.
"She is, and a very good one too," she said.
That was news to me. I did not know how she had come to that opinion for she had never seemed to bother anything with me up to then.
Then Millie threw in her tuppence worth, God love her.
"Sawey Anne is Ma'hew's new girl," she said with a teasing smile, like she was in the know and this was the time to be sharing it with the circle of the world.
An awful hush fell into the middle of us.
A sinking feeling in my stomach, my heart doing double time, likely as it pumped extra blood up to the white of my face.
'Oh Máire, Máthair Dé!' I whispered in my head.
Unfortunately, instant prayers to Our Blessed Lady do not always work. Matthew's neither, whoever he was praying to. The ground did not open to swallow me. It did not even make a groan of sound to break that stunned silence.
Victoria looked at Matthew. Stanley, the 'surprise Stanley', who had not spoken yet, looked at me. Mrs Henderson opened her mouth to speak but thought better of it. Jane put her hand over her mouth as if to catch the stream of words that her twin had let escape. I looked at Matthew, his neck reddening up like a rose. To give him his dues though, he did manage to say the right thing and break us out of this frozen moment.
"Ah Millie! You say the daftest things," he said with a forced laugh. "Pay no heed to her Victoria."
Victoria's face was all of a muddle and I saw her eyes go to her man. Stanley came riding to the rescue.
"Must be smashing to have a maid, Matthew," he said in that strange accent they all seem to have in England. "'Specially one as pretty as this one."

With that he stepped forward, very mannerly like, and stuck out his hand to me.
"Nice to make your acquaintance I'm sure," and he shook my hand in a wet-herring sort of way.
'What a slabber this one is?' I was thinking. Then, without really meaning to, I found myself bowing my head to him; just a tiny bit, but I bowed to the *Sasanach!* An old instinct in me that I was not even aware of had prompted me to this impulse. I instantly wondered how and why it was there at all. After the experiences I had had with Englishmen in my own home a while back I thought that there would not be a whole lot of respect left in me for people from their country. But there I was, still acting as if he was from the master race across the sea.
The attitude was not long of changing in me. Out of the corner of my eye I caught him taking a private look down at his hand a second or two later, likely to check for contamination. I wanted to ask him, "What is the matter, Mister Stanley? I am sorry. Are the English allergic to dirt, are they?"
Instead I let it pass and made a point of saying to Victoria, "You must be very tired and hungry. Will I make tea? After I have washed my hands."
"Thank you; that will be smashing," Stanley answered for her.
'Two 'smashings' in his first two sentences,' I thought. I translated the word in my head. 'For 'smashing' read '*iontact deas*'. I stored it away in case it ever came up again.
I wondered straight away about this man. Why had he arrived with Victoria without so much as a letter, a warning? Had it taken Matthew by surprise as much as me or had he just forgotten to tell me? This was my first Englishman to ever meet or talk to in a sociable way. You could not describe the soldiers who had searched our cottage at home as 'sociable'. It was going to be very interesting.
Both he and Victoria were very tall. That was the first thing I noticed about the appearance of the pair of them and it was probably the only thing that I could see they had in common. He was much older than she was, maybe ten or fifteen years, but then she was near enough the same age as Matthew, if I remembered correctly. While Stanley was black-haired, with skin the shade of peat ash, Victoria had a full head of hair, the colour of butter, and a complexion like the cream on top of a churn of milk. His eyes were a dull browny-grey colour; hers were as

blue as the sky. Stanley wore one of those big black moustaches with such pride that it gave you the feeling it was a pet that he had reared up since it was just a dark shadow. His eyebrows were two smaller versions of the same thing but were well on their way to matching the 'pet' for size.

From the start I had the feeling that they were an unusual couple and not what you might call 'best-matched'. Ah well, who was I to be making judgements about 'best-matched'? I wondered how they had met. I wondered what he, as an Englishman, was doing in Ireland, especially after the war we had just fought to put them out. But then, of-course, this was Northern Ireland and this place was still very much seeing itself as a part of England.

After making tea I could not wait to get away from them to the clear air of the farmyard, then to the hay-shed at the back where I understood everything and where there were no surprises and no strange foreign accents, be they English or Belfast. I could think of nothing to be doing so I just sat on a pile of hay, swinging my legs, thinking, worrying. I was not even sure why I was so concerned if I am being honest. What Millie had said could not be unsaid. How would it change things?

That was how Matthew found me in the shed half an hour later.

"What are you doing out here?"

"Just thinking."

He made as if to kiss me but I stopped him.

"Did you know that Englishman was coming?"

"Not at all. I would have told you. He just arrived off the tram with her. I knew nothing about it. She says she wrote me a letter to tell me. It never came."

"It feels very strange to me," I said.

"It's strange surely. Victoria engaged to an Englishman."

"Engaged? And him nearly old enough to be her..."

"Naw," he interrupted. "He's not that old. Maybe ten or twelve years older than her. Just that he's English, with that accent. We don't get many Englishmen around here. He seems alright, mind you."

"Does he?"

My prejudices were about getting the better of me. But there was worse to come. Matthew looked a bit uncomfortable for a moment and then he took my hand.

"I was trying to work out where he can sleep," he said.

I waited.
"And what did you decide?"
"Well, she'll be in the guest bedroom. The only other place is the wee box-room up beside you in the attic."
I jumped down off the hay, too quickly, forgetting about my ankle. The spasm of pain was nothing compared to the panic running through my mind at that very moment.
"You are not putting the Englishman in the room beside me!"
"No, no. I wouldn't be doing that to you."
"Well....what then?"
"He can go into my room. I have new sheets left out for him if you can put them on for him."
"I will," I said.
That's all I said. I could not bring myself to ask the obvious question. It sat with us in the hay-shed like the apple did between Adam and Eve. Who would bite first?
I could see he was as embarrassed about it as I was. We stood in the quietness of our private fears, four feet apart but staring away from each other into the spaces of our own expectations.
He broke first.
"That's alright, isn't it?"
"What is?"
"If I sleep in the box-room?"
"It's your house. You can sleep wherever you want."
He gave me a long look which I did not return.
"Can I, Sally Anne?"
'Oh dear God,' I thought. 'Far too much meaning in that question. No, no, no!'
I did not want to hear this, to think this.
I turned away from him. It was getting out of hand, this intense closeness that he was determined to be leading me into. I had always thought I could handle myself, that I could handle any situation. Now I was in serious deep water.
"That's not fair of you," I said and I could not believe the tremble in my voice as it came out.
"Don't be worrying yourself," he said. "I'll be in the box-room. You can shut the door."
I decided to go back to the house.

~~~~~

As the day wore on I was as nervous as a kitten concerning how close to each other Matthew and I were going to be sleeping that night. Don't be thinking that I had been able to put it from my mind. I had even taken time to run upstairs just to check on that door between the two rooms. It had never shut properly since I had arrived. Maybe it had not shut properly since whoever had hung it there in the first place. Tonight I wanted it tight shut but the more I tried to make it close, the more it seemed determined to resist me. I tried lifting it by the handle. I tried forcing it with my shoulder. To no avail. It was an ill-fitting door and it was not going to be obliging me. It stayed ajar. Sure it didn't even lock anyhow, so what was I worrying about? If anybody wanted to come in all they had to do was push it open. The screech of its old hinges and the creak of the floorboards would have wakened the dead. I looked around for a box or something heavy to set behind the door but there wasn't a thing I could use.

Anyhow, what was I being afraid of? I trusted Matthew. If he had wanted to come up to me in the attic in the night hours he had had every opportunity in the months before now, creak or no creak. It was just the fact that he had asked that stupid question, and that he would be so close to me that night, a matter of ten feet away on the other side of that wall. A thin wall, so thin I could imagine hearing him changing his clothes, maybe even changing his mind. Well, if he changed his mind and decided to try to take things further with me I would just have to handle it when the time came. The very thought of it was causing me flutters of fear in the pit of my stomach.

Later that night I lay awake waiting for him. If that sounds bad what I mean is that I lay awake as long as I could, waiting for him to come to his bed next door. The nervousness in me, like a mother watching the door for a wayward child coming home late from a dance, but worse. Much more nervous, believe me.

I had gone up to bed at the usual time, after the excitement of the family meal together. The Henderson family together, I mean....along with this Stanley fellow. I had eaten with them every other evening at that table, in fact every mealtime since I arrived. This was the first time I did not. There was no room for me at the table. Matthew and Stanley were at either end, Millie beside the mother and Jane beside the 'princess'; Victoria, I mean. I had made a stew, with beef, carrots,
~~~~~

onions and potatoes. It tasted good, if I may say so myself. It would have fed three families in the Rosses. But, when it came to the eating of it, I ate mine standing up by the work-bench. I accepted that, all the more so when I had a lovely little gesture from Matthew, just the tiniest hint of a wink when everybody else had their eyes closed before he said the 'blessing'. I read it as an affectionate wink of appreciation; it was all he could communicate to me in the crowded circumstances of the kitchen.

When I served the Englishman and I was standing behind him I noticed that he had a bald patch on the top of his head. It was something that obviously concerned him, I thought, because he had allowed the surrounding dark locks to grow really long so that he could brush them over the thinning part where the white skin shone up through. I smiled inside myself at his pride.

'He could be doing with a good thatcher,' I thought to myself. 'It is a pity he can't take that moustache off and spread it out on the top of his skull. It would fit him better. I wonder what this Victoria sees in an old fellow like this, and him going bald?'

I listened to them talking. I suppose I was listening for clues. Clues about all these relationships, especially Victoria to Matthew and the other way round, but also Victoria to Stanley and Stanley to the place he found himself in. From what I saw during that meal, Matthew still had a soft spot for her, a more-than-cousinly soft spot in my opinion. I could see how easily he had been under her sway when he was younger, for she was a striking looking girl. She must have been a full foot taller than me for a start. And the big full lips on her, like she had dipped them in a tin of red lead paint.

Stanley said very little during the meal. The only thing he said of any note was when Matthew was asking him about how he was enjoying life 'in this country'.

"It's a lot safer up here than in the south, that is for certain," he said.

"Really?" said Matthew. "In spite of all this bother in Belfast? You must see a lot of that."

Stanley just laughed, a strange snort of a laugh through his nose, as if he knew something nobody else knew.

"You could say that," he said. "But the south was something different. I must tell you sometime about how it was down there."

'The south?' I thought. 'What was he doing in the south?'

I had my suspicions but, no matter how closely I listened in to the rest of the chat, there was never any further mention of it.
At one point Matthew announced to the visitors that the following day he planned to yoke up the new binder for its first outing.
"Wot is that? A binda? Wot does it do when it's at home?" asked Stanley in his thick English tongue.
"Victoria," said Matthew, a teasing smile on his face, "you tell him."
"Tell him what?" she said, turning from chatting to Jane.
"A binder. Tell him what a binder is for," he said. Then to Stanley, "Victoria is a real fount of knowledge on everything to do with farming."
"That is not fair....cousin," she said, fiddling with her knife and pointing it at him in pretended menace as the girls giggled and Matthew sniggered.
"We have some good yarns to tell you about Victoria and the farm," he said to Stanley. "She is a great expert on how the Shorthorn heifer gets a mate."
"Oh Stanley," she pouted, "stand up for me please. They are really horrible to me sometimes down here. How am I supposed to know about what goes on on some back-woods farm?"
The girls were loving this. Jane especially.
"Milk comes from cows. Bacon comes from pigs. Eggs come from hens. Wool comes from sheep. Honey comes from..." she rhymed as if reciting some farmer's creed.
Her mother interrupted her. "That's enough, Jane," she said. "Let poor Victoria alone. They don't have all those animals in Belfast."
"No they don't," Victoria protested. "In Belfast milk comes out of a bottle and wool comes from a shop and bacon from the butcher and honey from a pot. We don't go in for all that messy stuff. Eggs from a hen? Just imagine how! From the hen's...you-know what, for goodness sake! So unhygienic."
'Whatever that word means,' I thought but at least she was joining in the laughter against her own pretence of innocence. The same girl had little to learn about birds and bees, I was fairly sure.
"So what is this binda thing?" Stanley asked.
"It is a new machine for cutting corn. I just bought it. It's a top quality implement. First one around here. We ordered it in from the mainland. You'll see it the morrow," answered Matthew.
'The mainland?' I thought. "What does he mean by 'the mainland'?'

"Good for you," said Stanley. "I look forward to seeing it. You have a tractor then?"
"No, no; it's a horse-drawn one. No tractors about here. No need of them when you have two good horses. They might have a tractor down about Baronscourt estate, I'm led to believe. Sure there's hardly even a motor car around these parts," said Matthew.
"Ah well, when I get my new car I look forward to bringing it down here to show you. We could go for a spin in it, couldn't we Victoria? Take Matthew and the girls. They would love it. Where is there to go around here?"
"Plenty of places," said Matthew. "We're not that far from Donegal town and the beach at Bundoran."
"Ah, wait now," said Stanley. "Bundoran and Donegal town? Those are in the Free State. With the amount of IRA troops in Donegal at present it would not be advisable. I would not be allowed you see. Security and all that."
"Ah right," said Matthew. "I never thought of that. Well, we could go north to Derry or somewhere if you like. Walk around the walls maybe."
"Yes," he said, "Londonderry might be a safer bet."
"So when are you getting this new car then?" asked Matthew.
"The car? I have it bought actually. It's a Morris Cowley. Two years old. Not a scratch on it. Just waiting to take delivery of it."
"Sounds like a brave car," said Matthew. "I'm looking forward to a spin in it."
'A spin in it!' I thought. 'The Englishman is only here an hour and Matthew is starting to sound like him already.'
All this conversation was running through my head again as I lay in my room. I could not make a lot of sense of it but I was beginning to have my suspicions about this Stanley. What did he mean about not being allowed in the Free State? What sort of job did he have that he could afford a car? Goodness, he would be the first person I knew who actually owned one.
I would have to keep a close eye on somebody like him. I felt a long way away from the safety of my wee home in Ranahuel, from the wisdom of my father's advice and the constancy of my mother's stare. What I would have given to hear the sweet comforting sound of her whistle.

I recited the Rosary in my bed as usual, the room being very cool at that time of night. I heard no creak on the stairs, nor in the room next door, nor from the squeaky hinges of my door. I saw no sign of a candle. Matthew did not come to his bed. Despite myself I drifted off to sleep, the beads twisted in my fingers and a prayer to Our Blessed Lady for protection echoing around the corners of my mind.

Chapter 21

Matthew Henderson

The day of the corn-cutting

I was feeling tired all that day.
The night before I had sat up talking to Victoria and her man, catching up, remembering old times. I sat on with Vic whenever he went to bed, which was very nice.
I found Stanley's conversation hard going. After knocking back a couple of glasses of whiskey his English reserve began to wilt. I had to listen to him boasting about his involvement in the war in France. He had no feeling for the fact that my father had fought and died there, that he still lay there. I did not want to be hearing about his heroics at some place called Messine Ridge.
Then, when he was finished with 'the Kaiser and his Huns', he waxed on about how he countered the Irish rebellion in Cork and Kerry. After an hour of that I had had enough but how do you stop somebody so full of himself and so in awe of his own 'military capabilities'? He told me he had been a member of the Auxiliaries. I knew that this group had a fearsome reputation, even here in Ulster, and, if half the things he told me about what the Auxies had done in Cork and Limerick were true, their reputation was well-merited. I wasn't disagreeing with him; in this form it would have taken a brave man to disagree with him. At the same time I did at one point ask him if it was true that they had razed parts of those cities to the ground, as I had been led to believe.
"Absolutely," he said. "It was the only way to make the rebels see sense. If they were intent on killing British soldiers then they had to be taught that we wouldn't stand for it."
"But those people in the wee streets, they hadn't done anything wrong, had they? Were they not just ordinary civilians going about their business? Women and children in some cases? Surely they weren't the gunmen?"
'Lord above!' I thought, shocked by my own courage. 'What am I doing asking a British soldier a question like that?' But I had read some

reports somewhere and I wanted to know the truth of it, for it was hard to believe all you read at times like those.

"Look Matthew. The Empire was at stake here. We couldn't let a bunch of Irish peasants defeat the might of Great Britain. We were fresh back from the trenches; we had just won a major European war against Germany. We were hardly going to lie down against a bunch of Irish farmers and school-teachers, were we?"

The whiskey was doing a lot of talking.

"No, I understand that," I said, "but in the end they did defeat you, didn't they? They got what they wanted."

"Not all of it," he said with a touch of resentment. "There is still a British presence in this part of Ireland and that must be held. It is strategic, apart from anything else."

"I agree," I said, "but it is going to be tough in areas like this, with this Border Commission threatening us and with all these attacks and killings. There was people burned out of their farm in Raphoe the other day; a Protestant family; had their car stolen too. It's happening all over.

"Raphoe?" he said. "Where's that exactly? Near you?"

"Near enough. Just across the border in Donegal. But we had a farm burned beside us here just a few weeks ago."

"Really? Tell me about that," he said.

"People by the name of Bond. Good dacent folk. Never did anybody any harm," I told him. "They had an outhouse set on fire. Lost all of their pig-herd."

"And did they find the culprits?"

"Agh no. We are so close to the border. The IRA can run back over there and we can't touch them."

"Do you feel unsafe yourself, Matthew?" asked Victoria.

"Not at all. I just keep my head down."

"But do you have a weapon to defend yourself with?" said Stanley.

"I have a shotgun, that's all," I said. "The thing about it was, the ruffians came here first. One of them actually came inside the house. Sally Anne disturbed them or it might have been my sheds that were burned down."

"I take it there were some reprisals though, some revenge?"

"Nothing. The Bonds didn't even report it. They said they didn't want anybody else to suffer the same as them," I said.

"Now that is where I disagree. You cannot let these blighters off with it," he said, lighting up his third cigarette. "And you say all you have is a shotgun? What use is that if you are up against a trained volunteer? You need a proper gun, Matthew. I must see if I can get you something a bit more substantial."
"How can you do that?" I asked.
"No problem at all, mate," he smiled.
"Stanley holds an important position in the intelligence department in the barracks in Hollywood," said Victoria.
"All I have to do is vouchsafe for your character and credentials," said Stanley with that arrogant confidence of his. "Why don't I bring you down a proper weapon whenever I get the chance? Show you how to use it too. We gotta look after each other, now that we are going to be related, yeah?"
"Don't be telling too many people around here about your position," I told him.
He laughed.
"Now you are teaching your grandmother to suck eggs," he said.
When he went up to sleep in my bed I was glad to see the back of him. It gave Victoria and me the opportunity to talk.
"Well," she whispered excitedly, "what do you think of my fiancé?"
"He's alright," I said.
To Victoria this was understating the case and she showed it in that typical pout of hers which I had seen so many times in our childhood. I tried to bail myself out.
"He seems like a very nice man," I added.
That didn't seem to redeem me to any great extent. Then I made it worse.
"For an Englishman, I mean."
"Matthew Henderson! I never thought that you would have an attitude like that, you of all people," she said, blinking back the hurt that had sprung up behind those long eyelashes of hers.
"I didn't mean that the way it came out," I said. "All I meant was that he is a nice man for somebody who is....who's not from around here. You know what I mean? I don't know many...."
"What gave you the impression the only decent human beings on this planet are from County Tyrone? You can be so narrow-minded, you country folk," she said.
"Ah, come on, Vic," I said. "You didn't always feel that way about us."

"That's as maybe," she said, standing up suddenly. "Anyhow, he is a dammed sight better match than your wee servant girlfriend from Donegal."
Now this hit me like a thump from a shovel. I felt the blood rush to my face. The words I wanted to say scraped around in the dryness of my mouth and came out in a confusion of vowels.
"Whaaat?" I said. "Naaaw Victoria. You can't believe that. That was just some silly comment from Millie. Pay no heed to her, for goodness sake. Sure she has little wit about her. You know what she's like."
She made as if to leave the kitchen and go to bed.
"Hold on, Vic. Come back here and sit down. If I said anything to annoy you I am truly sorry. I have nothing against Stanley. If he is the man you want and if he makes you happy, then I am delighted. I could wish only the best for you. You know that. Come on, sit down here and tell me about yourself."
She sat down reluctantly, her head averted from me. How pretty she still looked, how glamorous, such a modern woman-of-the-world. How far she had advanced from the leggy teenager I had had such a fancy for.
"That's better," I said. "So what about this new job you're in?"
"Don't change the subject," she said. "You and this hired girl? What have you been doing with her?"
"Oh for God's sake, Victoria," I said. "I have been doing nothing with her. Why are you going on about that? Millie and Jane have been dreaming up stories as usual. They are always at it. It's a load of nonsense."
"If it is nonsense why have you coloured up with embarrassment?" she said. "You're as red as a beetroot."
"No I'm not," I argued. "You are just annoying me, that's all."
"So look me in the eye and tell me you haven't kissed her," she said, adjusting her position opposite me to stare me in the face.
"I haven't touched her," I lied, feeling the crimson stain on my neck deepening by the second, "and would you ever stop going on about this. It's not as if it is any of your business anyway."
"Yes it is my business. I love you dearly, cousin. I have every right to be interested in you and your love life. Who else do you have to be advising you? Your father is gone and your poor mother isn't able to see what I see, and I am only in the door a matter of a few hours."

"You have the greatest imagination," I said. "There is nothing going on. Do you take me for a fool?"
"Oh Matthew, I hope you are being truthful with me. You are far better than any servant girl. Think about her background. She is as different from you as day is from night. Don't be falling for her charms, whatever they are. I saw how you looked at her. I can read you like a book," she said.
"You are reading a story that's not there then. I am not falling for her charms, Victoria."
"But you have kissed her, haven't you? Maybe more," she said.
I just shook my head this time. She was wearing me down and I was starting to flounder in self-pity and resentment; until her next sentence.
"I don't know what you see in her anyway. She's as scrawny as an alley-cat. A pathetic wee face, brown as a nut. And all the size of her! She has the figure of a ten year old, for goodness sake. A ten year old tramp!"
Whether she meant to draw me out with this or not I do not know but I rose to the bait. Sally Anne's face and figure and honour called for gallant defence and I stood up for her. Literally!
"Now wait a minute Vic! Sally Anne may not dress like you do and she may not paint her face the way you do but she is a great girl and one of the nicest people I have ever met," I said, "She is my servant girl and I'll thank you to show her the respect she deserves when you are in my house."
I was surprised by my own shortness with Victoria but if she was, she didn't show it. She smiled and stood up herself, close to me; she put her hand on my shoulder, almost seductively I would have said if I hadn't known her better. Her bosom was very close to my chest, her perfume suddenly strong in my nostrils.
"Good for you Matthew," she smiled; there was just a hint of scorn in that smile of hers; she couldn't disguise it. "I wanted to see if you would stand up for her and you did."
"You would like her too, if you knew her the way I do," I continued. "She is kind and gentle. She gets on great with the girls... and with my mother. Joe Kearney, all the Kearneys like her. She just has a great way with her. And she can play the fiddle like nobody you've ever heard."
"I doubt it's not only the fiddle strings her fingers have been plucking at. She has worked them around your heart-strings too, do you not

think?" she said, her hand now reaching up to my neck, playing with my shirt collar.
'Oh, you are so clever with your words," I thought.
"She is not like that," I said weakly.
"Maybe she is, maybe she isn't. Defend her all you want to, Matthew, but promise me that you won't let her any closer into your affections than you have already. Think about who you are. Think about what your poor father would feel if he knew you were falling in love with a Catholic servant girl from the Free State. He would turn in his grave."
I was annoyed at this tasteless comment. I was even more annoyed at the weakness in my reaction to her. I turned away abruptly and lit a candle from the embers in the hearth.
"My father's grave? Sure we don't even know where he's buried," I said.
"I'm sorry," she said. "That was clumsy of me."
"It was all a bit clumsy, if you ask me," I said. "Goodnight, Victoria."
"Goodnight cousin," she said. "But think about it."
Think about it I did, especially when I reached the attic and gently pushed open the door between Sally Anne's room and mine. The hinge creaked but she didn't stir. I looked down at her sleeping so soundly, her hair tousled across her face and her breathing as gentle as a summer air. In the candlelight I noticed a glimmered reflection from something in her hand. She had her rosary beads twined in her fingers.
'She must have fallen asleep saying the rosary,' I thought. 'Or does she always sleep with the beads in her hands, maybe for protection from whatever might happen in the darkness? Or maybe it's just tonight that she felt she needed special protection?'
I made up my mind to ask her about that in the morning and I stooped to place a light kiss on her head, Victoria or no Victoria. Was I tempted to wake her, to take her in my arms, to lie with her and stay beside her through the night? Of-course I was. But I resisted; I left her sleeping and went to my own bed and to lie awake in a no-man's-land between the two women.

~~~~~

Come the morning, I was up at six o'clock and away out to the binder before she stirred, I was so curious and impatient to get the machine into action. There was a reporter to be coming from the local paper to
~~~~~

take a photograph of this new machine, this novelty. I wanted to keep an eye out for him.

It was going to be a beautiful autumn day. The air was clear and scented with hedges and ripe oats and wholesome farmyard smells. A couple of thrushes were warbling to each other across the breadth of the cornfield; such a beautiful song they were making. The western breeze was beginning to freshen, just enough to bend and sway the corn-stalks and to shift the thin layer of autumn mist which lay like a bridal veil in the Derg valley below.

I fed the two horses early so they would be ready for the task ahead of them. It would be their first time to pull a binder behind them but I was fairly confident that they could handle the weight of the thing and that the clattering noise it would make would not alarm them too much. Joe and Sally Anne had already helped me open the field up, ready for the machine. This had meant cutting a swathe all around the field, using the scythe in the traditional way, so that the horses could walk on the cut sward and turn the machine around at both ends without tramping over the ripened corn.

After we filled ourselves with Sally Anne's breakfast and finished the usual chores around the yard, I yoked the horses to the binder and we followed them as they pulled it from the shed, down the back lane and into the field. Three of the Kearneys showed up to help, Anthony hobbling along behind the eager Kate and Joe. Sally Anne and the twins were there already of-course and all eyes turned to watch the arrival of Victoria and Stanley, arm in arm and looking like they would have been more at home shopping in the Royal Avenue in Belfast than working in a cornfield. As Stanley strode across towards us he bent his head down against what breeze there was in a curious-looking manner.

"Why is he walking like dat?" asked Millie, a question she voiced for most of us. Jane had the answer, the impudent child that she was.

"He's trying to keep his hair in place," she said, "so it will cover the areas where it was sowed a bit thin."

"You're a case, Jane," said Anthony as we all tried to suppress our laughter at her childish wisdom.

Thankfully our giggles subsided before the loving couple approached us. We made the introductions to the Kearneys, a bit of an awkward moment for some reason. As we were doing that I saw a pony and gig arrive in the lane above. The photographer had managed to find us up here in Lismore. In no time he had us all lined up for the picture, the horses and binder in the middle with the family and workers at the sides. A strange looking five-legged beast he was, with his head under a dark sheet as he looked through the camera and shouted instructions to us. After the big group photo he said he wanted one with just me up on the binder. I had no objection to that and I clambered up onto the narrow seat for the first time and looked down, proudly I suppose, as the others watched with happy faces. Whatever way the machine jiggered and clinked as I shifted my weight up there, the horses didn't like it much and began to fidget a bit.

"Here girl," the reporter said to Sally Anne who was standing beside him. "Go and hold the horses' heads and settle them."

She did as he asked and so, when it appeared in the paper, instead of it just being a picture of me on the machine, it was a photograph of Sally Anne smiling her loveliest smile at the camera from the front of the horses and me, a small figure up on the binder away at the back. I remember looking at that picture years later, cut out of the paper, framed and set high on our mantle-piece, and thinking that most people glancing at it would have had trouble seeing past Sally Anne to me in the background. It didn't concern me that much either. She made a much better picture than me.

The tall photographer stalked his way back up the field with jerky steps as he tried to keep his shiny shoes clean.

"He walks like a hen," Millie said as she watched him go. I could see what she meant.

"So what would you like us to do, Matthew?" asked Stanley.

"Well, I suppose the first thing is just to watch," I said and I climbed up on to the seat again at the back of the binder. I took the reins in my hands and flicked them against the flanks of the horses.

"Git up there, Dobbin."

As he lurched forward and as Peggy, beside him, responded I felt very exposed and quite unsafe perched up there like a crow on a post, staring down at the workings of the machine below me. The binder was geared to work at the normal pace of two strong horses, its huge, broad wheel driving everything, the turning flails, the cutting blade, the canvas belt and the binding mechanism. Into the corn we went.

The fresh dusty smell of the falling oats rose to my nostrils and immediately stirred a memory in me of my father swinging his scythe in this very same cornfield years ago. How pleased he would be with me if he was here today. I could picture his broad shoulders, the long legs of him striding along beside the sward, his arms behind his back. I could see him glance up at me, wink and smile, pull the cornstalk from his mouth, cough in that way he did and spit on the new stubble appearing at his feet. What a shame he wasn't here to enjoy this. What a tragic war that had been, for so many men to have been mown down in their prime, a generation of them that never got to return to their people to see the results of the seeds they had sown in their own families and neighbourhoods.

I looked down nervously at this clattering contraption below me but inwardly I was thrilled at the chance to show off my new implement. The blade shuttled back and forward in its forked sheath and the stalks of corn seemed to shiver in fear of it. As they were cut, the arms of the flail pushed them backwards in a uniform direction and they fell over perfectly onto the canvas floor to be carried up into the binding section of the machine. A few clicking sounds and the first freshly-tied sheaf was fired out from the side onto the stubble, to the cheers of the following labourers. Others followed in very quick order of-course; I think that was what surprised us all. One sheaf, perfectly tied, seemed like a bit of a miracle but the real thrill was the endless stream of them, laid out in a near perfect row down the field. It was a lovely sight. I was sorry the newspaper man had taken his camera away so quick for this would have been a picture worth taking.

When we reached the bottom of the field I needed help from someone to lever up the blade so that the horses could back up and make the turn. Joe was at hand and I called on him but he was too slow to move; Sally Anne was following me closer and she beat him to the task. I was unsure about this.

"You have to take hold of that lever thing and hold it down while we get round the corner," I told her. "Maybe you should let Joe do it. It might need more strength than you have."

"I can manage it," she said, grabbing the wooden lever and wrenching it downward as if she was born to it. The blade and the canvas floor lifted smoothly.

"Good for you," I said and we exchanged smiles.

All would have been well if Victoria hadn't decided to become the Charge Hand at that point.

"Joe, go and take over there," she said. "That wee lass is going to rupture herself with that thing."

Joe moved to obey but the horses were already backing up and the binder was creaking round into position.
"I'm alright, Joe," said Sally Anne. "Leave me be. I'm not as wee a lass as I look."
So the morning continued. The binder was a great success. Farmers from all around the district stopped along the road and came down to the field to watch it operating. I was as proud as punch and I got the feeling, from the grin that stayed on her face through it all, that Sally Anne was as well. Joe resigned himself to joining the others in setting up the corn-stooks, groups of four sheaves tied together at the top and left to the weather to dry out.
I looked up at the sun. It was definitely coming close to lunchtime. We would eat together in the field as normal custom would have it. I spoke back to Sally Anne walking behind me.
"Do you think you could drag yourself away long enough to go in and bring the food out to the field?" I said. "Take the girls with you to help. Maybe Victoria too. Joe can help me till you come back. If you trust him to, that is?"
She laughed up at me. Lord but I loved that laugh, the white teeth of her shining like pearls; I loved the green light glistening joyfully in her eyes at times like this. She was just in her element, working with me in the cornfield.
"I will surely. Wait till we finish this row," she said. "But do me a favour Matthew, please?"
"What's that?"
"Keep Victoria out here in the field. I can manage better with just the twins."
"Alright," I said. I understood.
"Thanks," she said.
I looked around the field. Everyone was working, backs bent and heads down. Nobody seemed to be listening to us. I was fairly sure that the noise this binder was making was enough to muffle our conversation anyhow.
"Oh, I meant to ask you," I said. "Do you always sleep with them rosary beads tied round your fingers or were you just trying to scare me away?"
"What?" she said in mock panic. "Did you come into my room last night?"

"Of-course I did," I said. "You surely didn't expect me to sleep in the room next to you and not come in for a goodnight kiss?"
"You are lying," she said. "I would have heard you. That door makes a racket. You never did. Did you?"
"How did I know about your rosary beads if I didn't come in?" I said.
"God help me," she said, scampering along beside the binder on the stubble side, dodging the sheaves as they were fired out towards her. "You should not have done that."
"I thought you would be delighted," I said. "You even smiled in your sleep when I kissed you."
"You did not kiss me," she said, laughing but trying not to. "I would have known. Tell me you are lying? You should not be taking advantage of me like that."
"I didn't take advantage, Sally Anne. I just kissed you. And, come on now, you would have been disappointed if I hadn't."
"You are terrible. I should report you to your big Belfast cousin. She will put the brakes on you," she said. "Likely report you to the 'B' Specials or something."
She didn't know the truth of what she was saying. As we were laughing together I had one eye on Victoria as she worked on the other side of the standing corn. Now she stood up to straighten her back; she looked over at the two of us like a hawk. Aye, a hawk, beady eyes, beak, claws and all. I just hoped that the clunking of the binder and the rustle of wind in the corn had drowned out our conversation.
After a while Sally Anne returned from the kitchen with a whole spread of soda farls, buttermilk and tea. The work stopped and everybody gathered at the head of the field. I used to love those times when you could relax together, eat a bite, tell yarns and listen to others trying to better the last one. Folk would find a place to sit on the grassy dyke that ran between the two fields and rest their weary backs. Everybody except Stanley, that is. Even Victoria managed to find a clean place to rest her pretty rear end. Stanley couldn't manage to bring himself to place his proud English arse on cold Irish soil.
"I don't mind standing," he said, trying to pick some thistle barbs out of the palm of his hand.
A strange man, this Stanley. I still couldn't work out what Victoria saw in him. The fact that he was going bald, in spite of his best efforts to hide it with that flap of hair, made him seem older than he possibly was. No, it wasn't the age difference so much as the difference in his

way of going on. He was certainly coming from a very different part of the world to most people I knew. When I was talking to Anthony about a bit of fencing that was needing to be done I saw Stanley's eyes light up, until Victoria whispered to him, "Putting up a fence, he means. Not..."
"Ah," he said, with just a hint of embarrassment.
"Aye, fencing," I said.
To be fair to people, nobody really laughed at him nor took much notice of him, the way they might have done if it had been Victoria putting her foot in it like that.
During the second half of the day Joe and Sally Anne swapped roles, mainly as a result of Victoria working things to her own ends. She noticed that Sally Anne was starting to favour her damaged ankle.
"You're limping," she said. "Let Joe take over from you and come and work with me for a while."
So while Joe followed me faithfully around the stand of corn as it slowly got smaller, Sally Anne found herself setting up sheaves in harness with my clever cousin. I could only watch from a distance as Victoria nattered on at her. I was more than curious about this, worried even. Looking on, I got the feeling that Sally Anne was getting a right going over. She appeared to have her head down to the work most of the time, but a couple of times I saw Victoria standing over her, looking like she was cross at her, I would have said. Whiles Sally Anne would straighten up and stare her out, either that or she seemed to be arguing back against whatever point was being put. I wished I could rescue her from the situation but I was stuck up there on the seat of the binder and had to let the conversation take its own course.
We harvested that entire field before nightfall which was amazing; it normally would have been a two or three day affair, and with much more back-breaking work. The last few swards were left to Joe, Katie and myself as Anthony went home to tend to his cattle and Sally Anne went to the milking. Stanley, Victoria and the twins had already trudged wearily away; from my hoisted position I could tell by the droop of their bodies that they were exhausted and had had enough.
Enough labour but, in Victoria's case, not enough interference in my affairs.
She could barely wait until the supper was over to take up her regaling of me again. My mother and the twins had gone to bed. Stanley was wandering about outside having a smoke in the moonlight. I had

suggested that Sally Anne bring down her fiddle and play us a few tunes after she cleared up the kitchen. Victoria wouldn't hear tell of it.
"Not at all," she said bossily. "I am sure that girl's hands are sore after all the work she did today. We will have enough music at the dance tomorrow night. You must be tired out, Sally Anne. Away you go to your bed; Matthew and I have a lot more catching up to do, haven't we Matt?"
"Have we?" I said quietly, resigned to more of this Spanish inquisition of hers.
"We have lots more to talk about, believe me," she said.
Sally Anne looked long and hard at me, a silent longing in her eyes, but there was nothing I could say at that point. Not a thing. I was dying to ask her what Victoria had been saying to her in the field but I couldn't do that now. I wanted to ask her what she had given away about our relationship but my crafty cousin had made sure that I had not had the opportunity to be alone with Sally Anne since we left the field. I was feeling very trapped and I was already starting to feel the ground shifting under me where before I had thought myself to be on a firm footing.
Sally Anne still waited, still looked at me like a faithful collie looks at its master for his approval, for his bidding. Everything in me wanted to have the courage to take charge of matters in this my own kitchen. I wanted to say, "Sally Anne, go and bring your fiddle and play me my favourite tune; if you don't want to hear it, Victoria, you can just go to bed yourself!"
But I did not say that; of-course I didn't. Instead I diverted my eyes from her and muttered something like, "Go on to bed girl."
She shuffled towards the hall, a shadow of dejection in the tilt of her tired back.
I wanted to tell her that I was proud of her, of how she had worked so hard that day. I wanted to tell her that I had loved her enthusiasm and the joy in her as she helped me with the binder. I wanted to tell her that it had felt so good, the two of us being a team together in the harvest, with the new machine, a symbol of what the future could look like around here. I wanted to tell her that I was delighted that she was in the photograph with me and would be seen all over the countryside. I also wanted to tell her, though, that, with everybody else around, I had missed her touch, her physical closeness during the day... something that I had become used to over the last few weeks. I wanted to assure

her that I would see her later, that I would hold her, comfort her, when I came up to our attic. But I couldn't; not even in a look. Victoria was chaperoning me, watching my every gesture, censoring the smallest flicker of my eye, the least shade of a smile.

One brief backward look and Sally Anne was gone.

I was furious but it was an anger I had to wear deep below a pretence, a crust of indifference.

"You didn't have to do that to the girl," I said, the mildness of my tone in contrast to the depth of my annoyance.

"Do you think not?" she said. "Somebody has to let her know her place."

It was on the tip of my tongue to come clean about this whole matter, to say something like, "Her place is with me; her place is beside me, here in this my own house. She is more to me than you ever were."

It almost came out. The only reason I held it back was that at that moment Stanley pushed open the back door and came into the kitchen.

"Beautiful out there," he said, a shiver running over his shoulders. "Beautiful starry sky, so quiet, not a sound to be heard....apart from one owl that I heard hooting nearby. Lovely night, but getting rather nippy."

"Aye, it's nice here at this time of year," I said.

Victoria went to him and they embraced, right in front of me, far too intimately, I thought, her knee rising against the inside of his leg briefly and her foot hanging out behind her.

'Likely got that from seeing too many of them new movie things,' I thought, turning away.

"You must be tired darling," she whispered. "After all your hard work today. Why don't you just go on up to bed. Matthew and I have matters to discuss."

She had a great way of clearing a room, our Victoria.

Stanley obeyed his commanding officer with little protest.

"I'll leave you to it then, shall I?" he said. "Let me just warm my bones by the fire for a moment though. You wouldn't have a nip of whiskey, Matthew? Help me thaw out."

I obliged and poured him a half glass. We waited in silence while he sipped it, his other hand pushing the poker around in the embers to try to draw out some of the remaining heat. Eventually he straightened up, gave Victoria another lingering kiss and headed for the stairs.

The decks were cleared for this show-down that she had planned. Stanley's presence had given me time to think how I was going to handle this. I vowed in my head to resist Victoria's probings and not to be drawn into an argument. Better to play innocent and silent. Better to follow the old country wisdom, 'Whatever you say, say nothing!'

Victoria began her pitch from the gentle slopes of flattery; not flattery of me but of Sally Anne. I was a bit surprised by this tack, unnerved by it, I would say.

"So… I had a good talk with Sally Anne," she purred. "I have to tell you, Matthew... I was very impressed by her. There is a lot more to that girl than I imagined at the start. She has a nice way with her, as you tried to tell me. There's more there than meets the eye. You were right."

"I am glad," I said.

The fewer things I said, the quicker this would be over and the less bother I would have in fending off whatever it was she was going to be preaching at me, I thought.

"Yes, she is quite a girl, this maid," she continued. "Intelligent, hard-working....goodness, I don't know how she was able to keep going at such a pace today. She obviously has great strength in her, great stamina."

"She has that, I agree," I said.

"And pretty too, when you get a chance to look at her close up. Lovely eyes. Still a bit thin, I would say, but that is probably because you have been working her far too hard."

"Maybe," I said.

"So, quite a girl. For a hired hand, I mean."

She waited for a response but I did not oblige.

We just looked at each other.

I wondered what she might throw at me next.

"Matthew," she said earnestly. "That girl is in love with you."

I opened my mouth but could not decide why. So I just closed it again. Better to say nothing. I would not be drawn in to incriminating myself.

"You do know that, don't you?" she persisted. "And the thing is, it is entirely your fault."

"How is it my fault?" I said.

'Oh, you fool!' I thought immediately. 'Why did you have to say that? Say anything? You have given her a way in. Why did you have to be so defensive?'

"It is your fault and you know it," she said. "You have simply been yourself, your usual kind, generous, loving self.....like you have always been. She couldn't help falling for you. It doesn't help that you are just about the most handsome young farmer in County Tyrone, for goodness sake. That part you couldn't help, short of growing a beard or wearing a bag over your head. But you could have helped how you behaved towards her. You could have helped how you led her on."
"I haven't led anybody on," I protested.
"Have you not? Do you seriously expect me to believe that?"
"Believe what you want," I said.
"I am not blind, Matthew. I see how the two of you are together. I see how she looks at you, like you had just dropped out of heaven into her lap. You have swept her off her feet and that was cruel."
"I haven't done anything cruel to her," I said.
"No, of-course you haven't. That's the point, don't you see? She is your hired hand and, instead of being the usual harsh master, you go out of your way to make her feel the most special girl who ever came out of Donegal to work on a farm."
"I haven't made her feel special," I said.
By strange and unfortunate coincidence, this was the very moment when the faint sound of Sally Anne's fiddle descended, gentle as floating thistle-down, from the attic far above us. The tune? 'Eleanor Plunkett'.
We both paused to listen.
I was thinking, 'She is talking to me, the clever girl. She is saying, "Remember me, Matthew. I am still here, I am not going to sleep tonight. I am waiting for you, so come soon".'
I wanted to say to Victoria, "That is a tune she plays often for me of an evening; she knows I like it."
Instead I said with faked concern, "I hope she doesn't waken anybody with that thing."
"Alright," Victoria said, a smile playing behind her eyes. "Answer me this. Where did Sally Anne get that fiddle? Don't tell me she brought it with her because I already asked her that."
"So if you asked her then you will know the answer to the question."
"She wouldn't tell me," said Victoria. "All she would say was that it was given to her. She wouldn't tell me who gave it to her. But I think I know."
"Do you now?"

"I do. It was the lovely, kind, handsome, generous Matthew Henderson who couldn't resist the opportunity to impress his wee servant girl. And you say you haven't made her feel special? Can't you see how stupid that kindness was? You went and bought your maid a fiddle. What is she meant to make of that?"

"I didn't buy her a fiddle," I said without thinking where that might lead the conversation. Too late I saw my mistake.

"You didn't buy it for her? Where did you get it then?"

"That is my business."

"Oh Matthew Henderson! I do not believe you! You gave her your father's fiddle?"

"I didn't give it to her. It's just...I loaned it to her, just while she is here," I lied.

Aye, I lied and as usual it showed on my face like ringworm. I never learned how to lie without the giveaway signs.

"You are lying to me! You gave your father's fiddle to a wee servant girl that you barely know?"

"It is not a crime, Vic," I argued. "I can do what I like with my father's fiddle. It was only gathering dust and anyway, it's just while she is here."

"I can not believe you are so stupid Matthew. Will you just admit it! You are so struck on this Sally Anne that you have forgotten who you are."

"Nonsense Vic," I said lamely. "I'm not struck on her or anybody else."

"Listen to yourself, you silly fool. You cannot go on denying it. I was in that cornfield today, remember? I saw how you watch her. If you were a dog, your tongue would have been hanging out. And her? She's like a bitch in heat. The pair of you are on thin ice."

"That's not nice," I said but I felt in myself that I was wilting; I couldn't withstand this any longer. My head went down on my hands, partly from tiredness, largely from defeat.

"I am just glad we came when we did," she said. "Dear Matthew, can't you see how silly this is? Where can it lead to? You cannot seriously tell me that you want to marry this girl?"

"Who is talking about marrying anybody?" I mumbled from the cup of my hands.

"So you draw this lovely girl right into your heart, into the delusion that you and she can be together for the long haul...and then, what? You tell her to go away back to Donegal and never come back? Is that what you

plan? Because, if it is, it is not worthy of you, Matthew. You are a decent human being. It is not in you to be so cruel."
"I don't want her to go," I breathed and, as soon as I had said it, I was wondering, 'Who gave my deepest thoughts permission to sneak out into the open like that?'
"So what is the alternative?" she said.
"Why should I not just keep her on? Manys a hired hand is asked to stay on for another season," I said.
"I wouldn't know about that," she said, "but you may be right. Maybe they do. And if you ask her to stay on through the winter, and then the next year and so on....how long before her belly starts to swell and a baby arrives?"
"What?" I said, my head coming up from my hands as if I had seen a ghost in the ashes. "That is out of order, Victoria. I have not....I am not doing anything like that with her. I am not that kind of man."
"Listen, dear cousin," she said. "There is not a man alive who is not that kind of man. Don't tell yourself that you are above it. I'm not saying that you are at that point already but, given a cold evening in that wee attic up there, given the human need in both of you....believe me you and Sally Anne will come together. What's more, I couldn't blame you, Matthew. She is a nice girl. You were right about that."
"I am glad you like her at least," I said in the face of my desolation.
"A nice girl but not the girl for you. Think about who you are. You are a Henderson, your father's son. You cannot give yourself away like the way you handed over his fiddle. You are well respected in this whole community. How do you think people in your church would react to you taking up with a girl like this? A Catholic maid? She would ruin you, for all her niceness. You can do so much better."
"She is all I could ever want in a girl," I said softly.
"But you know it cannot be, don't you?" she said. "You need to stop this thing now, before.... before you know what. It just cannot be, Matthew."
Victoria stood and hugged me as I sat. Then she put her face down close to mine and, with those big wet lips of her, she kissed me on the cheek.
The thought crossed my mind that Judas Iscariot had kissed Jesus a bit like this. Mind you, our Victoria's kind of kiss felt more like a Mary Magdalene.
"I still love you, cousin," she whispered into my ear.

'My God," I thought, "where has she learned all this?"
We left each other. She went to her room behind the parlour and I climbed to the attic, candle in shaking hand, with her words echoing in my tired head.
'It cannot be! It cannot be!"
There was still a flicker of light from beyond the door into Sally Anne's room.
'Oh dear!" I thought. "She has stayed awake for me. I sort of thought she might. Is her candle lit as an invitation to me or as a protection from me? What do I do now?"
For days past, I had been imagining this moment; everything in me had been looking forward to it. Since I had watched her asleep the previous night the thought had been even stronger. All day long I had been thinking about this very situation, this very minute in time. Was this to be the night, even after all that I had just heard? Even with Victoria and all those other people asleep in the house below me? Was Sally Anne feeling the same way as me? I was sure she loved me and I believed that she still wanted me; that was what the tune had been about; that was the reason her candle was still burning through the crack of the door. Sally Anne shared the deep thought in me, I imagined, that tonight we would be together. I saw it in the longing in her eyes as we worked in the harvest field. I could read her hunger like a book. She was missing our physical closeness as much as I was. As our touches had grown more intimate in our courting of late, so the need for each other had grown stronger and stronger by the day. There hadn't been a single physical touch today, not even a brushing together of our arms, as we had kept a deliberate distance in an unspoken tryst.....for the benefit of Victoria, for the benefit of everyone watching, I suppose. The need was building up in me like a brimming lint dam, ready to burst out and flow into freedom over its sluice gate.
I had just witnessed Victoria's intimacy with her Stanley, the way she raised her knee against the inside of his thigh, the way his hand drifted down towards her side before checking himself. The sight of it had aroused me as much as it had disgusted me. Now it annoyed me to my core. So it was alright for her to be so openly like this with her Englishman, right in front of me. It was alright for him to kiss her mouth to mouth as if he was sucking the spittle out of her. But it wasn't allowed for me to be thinking similar thoughts about this girl

that I had fallen in love with, this slender, beautiful being who was wanting me, I hoped, as much as I was wanting her.
I set my candle down. I stood in the centre of the room facing her door. Slowly I took off my shirt but I stopped there. The air was very chilly under the thatch of the roof but I felt nothing other than the heat of my own virility. The floorboard creaked as I went to the door, standing ajar for me in invitation. I hesitated there. The hesitation turned into several minutes as Victoria's words echoed through my head with the beating of my pulse.
"It cannot be! It cannot be!"
'Why shouldn't it be?' I argued to the echo. 'I am a man. She is a woman. We love each other. It is how the world works. We are drawn together by circumstance, by affection, by love, by desire. We cannot back away from that. It is meant to be. It must be meant to be. Otherwise why would I have hired her in Strabane Fair? Why did I hire her, a wee weakling of a girl, when I could have hired any decent labourer? It was her eyes that drew me in. Those eyes....."
How much I wanted to push open that door and see her lovely eyes, to dive into their green waters, to spend the night looking into them with her in my arms. To look into those eyes would have brought my surrender to her, with no turning back. I knew that. The step out over the precipice. But still I stood there.
'This should be the most natural thing ever,' I was thinking. 'Why is it so hard to open this door? My darling Sally Anne; help me here. I am drowning in my own doubt."
"It cannot be! It cannot be!"
The voice! I looked behind me at the door to the staircase, almost surprised that Victoria was not standing there. It was still shut. But it wasn't the problem. This other door was.
'Why can't it be? Why can't it be?' I raged back at Victoria's spirit. 'It is my right to choose who I am and who I want to be. It is my right to choose to have this girl, no matter if she is my servant girl or not. I owe it to myself, don't I....be it right or wrong? I owe it to myself, either tonight or after Victoria has gone home. It doesn't matter that Sally Anne is my hired hand. It is my right as the man who loves her most in all the world, as the man that she loves most in all the world, as long as I am not forcing her to do something against her will. And I don't think I am doing that. If she wants me to stop short of the whole works then I will stop.'

But still I stood, the door a matter of a foot from me.
Victoria had shocked me earlier when she mentioned the point about a baby. I hadn't thought about that. I didn't really know much about whether it was inevitable or not but, for the first time, the notion scared me. If Sally Anne was to end up in the family way because of me, that would put a whole new slant on it. What would I do if that happened?
'I would marry you, of-course I would. I would do the decent thing, Catholic or no Catholic,' I told her in my head. 'No stupid religion would keep us apart. You could be my wife and people would just have to like it or lump it. It has happened before in this country and it will happen again. I don't give two hoots about your humble background.'
I said all this in my head but I knew I was lying to her in my imagination. In my eyes she could be the most wonderful girl in the world but, in the eyes of more or less everyone I could imagine around Castlederg, she would be forever 'his wee, Catholic, servant girl from Donegal!'
Victoria was right in that respect.
People would still smile at me but they would be laughing behind their smile. Laughing at my stupidity. Most of them anyhow. A few would do a lot worse than laugh. I could hear them.
'Him and his wee Donegal hoor!'
There would be plenty of folk around here who would cut me off completely, maybe worse, if I was to marry a Catholic.... and a Catholic servant girl to boot.
'But what is all this fuss about marrying,' I said to myself, in my head of-course. 'There is no question of marrying, not at this stage. Let that look after itself whenever the time comes. Tonight is not about marrying; it is about love, and I love my Sally Anne, so.....here goes! And to hell with the consequences!"
I leaned my head against the door for a moment, sort of to calm myself. I went to push it open but the fingers of my right hand seemed to have a mind of their own and simply grasped the edge of the door, extending around it into Sally Anne's side of the room.
"It cannot be! It cannot be!"
I stood in the flickering candlelight listening to the sound of the blood in my ears, but above that sound I thought I could hear faint breathing from the room beyond...Sally Anne's breathing from the other side of

the door, really close to the door. She was standing there, waiting for me.
My heart was fit to burst. She understood my hesitation. She was impatient for me. She was inviting me to come to her. She....was inviting me to come to her?
Something I didn't expect happened me at that moment.
I had another thought, a darker sense rising unbidden in me.
'Is she not being a bit too bold here, standing behind the door waiting for me when she should be in bed asleep? Am I the fly caught in her web?'
It was a sudden thought flashing like a warning light across the picture of my imagination.
"It cannot be! It cannot be!"
'She is making a big, presumptuous leap to be encouraging me like that, isn't she?' the Methodist in me began to think. 'It's the next thing to seduction.'
"It cannot be! It cannot be!"
It was my father's voice I heard. The shock of it made me jump back from the door. The pounding of my heart against my ribs and in my ears was mighty. My father's voice, as clear as a bell, speaking to me from beyond the grave, wherever he lay.
How could I be about to do this to him? What on earth would he think of me?
I looked back at the door, listening. I could not hear Sally Anne's breathing any longer. Had it even been there at all or had I imagined it, I wondered. I stood shaking in the middle of the room, my hardness disappearing by the second. There was a deep dread in me but it was all mixed up with a growing sense of relief. How close had I just come to disaster, possibly a life-changing disaster? I had an urge to open the door and tell Sally Anne about it, to apologise to her for how my lust had almost overcome me, to thank her for her understanding....but I thought better of it. She might not appreciate what I would be telling her. She might resent the implications of it and I had no wish to hurt her any further. Hurting her was what I was trying to avoid. We could talk about it some other time. Maybe I would get a chance to explain it to her tomorrow. I had no doubt that she would understand. She would appreciate me all the more for my self-control, I was sure of it.
I was shivering. I gathered up my shirt again and put it back on. I knew I wouldn't sleep if I stayed there in that room, so close to her, so close

to catastrophe, so I slipped out and went back down to the kitchen. I curled myself into my mother's chair by the cold hearth, pulled a rug over myself and eventually drifted off into sleep. If I am being honest though, I would have to admit that it was the worst night's sleep I can remember. The clickety-clacking noise of the binder was rattling about in my head all night and, no matter what I tried, I couldn't shift it. Nor could I seem to shift the thought of Sally Anne, lying up there in her nightdress, waiting for me.

The whole thing defeated and confused me until I had to get up after an hour or two and take a walk up the loanen in the moonlight.

Chapter 22

Sally Anne Sweeney

What happened at the Harvest Dance

What occurred at the ceili in Castlederg left a scar on my soul that would take half a lifetime to heal. Coming on the heels of what had happened the previous night and my confusion over it, the Harvest Dance gave me a harsh dose of reality. It left me feeling like I had woken up from a lovely dream but, instead of romance, I found myself alone on a cold rocky island, looking at the faceless ghosts of people I had thought were my friends.

When I sensed him pull away from the door on the night before I nearly went into a swoon of confusion. I did not have the words in me to describe how I felt. It was the strangest mixture of relief and wondering what had happened on the other side of that door.

According to what he told me when we were working at the corn, the previous night he had come in and looked at me when I was asleep. The very thought of him standing watching me, and me knowing nothing about it, made me quake with nervousness. Nervousness and yet a warm feeling of appreciation for him, that he could stand there watching me at my most innocent and not take any advantage of me. All he did was kiss me on the head, that is what he said and I believed him, of-course I did. If I had wakened up at the time I wonder what I would have done? Would I have clutched the blanket around myself for protection or what?

Well, that was two nights ago. I had thought about it all day in the cornfield. Even when that Belfast accent was buzzing in my ears like a nest of wasps I was thinking about it. How that woman grilled me! All that day as we worked I was thinking about what might happen later. I was determined that I would not be asleep this time. Victoria could talk to him into the wee, small hours to delay him but she would not see me off. It didn't take much imagination to be knowing that she was going to be warning him to steer clear of me. Her whole attitude to me put such a temper on me. It was plain that she looked down her nose at everything about me, my accent, my religion, how I looked, where I came from....everything!

But I would wait for him. I would talk sense to him and console him when she had done her worst.

And wait for him I did. Mind you, I was more than tempted to sneak back down to the hall and listen to whatever venom she was trying to sting him with. I even went down the ladder to the head of the stairs and tried to listen on the top step. All I heard was the drone of her. The creaking of the second step put me off and I just went back up, took out the fiddle and played him his tune. I even left the door open so that he could not miss it. A bit of a risk but the twins sleep very soundly, just like their mother. It never struck me to be in a worry about disturbing the Stanley fellow.

So what had happened to Matthew that night?

I had missed him during the day, even though I had been working with him, talking to him. I had missed having him to myself and I wanted to tell him that.

I had heard him come in. I heard the rush of him, undressing I imagined; the rustle of his clothes above the fuss that my heart was making, thumping, thumping and nearly coming out through my chest. It was a mixture of nervous excitement and fear.

'Don't dare come in to me like that,' I was thinking. What on earth would he look like if he came in wearing next to nothing? I hoped to God he would never be so bold. What would I do if he did? It brought me up off the bed where I had been sitting, still fully dressed. I was not going to be taking anything off me, just in case. It was chilly enough anyhow.

I was desperate to say to him, "Forget about your precious Victoria; forget about what she has been saying to you; don't be poisoned by her advice; remember how happy we have been with each other for the last while."

But I hesitated; it would have meant going in to him and he changed out of his work clothes and maybe standing there half-naked. That could have been dangerous and he might have misunderstood me. I stood behind the door, waiting and listening to his heavy breathing. There was something about it that started to fill me with dread, something of an animal, a bull or a ram, and I became suddenly worried. What if he was in some kind of temper, some driven state of mind, maybe determined to have his way with me whether I liked it or not? Would he force himself on me? I didn't think he would but I had never heard him like this before. I could imagine his face, red and wild and determined. I saw his fingers grip the side of the door and instinctively I stood with my back against it, ready to try to block him coming in to me. At the same time I was thinking how much I wanted to hold him and gentle him into peacefulness again. He needed soothing and all my instincts were to do just that for him, to calm him down and let him know he was loved and it would be alright when Victoria left. Fear fought with love in my deepest heart. I have never experienced such a swirl of opposite emotions and urges all at the same time, all pushing and pulling me in different directions.

Then....nothing.

Nothing happened.

The door was still ajar, despite me leaning against it.

Everything was as silent as the grave, except for the rhythm of his breathing and my heart beating in my ears.

My back against the door, I thought I could feel it move a fraction towards me.

'He is coming,' I thought with a sudden leap of the heart.

I could sense myself flush here and there; I am sure my face was the colour of a sunset. But he still did not come in to me. Out of the corner of my eye, I studied his fingers gripping the door above, white-knuckled and tense. There was something about them that told me Matthew was struggling, just a twitch of uncertainty.

Every bone in my body wanted to help him, to comfort him in whatever turmoil he was going through, to tell him it would be alright. Even if I knew in my heart of hearts that it might not be. But I could not give in to that temptation; I dared not open the door to him. All I had ever been taught as a child rose up in me, my father's warnings especially, and I fought down those other instincts, holding tightly to my stomach with both hands and saying the Rosary silently in my head. Suddenly the gentle pressure of him from the other side of the door seemed to relax. I looked up at where his hand had been pushing and it had disappeared.

'What?' I wondered. 'What happened there? Is he just playing some sort of joke on me?'

I waited, standing very still, watching for him. Maybe he would try again when he had picked up the courage. I waited and I listened. He was doing something with his clothes again I thought. What was he doing? What was his game? Then I heard the outer door creak on its hinges and the sound of his footsteps going down the ladder at a serious rate. I was confused, greatly relieved but disappointed in him all at the same time.

'Good; maybe he is away to the toilet,' I thought. 'That has to be it. Either that or his conscience has been undermined by Miss Victoria, the Belfast protector of his mortal soul.'

I hoped it was not that. I hoped it was the other explanation.

I sat on the side of my bed, wondering if he would return.

He was taking a long time, wherever he had gone.

'Maybe some wee problem has come over him after the meal,' I thought and the more I considered it, the more I thought that that had to be the explanation. His nerves had got the better of him. A wee bout of diarrhoea or sickness or something like that had taken him.

The tension gradually drained out of me as I lay there; the ache in me eased and the dread of what might have been melted away. I did my best to stay awake and listen but the next thing I heard was the birds singing for themselves outside, my daily alarm clock, and I woke to find the candle burned to a stump.

I remembered. He would be still asleep in the bed next door. I would go to him and wake him. It was my turn this time.

I glanced through to the box room and the sun shining in through the small skylight half-blinded me. But he was not there. The bed had not been slept in.

'Where has he gone?' I wondered.

I found him asleep on the big chair in the kitchen.

"What are you doing, sleeping down here Matthew?" I said. "Are you not feeling well or something?"

"Something like that," he muttered grumpily. He lifted himself stiffly out of the chair and went outside to the water pump.

I looked at him closely when he came back in. Something was different about him. He could not meet my eye. I was dying to ask him about last night but the subject felt more awkward between us than anything I had ever experienced with him, and there had been many. He had little to say and, when he did speak, it sounded very strained. It was also a disappointing instruction he gave me.

"When I am over at Kearney's today you would need to be cleaning out those sheds and putting in new bedding. And do a bit of baking for these folk for tomorrow," he said. "You will not have time later with the ceili tonight. That is if you still think you should come?"

There were a couple of things in what he had said that confused me. Of-course I was going to be going to the ceili. He knew that. We had talked about it often enough. He himself had asked me to bring the fiddle and play with Tam Glenn and whoever else showed up to play. Why would he now be doubting that I wanted to go? It left me in a muddle of quietness for a minute.

"Do you not want me to go over with you to Kearney's to help with the binder?" I asked. "I thought you said..."

"It doesn't matter what I said," he said. "You need to be here today. Victoria and Stanley will be about. I can manage with Anthony and all the wains. We'll not need you. It's only a wee field."

"Alright," I said tamely.

Bafflement rose in me like the tide. What had I done wrong yesterday, on that glorious day of working so well together with *mo bhuchaill* to have him brush me off so coldly today?

"And the ceili?" I said. "What did you mean, 'If I still think I should come'? Of-course I am coming. My friend Ailish is coming from Newtownstewart; Joe is going over for her."

"Alright," he said. "Suit yourself."

"And you will be there, Matthew," I said. "I have been so looking forward to it; for weeks I have been looking forward to it, to dancing with you and...."

"Whisht!" he said softly, still without looking at me.

He walked quickly to the back door. Then he turned and looked back at me. There was an ocean of hurt and regret in his eyes. I could have sworn he was close to tears, so intense was that look. He just stood for a bit, his fingers working at his eyebrows as if he had a headache. So helpless he looked, so defeated. I moved towards him. He held his hand up against me in a gesture that said 'Stop, just stay there!'

"Don't," he said. It sounded more like a gasp than an order.

"What's wrong, Matthew?"

He dropped his eyes to the floor as he stood there. Such a strange sadness grew in his kitchen at that moment; I felt I could reach out and touch it, strong as a remembered grief.

"Nothing, Sally Anne; it's just....I can't....I don't see..."

With that sigh, he turned on his heel and fled from me like I had the plague.

I was completely floored by this. Something had altered him in his attitude to me over the past few hours. How was I going to handle this? Handling his advances was one thing but handling this fickleness in him was another. With Matthew I never knew the way the wind would be blowing but it had changed from yesterday.

As I worked through my tiredness and low spirits during the course of that day, I made up my mind not to panic. I would see him through this... this swinging back and forward in him. I would see the back of this Victoria and her hold over him. She would be gone soon. I would not give him up. I would not be brushed off so easily. Over these past few months I had put so much of myself into surviving his shifting moods and his strange attitudes. Above all, I felt such a deep love for him that I believed for the best in him, the best for both of us, both of us together.

'Tonight at the ceili,' I thought, 'when he sees me in this dress it will all be alright again.'

I did my chores outside with little else in my thoughts. I came back inside and baked several wheaten farls for Sunday's meal. I prepared everything for the evening meal and for cooking the next day. When I felt I was on top of everything I ran upstairs to my room and held up the dress that I had been making for the past few weeks. It was the colour of a field of ripe corn, and lovely and light of itself. Mrs Henderson had told me that it was 'calico'. She had rubbed it affectionately between her thumb and fingers.

"Aye surely, daughter," she had said to me when I asked her about it. "You can make yourself something out of it surely."

I was not sure if she really was mixing me up with one of the girls or if that was just her way of talking but I appreciated her generosity anyway. It was great material, the like of which I had never seen in Donegal, let alone get my hands on to fashion a garment from. I loved the flowery pattern that was woven into it. It went so well with the red *geansaí I* had been knitting to wear over it when I was lying upstairs with the bad ankle. Now I took the dress downstairs to put the finishing touches to the stitching and run the warm iron over it to take the creases out of it. I hung it on the door back up in my room and went to the bathroom to give myself the first good wash in weeks. Feeling much fresher when I came down again, I have to confess that I was suddenly overcome by the temptation to sneak into the guest bedroom to see if I could find some of Victoria's grand perfume. Find

it I did but, just as I was about to dab some of it on my neck, I had the wisdom to realise that it would not be Matthew alone who would smell it. Victoria would too, not to mention Stanley; I would have given myself away and established myself in her eyes as a thief. Matthew would have to love me smelling the way I always did or not at all. I would be fine; he had not objected to anything about me so far. I did not need to be using any help that had been purchased in a Belfast shop, I thought.
The four of us travelled together in Matthew's trap. He had the reins, of-course, and he seemed very intent on the road, his concentrated gaze diverted there for almost the entire journey. Only at one point did he engage with me and then only to look at my new dress. I tried to catch his eye. I wanted to say, "Do you like it, Matthew?" But Victoria was filling up all the conversation space with pointless little observations about this and that. Stanley answered her at times and, to be fair to him, he was the only one to make any reference to my dress. He took the material between his fingers and praised my choice.
"Very nice material, Sally Anne," he said. "Did you make this all by yourself?"
"That I did," I smiled.
"Where did you get the cloth though?" asked Victoria, her tone suspicious. "I'm sure a girl like you can't afford material like this? It's not another gift from Matthew I hope, is it?"
I did not like that comment, not one bit. I looked away from her, *bitseach* that she was.
"My mother gave it to her," Matthew said in a strangely tense voice that had a tinge of annoyance in it. "She told Sally Anne she could use it to make a dress for tonight."
'Thank you, *mo ghrá,'* I thought.
"Ah, I see," said Victoria. "What is this hall where the dance is being held tonight?"
"The Temperance Hall," answered Matthew. Then he caught my eye, only for a second; a lovely wee Matthew kind of smile, short and sweet and then he spoke very quietly.
"You did a good job with it. It suits you well."
This was music to my ears; it and the smile warmed me inside again; it gave me hope that his coolness had been yet another passing phase; it brought me encouragement for the night ahead.

I carried my fiddle shyly as we entered the hall. The first thing to strike me was the brightness in there. This was the first time in my life I had ever set foot in a place which was lit by this new electric lighting. Electricity had come to Castlederg just eighteen months before, according to Matthew, and a great thing it was. I could see every corner of the hall so clearly you would have thought they had taken the roof off and let in daylight.

I saw that many people had already gathered there. Most looked to be farming types. You could tell by the roughness of their hands, the ruddiness of their faces and the general shape of the clothes they wore. On the other hand, there were many from the town, their outfits a good deal brighter and of a tidier cut, their hair more neatly styled. I met John Sproule nearly as soon as I set foot in the place. He gave me a very funny look, a mixture of curiosity and scorn, I thought. I stepped around his stare and made my way through the crowd. Amidst them all though, the untidy figure of Tam Glenn stood out as one of a kind. He approached me warmly and gave me an unexpected hug. He did not smell any different to his usual smell, and why would he?

"Come on up here to the stage," he said, "and meet the other musicians."

So I followed him. There were three others already on the platform, tuning up; Jim, a banjo player, Rose, who had a battered set of uilleann pipes and a huge man called Pat who seemed to be far too big for his puny wee side drum and cymbal. Tam introduced me to them like I was God's gift to dance music.

"Go easy, Tam," I said. "After that chat I can hardly wait to hear myself play."

Sitting up there, a few feet above the dance floor, I had a grand opportunity to observe everyone and everything that was going on. I was able to see the cliques forming, the men and boys clinging around the walls like ivy while the girls were preening themselves in the middle of the floor, doing their best to attract attention. Flowers and bees, I thought. There was still no sign of Joe and Ailish. I hoped he had been able to find that farm that she worked at and, more importantly, had not run in to any objections from farmer Spence.

Matthew was in my sights most of all. He stood out from the crowd, partly due to his height but mostly because he obviously had big pulling power with all the local girls. His natural shyness served him well though and he seemed to be able to bounce most of the lassies off of

him fairly quickly. All except one. It did not take me long to notice that same girl who had been beside him at the fair several weeks back, the one with the head of dark hair who looked far too young to be making a play for Matthew.
"I hope you don't be wanting me to play all night," I said to Tam.
He laughed. "Not on your life," he said. "Something tells me you'll be after a bit of a dance with a certain young gentleman. It would never do to deny you that, would it now?"
I smiled and I noticed that I was well past the stage of being embarrassed about it.
The Master of Ceremonies shouted for attention and launched the first dance. Couples lined up for the 'Waves of Tory' and we played a selection of barn-dance tunes, all of which I was able to make a reasonable job of. Matthew, I noticed, danced with Joe's wee sister, Kate; he danced well too, from what I saw of him, not that there was much to this warm-up of a dance. Half-way through I was pleased to see Joe arrive; he had Ailish with him and I watched the two of them team up together and join the line.
'A nice pair they would make,' I found myself thinking as I waved down at them. At the same time, I could not help noticing that Ailish looked very bedraggled and tired. Her skin was weather-beaten to a rough brown colour and the dress she had on her looked as if it had not seen a decent wash since she left Donegal months ago. She could have been so much prettier if she had made the effort but she just looked a bit saddened and flat of herself. It made me feel all the more glad of the decent treatment I had received at Henderson's place, all the more so when I saw some of the looks that the local town girls were directing at Ailish. She stood out from the crowd like a shabby rag doll in a shop-window display of brand-new Crolly dolls.
Between a couple of the dances the MC suggested that folks take a rest and that the band would play a tune. Tam looked at me and winked.
"Away you go, girl," he said. "Give Eleanor a birl there."
"You too," I begged and he joined in. As we played I scanned the dance floor for Matthew, to see if I could catch his eye and get a smile from him as I played his tune, our tune, on this fiddle, his gift to me. The neck of the violin lay snug and smooth in the hollow of my left hand. My chin rested on its brown-stained body and I looked down along the strings as they vibrated under the teasing of the bow. His father's fiddle felt so natural in my hands, so lovely and so alive, in a

way that made it seem to me to be a symbol of our mutual but secret love. But he himself was nowhere to be seen, no matter where I looked. I had not seen him leave. I was disappointed that he hadn't heard this our tune, hurt even. I finished the air and stood up.
"I will be back for more in a bit," I told Tam. "I need to go and speak to my friend Ailish."
"Aye," he said. "Of-course you do. And then go and find that man of yours and dance the legs off him."
"Tam!" I said. "He is not my man."
Whether he was or not, I could not find him. I met Ailish and Joe and we chatted. He was still looking after her well. But when the MC called the next dance my eyes were still searching. Joe took me by the arm. He had noticed the forlornness hiding behind my pleasure at seeing Ailish.
"Come on; you promised me a dance," he said. "What's the matter with you anyway?"
"Nothing," I said. "I was just looking for Matthew."
"No idea where he is but are you dancing or not?"
"We will be back in a minute," I said to Ailish. "If I survive this."
We danced and I could not help smiling at Joe's odd way of moving. He had the rhythm of a heather bush flapping about in the wind. I counted three times that he stepped on my feet during that one dance. Normally I would have found it funny and would have laughed at him but this night, given the state of my agitation over Matthew and the soreness in my ankle, it simply hurt me more. The third time it happened I nearly kicked him back on the shins.
Towards the end of the set I caught a glimpse of Matthew arriving back in the hall. I was so curious that it was all I could do to stop myself breaking off from Joe to ask him where he had been. As it happened, it looked to me that I would soon get my chance with him.
"This next dance is a waltz and it's 'Lady's Choice," shouted the MC above the clamour. "Girls, go and find your man."
'Great,' I thought and I went hobbling straight across the hall towards Matthew.
But I was not quick enough. That young girl with the dark hair had him first. Had him by the hand too and was dragging him, against his better judgement, I thought, towards the centre of the dance floor. I cursed my slowness off the mark. I cursed the fact that I had been standing so

far away from him across the hall when the waltz was announced. I watched the two of them dance and cursed the closeness of her to him. 'Has nobody ever told her not to be rubbing that brazen bosom of hers up against a fellow; after him having the decency not to turn her down when she asked for a dance? Far too pushy altogether, that one,' I thought.

Joe was back dancing with Ailish. Stanley was showing off his superior moves to all who wanted to watch as he danced with Victoria. I was left observing, like a drooping wall-flower. Still, I would wait my turn.

I saw a group of young men arrive in the hall. They stood staring around at everyone. They looked like country fellows. There was something about their attitude and how they sneered at the couples dancing and the onlookers like myself that I did not like. I moved away from them and stood close to the stage.

'Surely with the help of God I will get another chance to dance with Matthew before the night is out,' I thought. 'Maybe he will ask me for the next dance?'

When the time came, though, he bypassed me yet again, asking Victoria instead. I was getting more and more annoyed and disappointed. It did not really help that her Englishman made a big show of inviting me out to the floor and partnering me for 'The Siege of Ennis'.

"You will have to talk me through the various steps and turns," he said loudly as we began to circle past the gang of young fellows that I was wary of. "I'm afraid I will be completely at sea here. This would not be my forte at all, you know. 'The Gay Gordons' is about my limit, bless them."

That fine accent of his, along with the cut of his clothes, his whole bearing, made him stand out from the crowd in Castlederg that night. A few dirty looks followed us around the room. I was very aware of them but Stanley did not seem to notice. As far as the dance was concerned, he learned quickly though, and my feet suffered no more damage. When it was over we moved towards Victoria and Matthew but, while she came into Stanley's arms for a warm embrace, Matthew's eyes would not meet mine for any longer than a second. I stood in front of him, my gaze up to the stubborn jut of his jaw. Looking over my head, he scanned the four corners of the hall.

"What is it, Matthew?" I asked.

"Nothing," he said. "I'm just keeping an eye on those rascals."

That was the height of his conversation with me. He was so edgy, in the middle of yet another of these episodes of awkwardness.
"Now, an old favourite," came the voice of the announcer. "Form up in two big, wide circles for 'The Farmer wants a Wife."
My eyes flicked up and met Matthew's but, whereas there was a tiny smile forcing its way around the corners of my mouth, there was some sort of a dark shadow of gloominess about him.
We joined a circle of laughing faces. Matthew found himself pushed into the middle, 'volunteered', against his will to act as the first farmer for this old country game. The music started and we danced around him, all of us holding hands and singing.

'The farmer wants a wife,
The farmer wants a wife,
Hey ho my deario,
The farmer wants a wife.'

Matthew made his choice of 'wife'... and it was not me. He played safe again, pulling Kate Kearney into the centre of the spinning ring of dancers. A ripple of disappointment went through me but I could understand what he was doing. Everybody watching him would know that Kate Kearney would never be in the running to be Matthew Henderson's wife. As the dance progressed I found myself side-skipping in time to the music but singing inside myself,

'And the maid wants her man,
The maid wants her man,
Hey ho my deario,
The maid wants her man."

Can you turn such a frivolous rhyme into a prayer? If so, I think the words of that silly verse became something of a novena to me as I tripped around in that monotonous circle. I wanted Matthew's attention. I needed his touch again, a smile of reassurance, a little glimmer of love kindling behind his eyes. I longed for a sign of his ownership of me, some expression, however insignificant to others watching, of his affection for me. I was finding this distance just too hard to bear and the frustration was building up in me.

There was some sort of a ruckus rising up at the back of the hall. The dancers were becoming distracted. The band was faltering and the tune broke up into chaos. The Master of Ceremonies held up his hands and shouted for calm. We all looked around to see what was causing this interruption.

Standing tall against the wall was the figure of Stanley, his hair askew on his head and a determined look on his face. He had a chair in his hands and he was using it as a defence against a number of attackers, waving it about from side to side to block their advance. It did not take me long to realise that this was the group of youths that had arrived together earlier, about six of them. I had no idea what had started the row but it was not hard to guess. Stanley's English accent had attracted their attention. Insults were still being shouted at him as he prodded off their attacks.

"English bastard!"

"What are you doing over here anyhow? Go back home or you'll be sent back in a box!"

"Are you a soldier, are you? Or a peeler?"

"Likely a Black and Tan!"

Matthew went straight to his aid, as did several of the local fellows who had been dancing with us.

Arms grappled with the attackers from behind. Fists were swung in retaliation. Matthew took a kick from one of them in a painful part of his person and came lurching back out of the affray holding himself. I went to him of-course.

"Leave me be," he said but I stayed with him and stroked his hair as he groaned and knelt down on his hunkers. Nobody was paying any attention to us anyhow. I might as well have been his mammy there, trying to console him. "I'm alright Sally Anne; go on back up to Tam."

I was not for going anywhere. I watched as the gang of fellows was slowly brought under control. Some of them had their arms twisted up behind their backs by the stronger farmers. One was pinned to the wall by Stanley's chair, captured between its legs. He was fit to be tied with rage and humiliation.

"You British bastard you. I'll swing for you, so I will. Just you wait!"

"Why wait?" said Stanley grabbing him by the throat in what looked like a very expert and aggressive manner, I thought. "Why wait when you can swing now?"

I swear I thought he was going to choke him. Victoria was trying to pull him off from behind. The fellow was spluttering, his tongue sticking out and his face turning forty shades of purple above his black beard.

"Leave him, Stanley; please stop!" she shouted in his ear.

Stanley stopped and the poor fellow fell to the floor, gasping for breath on his hands and knees. He could not speak a word, not for ages. Stanley stood over him, sort of to underline his victory, I thought. The fellow eventually crawled towards the door, a pathetic looking sight, with everybody staring at him. He reached the exit and grabbed the door-jam to help pull himself to his feet. He looked around for his friends but they had all been thrown out into the night. He was the last of them and he was a sorry sight. He tried to speak but what came out was just a scrape of a sound, like a hen having its neck pulled.

"You'll live to regret this night," he said to Stanley and then he looked around the whole group. "All of yous!"

"Bugger off, you rebel dog," said Stanley with an ugly grin on him.

'God but he is an arrogant man,' I thought to myself. 'He nearly killed that chap and he is not in the least bit sorry.'

The Master of Ceremonies took over again.

"Right, come on everybody," he called. "The fun's over and there's still a lock of dancing to be done. Will ye all take your partners for 'The Flyin' Scotsman'. Strike up the music there, Tam."

"I take it you don't want to dance?" I said to Matthew.

"You take it right," he said.

"Are you still very sore?"

"Just what you would know," he groaned. "Away and play your fiddle."

"Did you hear me playing your tune?"

"Aye, I heard it. Now go on with you," he said still bent over, holding himself.

I was not sure how to take this. Did he want rid of me because he was hurt in that embarrassing place? Was I annoying him by my desire to look after him or did he seriously want me to be playing the fiddle? I could not make sense of him that night. Anyhow, I took his advice and headed back to the stage. On my way I passed the MC. On a whim I said to him, "Will there be another 'Lady's Choice' later on?"

"Why?" he said.

"Just wondering," I said.

"I can call one if you like."

"Would you?" I said.
"Alright," he said with a grin, "so long as you choose me."
I played a few more tunes. The dance was in full swing and the fight had passed into history. The atmosphere was great and people were enjoying themselves. After a while I saw Matthew get to his feet and join in one of the dances with some wee red-haired girl.
'Good,' I thought. 'He is back on his feet. He will hardly refuse me this next dance, when the time comes.'
I was ready this time. The MC gave me a considerate early wink. I put the fiddle down and made my way towards Matthew.
"Now, young friends, we have a request for another 'Lady's Choice' from our young fiddle player here. I thought she was maybe going to choose me but she has just walked past me with her head in the air, so let's see who she is for choosing."
'Oh mother,' I thought. I was more than affronted. Every eye in the place seemed to be on me. This was not fair. It was not what I had intended, in fact every instinct in me cried out against it. And, if that was true for me, how much more was it going to be true for Matthew? I felt badly let down by the MC's silly attempt to be funny. I felt the stares of everyone in that hall as if they were knives going through me. There was a strange calming in people's chat, followed by an 'ooohhh' of sound from the dancers, a sort of put-on curiosity as they watched me to see who I would choose. I wanted to run a mile from that place but I was stuck.... stuck between my own scheming, my desire to have Matthew acknowledge me as his girl and the knowledge that this was such a make or break moment in the course of our relationship.
"Go on girl," said the MC. "Who is this man of your dreams that you want to dance with?"
A few other voices rose from the crowd.
"Go on girl!"
"Let's have you!"
"Don't be shy!"
"Pick me! I'll dance with you! I'm blind anyway," called one joker.
I stood frozen to the spot, all those eyes boring into me, as if to read my mind. And my mind was not going to be easy to read.
'I have put myself in this stupid position,' I thought. 'I can't back down now. I have to go for it. If I pick somebody else, to spare his blushes he might misunderstand. If I pick Joe, just to get myself out of this mess, his jealousy might take over again and make him mad at me. I

have to go through with it. Anyhow, he loves me. I know he loves me. So he will not be angry with me. He will take it all in good heart, so he will.'

Slowly I moved towards Matthew. I saw Joe out of the corner of my eye and I swear he was stroking down his hair, sticking his head forward so I would notice him. I went past him. The noise of the crowd's roar of anticipation grew in my ears, fighting with the thudding sound of my own heart. I arrived in front of Matthew. Suddenly there was silence.

I looked up at him. There was an expression of dread in his eyes that I had never seen before.

'Don't, Sally Anne,' it begged.

But I had come too far.

"Will you dance this dance with me?"

He looked away to the back door of the hall, as if trying to decide whether or not to make a run for it. He did not say anything.

"Please," I whispered.

"No Sally Anne," he said quietly, through his teeth.

Cousin Victoria came to his rescue, pushing through the crowd towards the pair of us.

"Matthew promised me this dance," she said, sounding more haughty than ever and moving smartly in between us.

I stepped back.

"I am sorry," I said. "I didn't know."

"Ah go on, Matthew," called a few voices from the crowd. "Go on! Dance with the girl!"

"Dance with your wee hired hand!" called another.

'Why don't they leave him alone?' I thought in a panic. 'This is not fair. They're all going at him here like a pack of dogs and he is going to blame me for it.'

"Go on Matt! Sure you do more than dance with her every night, up there in Lismore," somebody laughed.

"Give her a birl, Matt," said John Sproule, really enjoying this moment of my disgrace. "Spin the Papish outa her!"

He was not a nice fellow that.

The onlookers were laughing now, pushing forward to stare, as if this was some grand drama they were being privileged to witness. There was nothing I could do now to help the situation, to save my Matthew from these fools.

He stepped forward from the wall, pushing Victoria to the side. There was a look on his face as he glared down at me that I had not seen before.

"Leave me alone," he said through his teeth.

"I am sorry for whatever I have done wrong," I said. "I only asked you for a dance."

"Leave me be and mind your place."

His words went through me like a cold wind.

"You're forgetting who you are," he said and with that he stormed away from me and marched out of the Temperance Hall.

I have no idea what happened after that. For a while I just stood there. I must have looked like a marble statue of Our Lady at the Cross. At that moment my heart felt as if someone had cut it down the middle with a kitchen gully knife. My world collapsed in on itself in a sudden realisation that I had been living in a false dream for the past few months. I felt nothing but the deepest sorrow.

The big tears started to escape my eyes and trickle down my cheeks. I had no more control over them than I had over the rain that fell from the clouds.

'Mind my place,' he had said. The pain of it.

People were still looking at me; I knew that by the strange silence, a silence of sympathy and disappointment, I thought. It was of no consolation to me. I did not know what to do. I just stood there as I had when he had fled from me. I could not move a leg muscle to go anywhere, it seemed. If I had had that fiddle in my hand I would have played the most mournful lament I have ever played, either that or broken the damned thing in half over my knee.

The Master of Ceremonies spoke again. "Sorry about all that," he said. "These things happen. All is not fair in love and war. But we still have a few dances to do....so ladies, take your partners then for a two-step. Strike up the band there."

Sproule's face appeared through the blur of heads and bodies around me.

"Serves ye right, ye stupid wee bitch," he sneered. "You have a right cheek on you!"

Suddenly the words were a distant echoing noise and the whole place seemed to go spinning around me. I felt myself falling but it was as if it was happening to somebody else, not me.

The next thing I knew was Tinker Tam speaking down to me and Joe Kearney by my side, stroking my face.
"Sally Anne, talk to us. Are you alright girl?"
Tam's Antrim accent made its way into my fuzzy consciousness and I saw his concerned eyes looking down at me.
"That was a terrible thing happened to you," he said.
"You just fainted, that's all," said Joe. "You're alright now."
Ailish was offering me a drink. I sipped it and sat up.
"God help me," I said to them, "I have made a complete fool of myself."
"Not at all," said Tam. "Anybody can faint."
"That is not what I meant," I said.
"I know what you mean," said Joe, anger in his voice. "It's not you is the fool. It's bloody Matthew Henderson. I thought he had more in him than to treat you like that."
"He only did it because I disgraced him," I said.
"How did you disgrace him?" said Joe. "You only asked him for a dance. He should have been delighted."
"You would have been, Joe, wouldn't you?" said Ailish and smiled at the comical face that Joe pulled at her.
"We are taking you home with us," said Joe. "I am not allowing you to go home with that bastard."
"Don't call him that, Joe," I said. "He is your friend."
"He was," said Joe. "Not after tonight. He had no right to insult you the way he did tonight. And in front of all those people."
"But how can you take me home?" I asked. "Are you not taking Ailish back to her place?"
"I am," he said. "And I'm taking Tam too, and our Kate. There's room for five of us in the trap. It's a nice night."
So that is how I got home to Henderson's, in the middle of the morning. It was a beautiful night to be travelling along the wee lanes of west Tyrone with the stars blinking up above us and the smells rising from the verges beside us, but it was cold. I huddled down on the floor of the trap, between Joe and Kate for heat. It was not how I had imagined the evening ending and, when I thought about that, the tears flowed silently again, unnoticed by my fellow-travellers.
"Will I come round for you in the morning for Mass as usual?" asked Joe when he was dropping me off at the end of Henderson's lane. "Maybe you'll be too tired to be going."

"No, please come for me," I answered. "I will not be any more tired than you."
"Fair enough," he said. "We will go for a dander up the mountain in the afternoon as well, if you like?"
"Great," I said. "It will get me away from Victoria for a while."
"That's a deal then," he said.
We said our 'Goodnights' and I walked slowly along the lane, fiddle under my arm like a bad conscience. It was all I could do to restrain myself from throwing it over the hedge. I staggered along, exhausted and feeling as flat as a pancake.
I went into my own language to curse my foolishness for I could not put words on it in the English.
I wondered if Matthew would have waited up for me.
I need not have bothered.

Chapter 23

Matthew Henderson

How things developed

It was a desperate business, that night of the ceili. There's no doubt about that. On the one hand I felt bad that I had affronted Sally Anne. It nearly broke my heart to have done it to her. It must have seemed so cruel to her; I suppose I had to be cruel to be kind. If I am honest with myself, I had known all along, in my heart of hearts, that it might bring some disaster like this. All the same, it was just a pity that it all had to be so public....but then that wasn't my fault. It was her that painted me into a corner. I know she did not mean to but she had made a laughing stock of me in front of everybody, all my friends, all those folk from the town who see me sitting in church Sabbath after Sabbath, the good wee Methodist Christian: Alice Porter especially. What would Alice have thought of me, dancing with a servant girl from Donegal, my arms round her and her holding me close the way she would have been doing? Folk would have been putting two and two together and guessing that we were a couple.

Victoria, my old friend; I wish she had stayed in Belfast, to be honest. She had turned my head on me, with her smiles and touches and clever words. What made her think it was within her rights and duties to be trying to sway me against Sally Anne? It was her that put me in the wrong frame of mind for the ceili. If she had not been there, with her eye on me all the time, her pulling and prodding, maybe I could have danced with Sally Anne and it might have passed off unnoticed. And if I hadn't had such pain down below after thon kick, maybe I wouldn't have been in such bad twist, maybe I would have even enjoyed the dancing with her, even with everybody looking and laughing at me.

Mind you, all that logic didn't help me to sleep that night. I couldn't face another night on that chair in the kitchen so I went up to the attic again, thinking I would sleep better there.

But of-course I lay awake, tortured by the memories of what had happened. It was a mixture of my anger and regret and resentment.... against her, and against Victoria, against the circumstances of the night...and yet, from another part of me came the deep, deep longing to hold my girl again, to look into her eyes and find some understanding there, some forgiveness. Could we not just have been friends, lovers even, as long as it was in secret? Could we not just have had an understanding between the two of us? Victoria would be gone tomorrow; how was I going to cope with the tangle of my feelings, with this attraction, this desire for Sally Anne which had become my constant master?

In my fury when I left the dance, I had gone straight to the pony and trap and made ready to leave. I could hardly wait to be out of Castlederg. Apart from anything else I was still suffering, walking like some old fellow with gout. Victoria and Stanley followed me of-course, speaking reassuring words, supporting 'the firm stand I had taken'. I barely waited for them to sit down before I had that pony gathering pace to a full gallop.

I was a good half mile up the road when it suddenly came into my head that Sally Anne would be waiting on me to bring her home; that is how far past myself I was. I pulled the pony to a stop at a lane-end.

"What are you doing now?" Victoria said.

"I forgot Sally Anne," I said. "I need to go back for her. She'll have no way home."

"She will have plenty of ways home, the same girl," said Victoria. "Joe Kearney for one. He'll be dying for the chance."

I thought about this as I got down from the trap to back the pony into the lane. "Naw, I should get her," I said. "She would be expecting me to...."

"You will do no such thing, Matthew. That girl has you twisted round her wee finger, so she has. Let her be, for once; let her think about tonight; let her think about what she did to you. It will not do her any harm."

I hesitated. I was still feeling the shame of the night.

"What will those friends think of you if they see you arriving back in the Diamond to look for your maid? 'Ho, Ho! Good old Matthew has had second thoughts, has he? He's come back for his wee Donegal woman!'" she taunted. "Joe will bring her home."

I got back into the trap and drove on up the hill.

"You're doing the right thing, Matthew. I am proud of you. Now everybody knows where they stand," she said. In fact she cooed these reassurances several times as we raced back up to Lismore till I was nearly scunnered listening to her. I said not a word.

Victoria had been right; Joe did indeed welcome the chance to be Sally Anne's knight in shining armour and see her home safely. There were no flies on our Victoria when it came to reading men.

I lay awake waiting for Sally Anne. I kept going over my apology in my head. I thought of the most gentle and genuine words I could muster and whispered them up to the thatch. She would understand what had happened. She would see the sense of the thing and realise where she had gone wrong. Her eyes would twinkle with forgiveness and she would look at me again with that special look in her eyes. I would hold her again and comfort her.

The minutes ticked by into hours. Where was she to this time of night? Had Joe Kearney taken her to his house, the sneaky devil? Then I remembered that other maid that he had had with him, the friend of Sally Anne in the brown dress. Of-course! He would have to take her home first to wherever she was hired. I tried to stay awake as long as I could. I even lit my candle again and went down to the kitchen at one point to see if there was any sign of her. Now that was a decision that brought me a quare gunk.

On my way down, as I passed my own bedroom, it struck me as strange that its door was lying half open. Curious about this and out of a natural concern to keep any draught away from Stanley, I looked inside. Even in the faint light of my candle I could see that there was no Stanley in my bed. Another missing person! Surely he wasn't out for a smoke at that time of the night? I reached the door from the hall to the kitchen and paused. From the guest bedroom ahead of me came faint giggling sounds. I listened for a bit and there was no doubt about it; the tell-tale sounds of a man and a woman laughing and the regular creaking of ancient bedsprings. I was so shocked that I nearly shouted her name.

'Victoria! My Victoria! You hypocritical bitch! You have the gall to lecture me about my affair with Sally Anne and all the time you are doing this with your English Jack-The-Lad? One rule for me and another for you! Aye, I know you are engaged. It doesn't matter a damn! You should not be doing this with him! How do you know he is going to marry you, you stupid girl? You lecture me about swelling bellies and you call Sally Anne a 'tramp'? You are a fool and my respect for you has just gone down the drain. In our house, the house where

you are guests! You think it is alright to be at it like rabbits in this my house, maybe even my bed too, for all I know?'
This was what I shouted at her from the very bottom of my betrayed soul; the words, of-course, bounced back down my throat from my clenched teeth and firmly closed lips.
'Oh Sally Anne,' I thought. 'I have been so misled, so deceived. She turned me against you and all the time she is nothing but an immoral hussy herself! Please, please, please can we go back to where we were before those two arrived in my street? Please forgive me and take me back...I have been such a fool.'
This was what I wanted to say to her, on my bended knees if necessary, but she was nowhere to be seen in the kitchen, on the street, on the lane.
'If Joe has taken her to his house I will lynch him,' I thought in my annoyance.
All I could do was go back upstairs and lie down to wait for her return, or for the morning, whichever came first.
The morning came first. She had not returned. Her bed was empty. I waddled down the stairs in a daze of self-remorse and despair. When I opened the kitchen door though, she was suddenly there. She leapt up from the chair where she had been sleeping, still in her lovely dress, now well crumpled, her hair tousled and her eyes sore red from crying. She looked very scared and not at all pretty.
"Sally Anne," I began, "I want to say sorry for..."
I got no further.
She rushed past me at the door, her body stiffened and her head turned away from me as if I was the rotten carcass of some dead animal. She ran up the stairs without a word.
Every time I came near her that morning as we worked at the animals she moved away. She did not meet my eye once. She had not a word for me, not one, and, when I tried to speak to her, she almost ran from me. Somehow we completed the morning routine. It wasn't quite so strained when we were at breakfast; the presence of the twins and my mother helped in that, not to mention Stanley and Victoria, who arrived from their respective bedrooms, I noticed. I found it very hard to look at them, the pair of them.
"Did you sleep well, Matthew?" asked Stanley.
"Aye," was all I could manage through the choking sound of disgust fighting with a spoonful of porridge in my mouth.

"I slept very well. Did you Victoria?" he said. Just the faintest wee smirk between them in that fleeting glance. It near turned my stomach. 'You are pushing this too far,' I thought. The cheek of him, in front of our girls too. But then he didn't know that I knew, did he?
"Matthew, I was thinking about that affair with those ruffians last night. I take it you know who they were, do you?"
"No I don't. Why?" I said.
"Really?" he said. "I thought you would know everyone from around here?"
"Not those fellows," I said. "They are likely hired hands from various farms about the locality. The only one I thought I recognised was that chap you had pinned to the wall."
"The one with the beard? You knew him, did you?" asked Stanley.
"I don't know him but he looks a bit like a fellow that Kevin Duggan would have been friendly with. I might have seen him last year at a fair or a market somewhere," I said.
"Kevin Duggan? How do I know that name? Kevin Duggan?" he mused.
"You wouldn't know him," I said. "He was my hired hand last year, that's all."
"Rings a bell. Don't worry; it will come back to me."
"He has a great memory," said Victoria.
'Pity he couldn't remember where he was supposed to sleep last night,' I thought.
Sally Anne looked very downcast as she went around the table, pouring the tea into our cups. All the joyful light had disappeared from her eyes.
"You know, Matthew," Stanley continued, "I wouldn't be at all surprised if those ruffians aren't involved up to their necks with the rebels."
"You may be right," I said.
"It makes me uneasy for you, up here in this isolated area."
"Don't be worrying yourself about me," I said. "I can look after myself."
"With what? A shotgun? No, no, no, Matthew. Look mate, I will be back in the North-West within the next two or three weeks. I have a review meeting in Londonderry. Why don't I come in this direction first and drop you in that.... that item that I was talking about?" he said with a quick glance at Sally Anne.

"Don't be doing that," I said. "It's well out of your way. I wouldn't have a notion how to use it anyway."
"I will have the car by then. I don't have to go over Glenshane. I can come via Omagh and make a small detour through Castlederg. It's no problem. I would feel better if you were properly armed and ready to protect yourself if any of those rascals decided to pay you a visit. Such things have happened before, as you well know from experience. And let's face it, you came to my defence last night. They noticed that. That chap even made a specific threat."
"That was just his pride talking," I said.
"Perhaps, but I wouldn't be so sure. Best be prepared," he said.
'Aye,' I thought. 'You would know about that.'
Shortly after breakfast Joe arrived on the street in the trap to take Sally Anne to Mass. She managed to slip away without saying 'Goodbye' to Victoria and Stanley, which I thought wasn't the best example of her manners. I had not managed to speak to her alone, to try to explain last night. She hadn't bothered to take her leave of me either which was the first time that had happened. She was usually very good at letting me know she was going.
On my way to morning service I took Victoria and Stanley to the station to await their tram. As they took their leave I had to listen to some more congratulatory chat from my cousin, now badly shop-soiled in my changed opinion of her. She gushed on about how proud of me she was the previous night, what a man I had been, how pleased my father would have been of how I had taken my stand. I wanted to reply that her mother and father wouldn't be exactly proud of her if they knew what I knew but I kept my powder dry and said nothing, apart from the usual 'Goodbyes' as they left me.
Stanley's final words were about his promised return and this weapon he would bring me. He seemed determined to make a Davy Crockett type of hero out of me. I think he was imagining Lismore turning into another Alamo. I couldn't see it myself, not even with the recent newspaper reports that the Border Commission was petering out and that the boundary with the Free State would probably stay where it was. Now that was something that was bound to annoy the hardliners on the Anti-Treaty side of the Civil War that was going on in the Free State.
Alice Porter came to me after church. Actually, if looks could have achieved it, she came to me several times during the service as well. She

wanted to know how I was. Last night had been so difficult for me, she said, especially the injury I received when helping my friend. Then the difficult position that that silly servant-girl had put me in. She was the second one to be telling me what a hero I had been and how proud she was of how I had dealt with it. They were all so delighted with the way I had publicly insulted the loveliest person I had ever met; it nearly made me sick, listening to it. Even that seductive stroking of my arm and the flickering of her long eyelashes over those dark eyes of hers left me cold.

"Would you not come down to the town this afternoon and we could go for a walk along the river?" she asked me. "It's lovely down there, with the leaves turning to brown. We could have a picnic in the old castle. It would lift your mind, Matthew; you would enjoy a walk with me, wouldn't you?"

'No I wouldn't,' I thought. 'No walk with you would lift my spirits this day.'

My mind was focussed on an afternoon spent with Sally Anne, a time spent getting our relationship back on a proper footing, explaining what had pushed me into saying those things last night and why I had had to treat her in that cold way.

"I have a few things to fix up at home, but thanks anyway, Alice," I said and it wasn't a word of a lie I was telling her. Those were my firm intentions. I had even spent the entire duration of the sermon readying the words in my head to bring about our reconciliation. I had no idea what his reverence was rambling on about but it wasn't the first time that that had been the case.

The trouble is that it takes two to be reconciled. It takes the other person to want to be as well. It takes the other person to actually be there and that is where my plan went wrong. Sally Anne did not show up all afternoon. I waited for her; I sat by the hearth; I stalked about the farmyard and the lane; I even went over to Kearneys to bring her back home, if she was taking refuge there.

"She's not here," Monica said at the door. "Joe must have taken her up the mountain for a walk."

Well, they could walk, the pair of them. I wandered back across the burn, through the gap in the hedge and up the back lane to our place. I sat in the barn. I climbed the fort and remembered that day of closeness, just a few weeks ago. I tried to recall the scent of her hair as

I carried her home with her sprained ankle. I would have given away half of Lismore Farm to be able to turn the clock back to then.
I went to the milking early. Maybe I could have it finished by the time she got home; that would please her; it would also give us time to talk. I finished the milking. Still no sign of her. I had a sudden panic and I ran up the stairs and climbed to the attic. Her things were still there, I saw with relief. Her bag was on the bed and the fiddle stood in its case in the corner.
It was nearly half six by the time her and Joe came around the side of the barn into the street. I was standing with my hand on the pump. They walked across the cobbles past me without so much as a look at me, never mind a word. Had I turned into an object, like the cast-iron pump? Why would they ignore me like that?
"Sally Anne," I said, "I have been looking everywhere for you. What kept you to this time?"
I likely sounded more like a factory foreman or a bailiff than somebody who wanted to apologise for his actions.
She stopped in her tracks, close to the back door. She just stood there, head erect, not looking round at me. She didn't say a word.
"What kept you, Sally Anne?" I said, thinking at the same time, 'Why am I the opposite of what I want to be in this conversation? Why am I antagonising her when all I want to be doing is bringing her back to me?'
"She doesn't have to answer that," said Joe sullenly.
"Stay you out of this," I said. "It has nothing to do with you."
"It has everything to do with me," he said. "She doesn't have to tell you where she has been or what she has been doing on her time off. She is back in time to do the milking as usual, so it's no concern of...."
"She is not back in time to do the milking," I said. "The milking is done. She is late."
She looked at me briefly, the coldest glance I could ever have imagined from her.
"This is none of your concern, Joe," I said. "You can go on home. Me and her have to talk. She has the tea to make."
"Are you telling me to leave?" he said. "If that is what you are telling me, that is the first time ever a Kearney has been asked to leave Henderson's farm, as far as I know anyway."
"Whatever you say," I said.

"Well, I'll go," he said, "but not before I tell you one or two home truths."
"Don't Joe," said Sally Anne. "Just leave it."
"No, I won't leave it," he said. "Somebody has to tell him what an ignorant, ill-bred bastard he has turned out to be."
"Don't," she said again.
I was flabbergasted by this outburst from him. It was not like him to be talking so bold.
"What you did to her last night," he said, "was not the way a decent man behaves. She did not deserve that, to be treated so cruel in front of that whole crowd of people....and all she was asking for was a dance. I would never have thought it of you. You are not the fellow I thought you were and I am hurt for her and for myself, for I thought I knew you better than that. It was a bloody disgrace, what you did. You treated Sally Anne like dirt and there is nobody deserved it less than her. How would you feel if somebody humiliated you like that in front of all those folk?"
"But it was me was humiliated," I said. "She kept pushing in at me, asking me to dance and all. I couldn't dance with her, not after... She went too far."
She stood, her back to me, her head held high and steady. I saw that she had her hair pinned up on top of her head in a manner that I had never seen before. It looked very different, very elegant altogether, the long neck of her. She looked changed. Maybe Kate had styled it for her. She stayed silent and still, like somebody had carved her from bog-oak and set her on my doorstep as a sort of ornament.
"She went too far?" Joe had a taunt in his voice. "So it is alright for you to be carrying on with her the way you have around here, behind the barn door or up on the fort, up in her room...but you couldn't even bring yourself to hold her hand in a dance in public? You couldn't even pass yourself like any other decent person would?"
I looked at Sally Anne.
"What did she tell you about us?" I said.
"She didn't tell me anything, you hypocrite. She didn't have to. I have eyes. I didn't need to be Sherlock Holmes to be noticing what was going on between the two of you."
"You low-down rat," I said to him. "You were running around spying on us. Had you nothing better to be doing with yourself? Were you just so jealous that you had to watch us?"

"I was not spying on you; give me some credit. The very dog on the street could see what you were up to. And, as for jealousy....aye, I'll admit it! I was annoyed at the two of you at the start, especially that night of her birthday. I couldn't see it working out for yous and I didn't want to see her hurt. She is ....well, she didn't deserve to get hurt. But then I started, inside myself and nearly in spite of myself.... I started to wish the best for the pair of yous. If it was going to make her happy, then that was all that mattered to me....but I was wrong. It has ended up like this and now she is badly hurt, by you."
"I didn't mean to hurt anybody," I said.
"It's a bit late for that now," Joe said.
"So what's to be done? Sally Anne, I need to talk...."
"Will you give me my money and let me go?" she said sharply, still not looking at me.
I was shocked by this, I have to say. I opened my mouth to speak but I couldn't find any words to put into it.
"Give her her wages," said Joe. "She wants to leave. Let her go."
"I will not," I said, "And I'll thank you to stop interfering in my affairs. It is none of your business what happens between me and my.... me and Sally Anne. It's time you were away home. You've said too much and done enough damage."
"My father and mother will be more than hurt when I tell them how you have behaved to her," he said as he turned to leave. "You're not the fellow I thought you were. Your father would...."
"Will you shut your gob about my father!" I raged at him. "Everybody keeps going on about my father. First Victoria; now you. Why can yous not just leave him to rest in peace and let me live my own life? Just go home, Joe!"
He did. Sally Anne turned to watch him. She did not look at me once.
"Will you let me go?" she said.
"Oh Sally Anne," I said, "don't be doing this. Let me just explain to you..."
"Stop," she said, lifting her hands against my words. "Will you give me my money and let me go?"
"I can't do that," I said. "Look, Sally Anne, I want to talk about this. I need you to see it from my point of view."
Her name was becoming like some sort of charm; the more I said it, the more I thought she might see sense, see my true heart and stay.
She looked up at the sky, as if asking for help from above.

"Please just listen to me for a minute. I am sorry about all that happened last night...." I tried again.
"I do not want to hear about last night. Will you let me go?" she barked.
"I want you to stay," I said. "I can't make you stay but listen to me a minute. There are only a few more weeks to go until your six months is up. I really need you to see it through until then. Please, Sally Anne. Don't talk about going. Look, I am trying to apologise for what...."
"Aahhh!" she said, adding what sounded like some swear-words in her Gaelic tongue. "I told you I do not want to hear about last night."
Her voice rose up like the screigh of a pheasant.
"Alright, alright," I said. It hadn't been often I had heard her take to her native Irish. I wasn't sure whether it was some sort of curse or what it meant but I did see the fury rising in her like a furnace. Anything I was going to say would only fan it hotter.
"Anyway," she said, "it is Joe you need to be apologising to. He is your friend and you treat him like that? I am just your hired hand."
With that Millie came out the back door to see what was going on.
"What yous shouting about?" she said. She went to Sally Anne. I thought that this was an interesting thing in itself. Millie always had that sensitivity about her that could home-in on hurt, be it a bird with a broken wing or a spider trying to climb out of a bowl. Where I would have squashed the spider she wanted to save it, protect it. The motherly instinct in Sally Anne responded and she put her arm around my wee sister, her head bending down over her.
"Sally Anne wants to stop working here," I said. "She wants to leave us."
I knew what I was doing. I wasn't ashamed of myself. This situation called for every trick I could find, emotional blackmail included.
"No," said Millie horrified. "Why you wanna leave, Sawey Anne? Is you and Ma'hew fighting?"
Sally Anne's response was as clever as it was kind.
"No, no; we aren't fighting, Millie," she said quietly. "And I don't want to leave you. It is just that I am missing my Mammy. I want to go and see her."
She gave me a scornful look over Millie's head as she hugged my little sister. I saw those emerald eyes of hers, wet with big soft tears like morning dew on the grass.

"You stay," Millie said, her voice muffled in against Sally Anne's bosom.

I went to join them, to put my hand on Sally Anne's shoulder. She twisted away from me. Her eyes flashed me a look that would have lit a candle.

"Don't," she breathed. Then to Millie, "Go on in now, Millie. I am coming in to make the tea."

"You has to stay," said Millie. She went inside with a slow, hurting look over her shoulder.

"Please?" I said.

"Just don't ever touch me again. Don't expect me to talk to you, to answer you, to even look at you," she said. "And don't ever try to stop me going over to Kearney's when I want to, or question me about where I have been. That is my condition. I will work as hard as I have always worked. I will take my money and leave you when the time comes, and it could not be soon enough."

She said all this without once looking at me. She made me feel like I was the servant man here, like I was the one who had caused all this misunderstanding. I watched the stiffness of her hips as she stomped in through the back door to make the evening meal.

'Well, we'll see,' I thought.

Chapter 24

Sally Anne Sweeney

How the gap widened

That following week was all about the gap between us widening, in more senses than one.

I dragged myself through my daily work. It seemed to take more out of me after that night and I was not the better of it for a long time.

'How come,' I thought to myself, 'that only a week ago I was loving this? Every one of these jobs, every meal time around Henderson's table, every bird that sang to me in the fields.... Every joy that was in it.... gone.'

My only motivating thought was how to avoid being alone with Matthew Henderson. This was what I spent my time scheming about. If he was at the milking first, then I would go and prepare feed for the pigs. If he was cleaning out the byre, then I would go collecting eggs. Only when he was away from the farm, delivering the milk or some such errand, did I feel comfortable.

There were times when I had to be with him of-course. Gathering potatoes, for example; that was very much the two of us. There was no sign of Joe coming over; I understood that. Anytime Matthew tried to start a conversation I either walked away from him or just played dumb. He would not get a word out of me, of that I was determined. He would suffer for how he had misused me and I did not give a damn how he was feeling.

Or so I told myself.

Inside I was just very hurt, very disappointed. I did not think I had done anything to deserve the scorn he had shown me that night. Why had he been so weak and gullible in the face of that hypocrite of a cousin of his? And why, why, why had I not gone to him that first morning after they had arrived and shown him the pair of drawers, man's drawers, that I had found in her room when I was tidying it up? That would have put her in her place! She would have had trouble explaining that now, would she not? She would not have had the gall to be questioning me about how I behaved with Matthew after that, nor poisoning him against me either. Instead I had slipped them back up to Stanley's room and said nothing, just to protect her privacy. If I had it to do again....? I would have rubbed her nose in them, I am thinking.

Every evening that week I went over to Kearney's. As soon as my work was done I walked down the back lane and spent the night talking to Monica and Kate. If it was late, Joe would walk me home, right to the Henderson's yard. To be honest, I asked him to do that. I did not want to encounter Matthew waiting for me somewhere in the gloom of the evening.

Tam Glenn left the Kearneys on the Tuesday to continue his wanderings up in the Strabane area he said. He had a quiet chat with me before he departed. I could tell that he was truly disappointed in Matthew and that he understood my own confused feelings. For all his reputation as a hardened old bachelor, Tam had a well of goodness in him and I drank deeply from it those couple of evenings. He tried to encourage me gently, saying that it would all work out for the best, even if it was hard for me to take at the present. He told me not to be too hard on Matthew, that it was tough for him, not having a father to be guiding him, as Joe had. He agreed with me too, that Matthew turning his back on me had more to do with Victoria than with Matthew himself.

"Don't give up on it yet," he told me, "and remember the good times."

I was in no mood to remember any good times but I knew he was trying to get me cheered up.

Joe's father looked on and was curious; I could tell he could read that something had happened at the farm to be pushing me over to them every night. Joe had not told his parents anything about the events that night at the ceili and he had sworn Kate to secrecy as well.

"Will you bring your fiddle over tomorrow night and play us a few good tunes?" Anthony asked me.

I did not know what to say to this. That Henderson fiddle was the last thing I wanted to be playing. I would sooner have cut my wrist. After a second of wondering what to say I was rescued by Joe.

"She can't play it at the minute. Matthew broke a string on it," he lied.

'Lord above, Joe,' I thought. 'How did you come up with that one?'

"Is that so?" said his father.

I could see that Anthony was not taken in though.

"Is everything alright over there?" he asked after a while.

I looked at Joe again and yet again he answered for me.
"Aye," he said, "everything is alright."
"You don't seem to have been over much helping Matthew this week?" said father to son.
"No, I haven't," said Joe. "He hasn't needed me."
"Is he not at the spuds again?"
"He could be," answered Joe, "but he hasn't come looking for me. He knows where I am."
I could tell that the older man was puzzled, puzzled and concerned. Joe made an effort to change the subject.
"Sally Anne is going to come with me on Sunday to watch the match," he said.
"Am I?" I said. "What match is that?"
"I'm playing football for the parish. We always have a challenge match against Clady around this time of year. You'll come, won't you?" he said.
I laughed. "I can think of better ways of spending a Sunday afternoon than watching your skinny wee legs trying to kick a ball over the bar but, if you are asking, I suppose I will have to come."
And I did. Straight after Mass we rode off in the pony and trap to a field in the town-land of Tullymoan. Kate was with us and she had brought a basket of food. We stopped along the road and had our picnic beside a huge standing stone, an ancient thing in the middle of a rushy field. We ate our soda bread and buttermilk, sitting on the grass with our backs against the cold rock. It was a lovely October day, the blue of the sky sharpened by white cauliflower clouds and the brown Tyrone hills to the east of us, clear and lovely to view. A blackbird was performing its own special song for us from high above in the branches of a twisted Scots Pine tree nearby. I was reasonably happy for the first time in a week.
Joe played his heart out, bless him. He ran around the field like a mad March hare. At times, though, I had the feeling that he could be doing with some sort of spectacles. Maybe that nose of his was getting in the way of his vision but he did not manage to score a single point, despite being in the forward line and having several goes at it.
"Somebody shift those posts for him," I shouted.
Mind you, some of his team-mates were not much better and the boys from Clady won the match easily. Joe emerged from the field with as much mud about him as would have grown a patch of cabbages. We

got him scraped clean between the pair of us and we set off back towards Gortnagappel.

I stayed as long as I could possibly stay with the Kearneys that evening, as usual. And, as he loved to do, Joe decided to leave me back up to Henderson's around about six o'clock for I had the cows to be milking. He had had a wash and was looking more like himself. As we crossed the stepping stones over the burn and arrived at the gap in the hedge between the two farms we were met with a surprise.

There was no gap any longer!

An angry-looking Matthew stood on the other side of a barbed wire fence, a crowbar in his hand as hard as the scowl on his face. Joe stopped in his stride.

"What in the name of God is this?" he said.

"It's a fence. What does it look like?" said Matthew.

"But why? What do you need to be putting up a fence for?"

"If you had been here this afternoon instead of away scungin' the countryside with her you would have seen why I am putting up a fence. A lock of your half-starved bullocks broke outa their field and came through this slap into my land," said Matthew.

"I'm sure they didn't do any harm; you could just have chased them back through and told my father about it. He would have shut them in the north field again. No need to be putting...."

"But they did do harm," said Matthew. He nodded in my direction. "She left the top gate open and they came up the back lane and into my praties. Tramped all over them. Samuel Bond was over to see my mother; it was him noticed them in the potato field. I had to get him and the twins to give me a hand to chase them back to where they came from. She should have been here to help but she was away gallivanting with you. A lock o' my spuds are ruined, so they are."

"I am right sorry about that but there's not much I can do about it now," said Joe.

"Aye there is," said Matthew. "You can pay me compensation for the damage."

Joe shook his head in disbelief. I spoke for the first time in this argument.

"For goodness sake," I said. "It is not Joe's fault that his animals broke into your field. Catch yourself on."

"What did you say?" said Matthew, turning towards me.

"It is not Joe's fault," I said.

"Is it not? And you are standing up for him, are you? My word, that's a good one. Now that I come to think of it, you are right, it isn't Joe's fault. It's yours; if you had shut that gate they wouldn't have gotten into my spuds. So it's you will have to pay, out of your wage at the end of your time."

"God but you are a heartless bastard," said Joe. "Listen to yourself!"

"Wait a minute," I said. "When am I supposed to have left the gate open?"

"Whenever you went over to Joe's this morning," said Matthew.

"Joe picked me up at the end of your lane before Mass," I said. "After Mass we went straight to the game. We never called back in here at all. You can ask Kate if you don't believe me. I could not have been the one to leave the gate open because I did not go down the back lane today."

"There, you see," said Joe. "You owe her an apology, but I don't suppose you'll give her one. Just like after the ceili."

Matthew hung his head for a second.

"I'm sorry if I accused you in the wrong," he said, the wind taken out of his sails and his tone softened. "I am sorry Sally Anne. And listen, Joe; I seem to have spent the last week trying to apologise to her for what happened at the ceili but she is so high and mighty of herself that she won't listen to me."

"That's as maybe," said Joe moving forward towards the three strands of barbed wire. "How do we get through this fence?"

"You don't get through it," said Matthew sullenly. "You have to go round by the road."

"You are not serious?" said Joe. "That takes forever. This has always been a right-of-way as long as I have been here. You can't go shutting it off like this, just on some silly notion of yours."

"Can I not?" said Matthew. "Looks to me as if I just have. This is the march ditch and I can do whatever I want with it."

Joe moved on along the wire and beyond it, looking at the hedge.

"There must be another wee gap in your 'march ditch', along here somewhere, big enough for us to slip through," he said. "Aye, there's a bit of a gap here, if I bend down this branch...."

"You stay where you are," said Matthew aggressively. "I don't want the whole thing to happen again. Don't go making any more holes in that hedge. She will just have to stretch her legs and walk around."

"What are you thinking, Matthew?" Joe said angrily. "Sally Anne is tired. She has been standing all afternoon watching me playing football. Let her through here and don't be so pig-headed."

"Watching you playing football, was she? Gaelic likely, on a Sabbath afternoon! That is not something I want my hired hand to be doing," he said, the temper making him splutter his words.

"Listen to yourself, Matthew! For God's sake listen to yourself," said Joe. "Who are you? You are as crabbit as bedamned. Where is the craic in you that there used to be? Who have you turned into?"

"I am me!" he said, sticking his chin out in that proud way he had. "I am Matthew Henderson and I will not have her going off with you to a Gaelic match on the Sabbath, not while she is still in my employ."

"Is it because it was a Gaelic match? Or is it because it's your Sabbath? Or is it not because she is going somewhere with me now, rather than with you?" said Joe.

That one struck home better than any barb from the fence could have done.

"You bastard you," he shouted to Joe. "Don't you ever set foot across this fence again, you hear me."

"That's no bother to me," answered Joe. "And you remember that whenever you need me for some slave labour around your precious bit of land."

He turned to go back to his own house. I watched his back but did not follow him, not yet.

I was alone again with this fellow who was my employer.

I looked through the strands of wire at him. For the first time in a week I looked at him and I felt something for him; not the sort of blind affection I had had for him since I first saw him in Strabane fair; no, all that was well and truly gone; it was more of a sense of pity for the dour, resentful individual he was allowing himself to turn into. I could not help myself. Something in me changed at that moment and I wanted to stop this hate in me. The fellow needed mercy, I was thinking.

"I will be home shortly to do the milking and make the tea. I might be a bit late for I have to walk around by the lane and the road," I said quietly.

He just looked back at me, so sadly, so unsure of himself behind the mask of anger and toughness that he wore on his face, that same face that I thought so handsome just eight days before.

"Here girl," he said more softly. "Come on and I'll hold the wire down for you. You don't have to go the long way around."
I could have yielded; maybe I should have yielded. I could have moved toward him and stepped over the fence; maybe even given him a hint of a sympathetic smile. But I stood my ground.
"No it's alright," I said. "A walk round won't do me any harm. And I am sorry about the potatoes."
"Aye, well," he said, "it's no matter. They're only potatoes."
'Lord above,' I thought. 'It is true what they say; '*Níor bhris focal mhaith fiacail riamh'*. 'A soft word never broke a tooth!' That gentle tone of mine has disarmed him entirely.'
I turned and walked away slowly, back towards Kearney's lane.
"Sally Anne, please...." he called after me.
I walked on.
He had made his bed; he could lie in it!

~~~~~

It was a couple of days later that Anthony Kearney found out about the new fence between the two farms. Joe had kept the news to himself. Anthony had gone to speak to Matthew, something about the timing of the threshing this year, and found his normal route blocked. I was in Kearney's kitchen when he came back.
"What is that fellow thinking of, putting a fence across the slap like that?" said Anthony gruffly.
"I have no idea," said Joe without lifting his head from the table.
"Did you know about it?" asked Anthony.
"I did," said Joe.
"But you never thought it worth your while to tell me?" said his father.
"I meant to tell you; just never got round to it," said Joe.
"Never got round to it?" repeated Anthony. "And I suppose you have no idea why he did it or what is going on here?"
Joe was silent. The tension grew between father and son as the older man waited. I wondered if I should speak. After all it was because of me that the thing started, in a way. Monica came to the table, baking bowl in hand, staring at Joe, waiting for an answer. Joe had become strangely, stubbornly silent.
~~~~~

"There has been a bit of a falling out," I said into the quietness between parents and son. "I am afraid it all started over the head of me. It is not Joe's fault."
"What happened son?" said Monica.
So it all came out, the story of the ceili, the way Matthew had treated me, the shouting match on the next day, then the bullocks breaking into his potatoes and the confrontation at the fence on Sunday night. Joe told the most of it and I filled in the bits I thought were necessary to defend him. I was surprised, I have to say, at how angry and depressed Joe had become about it all. It was as if he was experiencing the death of something that had been precious to him, the tearing apart of this relationship which had defined him in this his neighbourhood. I had not seen it in that way before until I heard it from his lips to his father and mother. It was not just about me; it was this let-down with the character of the fellow he thought he knew, with the person he had always thought of as his friend. Both father and son were very affected by the whole thing, I could see that, Anthony especially. His head went down into his hands and he rubbed his eyebrows and scratched at the back of his neck as Joe recounted the saga.
"You should have come for me, Joe," he said. "I needed to know about this straight away. What possessed you to keep silent about it?"
"I don't know," he said. "I just knew you would be mad. I thought it might blow over."
"I doubt that, knowing how thick Matthew can get. No, we will have to go and talk to him and get this whole thing fixed," he said. "You will need to apologise to him and...."
"I will not be apologising, Da. I have nothing to apologise for and Sally Anne will back me up on that," said Joe. "It has all been his fault. I am not just saying that. If I was wrong in this in any way I would be the first to go and make it right but I'm not in the wrong this time. He has just turned into somebody I don't recognise. He is the one needs to come and say he is sorry."
"What does he have to apologise to you for, son?" said Anthony.
"For... for how he treated Sally Anne. For turning into an ignorant bigot."
"But he doesn't need to apologise to you for how he treated Sally Anne," said Anthony. "That is between him and her, nothing to do with you."

"Well, for putting up that stupid fence then. He has no right to be doing that," said Joe.
"He doesn't see it that way," answered his father. "To his way of thinking, our cattle broke into his potato field. We didn't know to do anything about it. So he has every right to put up a fence."
"No he hasn't. Sure that has always been a right of way between the two farms. Is he saying he doesn't want us helping him out with the work any more? What about the threshing? What about all the work he owes us?" Joe argued.
"It isn't an official right of way. I know we have always used it as that but everything is changing now, especially with this border running between the two farms."
"But Da," said Joe in frustration. "Things can't change that much surely, border or no border? And why are you taking his side in this anyway? Why am I having to argue with you as well as him?"
"I am not taking his side," said the older man. "I am on your side. I think it's terrible that things have come to this. I'm just trying to get you to see it from his point of view."
"You've always been like that, always sticking up for the Hendersons. Why do you have to be always defending the Protestants, for God's sake? Is it any wonder our Mary gets mad at you at times," said Joe with more bitterness than he should have.
Anthony Kearney looked hurt. He sat with his head back on his shoulders for a minute, calming himself, I thought, his mind seemingly far away, pondering some hidden issue. Eventually he spoke to Joe, to all of us in the kitchen, Monica, Kate and myself included. The younger ones were through in the bedroom.
"Sit down around the table," he said. "I need to tell you a story, Joe. You might as well hear it too, Sally Anne; you too, Kate. Your mother knows all this already."
We sat down, almost reverently. I stayed in the corner, on a stool by the fire. Joe's mother looked apprehensive.
"Don't be going into too much detail, Anthony," she said. "For the sake of the girls, please."
"I won't, don't worry," Anthony said.
"Details about what?" asked Joe. "What is the point of all this?"
"The point is to help you to understand me, son," said Anthony, "and, when I have finished, I hope you will be able to see why that last statement you made is very foolish and very unfair. You think I stand

up for the Hendersons? Well, if you are right, then I take it as a compliment and not as a criticism."
"That is just the strangest thing to be saying," said Joe. "I don't understand."
"You will, son," said Monica. "Just listen to your father."
"This is a story I have never told anybody but your mother and Matthew's mother. It is not a thing I like to think about but, believe me, I do think about it, every single day of my life, especially in my prayers. It is not an easy thing to speak about. If I had the choice now I wouldn't be talking about it at all. But I think I owe it to you, and to Matthew Henderson."
He paused and cleared his throat a couple of times.
"You likely know bits of this already, Joe. James Henderson and me fought together in the war. It was back in November Nineteen Fifteen that we joined up. We went to Omagh and signed up for The Royal Inniskilling Fusiliers. At the time they were recruiting in Tyrone. We had talked about it often enough, for him and me were very close, so we were. The funny thing about it was that the pair of us went to fight in the war for opposite reasons."
This was very interesting to me. I had often wanted to ask Anthony what on earth had persuaded him to go to fight for Britain when, in the middle of it all, so many young men were giving their lives in the rising to free the country from the very power he was going to fight for. I was all ears.
"For James it was all about the Empire and Great Britain and being patriotic. Britain needed him. Matthew was old enough to manage at home till he came back. Eliza had all her wits about her at that stage and she could have run an army, the same woman. They had a very good servant man who had been with them for years, a fellow by the name of McLaughlin from Convoy, so the farm would be alright. For me, it was very different. We talked about this, the two of us, for we had always been the best of friends; we talked about everything; sort of the way you and Matthew are."
"Were," said Joe.
"Why did you want to fight for the British?" I asked him bringing my stool in beside the table.
"Well, you see Sally Anne, this country was on the verge of having Home Rule. It had been promised to us but the war more or less interrupted it. At that time, even our politicians, like Redmond for

example, were supporting Britain in the fight against Germany. The Germans had broken their promise and invaded Belgium. They had done terrible things to Catholic women and children there. I joined up as much in protest against that as anything else."

Joe was shaking his head. I could see that he was not impressed by his father's reasons.

"And you expected the British to honour their promise to us whenever the war was over? Surely that was a vain hope. Instead of Home Rule, we get a Protestant parliament in Belfast. The country split in two," he said. "You were fighting on the same side as Carson's Ulster Volunteers, for God's sake."

"Well son, it's alright saying that with hindsight but I felt at the time that it was the right thing to do. I'm not sure I would do it again. I am very lucky to be here at all," said Anthony.

"You'd better tell him what really happened," said his wife. "Sally Anne has to go back to Matthew before it gets too dark."

"Alright, to cut a long story short," began Anthony again, "after our training over at Finners Camp in Donegal we were transported across to England, then on to France. We hadn't a notion what we had let ourselves in for. After a week or two of more training near a wee town by the name of Albert, we found ourselves being pushed up the line to the front at this place they called 'The Somme'. We were part of the Thirty-Sixth Ulster Division. We lived in these trenches that were like massive deep sheughs, running for miles and miles. We were in there for weeks. Our section of the Front was in a sort of forest, or what was left of a forest; it would have been a lovely place if it hadn't been for the shells that were falling all round us. Fierce noise. You were always scared one of them was going to land on you and your number would be up if it did. Our feet were wet and cold; the worst smell you can imagine in your nose, morning, noon and night, coming from the latrines in the trenches and decaying bodies in no-man's-land; rats everywhere; they would be feeding on the corpses; they grew to the size of cats; they would be running over you when you were sleeping, even when you weren't sleeping. James used to joke with me that it was like threshing corn back at home with the rats escaping from the bottom of the stack. It was a shocking place to be in. Brutal! You wouldn't ask your cattle to live in it, so you wouldn't. Hell on earth; I'll never forget it."

The more he talked, the more I noticed a change in his body, his face in particular. There was a shake in his head and the skin seemed to draw itself tighter over his jaw and around his mouth. It was strange to watch this in a man I thought I knew well. Even his voice seemed to be straining to stretch itself around the sharp edges of the words he was having to use.

"Anyway, as June started, so did rumours of a big push against the Gerries. We knew by the increase in the bombardment from our big guns behind us. It was constant; I thought I was going to go deaf. Come the First of July, we were told, we were going to be going over the top....that meant climbing up out of the trench, you understand, to take on the Germans. That morning we heard the most almighty explosions going off. It was these huge mines that our boys had planted in tunnels in below the enemy lines, although we didn't know that at the time. It could have been the end of the world, for all we knew. It was terrifying. You could feel the ground rippling under you like it had turned to clabber in a bog-hole. Then we heard the whistle, the signal to attack.

It was like climbing up over a turf bank, except that when you got to the top there were bullets flying at you from German machine guns and your mates were dropping round you like flies. James was beside me, running through this ploughed field of a place with shell craters everywhere; it was hard to keep your feet for you were slithering about on this soft yellowy muck. Our orders were to attack an enemy position called... Agh, I can't remember its name. Schwaben or something. It was up behind a ridge about half a mile from us; they were very well dug in up there and all we could do was hope that the bombardment had destroyed their gun positions. Somehow we made it right up across this slope to the barbed wire, expecting it to be flattened by our shells but no such luck. We had to line up to climb through whatever holes there were in it and of-course that made us easy targets for the machine guns."

"Is that where James got shot?" asked Joe.

"No, we were very lucky there; a lot of the lads never made it through that wire. In some places the bodies sort of got stuck in it like sheep in a hole in the hedge. Hopeless! What was left of our platoon fought its way right to the German lines and we took over some of their positions. It was a miracle, so it was. But the trouble was, we had pushed too far and the boys to our left and right had been beaten back.

So we were in danger of being cut off from our lines. You can't get isolated or surrounded, you see. After a while the CO gave the order to retreat. We had fought our way through hell for nothing. And that was when disaster struck the pair of us."

Anthony paused and rubbed his stubbly chin in the palm of his shaking hand. He tried to clear his throat of the phlegm gathering there. He was back on the battlefield, reliving it, I could tell. We waited for him to clear his head and speak again.

"The next thing I remember was James shouting over to me. 'Just keep running all the way back to Gortnagappel,' he said. He was laughing. Then I took a hit. A shell must have landed over to my right and all I felt was this screaming pain in my back. I went down straight away. James ran on for a bit. I don't think he realised I had been hit. I lost sight of him in the haze. Maybe I blacked out for a bit. Then I could see him through the smoke. He had stopped. He was standing there looking round, with bullets flying past him. You'd have thought he was out for a Sunday dander and had stopped to count the sheep. I knew he was searching for me. I wanted him to run on and get to our trenches. At the same time I wanted him to come back for me. If I was going to die there I didn't want to die alone. I wanted to send a message back to Monica with him. Anyway, back he comes for me.

I'm shouting at him to go on, of-course. That's what you feel you should do. But he doesn't listen.

'We'll make it to the sunken road,' he says.

This was an old road in a sort of hollow, over to our left. He picks me up and carries me over his shoulder as if I was a bag of corn. James was a strong man, so he was. Then he's running up and down through shell holes, stepping over dead bodies, and he's dragging me back through that blasted barbed wire again. We were within fifty, maybe forty yards of the road and safety when the machine gunner must have spotted us and opened up on us from our flank. Rat-a-tat-tat, like the hammering of one of those Lambeg drums. James didn't stand a chance. He must have taken three or four bullets. How none of them hit me I will never know. He was killed instantly. He never said a word. I lay beside him, in agony myself but still able to talk to him. I said a prayer for him. I told him I would tell Eliza that he had died as a brave and kind man and a true friend. I told him that I promised to look after her and Matthew and the girls as if they were my own wains. You see, in my mind he had sacrificed himself to try and help me. If he had run on himself he might have survived; maybe I would have been the one in a war grave there in France instead of him."

There I was in Kearney's kitchen, hearing this sacred piece of their family history and feeling very strange about it. The atmosphere was something I could not describe. A touching hush took over the room; it seemed to go on for ages. Silent tears were running down Kate's pretty wee face and her mother put her arms around her. Joe was suffering too; I could see it. This challenged everything in him, in what he thought about his father and in what he thought about Matthew.

"How did you survive then?" he asked, in a soft, reverent tone.

"I lay there till nightfall. I was going in and out of consciousness. Some of our fellows must have heard me calling; maybe they saw me go down as they were running back. A couple of them came out under cover of darkness and dragged me back to our forward trench. From there I was sent to the Field Hospital. The nurses cleaned the wound but they couldn't do anything to get the shrapnel out. The doctor thought it was too dangerous to try. Too much risk of infection. So they parcelled me up and sent me home. England first and then later on home to my wee wife. Home to all of yous. And home to explain it all to Eliza," he finished, his voice becoming very brittle with emotion.

"Why did you never tell me this before, Da?" said Joe.

"I don't know, son. I didn't like to talk about it; still don't. I told your mother but we made a deal never to speak of it again. You see, it was like another world out there, a strange place where the suffering and stupidity of it all was beyond putting words around. The only way I could survive it without going mad was to lock it away in a secret place in the back corner of my mind. If I had to think about it at all, then I would do it myself and try and handle it alone, rather than bringing yous all into it. That was my way of working with it. Others were different. Do you know, when the whole locality were all down celebrating in Castlederg on Armistice Day I never went near it. None of us did. I went for a long walk in the mountains by myself that day and listened to the birds."

"But can't you see that I needed to know about Matthew's father; I should have known what I owed to him?" argued Joe.

"No, that's not how I see it, Joe," said Anthony. "I wanted you to respect Matthew for his own sake, not out of some duty to his father. If I had told you what James Henderson had done for me, you would have been for ever feeling you were in his debt. That is no way for a

friendship to be built. You have to get on with him for his own merits, if you see what I mean."
"I do see that," said Joe, "and you might be right, but what do I do now that he has turned out such a bastard? I can't see any circumstance that would bring him to make a sacrifice for me, or the other way round, for that matter."
"Fair enough. That might be true at the minute, for you, Joe, but can you see why it would annoy me if our two sons turned into enemies? After all I went through with his father?"
"So what do you want me to do? I am not going anywhere near Matthew until he sees some sense. I am not apologising for something I am not responsible for."
"Alright," said Anthony, "but take my advice and let it rest. Don't be doing anything to make it worse. He will maybe come to his senses and see what side his bread is buttered on."
I wondered if I might play a part in this myself. Maybe I could talk to Matthew, as an outsider? I went to Joe.
"I could speak to Matthew about this, if you like," I said. "I could try to explain it to him. He might take it from me."
"You will do no such thing," said Joe. "After how he has treated you, that is the last thing you should be thinking about. If he doesn't have a conscience of his own, what is the good of you trying to become a conscience for him? He'd likely just remind you again that you are the servant girl and to stop meddling in his affairs."
"But he needs to know how he has hurt you; he needs to see this from your father's point of view, do you not think?" I said.
"Don't you dare tell him about what you heard here in this kitchen tonight," said Joe. "That would be the last thing I need, him lording it over me that his father sacrificed himself for my da."
"I think Joe is right," said Monica. "Just let it rest and see if time will heal it in its own way."
I could see Joe's point. I just hated being the cause of a fall-out in their friendship; yet here I was in Kearney's house, privileged to be hearing the hidden history of their family, seeing the nature of their relationships through their eyes. I started to think how I might see it through Matthew's eyes, even if that view of things would be one that I would have no time for and would completely despise.
This was what I thought about on the way home that night, the long way home by the road, of-course.

Chapter 25

Matthew Henderson

When Stanley returned

I had very mixed feelings about Stanley's return.

He came back to the farm on the Friday after I had fenced the slap between Kearney's land and mine and what a grand entrance he made. I was in the pig-house putting down new straw but I heard the rip-roar of his new car coming up the road from the valley when he was still a good few field-lengths away. Mind you there wasn't a person for miles around that didn't hear him coming, such a din he was making. He came honking into the street and I thought my collie dog was going to swallow herself with fright. The hens scattered from their scavenging and the very horses were galloping around the front field, whinnying in terror.

The hood of the car was down, for best effect, I thought. Stanley's flap of hair was blowing out behind him like a dark coxcomb, not fulfilling its key purpose in life at all, as he rounded the corner into my sight. He wore a pair of goggles and broad grin of pride underneath that brush of a moustache.

Sally Anne was the only one to take the arrival in her stride. She was rinsing out clothes by the pump and she hardly so much as lifted her head when this gleaming machine came across the cobbles and rumbled to a halt beside her. As I crossed the street I saw Stanley look sideways at her and shake his head in disbelief; how could anyone resist such an impressive arrival and ignore such a wonderful car?

That was Sally Anne. She could play the cold fish the best ever you saw; I had been living with it for two weeks, waiting for her attitude to warm to me again and I was just about at the end of my tether with her. Surely she should have been over the disappointment of the dance by now? It was not as if I hadn't tried to apologise to her, for I had, several times. Surely she couldn't be holding against me that I had offended her 'best-friend', Joe, by doing the logical thing and putting up that fence between the two farms? It was long overdue anyways. Why was she keeping up this iciness towards me? She had been the love of my life for months. Even before that, we had always treated her as one of the family, for goodness sake. Hadn't I gone out of my way to show her great kindness, giving her my father's old fiddle after she arrived? Come to think of it, I had not heard her playing it recently. Hadn't I been a gentle lover to her, never forcing myself on her and, indeed, resisting with all my strength the natural urge to take things to a closer level, as manys a man in my shoes would have done? Why wouldn't she try to see my heart again and thaw out a bit? I was disappointed in her but there did not seem to be any way to bring her back to me. Why could she not see my heart?

Warm shaking of hands with Stanley though, and we stood surveying this shiny new car of his.

"A Morris Cowley," he announced. "Manufactured in Nineteen Nineteen and known as 'The Bullnose', on account of the shape of its radiator grill at the front here."

"Very nice," I said. He sounded like a salesman.

"I would have preferred a darker colour but this sky-blue was all that was available."

"It's a nice colour," I said.

"Great engine. She'll do forty miles per hour with ease," said Stanley. "I don't want to push her too hard though, especially with the roads around here, but on a good straight road, with a bit of a down-slope and a following wind, she can really fly. I can't wait to take you for a spin."

"That'll be great, Stanley," I said, "but come in first and Sally Anne will make you a cup of tea. I'm sure you are thirsty after that long journey."

Sally Anne seemed reluctant to leave her washing but she followed us in and did the needful without so much as a word to either of us. Stanley put his suitcase in the guest-room and joined us in the kitchen. My mother, God love her, had forgotten who he was. She thought he was from 'The Ministry', which, I suppose, he was... in a sense.

When Sally Anne left us to go back to her chores Stanley brought up the subject of the firearm he had got for me.

"I won't bring it in from the car at the minute," he said with a nod in my mother's direction. "I don't want to be scaring anyone but, if you have time this afternoon, I want to drive you down to Baronscourt, to the firing range they have there, and show you how to use the thing. I wouldn't want you to have it without a little basic training."

"Do you know the place?" I asked him.

"Not really," he said. "I haven't been there before. I'm hoping you will know the way."
"I know the way alright," I said, "but I have my doubts that we will even get into the place."
"Why's that?" he said.
"Well, for a start, do you know who lives there?" I asked him.
"Of-course I do," said Stanley with a smile. "Mr Hamilton, the Third Duke of Abercorn."
"Aye, but he's not just that," I said. "He happens to be the new Governor of Northern Ireland, for goodness sake. The place will be hiving with police and soldiers and the like."
"I am aware of all that Matthew," he grinned. "Isn't it just as well that I have contacts. I have already been in touch with the Duke's security chief. I have his letter here. Don't worry yourself. It will be fine."
"You have a letter?" I said. "And they allow you to arrive with some raw farmer that hardly knows one end of a gun from the other to practise shooting? My goodness! Do they know the danger they will be in?"
Stanley laughed. "They are used to this kind of thing," he said. "Did you know that the Ulster Volunteer Force did a lot of their training there in preparation for the war?"
I did know that. Everyone around here knew it. It didn't make me any less nervous about what was ahead of me. But, after I changed from my working clothes, that is exactly what we set off to do.
My first time in an open-topped car, I seemed to be flying along between the hedges with the wind blowing in my hair and snatching words away from my lips as soon as I had spoken them. I soon gave up trying and just sat back and enjoyed the ride. The bitter odour of Stanley's cigarette smoke mingled with the rich smell of these new shiny leather car-seats. Both of my hands gripped the sides of these seats tightly; I hoped Stanley wouldn't notice this. Small birds flew in panic from the hedgerows and rabbits scurried for safety into the ditches as we passed. Stanley seemed to be a good driver and all was going well until we rounded a bend somewhere near the village of Ardstraw and found ourselves confronted by a herd of cattle being driven along the narrow road in our direction. Stanley swore and jammed on his brakes, skidding to a halt just in time. He looked over his shoulder and stuck the car into reverse gear.

"Damn them," he said, beginning to back up. "I don't want some shitty-assed bullock making a mess of this car."
He stopped where the lane broadened out a bit and there was a grass verge at the side. He pulled the vehicle up onto this verge and waited for the dozen or so cattle to pass on the road which they did without any problem. The engine was still running of-course and, just as we were about to move on, I happened to look at the fellow who was driving the herd. I found him staring at our car and, in particular, at Stanley. He was a tough looking fellow, stick in hand, black-bearded and familiar for some reason. The Cowley gentled its way back onto the road. The fellow stepped back briefly and then moved forward towards us, suddenly aggressive, his eyes staring and his stick raised.
"You're the English bastard!" he shouted.
Stanley put his foot down hard on the accelerator and his car jerked forward, just in time as the drover's stick came swinging in our direction.
"Let's get out of here," he said as we picked up speed. "Who the hell was that chap?"
I had had time to think and now I remembered.
"That's the fellow you had the fight with at the Harvest Dance," I said. "He must be a hired hand at a farm in these parts."
"Well, well," he said, "what are the chances of that happening? That was a close run thing."
"It certainly was," I agreed. "You never know what sort of trouble you are going to run into around these parts nowadays."
"Maybe," said Stanley, "but that fellow doesn't know how close he was to serious trouble."
I didn't follow him there.
"How do you mean?" I asked. "You wouldn't have run him over, would you?"
"No need for that," he replied. "I wouldn't have risked damaging my car on him."
I was none the wiser but I said no more.
Soon we were entering through one of the lesser gates into the Baronscourt estate. I had been past this neat wee gatehouse a few times before but had never been inside, even though we lived less than ten miles away. It wasn't a place people like me would have any cause to go to. At the gate we were stopped by two soldiers and questioned about our business. Stanley's letter did the trick and we drove on through

some beautiful groves of huge trees, oak and chestnut and sycamore; their leaves had largely fallen by this stage of the autumn and were strewn across the vast lawns. The place was like an oil painting in browns and yellows. A long stretch of water in the valley below glistened in the sunshine. Through an impressive arch and into a square courtyard we drove. Stanley seemed so comfortable here and was not in the least intimidated by these grand surroundings. He told me to wait in the car and, taking the letter from his inside pocket, he went to chat to a couple of uniformed officials in a small office. It all seemed very friendly. One of these soldiers returned with him and looked me over.

"Your name, sir?" he said in an English accent.

I obliged.

"Very well, Mr Henderson sir, enjoy your shoot."

He saluted and stepped stiffly back. I was fairly sure that it wasn't me he was saluting.

I gathered that we had the all-clear to drive to the shooting range which was situated some distance away in what looked to me to be a disused quarry.

There Stanley opened the boot of the Cowley and took out two identical rifles.

"This one is mine and this one is for you," he said. "These rifles are called S.M.L.Es., Point Twenty Two Short Magazine Lee-Enfield Service Rifles, the best in the business. They are our standard training rifles. This should help you feel a bit more protected, don't you think?"

I wasn't sure what to think, to be honest. I don't recall ever being so nervous in taking any piece of equipment in my hands, even though I am well used to my old shotgun at home. I carried it carefully for a good distance as I followed him to the range. He spent the first while telling me the names of all the parts, only some of which I could remember and that only because they were the same as my own gun. I learned about the stock and the muzzle, the trigger and its guard, the bolt action, the cocking piece, the firing pin, the sights and so on. He showed me the best ways to load and unload, to clean the thing and service it. Then it was on to some target practice. I was amazed at the power of it, the kick-back against my shoulder. It took a bit of getting used to but when I got the hang of the sights and got my eye in I wasn't too bad at all at hitting the target. Nowhere near as impressive

as Stanley of-course but then he was an expert with years of experience, as I recalled him telling me on several occasions.
My own feelings were that this was all a bit of a waste of time.
'The chances of me actually needing to use this gun are next to nothing,' I was constantly thinking during that morning. That was my sincere hope anyhow. Despite the fact that my father had taken the gun in his hand when he joined up, I had little interest in guns. I was not inclined in that direction. What was more, the lesson from Stanley had failed to light much of a spark of fascination in me.
We drove back by a different road, west towards Castlederg and then up to Lismore.
"I don't want to be running into that beard again," he explained. "We are trained to be aware of the need to change our route when circumstances demand it."
"I'm sure some of the men who joined the 'B' Specials around here do the same thing," I said.
"Most likely," he agreed. "What about yourself? You ever think of joining them? You'd be ideal."
"Not for me, thanks," I replied.
"Why ever not?" he asked. "Your father was in the Services, wasn't he? What was good enough for him should be good enough for you."
"My father would never have approved of me joining the 'B' Specials," I said. "He always told us to keep our heads down and not take sides."
"But he took sides, didn't he? He joined up."
"That was different," I said. "He joined up to fight the Kaiser. I'd be fighting people in my own community."
"Your own community? That's a remarkably naive view of them, if I may say so. Far too generous, Matthew. Many of the people in your own community are enemies of the State of Northern Ireland, don't you realise. Incidentally, talking about enemies, I forgot to tell you about your friend Kevin Duggan."
I had to sit over closer to him to be able to hear him, with the breeze blowing around us as we picked up speed on the straighter road.
"What about him?"
I kind of guessed what was coming.
"He is a well-known volunteer; I checked out his name in our records. It came up several times. He may even have been an Intelligence Officer in the Donegal IRA, so you are as well rid of him, aren't you?"

"I could believe it," I said. "I have heard the odd rumour and his girlfriend more or less admitted that he was active. She is a sister of Joe, you know? Well, he hasn't been around these parts this year at all. The last time I saw him was in Strabane at the Rabble Fair in May."
We drove on in relative silence for a while, then he looked over at me again.
"What about Sally Anne?" he said.
"What about her?"
"Do you think she might know Kevin Duggan?" he said.
"Not likely," I said, surprised at the strength of my own defensive reaction. "Why would she know him?"
"Why would she not? How can you be sure? They are both from Donegal. For all you know he could be her cousin. Maybe even a volunteer in the same...."
"Not at all," I said, interrupting him. "Sally Anne is not involved in any of that stuff. She hasn't a political bone in her body."
"You are sure of that, are you Matthew? How can you be so adamant?"
"Of-course I am sure. I know her well enough by now, for goodness sake. She's a good, sound girl. I would trust her with my life," I said.
"My word!" said Stanley. "You really are still struck on her, mate, whatever Victoria says. You would trust her with your life, would you? But not trust her enough to dance with her, eh?"
'He is laughing at me,' I thought. 'Goading me. This is hardly fair.'
I sat silent for a bit, staring at the road ahead. I was conscious that he was still glancing at me and with a smirk on his face.
"So you are still in love with your servant girl?" he said in a clearly mocking tone.
"No, I am not in love with anybody," I said.
'Why doesn't he mind his own business?' I was thinking. 'The dirty, debauched dog that he is!'
"But you are still getting a bit from her up in that attic every night, aren't you?" he laughed.
"No, I am not and I'll thank you to mind your own business," I said firmly.
"You're not? My goodness!" he said. "And why not, may I ask? What's wrong with you, man? She may not be Victoria but she has all the right equipment in all the right places. What's holding you back?"

"Sally Anne is not that kind of person and neither am I," I said. I was barely holding onto my temper by this stage. What sort of a man had Victoria fallen for?
"'Course she is, Matthew," he continued. "Just give me one hour with her tonight and, when I leave tomorrow, she'll be all over you for it."
I had had enough. I did a foolish thing. I grabbed the steering wheel of the car so that it swerved off the road. I hadn't meant for that to happen. Thankfully we were slowing at that point to negotiate a tight bend. For the second time that day, the car bounced up onto the grassy bank and came to a stop before it hit a hedge.
"What the bloody hell are you doing, you fool?" shouted Stanley.
I was shocked myself at what I had done. It could have been a disaster. I looked him in the eye, coldly.
"You stay away from Sally Anne," I said. "You lay one hand on her and I swear to God that you will be the first one I use that gun on, you hear me!"
"Calm down mate, for pity sake. I was only having a laugh," he said. "You are lucky you didn't put us over the ditch there. Don't ever do that again when someone is driving."
We resumed the journey in silence, a silence that continued until we reached the house. It helped that the girls were back from school by that stage and Stanley was able to take them out for a little run in the Cowley. I was nervous about that until they returned safely but the twins loved it. They were bubbling with excitement and ran to tell Sally Anne by the byre door.
"He let me honk da horn," said Millie. "I scared a cow, so I did."
"It goes so fast, Sally Anne," said Jane. "We were flying, faster than the birds."
Stanley stood grinning beside the car, sort of posing with his hand on the steering wheel and one foot on the running board.
"Sally Anne," he said, "it's your turn now. Matthew was telling me how much you would love a ride with me. Hop in."
A dark fear came over me as I watched Sally Anne take a couple of steps towards him. I could see that she was curious and longing to experience what would likely have been her first journey in a car but she was hesitating. My tongue seemed to be stuck in my mouth. I could think of nothing to do to prevent this.
"Come on," he encouraged. "Everybody is nervous the first time."
'The bastard!' I thought. 'He is laughing at me.'

"Don't Sally Anne," I said weakly.
She stopped in the middle of the street, still looking at the car.
"Why not?" she said.
What could I say? I couldn't warn her of the danger she was in with this foul man, could I, and I wasn't thinking alone of his driving.
"Because....because....because I ...." I couldn't think how to finish the sentence.
She looked long at me. It was the first time in two weeks.
"What were you going to say, Matthew?" asked Stanley, smirking behind his moustache.
How I hated that smirk of his. I wanted to punch it the other way out.
"Because I ....I still have work for you to be doing. That's all."
She turned away and went inside.
"Had you worried there, old boy, didn't I?" laughed Stanley. "Don't fret yourself. I wouldn't touch her with a barge pole. She probably smells of pig shit. She's all yours mate."
That night I went back up to the attic to sleep. I didn't tell anybody. Stanley was in the guest bedroom so it wasn't that I couldn't have slept in my own bed. No, it was just that....
I waited until I judged that Sally Anne was sleeping; I pulled the makeshift bed across the door of the box-room and crept into it. I lay awake for a long time, thinking about her sleeping next door, thinking about how I would do anything to protect her and thinking that if that bastard as much as put his nose in through that door I would punch his leering English face all the way down the stairs and out to his precious new car and drive him out of my street at the sharp end of his Point Twenty-Two Short Magazine Lee Enfield Rifle, if need be.

Chapter 26

Mary's dilemma

Mary Kearney shivered in the damp, fusty air of her bedroom and pulled the blanket up over her breasts and shoulders. Her fists clutched the hem closely around her neck as she watched her lover fumble with his shirt buttons. Resentment churned in her chest. Yet again he was up and away to 'do his bit in the struggle'. The impatient sweet-talk and the urgency of his passion now felt to her like a betrayal, a stale after-taste of what she had anticipated. Unable to hide her annoyance, her smudged lips tightened over her teeth and the creases on her brow seemed to deepen.

"Kevin," she said.

In his silence he wondered how she could say his name with such a tone of disappointment and appeal at the same time. He stood abruptly, pulled on his trousers and buckled the belt, unable to trust himself to find the right words to soothe her.

"You always do this to me," she continued. "Get what you want and get to hell out of it! That's you all over Kevin; I'm getting fed up with it."

"Agh Mary," he mumbled. "Don't sulk now. You know I have to go. I told you that before we...."

"And where are you going this time?"

"You know I can't tell you that."

"I know you're not supposed to, but you have told me near enough every other time."

He sat on the bed and bent down to pull on his boots. Mary studied the back of his head, finding one or two grey hairs in the dark curls. She lifted her free hand and ran her fingers through them.

"Well, will you at least tell me about this letter you say you came across?" she said softly.

"There's nothing more to tell," said Kevin. "A letter to Henderson from his cousin in Belfast. The only thing of any interest was this Englishman she has taken up with."

"When was it that you found it?"

"A while back. Sure didn't I send Mick to the harvest ceili in Castlederg to see what he made of the fella."

"And why did you not follow it up at the time? What did Mick say about him?" she quizzed.
"Mick didn't say much at all. He got distracted; some girl or other; you know what he's like."
"I know what you're all like."
"Anyway, he was just some Englishman; we knew nothing about him then, except that he could handle himself when he got into a fight with Gerard Dolan."
Mary shifted herself in the bed so she could slip her arm around Kevin's waist, so she could look into his eyes. The blanket fell away from her shoulders and she cuddled against him instinctively, hiding her breasts.
"But you do now?" she said quietly. "You know about him now?"
"Aye, we do. We know a lot. He has a whole history in the Black and Tans, either that or the Auxies. A bad hound. He needs fixing, so he does."
"And how do you know that he is back around here?" she asked.
"By a bit of good luck. Dolan saw him and Henderson today, in a big flashy car, somewhere down about Newtownstewart."
"And he got word to you?"
"He did! He's to meet us tonight."
"Fair play to him," Mary said.
"Fair play is right," agreed Kevin, trying to untangle himself from her embrace so he could stand. "So now's our chance. Two birds with the one stone."
Mary released him suddenly, a shadow of doubt crossing her pale face.
"Two birds?"
"Aye, the two of them," said Kevin, reaching for his coat.
Mary clutched the blanket again, a deep shudder of cold fear in her head to match the chill shiver of her skin. Kevin was about to leave. She needed to delay him, to talk this through. As his hand went to the door-handle she leapt from the bed, gathering the blanket around her, and inserted herself between him and his intention.
"Kevin, wait."
"What?"
She hesitated for a second. How to put this?
"I was just thinking. There's no need to do any harm to Matthew Henderson, is there?"
"What do you mean?"

"Well...it's not as if he is... a target, an enemy like. He's not political. Aye, he is a Unionist, same as most Protestants, but he's not a bad fella; he's not even in the 'B' Specials."
"You're joking?" he said with a half-sneer.
"I'm serious. You should leave him be Kevin."
Kevin laughed disdainfully.
"You still got a soft spot for him, have you? Just because you used to chase him through the hayfield and cuddle him like he was your...."
"Don't talk rubbish. I don't even like the fella, even though him and our Joe are so big. It's just... he's just not involved in anything."
"Well he will be, like it or not. It sends out a message. We have to let the country know that we are serious, Mary. So, come on, let me go here," he said struggling to move her from the door.
Mary moved. She had no choice, Kevin's brute force suddenly lifting her and crushing her to him for a rough kiss before abruptly setting her back on her bed.
"Kevin," she said, "leave Matthew alone, right? His mother needs him; so do the wee girls. He was good enough to you last year."
"Was he, do you think?" Kevin said sarcastically. "I worked my guts out for him. I never had one word of thanks. He made me feel like I was lucky to be allowed to walk on the same planet as him. Like I should really appreciate the privilege of working on his precious bit of land. He's a stuck up Unionist bigot, so he is. It was all he could do to give me my four pounds ten shillings at the end of the six months."
"But his mother isn't well. She has nobody except for Matthew. No man since James was killed. And the twins...."
"Her man was stupid enough to go and fight for King and Country! What did he expect?" Kevin interrupted.
"That's not her fault though, is it? My father went too, remember? Fool and all that he was! I suppose you'll eventually have to kill him as well," she said, her features twisted as she glared at him.
"You are defending your father over me, are you?" roared Kevin. "Your father was an even bigger eejit than Henderson. Him supposed to be an Irishman. He was a traitor to his own nation....are you forgetting that? I am starting to wonder about you, Mary Kearney! What side are you on girl?"
"I know all that," Mary said. "I am on the side of Ireland, you know I am, but I am on the side of a decent Ireland, a fair country.... where it

won't matter about all that stuff that has gone before and where ordinary folk get to live beside each other in peace."
"Aye well," he said, pulling the bedroom door open, "there's a long way to go and a few scores to settle before we get there."
"So this is just you trying to settle a personal score, isn't it? You have to get back at your Protestant master. What sort of Ireland is it going to be if that is the way we get on?"
"Shut your mouth, woman. You are concerning yourself with things you have no right to be talking about."
"Because I am a woman, like? Is that what you mean?"
"Because it is none of your business. Right, I am away here."
"So where are yous meeting tonight?" she asked more meekly.
Kevin paused in the corridor.
"That is none of your business either," he mumbled in a flat tone.
"Ah, so it's the usual. O'Brien's? Ten pints o' stout in the cause of Irish freedom?"
No reply.
"You might at least say goodbye?"
"You stay out of this, you hear me Mary?" he called.
She heard the kitchen door open and close, before silence overtook her home again. He had only been with her a little over an hour.
'A hasty fry and a hasty lie. Satisfy your man on all counts... and count yourself lucky to be doing your bit for the Volunteers,' she thought as her head went down to rest against the peeling wall-paper.

Chapter 27

Sally Anne Sweeney

What happened on that night

It gave me such a shock, finding Matthew back in the bed next door to me. I had wakened as usual that morning with the rising of the sun, got myself dressed and was half-way across the floor when I sensed him lying there across the door looking at me. My heart gave a jump in my chest.
"What....?" That was all I got out of me.
"Don't be panicking," he said. "I'm sorry if I scared you. I meant to be up and away before you woke."
"But why....what brought you back up here?" I stammered.
"I had my reasons," he said.
"Sure that Englishman is in the guest room?"
This was the most conversation I had had with him since the night of the fencing, I realised. His face was still blotchy from sleeping; his hair was too long; it could have been doing with a wash and was badly disordered; he rubbed red, baggy eyes and yawned at me. He looked a mess to be frank, very different from the handsome fellow he was when I had first set eyes on him.
"Aye," he said. "He's in the guest bedroom."
"What is wrong with your room?"
"Nothing."
"Well why are you back up here then? I don't want you anywhere near me when I am sleeping," I said, my annoyance at him lacing the tone of my voice.
"And I don't want him anywhere near you when you are sleeping either," he said, shifting the mattress.
At the time I could make no sense of what he was saying so I left him there and went to my work. It was only later that morning that I worked out that Matthew must have thought I was in some danger from the Englishman, that he suspected Stanley might have tried to get to me when I was sleeping. How silly of him. That chap was not in the least bit interested in me; he was getting all he needed from his

intended, that I knew, but of-course Matthew did not. Anyway, I could have protected myself if anything like that had happened. I would like to have seen him try!

I had no idea how long he was going to be staying at the farm. I hoped it would not be long; I could not wait to see the back of him, him and his flashy car. Victoria was welcome to him. He was so sure of himself, so slimy, so buttery. Matthew was as wholesome as wheaten bread by comparison and that was saying something.

So Matthew had been trying to save me from Stanley, had he? That was interesting. He did not mind humiliating me and breaking my heart but he would deliberately give up his comfortable bed in some misguided attempt to protect my honour? I would have loved to ask him about this but of-course I would say nothing. He would only misunderstand again. What a contrary character he was.

I was churning butter in the wee dairy shed behind the byre around midday when I heard the commotion in the street, the starting up of the engine, the sound of it wailing up like a siren, time after time, the screams of the twins and then the screeching of the tyres. I looked out in time to see the tail-end of Sir Stanley and his chariot driving out of the street and disappearing behind a following cloud of smoke and dust as he sped down the lane. Was that him gone already? By the sound of the excited farewells from the Henderson twins I gathered that it was.

"Good," I said out loud. "Good riddance. I hope that is the last I have to see of you."

I was telling Joe about it all later that day. In the evening I went to Kearney's as usual, walking around by the road and the two lanes because there was still no sign of a thaw in the big freeze between the two of them. It pained me every time I thought about it, especially my part in it all, but there was no point in mentioning it to Joe and I would not be for talking to Matthew about it. I only had a couple of weeks left to work and then I would be away from the pair of them, leaving them to sort out their issues in whatever way they could. Or maybe never sort them out. That possibility really concerned me, even though it was none of my business. Except, of-course that it was my business, due to the fact that I was the main reason for their falling out.

Maybe I could hint about such a horrible possibility to Joe.

We were alone together in the hay barn. I know that sounds like a cosy sort of setting, ideal for all sorts of carry-on but, believe me, there was no carry-on. I was not interested and Joe, to be fair to him, knew that.

It did not stop his sweet-talk, mind you, but he was always the gentleman and never made any attempt to lay a hand on me. The hay barn was neutral territory, comfortable and warm, even as the October evenings shortened. It was perfect for our 'heart to heart' chats which were becoming our habit of an evening, by way of comfort for each other, nothing more.

"*Seosamh*" I began.

"Cad é sin?"

"Do you think when I leave here....do you think you and Matthew will ever be friends again?"

"You are breaking two rules at the same time," he said in some annoyance. "You have mentioned him and you have mentioned your leaving. I don't want to be thinking about either of those things."

"But you must talk to Matthew; it was all such a daft thing and all over something so completely pointless. You need Matthew; you know you do. You grew up in the lee of him. You have always depended on each other. You can't cut the cord that binds you that easily. You are his friend whether you like to admit it or not. Promise me when I go you will try to make it up with him."

"When you go! When you go!" he groaned. "I don't want to hear that. Will you stop going on about it, for goodness sake. Talk about something else."

"Alright," I said. "What will I talk about?"

"I don't know," he said.

We sat there quietly for a bit, side by side, our hands inches apart, fiddling with the dried hay.

"Why do you keep talking about going home anyway? What is so good about it over there?"

"It is not that there is anything special about it," I said. "It is a hard enough place to be living, a lot of the time, not like around here with all these big rich farms. People don't have a lot. I suppose it is just that it is home and it is far away from here."

"Aye," he said sourly. "Far away from here, far away from us."

"I did not mean that. You know I did not mean that. I meant far away from Matthew Henderson, that is all."

"Will you miss....?" He stopped short.

I smiled to myself. Poor Joe; he could not even finish the sentence.

"Of-course I will miss you," I said. "I will miss all of you, all your family, the twins and Mrs Henderson; I suppose I might even miss him a bit, if I brought my mind out into the open."
"How can you say that? After all he has put you through! You are mad, Sally Anne."
"I will miss how things were and how they might have turned out," I said. "I won't miss the strain there is working at Henderson's now."
"Well I will miss you too," he said. "More than I'm fit to tell you."
"Don't Joe."
"I have only so many more of these nights to be telling you, so you are going to have trouble stopping me," he said with that stupid smile of his.
"I will stay away."
"No you won't," he said.
Then the silence of the barn was all around us for a while, the softness of the hay and its musty scent strong to us. There was only the last dregs of daylight still ebbing in through the open slats around the top of the walls. You could just about see the moths and midges that flitted in and out of the gaps; some found themselves entangled in cobwebs, fluttering and spinning in vain and attracting the attention of waiting spiders. In the distance a dog was yapping hoarsely at some unseen presence. The sound of Kearney's cattle settling for the night filtered in to us, the hollow rasp of a cow coughing and some low contented moanings.
"Do you think you will come back in this direction next year?" he asked, his face close to me and his eyes screwed up as he squinted to see mine in the gloom of the barn.
"To be hired, you mean? I don't know about that Joe. I might try my luck elsewhere, if I go to the hiring at all. You never know, I might take a notion and emigrate altogether," I said, realising that this would not be something he would want to hear but careless of the effect of my words on him as always.
"You won't do that," he said. "You still have your mother to think of, and your father. They'll be getting older. They'll need you. You wouldn't be for leaving them."
'Typical of Joe to be thinking himself into my shoes and worrying about my folks back at home. If only he would take a bit more thought about how his life is going to be in the absence of Matthew Henderson's support and friendship,' I thought.

I got down from the hay.
"It is time I was going back," I said.
"I will walk you over," he said.
"Not at all," I said. "*Tá oíche dheas ann.* It is a lovely night. Sure look, there is plenty of moonlight for me to be walking in."
"Are you sure?"
I was sure. I wanted ten minutes on my own in the peace of the evening. I left him at his back door, the intensity of the love-light in his eyes such a rebuke to me. But what could I do? There was no point in pretending that I returned his affection at this stage....that would have been even more unkind. I would just have to see out the next couple of weeks and then bid him a fond goodbye. A good friend he had been, for all his doting on me.
As I walked out his lane that night a full round moon had risen and was sitting comfortably on the dark horizon of Bessie Bell mountain. Out of its sober face, the colour of ripe corn, two grey hollow eyes were staring in my direction. They gave me the feeling that they were disappointed in me, near enough ready to rebuke me.
'What is a young girl like you doing out walking the roads at this hour?' they seemed to be saying. "Have you no self-respect about you?"
A river of pale light poured directly down the full length of Kearney's lane. Running towards me on the glint of it I was able to make out the form of a beautiful fox, its red coat turned to a pewter shade by the moonbeams. I stopped and stood completely still. For whatever reason, maybe because what breeze there was was blowing in my face, the animal was not aware of me until it was only a matter of a few yards away from where I waited. It jolted to a stop and seemed to turn into a marble statue for a second, staring back at me motionless. It studied me with bright eyes that, even in the small light of the moon, were the colour of light on the sea. They looked at me without fear, fascinated, as I was myself. It was one of those sacred sort of moments when an animal and a human being seem to see and respect the specialness of each other. There was no panic in this animal; it just looked around slowly for a gap in the hawthorn hedge and slipped away through there, the proud brush of its tail raised and waving behind it like it was blessing me with the sign of the cross.
I wondered about this unusual meeting. If I had been fearful I would have been asking if there was some meaning to this meeting. What would my grandmother have said about it? She would likely have had

some explanation for the mystery of it, some superstitious link to the ebb and flow of life, but I was at a loss.
I was still marvelling at this, walking along the road towards Henderson's lane when, strangely, I thought I heard my name being called from some distance behind me. I turned to listen, thinking it might be Joe coming after me, or maybe his father. The voice did not sound like either of them. Who on earth around here would know my name and would be out on the road at this time of night? I watched as a figure emerged into the moonlight from the shadows of some high bushes. It had a ghostly appearance to it, whatever it was; a halo of glistening white about it, like foam on the beach after a storm. For a second I remembered Joe's story about the Tullymoan ghost and wondered to myself.
"Sally Anne!" came the voice again.
Now I knew that voice. What in the name of God was Tam Glenn doing here? He was hurrying towards me but hobbling as if his feet were sore on him, like from walking for a good distance.
"Tam? Is that you?" I called. "Take your time; you look worn out."
"It is me, alright," he said, "and I am worn out but...." He seemed to need to catch his breath, bending over with his hands on his knees and wheezing like a man on his last legs. I noticed that his fiddle case was strapped to his back but there was no sign of his parcel of tin or his bundle of possessions.
"What is wrong with you? Where is your stuff?"
"I am alright," he said, "or I will be in a minute. My stuff is in Strabane. I thought I could walk quicker without it. I left it behind a stone-ditch."
"You have walked all the way from Strabane?" I said. "In the one go?"
"I have that," he said between gasps. "From Lifford, to be exact."
"Why did you do that? Is something the matter?"
"Aye," he said. "Something is the matter, Sally Anne. Something terrible. I had to come."
He paused to wipe the wet from his nose and beard with the sleeve of his coat.
"Go on then. What is wrong?"
He took a deep breath.
"The Englishman is going to be shot!"
"What? What are you talking about? Who is going to be shot?"
"The Englishman that was at the Harvest Ceili; you know, the one that caused the fight," he said.

"Stanley?" I said.
"I don't know what name is on him," he said, "but there's a few boyos are going to come here this night to shoot him. Him and Matthew Henderson too!"
"Shoot Matthew?" I said. "Why do they want to shoot Matthew? How do you know all this Tam?"
"I don't know all about it," he said. "I just know what I heard, that's all. That is why I came as quick as I could. I was just hoping I would make it before it was too late. Is Matthew still alright?"
"I think so," I said. "I have not been there since tea-time. I was over with Joe."
"You didn't hear any shots?"
"Shots? God no! Nothing," I said. "But how do you know about this?"
"I'll tell you the whole story," he said. "I was in a public house in Lifford. I let the temptation get the better of me. I know I shouldn't have but I had done well for meself up around Donemana and I had a good wheen o' shillings so....I went for a drink or two; then it turned into two or three hours, then into two or three days."
"And what does you going on the tear have to do with Matthew and Stanley getting shot?" I asked impatiently.
"I'm coming to that," he said, holding up a shaky hand. "I suppose I just stayed in the pub there. There's bits of it I don't remember a lot about but last night I woke up in a tight space. For a minute I thought I was in a coffin but then I heard voices and I thought to meself, 'I'm not as dead as I first suspected'. I lay still, sort of wondering where I was. I worked it out that I must have fallen off the bench in one of O'Brien's wee snugs and rolled in underneath it. Nobody disturbed me; maybe they didn't even know I was there. So anyways, I was just about to roll back out of there to the land of the living when I heard one of the voices mention the name of 'Matthew Henderson'. I very near put my head out to say, 'Aye, I know Matthew; he's a friend of mine.' But thankfully I had more wit than that. I just lay on and listened to them whispering."
"What did they say," I asked. "Who were they anyway?"
"Well dear," he said, "your guess is as good as mine on that one but you wouldn't have to guess very long to hit on what sort of boys they were. One of the voices... I thought I recognised it now.... but my brain was so befuddled that it was only later on that it came to me. There

was a fellow worked to Matthew last year by the name of Kevin Duggan."
"I know about him," I said.
"Well, it was his voice I heard and he has it in for Matthew too. There were two other voices but them I had never heard before."
"What did they say Tam?" I asked, hoping he could hurry up with his story.
"They were quizzing this fella. His story was that he had been driving cattle somewhere when this car came flying round a bend and nearly killed him and beasts and all. He said he recognised the driver. It was the Englishman, and Matthew Henderson was beside him in the front seat, laughing at him and his animals on the road. He remembered them from the fight at the dance. He was very worked up about it. One of them seemed to be the boss and he had to keep telling this fella to lower his voice. Anyway, between them they suspect that the Englishman is a British soldier, maybe even one of the Black and Tans. They know that he is staying with Matthew so it's a grand chance for them to shoot him. That's what they are planning to do tonight, Duggan and this other fellow that seemed to be the boss. Duggan said that he was looking forward to putting a bullet into Matthew's thick skull."
"But why?" I said. "What does he have against Matthew? He is no soldier."
"I know, but he has a soldier staying in his house. He's helping the British, according to Duggan. The same boy has no time for Matthew, you know. All the more so now, for he didn't give him his job back this year."
"He is not going to like me much either then," I said, "'cause I took his job."
"He doesn't know you, Sally Anne. You'll be alright. You're a Donegal girl. It's Matthew I am worried about. That Stanley fellow I couldn't give two hoots about."
"But Stanley left today," I said. "He is not there."
"He left?" said Tam. "So Matthew is there on his own? You didn't tell me that. Oh Lord above, what are we to do?"
"I don't know," I said. "I think I will go and tell Anthony and Joe. They will know what to do."

"Aye, that's a good idea," said Tam. "You go… and make sure you stay down there tonight. It could be dangerous to be in Henderson's. Stay safe down there, you hear me girl!"

I left him and ran all the way back down to Kearney's. I did not wait to knock on the door, just ran straight into the kitchen. I saw the shock on Anthony's face; he was alone there, halfway through undressing for bed.

"What in the name o' God is wrong?" he said.

"Matthew is going to be shot tonight," I spluttered out. "What are we going to do?"

"Calm yourself, my dear," he said. "You'll wake the wains. What has come over you at all?"

"I met Tam Glenn on the road. He knows about it....he has heard about it?"

Joe arrived in the kitchen.

"Heard about what, Sally Anne?" he said.

"Heard that Matthew is going to be shot. And the Englishman. He was drunk in some pub in Lifford. They are coming tonight with guns. What are we to do?"

My voice, I realised, was high and trembling. My shoulders, indeed my whole body had started to shake and shiver, although I could not have said I felt cold.

"Get her a cup of tea," said Anthony to his wife as she came from the bedroom.

"So you met Tam Glenn? How did you meet him?"

"Just after I left you Joe," I said. "He was exhausted. He had walked all day from Lifford."

"And was he drunk, you say?" said Anthony.

"No, he was not drunk. He was as sober as I am."

"But you said we was..."

"I know I said that, but he is not drunk now, honestly. He came all this way to warn us."

Joe spoke, a bit doubtful of my story by his tone. "You met Tam Glenn and he told you he had been drunk. And when he was drunk, he had heard some sort of rumour about Matthew Henderson being shot? Am I right so far?"

"Aye," I said, "but stop smiling about it; it is serious."

"And the shooting is to be tonight? Who is going to do the shooting? Why would they want to shoot Matthew? He's not in the 'B' Specials or anything, is he?"
"I don't know about that; I don't know anything much about it. They want to shoot that Englishman, Stanley, because they think he is a Black and Tan or something. He was at Henderson's today. Yesterday he had Matthew away somewhere with him in the car, I don't know where, but they were seen together."
"Who are these men, for goodness sake?" said Joe. "It's hardly going to be some gang of volunteers planning something and telling oul Tam Glenn about it in advance?"
"How did Tam hear this?" asked Anthony.
"He says he woke up under a seat and heard these boys talking," I said. I could see the quick glance between father and son. They were not believing me. Even I was no longer believing me.
"You don't think Tam was just making this up?" said Anthony.
"If he did, he then ran all the way from Lifford to here to tell us," I said. "That is how convinced he is that it is a real threat."
"Maybe he is just starting to hear voices," smiled Joe. "It happens after a feed of drink, I am told."
"Voices," I said. "Aye, he heard voices and he recognised one of them. It was the fellow who worked to Matthew last year."
The atmosphere in the kitchen changed as if I had just dropped a pile of crockery on the hard clay floor. The three Kearneys looked at each other and there was something different in their look.
"What did you say?" said Anthony.
"One of the voices in the pub was that fellow Kevin that Matthew hired last year."
"Kevin Duggan?" said Joe.
"That is what he said."
"Kevin Duggan was one of the men plotting to kill Matthew and the Englishman?" said Monica.
"Aye, that is what Tam said," I repeated.
There was a strained silence as they thought about this piece of information. Joe gave a little shake of his head.
"It could still be Tam imagining things," he said. "He would know about what happened with Duggan last year. He would have heard the rumours. This doesn't prove anything."
"Maybe not," said Anthony, "but I am starting to believe his story."

"But what do we do about it," I asked. "Those boys could be on their way here at this very minute; like as not they are somewhere close by. They don't know that Stanley left today. Matthew is on his own over there. Can yous do something to help him?"
"Of-course we will; we'll do what we can," said Anthony.
"What can we do though?" asked Joe.
"Well, we can warn him for a start. We can go over and help him barricade the doors. I'll take the shotgun; even if it only makes a bang it will maybe make somebody think twice," said his father.
"You can go if you want to," said Joe, "but I am not going next nor near him."
"What?" I said. "Joe, you have to help your friend, for God's sake."
"I don't have to help Matthew Henderson," he said. "I would help any of my friends but he has stopped being one of them."
"So you would take the same side as your sister?" said Monica painfully. "You would betray all that we stand for and take the side of Duggan? That is not how we brought you up, Joe Kearney and I am ashamed of you. Even Mary would be ashamed of you, if she was here."
"This hasn't to do with Mary," he said. "It's not as simple as you are making it out to be."
"It is as simple as this son," said Anthony. "I promised his dying father that I would do my best to look after Eliza and the children as long as I live. That is what I intend to do, whether you help or not. If ever I meet James up above how would I look him in the eye if I break my promise now?"
"That's grand for you, Da," said Joe. "I understand that but he has hurt me; he has hurt Sally Anne and he has never as much as said 'Sorry' in any way."
I spoke. "He has hurt me, I will not deny that Joe, but you would hurt me even more if you would not be a big enough man to stand by him tonight."
Joe stood head down in the middle of his kitchen floor. His foot kicked out at the table leg and then he lifted his head and looked at me.
"You are one good girl, Sally Anne Sweeney. I'll go with yous."
I smiled at him and the return smile that I got nearly split that wee face of his.
Anthony took the shotgun from where it hung above the kitchen dresser and put a couple of cartridges in his pocket from a tin on the

top shelf. Joe stuck on a coat and held his father's out to help him get his arms into the sleeves. Monica stood, arms folded, watching the two of them and I read a mixture of pride and worry between the lines on her brow.

We left their cottage, the three of us together, unconsciously huddled closer than we normally would have against the coolness of the night air, against the anxiety and the sense of threat which we shared.

Joe paused at the gable where the moon-shadow of the house fell across the meeting of street and lane.

"Here Da," he said. "Give me that gun to carry for you. You'll make better speed without it. Yous go by the road. I'm taking the short-cut as usual. He's not going to deny me that and me coming to his help tonight, is he now?"

"But how will you get through the wire?" his father asked.

"Ah, there's plenty of holes still in the hedge if you know where to look for them."

"Well, be careful with that gun. We don't want any accidents the night," said Anthony and he gave him the shotgun and the cartridges.

"I'll watch myself, don't you worry about me. Sure it's not even loaded yet," he said and disappeared into the shadows in the direction of the burn.

Chapter 28

Matthew Henderson

The regrets of a night

I was in the kitchen. Mother had long since gone to her room. Lately she had started to go to bed much earlier, so that now she went about the same time as the twins. There was still no sign of Sally Anne, whatever was keeping her. She was another one who had been changing her habits, coming home later and later, even as the days shortened.

I had been thinking about her… about us. Was I just going to let these last few weeks of her hiring here with us slip by and see her walking out of my life forever without making one more attempt to get her to see my point of view and take up with me again where we had left off?

There had been so many times recently when I had secretly watched her as she worked. The movement of her body fascinated me, every bit as much now as it did when we were courting, even more if I am honest. She had filled out beautifully in the six months, I thought. Our good food had helped the whole shape of her. There was a tempting fullness to her figure now; fine curves where there used to be straight lines. I would have given anything to hold her again, enjoy her form and feel that warm female response that I remembered with such mixed feelings.

Aye, the pain and the pleasure of it all; the thrill and the guilt. There were times when I was right proud of myself that I had resisted her charms. She had had me under her spell and I had loved it, despite myself.

Now, as the day of her leaving drew closer, there were far more times when I would have given anything to have taken her back from that place, back to the night up in the attic when I might have enjoyed her to the full. I found myself wallowing in self-pity and regret, regret for the opportunities I had missed. Often I allowed my imagination to take me back to that crucial night. I let myself dream of what it would have been like to have loved her with no limitations. I imagined myself slowly pushing the door open, taking her hand, our fingers entwining at first as I took in the look of her standing there in all her loveliness, the light in her green eyes inviting me in. Ah, regrets, regrets!

I often wondered what would have happened if Victoria and her man hadn't arrived in Lismore when they did. Would I have found myself spending nights in her bed? And what might that have led to? A child? A quick marriage? Would that have been so bad, after all? What would have been wrong with it? Being with the loveliest, funniest girl I had ever met or was ever likely to meet? Sure what could have been better? Suffering the slander of the bigots in the neighbourhood and my church would have been a price worth paying. Aye, my own family circle too. Ah, what a fool I had been.

That night, as I sat waiting for her to arrive back from Joe's, I had a sudden urge to tell her exactly how I felt. Maybe it was not too late. I would tell her how misguided I had been. Somehow I would find a way of breaking through this crust she had put round herself. I just needed her to look me in the eyes again, to remember what we had meant to each other a few weeks ago. That night at the dance was just a stupid mistake, her mistake to some extent but very much my mistake too. These things happen...the course of true love never runs smooth, as the man said. I needed her to see that. I needed her to understand the way Victoria had wormed her way into my head and changed me. I would beg Sally Anne to forgive me and forget about what had happened. And I would tell her that I still loved her, that I still wanted her.

Aye, and I would go further. I would ask her to stay on. Stay during the winter months. Stay on for good maybe.

Lord above but that felt good, to come to that decision.

What the hell, I would go the whole hog. I would ask her to marry me, damn it!

I would tell her that she didn't need to leave. She didn't need to worry about living in poverty and depression in the west of Donegal any longer. My mind was made up. Changed and made up. It wouldn't change back again, no not for anything, not for anybody. She would be mine and I would ride proudly with her beside me in the pony and trap through Castlederg, through the whole countryside. I would tell anybody who wanted to listen to me that she was my Sally Anne. I would shout it loud to my minister, to Alice Porter and her stuck-up, bank-manager father, to cousin Victoria, to Sproule and the holy Bonds, to Joe Kearney and all the Kearneys.

"This is my new wife, Sally Anne Henderson," I would say, "and I am not ashamed of it. So put that in your pipe and smoke it."
Aye, there would be folk in the neighbourhood who would see to it that we would suffer; we might be shunned, threatened even, but we wouldn't be the first. To my certain knowledge in the past there had been at least two other farmers in the county who had married their Catholic maid. How they had managed to get around the church problem I did not know but I could soon find out. It might have caused a bit of a commotion at the time but things had settled down and people got used to it. They could get over the shock of me married to Sally Anne just the same around these parts.
I was so roused and excited by my own enthusiasm that I rose from my chair and hurried upstairs to the closet. If I was going to propose to her this night I would want to be doing it looking my best.
I washed my hair, shaved and gave myself as good a scrubbing as I had ever had. I even gave my teeth a bit of a scouring. I put on a white shirt and a red tie. I found my navy Sabbath suit and put it on. I was looking at myself in the mirror, giving my hair a final brush when I heard Fly starting to bark in the street.
'Great,' I thought to myself. 'That will be her back now. I'll go down and open the door for her. She'll get the shock of her life when she sees me standing there looking like this.'
But, before I even got to the door, I heard it being banged by somebody who was desperate to get in.
'Who is that?' I was thinking. 'It couldn't be Sally Anne, making a commotion like that, enough to rouse the whole house.'
"Matthew!" I heard a voice shouting. "It's me!"
I knew that voice. I hurried to open the door.
"Tam! What are you doing here and why are you making such a commotion?" I said. "The door is open. Why didn't you just come in rather than trying to waken the whole neighbourhood?"
"Matthew," he gasped, "you are in danger. There's fellows out to shoot you. This very night!"
It is funny what goes through your head in strange circumstances like that. This old vagabond standing wheezing at my door in his smelly rags, me in my Sunday-best and all decorated up to be proposing to my girl and thinking, 'Bad timing, Tam. Surely you could have stayed away for just a few more hours 'till I get to the other side of this special

moment? Nobody's going to shoot me in the meantime, for God's sake!'

I examined his face. The panic in him shone brightly in his watery old eyes.

"Come in here and settle yourself," I said and he followed me inside.

"You need to bolt the door and get yourself into a safe place," he said looking around. "Close those curtains too. Don't be giving them an easy shot at you."

'Goodness,' I thought, 'he really believes this, whatever kind of state he has got himself into.'

"Tam," I said as gently as I could, "this is all some sort of a fit you are having. Nobody is going to shoot me. You are imagining things."

"I'm not imagining nothing'," he said. "This is the God's honest truth. It's going to happen this very night."

"Agh Tam," I said, "maybe you had a feed of bad drink and it's given you nightmares. You dreamt this."

"No I did not," he insisted. "Aye, I did have a feed of drink, far too much of it, and I slept far too long after it, so I did, but it was when I woke up I heard all this."

I smiled to myself. It is amazing what too many pints of porter can do to somebody. I had seen this in Tam before. In times past he would have gone on the drink for a few days and always after it his poor old mind would be very open to seeing things that weren't there, hearing voices that weren't real and imagining all sorts of disasters. I had thought that he was on the wagon this past number of years but you never knew with somebody like Tam. One wee thing could set him back on the bottle again. I moved to the hearth to put the kettle on for a cup of tea to console him.

"Tam," I said. "I'm right disappointed in you. You told us you had given up the booze and now, look at you. It's going to ruin you, my friend. In fact it's going to kill you, and soon, if you don't quit it for good."

"Well, if it does Matthew, at least you won't be having to come to my funeral," he said.

"Why's that?" I asked.

"Because you'll be dead already. It's tonight they are coming! Would you listen to what I'm telling you," he almost shouted.

"Whisht, Tam," I said. "Who is this that is supposed to be coming, for God's sake?"

"Kevin Duggan and a couple of other boyos."
The name broke into my consciousness like a church bell had just rung at the side of my head.
"Kevin Duggan?" I said. "What has he to do with this?"
"It's him that's going to be shooting you," said Tam.
"Did you meet him?" I asked. "How do you know about this?"
"I woke up under a bench and, while I was wakening, I heard him talking."
"Agh Tam," I said. "This is just a fool notion. You had a dream and you thought you heard his voice and you somehow connected it with me because he had worked here. And the effect of the drink had you all through-other. So you came to the conclusion that this man was out to get me....I can see how that all appeared to you after sleeping off a bellyful of porter."
Tam was quiet for a minute, thinking. You could nearly see the mist clearing in him.
"Well maybe you're right," said Tam, giving his eyes a good rubbing.
"Of-course I'm right. Here, sit down there and content yourself. I'm getting you a cup of tea for your nerves," I said.
"Alright, alright," he said sitting down at the hearth. I watched the poor man, his bones and muscles were obviously very sore and he looked as if another clean shirt would do him, so tired was he.
"Good," I said. "Put your head down there in a minute and have yourself a sleep. You look worn out. Have you travelled far the night?"
"Aye, from Lifford, all in one march," he said, kind of staring at me. "But...why are you all dressed up, Matthew? Is this a Sunday? Have I missed out more days than I thought?"
"No, you're not that far gone," I smiled. "It's not Sunday 'till tomorrow. Naw...I'm dressed up for a different reason altogether. I am going to ask Sally Anne to stay on here with me, whenever she gets back from Kearneys. What do you think of that?"
"Lord above, that's a good wan," he said, looking at me strangely. "That's going to give her the shock of her life."
"You think?" I said.
"I do surely," he said. "I saw her on the road there the night.... she was telling me that the Englishman has left. It's just as well for him for it was him that those boys were after, first and foremost. You were only a bonus."

'Oh dear!' I thought. 'Here he is, still as confused as ever, the poor oul tinker.'

"You saw her on the road? What was she doing?" I asked him.

"She was coming home here, but I sent her back down to Kearney's," he said. "I told her to stay with them. She'll be safer there."

I was just about to change the subject and ask him where his bag and fiddle were when I suddenly had a different thought. How did he know that the Englishman had even been here? Maybe he really had met Sally Anne and she had mentioned Stanley's presence and the fact that he had left. I knew that she had a bit of an attitude to Stanley, as I had myself, of-course.

"So was it Sally Anne mentioned the Englishman to you?" I asked him.

"Well, she just told me that he had left today. That fella in the pub was talking about him. He had been driving a herd of bullocks somewhere. You and the Englishman must have been out in a car or something and yous had nearly run into him. That was the reason they wanted to shoot the pair of you."

Suddenly a loud alarm was starting to sound in my head. How could Tam have known about that event? Not even Sally Anne knew!

"Wait a minute, Tam," I said with a bit more urgency. "Are you saying that these men knew about Stanley being here?"

"Now you're getting the point of it all," said Tam. "That's what I was trying to tell you. They know all about your Stanley man."

"And one of them was the fellow who was driving the cattle near Ardstraw? The same chap who had been fighting with Stanley at the dance?"

"That's the truth, so it is."

"And Kevin Duggan was there too? How did you know it was Kevin Duggan anyway? Did you see him?"

"No I didn't see him. I recognised his voice. Sure he worked here last year. I never forget a voice; it's like the sound of a tune, do you see? The drink didn't destroy all my senses."

"And what did they say they were going to do?" I asked urgently.

"Shoot him, shoot you! Isn't that what I am trying to tell you?"

"When? When did they say they were going to do this shooting?"

"Tonight! I told you that already but you wouldn't listen," said Tam getting more and more tired by the minute as we talked.

"Tonight these men are going to come here to shoot me and Stanley! My God, Tam, why didn't you tell me this at the start?"

He closed his eyes with something close to a smile.
"I did. That is exactly what I did tell you. Now, young fellow, would you ever pour me that cup of tay and let me lie here for a sleep before I fall down through myself?"
"Sorry Tam," I said. "You go ahead and do that. I need to think what to be doing."
The heart was now racing in me. The shock of Tam's news and the possible truth of it had my mind all in a turmoil. What was I to do? I tried to calm myself, to start to think clearly. At the same time, it was one of those times when to sit still and come up with a plan would have been time wasted, possibly a fatal delay. For all I knew, if Tam was right Duggan and his bearded friend could be coming up my lane right at this minute, armed to the teeth.
'Thank God Stanley was here and left me with a weapon,' I thought.
It was time for action.
I ran and bolted the back door. I took the oil lamp and ran upstairs to my bedroom. Kneeling down, I pulled the rifle from under my bed and took it from its sheath. My hands were trembling as I found the clip of five bullets at the bottom of my clothes drawer where I had hidden them.
I went to the closet and looked out over the back street.
'Twenty minutes ago I was in here washing myself to be ready for a life-changing marriage proposal. Now look at me,' I thought.
I loaded the clip into the magazine as Stanley had taught me. It didn't come as easy to me now, without his help and with these quivering fingers. If it came to the bit, would I ever be able to fire this thing straight? My hands were shaking like leaves in a thunderstorm.
'Take some deep breaths,' I told myself as I carefully opened the closet window. I clicked off the safety lever, pushed forward the bolt and turned it over. The Lee Enfield was cocked and ready for firing.
I settled myself, kneeling on the floor with the barrel of the gun resting on the window sash and trained on the corner of the byre. The moon was casting a beam of light over most of the street but it was also creating a deep shadow along the line of the barn. This could be a disadvantage for me if any intruder decided to slip towards the backdoor along that wall. Suddenly I thought of my own silhouette outlined in the open window by the oil-lamp burning on the table behind me. Anyone coming into our farmyard, either from the front

lane to the right or the back lane to the left, would surely see me up there.

'How stupid of me,' I thought. 'I wouldn't be much good in the 'B' Specials!'

I reached back and turned down the wick so that it went out with a quick splutter.

I sat there and watched for the smallest sign of movement. It is amazing the things you think about when you are in such a situation. One part of my mind still refused to fully believe what Tam Glenn had been telling me. It all seemed so far-fetched, so unreal. I had to keep going over the details of what he had said to convince myself that this wasn't just some daft notion of his.

So my suspicions had been right all along. Kevin Duggan was indeed a volunteer in the IRA, as Stanley said and as Mary Kearney had hinted. A dangerous man to have had working here last year. A gunman sleeping under my very roof! It was all a bit hard to believe. This time last year I would have given him as good a reference as I could have given any labourer.

'It just shows you,' I thought. 'Do you ever really know anyone and what is going on in the secrecy of their own heads?'

I was still listening intently to the silence of the night, trying to pick up any unusual sounds. The only thing I heard was the bleating of some sheep away up in the distant mountain behind us. That and the odd hooting of an owl somewhere below in the valley.

I shifted so as not to put a crease in my suit trousers. My mind began to wander back to the reason I was dressed up in that suit at all. I started to think about Sally Anne again. How did I really know what was going on in her pretty wee head all the while she had been working here? I had thought I could judge her well enough in the early days but of late she had stayed so tight into herself, not willing to listen to me, not able to forgive and forget. How could all that love that we had shared disappear so completely, and in such a short space of time? Maybe I had hurt her more deeply than I had realised at first, maybe destroyed her confidence altogether.

'Agh but I really need to talk to her honestly; I'll try again tomorrow when this commotion is over and she comes back from Kearneys. I need to listen to her side of things, try to understand her a bit better,' I thought to myself.

This gun was getting heavy in my hands. How good a shot was I going to be with it if Duggan appeared in the yard? Probably not great, on my first shot in anger. It wouldn't matter though, as long as it scared them off. Goodness, what was my mother going to think when the shot went off? And the girls? They were going to get the shock of their wee lives, I was thinking, and no Sally Anne there to be comforting them.

How I wished Stanley had stayed on tonight as well. This would have been right up his street, if he was the grand warrior that he kept hinting he was. I could have used his help alright...seen what he was made of. Myself? I will not deny that I was nervous, nervous and scared; at the same time, the initial shock had worn off me a bit and I was feeling strangely cold and calm. This would likely be a false alarm anyhow, a lot of fuss about nothing.

What was that movement in the street?

From the shadows on the right I saw our dog emerge into the grey light and begin to bark in the direction of the back lane. To begin with, it stood still in the centre of the cobblestones, halfway between barn and byre opposite. It was aware of something beyond the left hand corner of the street, where the back lane begins. I pointed my rifle in that direction and looked down the barrel. Fly was still barking, making darting runs in that direction.

So Duggan, with his knowledge of my farm, was going to come at me from the back lane, was he?

'He is in for a surprise,' I thought, my heart thumping like a drum against my ribs.

At the last minute Fly stopped barking and, subconsciously I registered that her head went down in that friendly, welcoming manner of hers and she started to wag her tail.

'Duggan's a clever bastard. He knows our dog and she knows him,' I thought and just as I thought that he came around the corner.

I saw the gleam of the gun-barrel in his hands.

He was on his own though, no sign of the other man yet.

He spoke to Fly.

It might be the last thing he would ever say if I could be accurate enough.

My finger closed on the trigger and the rifle exploded in my hands, the same thud as before against my shoulder.

Duggan fell backwards as the bullet took him, likely in the chest I thought. He never made a sound.

'God above, I have hit him,' I thought. 'My first shot in anger and I have hit the bugger!'
My ears were still reverberating from the noise, deafening in the stillness of the night and in the closed-in space of the closet.
I whipped the bolt back to load the next round. The second man could appear at any minute. I was ready again, sights trained on the corner of the byre.
Fly had taken off at the gunshot.
I waited for the next figure, stupidly. He was hardly going to walk straight in to the street having heard the shot and maybe having seen Duggan fall.
'What a shot that was. Stanley would be proud of me,' I thought.
But, as I waited in the still silence and as my ears stopped ringing, I began to realise that it wasn't exactly a silence at all.
What was that noise I was beginning to hear?
From the direction of the road, the front lane. A high-pitched screaming. Coming closer, toward the house; coming up the lane.
I switched the gun to the right side of the window and covered the entrance of the front lane this time, just in case.
That screaming! What was it? A girl's voice, it sounded like. Yelling and yelling, the sound of it carrying shrill and loud on the night air, wailing like the proverbial banshee.
What on earth was this?
Suddenly it came to me that the voice was Sally Anne's.
But why was she screaming and what was she trying to say?
I listened as it came closer.
What I heard near enough turned me to stone.
"Joe! Joe! Don't be shooting Joe! Don't be shooting Joe! Matthew, don't be shooting Joe!"
The gun suddenly felt very heavy and loosened in my hands.
What was she shouting that for? What had Joe got to do with this?
I saw her come into the street. She was running, full pelt. Straight across to the fallen body spread out there in the cold glint of the moon.
"Joe! Joe!" she was crying. "What has he done to you?"
'Why does she think it's Joe?' I was thinking. 'She'll see his face in a second and know that it is not Joe lying there. It's Kevin Duggan.'
I watched her as she put her arm underneath his head and cradled it.

"Agh, Joe," she was sobbing, "don't be doing this to us. Joe, Joe, Joe! Why did you not just come with us? Why did you have to go up the back way?"
My finger came away from the trigger and my thumb clicked the safety catch to on. I set the gun down on the floor, still staring into the street below. I saw another figure come out of the shadows and limp across the cobbles to the body.
'Anthony,' I thought, 'what are you doing here?'
"Matthew Henderson!" she was screaming. "Where are you? Come out here and see what you have done! You have shot Joe!"
But I was still stuck to the spot there in the closet. The horror of what I had just done was slowly boring its way into my head and was putting me into some sort of coma of dread. I couldn't move a muscle to leave this closet, to go down there to the street, as I knew that I had to. It was as if the walls of that wee room had closed in around me like some kind of shell.
The night was suddenly cool and I began to shiver. I pulled a towel off the rail and covered my head with it. The shivering deepened into a shake that I had no control over and I rolled over on to the floor, on top of Stanley's rifle.
"Damn him and his weapons!" I said aloud, like I was renouncing the devil and all his works. "Damn him! Damn him! Damn him!"
My throat and mouth and my lips had dried up completely. I couldn't get a spittle from anywhere to wet them.
'Please God,' I thought, 'let me waken from this nightmare. Let this be a punishment of some kind and let it lift off of me as quickly as it came.'
How long I stayed in that state I could not begin to guess. All sounds from the street I somehow blocked out of my consciousness. The first thing that brought me to my senses was the towel being ripped from my grasp and a jugful of cold water being poured over my head.
I looked up to see Tam Glenn standing there looking down at me with a terrible expression on his face.
"Get up, Matthew," he said. "Come down to the street and see what needs to be done now."
"I can't Tam. I can't face it. I just want to stay here," I said.
Another jug of water, this time thrown in my face with such energy it took my breath away.

"Get up and come this minute," he said. "The girls are in hysterics and your mother is badly confused. They're in the kitchen. They need you."
"Where is Anthony?" I asked.
"In the street still. With Sally Anne. And Joe."
"Is Joe alright?"
"No he's not alright. Come and see for yourself," he said.
"I can't face it."
"I know that," he said, "but you have to. You don't have any choice Matthew. He was your friend."
That was the final straw. Suddenly I was bawling like a baby. I couldn't do anything else. If you had offered me a thousand pound in my hand to stop I couldn't have stopped.
Tam left me. In disgust, I thought.
After a while I heard somebody else come into the closet behind me.
"Come here son," said the soft voice of Anthony Kearney.
I looked up at his dark figure and cowered back into a corner, pushing my back against the wall with all the force in my legs. There was no give in it. No escape. Only Anthony's eyes were visible to me and they were piercing me with their shining grief. I tried but I couldn't speak. I just curled myself on the floor again, like a hedgehog.
"Come here son," he said again.
I stayed where I was. He knelt down with a grunt of stiffness and I felt his big strong arms go around me and pull me into him in a hug of such violent care as there are no human words to describe. And it lasted for a long time.
A long time indeed.
I cried again, like a baby. So did Anthony.
"Ah, my poor son, my poor son," he kept saying over and over.
"I didn't mean to...." I said.
"I know that Matthew, I know that."
"Is he....?"
"Aye, he's dead," he said.
"I didn't know it was him. I didn't mean to shoot Joe."
"I know that, son," he said.
"I just saw the light on his gun. I thought it was Duggan. How was I to know that Joe would be coming.....what was he coming for anyway?" I asked.
"He was coming to help you to defend yourself against Duggan's boys.".

"Agh, for God's sake," I cried.
"I should never have given him the gun to carry for me. He was only taking it to make it easier for me to walk the road to you," he said.
"You were coming too?" I asked.
"Aye, and Sally Anne as well. I suppose it could have been any of us got shot."
"Sally Anne went to get yous all to help me?"
"She did. She's a good girl Matthew. None better. She's down there now... still holding him in her arms until the priest comes," he said. "Tam is away to get Samuel Bond to go down for Father Mullan and get the police."
"Father Mullan?"
"Aye son, for the last rites."
My despair was complete.
"Will you not come down and speak to Sally Anne?" he asked. "You owe her that at least, do you not think?"
"What will I say?" I asked him.
"That I don't know. You'll just have to look inside yourself for that one," he said.
"Alright," I said. "Does his mother know yet?"
"She doesn't. I don't know how I'm going to tell her."
"Can you and me go together to her?" I said.
"We can that," he said.
We helped each other to rise from the floor.

Chapter 29

Sally Anne Sweeney

How my hiring came to an end

I only set foot in Henderson's kitchen the once after that night. Even that once was difficult enough. It had seemed only right for me to be staying with the Kearneys from then on. It was a wake after all. They needed all the support they could get.

The community gathered around them. People came from far and near, such was the effect of this sad tragedy on the whole neighbourhood. People from every kind of background were at the wake, people from all walks of life, high and low, people of every type of religion that this part of the world seems to be blessed with. Blessed or cursed, depending on how you look at it, I am thinking. The sympathy and prayers that Anthony and Monica received from every single one of those visitors was lovely to see. I am sure it was a great help to them but there was no real way for anything to heal the pain they were in. In my heart I was suffering deeply too but the sorrow on me was nothing compared to theirs. I sobbed myself to sleep those nights in Kearney's and I was only a blow-in friend of Joe's.

People were sitting quietly in the kitchen and the bedrooms of the wake house. Not much was said. Nobody was going to discuss the tragic way that Joe had died in the hearing of his parents. No theories were put forward. No details disclosed. All the head-shaking, the gossip and surmising happened in other places, not in the Kearney homestead. I am sure that a thousand inquests were held nightly in homes all over the parish but nobody was going to be adding to the family's pain by bringing their makeshift verdicts into the presence of the innocent young man stretched out before them.

For three days Joe's body lay in the kitchen underneath the blinded window. The colour of his skin was near enough that of the white linen that covered him. Rosary beads were twined in his fingers.....my Rosary beads. I was thankful to Monica that she allowed me to do that. A little crucifix lay on his chest, right on top of where that cruel bullet had entered his poor body and stolen away his youth.

The man who fired the bullet came too. He sat at the head of Joe's coffin and the tears flowed silently down his big, rosy cheeks like trickles of rain on a window pane during a heavy shower. That is what Kate told me anyway. But I could not give a single look to the way he was on! Not for all the tea in China would I have looked at him. Anthony, Monica, even Tam Glenn tried to talk to me about that. They all said I needed to make my peace with him, rather than go on blaming him for Joe's death. They all said that it would eat away at me like a canker if I did not try to see what had happened from his point of view. I should make an effort to forgive him, they were telling me.

"Look at him, sitting there with his hand on Joe's head," Monica whispered to me. "Every couple of minutes he asks Joe to forgive him, again and again. He can't forgive himself, so he can't. Go to him, Sally Anne. You're the only person who can get through to him now. Go to him and tell him it's going to be alright. Tell him that Joe would forgive him if he was here. He's a Protestant, you see; he has nobody to forgive him, no priest, no father of his own to be comforting him."

Whether that was true or not I did not know but, no matter what the good woman said to me, I could not bring myself to talk to him, not even to look at him. I kept my gaze away from him for every one of those minutes that he sat there in his torture.

'Let him weep,' I said to myself. 'He has earned it!'

I would not play a tune on Tam's fiddle in front of him either. Monica had asked me to play the first night of the wake.

"Joe would love you to," she said. "Just play something he liked."

I was very slow about doing that. For a start, Joe always loved the reels and jigs. I would not be playing anything that jolly in this situation.

"Are you sure?" I asked her. "Maybe it would not be right."

"He would want it," she said. "Will you not go over and bring Matthew's fiddle and play it for him?"

"I will never play that fiddle again, but maybe Tam will let me use his, if you really want me to play."

So that is what I did. I played a slow air for him each night of the wake, an old Donegal lament. *'Coinleach Ghlas an Fomhair'* we called it, 'The Green Stubble Fields of Autumn' and the sadness of it suited. I played it on Tam's fiddle. The mourners listened as they supped their tea and whiskey. I think they were relieved that the silence was being broken by something other than sniffles.

Eliza Henderson had been down to the Kearney house once, on that first day. She was taking it very badly too and the confused state of her mind only made things worse, much worse. At times she thought it was Matthew was after being shot; other times she talked about it as if it was her husband James who lay in that coffin. It was very difficult to listen to her or talk to her, so muddled was her thinking at that time.

"This will only make her dote all the quicker," I overheard Samuel Bond say to another neighbour.

Anthony spoke quietly to me the day before the funeral.

"I think that Monica needs to go up to speak to Eliza in her own house. It would be good for her to get away out of here for an hour, do you not think?"

"You might be right," I said.

"The thing is, she will not go on her own. Would you go up with her?"

This was something I was not keen to be doing but he talked me into it. On that second morning after the shooting he told me that Matthew was to be away at the police station making a statement and answering questions. He would not be at home at all. Tam Glenn had volunteered to go with him, to give whatever evidence he could to try to explain the situation to the authorities, I suppose. The fact that my boss would not be there made up my mind for me and I went with Joe's mother, a slow, dejected walk, to the Henderson house.

It was hard enough for both of us to walk through that street and see the spot that still bore the bloodstains of Joe's killing, despite the best efforts of whoever had tried to scrub them away. You could not help but notice the dark of his blood between the cobblestones; now, a couple of days since it had flowed fresh and warm on my fingers, it was the same browny colour as the Rhode-Island Red hens that were pecking grain nearby. I shooed them away from the sacred spot and we arrived at Henderson's back door.

Mrs Henderson received us well enough but at times that blank, far-away look in her eyes told me that she was not quite sure what we were doing there. There was no sign of the twins and I was glad of that. I do not know who had taken them out of the situation but it was likely just as well. It was no place for children. Monica sat and held Eliza's hand and both women cried a lot.

I left them to go upstairs to my attic room, mainly to get my bundle, for I knew that I had no intention of ever sleeping in that bed again. I pushed open the door into the attic. I was surprised to see that the fiddle he had given me was lying neatly on the centre of the bed, almost as if it was resting peacefully. I can only imagine that he had been in there and had carefully made the bed and laid out the fiddle on top of it, as you would a sleeping baby. He even had the bow laid out across the strings, like some sort of feeble crucifix.

For some reason I reacted very badly to this strange sight. I picked up the fiddle and a fit of madness came over me, a wave of regret and resentment, against it and against him.

"*Scrios Dé air*", I screamed at it. "Damn him! Damn him and damn you!"

I threw it at the wall. It clattered to the floor with a twang. The twang faded and it lay still and silent. I stared at it and it seemed to stare up at me, a pathetic air of hurt about it.

I was annoyed at myself for it. I had never treated a musical instrument with any disrespect in the whole of my life. It was not in my character to be doing something like that.

"I am sorry," I said to it. "It is not your fault."

A part of me wanted to say sorry to him too, for he had been generous enough in giving it to me all those weeks ago. Now I had taken out my hurt and anger on an innocent fiddle, I knew that, and I was disgusted at what I saw in myself.

I picked it up from the floor and examined it. Apart from a bit of a dint to the underside it was not damaged too badly. The bridge had been knocked out of place. That and one broken string, the E. It could have been worse. I reset the bridge and tuned the other strings up to where they should have been but, without the tension of the missing one, the other three would not keep their pitch. I set it back on the bed.

I stuffed my belongings quickly into my hessian bag. The only item I took the time to fold neatly was the dress I had made for the ceili. I was not sure what I would be doing with it but it would not be me would be wearing it in the future, that was for sure.

'I could pass it on to Kate Kearney maybe,' I thought.

I picked up my belongings and left the room without a backward glance. Only when I was passing his bedroom on the way down the stairs did I feel any twinge of regret. I went in and stood by his bed for a second, the stale smell of his tangled bedclothes in my nostrils.

"You poor man," I whispered. "You poor, strange, pitiful man. If only..."

When I returned to the kitchen Monica was on her feet, ready to take her leave of Mrs Henderson. It was only as we walked out the lane that she reached me a small envelope.

"That's your wage," she said. "It's five pounds, I believe. Eliza had it ready for you. She may be doting but she had enough of her wits about her to know that you would hardly be back in her house and that you needed your money. Either that or it was Matthew's doing. You'd better check on it and make sure it's right."

I did, but I was thinking, 'She is wrong. It's not five pounds. We agreed on four pounds and ten shillings.' Sure enough, though, when I opened the envelope there were five single pound notes in it. I would have loved to know how that had happened. Was it Mrs Henderson's mistake, maybe on account of her memory? Or was himself so confused and distraught in the wake of all these terrible events that he forgot the agreed amount and put the five pounds in for me? Either way I was not in a mood for going back to the house to straighten it out. I had worked my hardest and I had got every last penny and more out of that job to take home to my own folk.

I left Lismore, or Gortnagappel, to be exact, the day after Joe's funeral. He was buried in St Patrick's graveyard. Most people said it was one of the biggest funerals ever seen in the town.

Some local men helped carry the coffin with Anthony, Samuel Bond included. His extra height tipped the weight of the thing down onto the grieving man's shoulder beside him. With Anthony's limp slowing him up it was a very slow procession up the lane, the arms of the two neighbours pulling them solidly together. It must have been very hard for Joe's father, that walk.

I even saw John Sproule in the crowd and I noticed that he carried the coffin too. Maybe that should not have been a surprise to me; looking at his face as he shook hands with Anthony and Monica, I did see that he had deep sorrow in him over what had happened to Joe.

'Fair play to him,' I thought. 'He is a person the same as the rest of us at a time like this.'

It was not the done thing for the women of the house to walk behind the coffin with their men but Monica could not bring herself to let the cortege out of her sight, and who could blame her. She gathered Mary, Kate, Rosie, Seamus and Hughie to her and followed the dark suits of the men, arms draped around each other's shoulders. It was a moving sight.

I wandered along behind, feeling very alone and desperately sad. There was hardly a word said; neighbours who would usually have been chatting about the weather or whatever they were doing on their farms shuffled along in silence. Heads down, we all followed behind the person in front of us. Hemmed in by the solemn stone ditches, we moved out the lane like a shoal of young fish in a narrow rock-pool. All you could hear was the cooing of pigeons in the trees across on the fort. Not a crow to be seen or heard, which was good. It was as if they knew to take their noisy crawing elsewhere for the day; in their place the pigeons were sympathising in their own quiet, keening kind of way.

We reached the road and turned right towards Castlederg. I thought the family might stop but they continued their slow walk along the road towards Henderson's lane-end. As we reached it I could not help myself and I looked away over the field to the front of the farmhouse. I don't know what I expected to see but what I am fairly sure that I did see was the tall figure of Matthew Henderson framed in the upstairs window of his mother's bedroom and him staring out at the funeral of his friend. As I looked I could swear that he saw me and moved back into the shadows of the room.

It would be the last time I set eyes on him and my heart groaned under the weight of so many deep emotions that I had experienced in those months with him.

The next morning, after a long parting from Monica and her children, I got up into Kearney's trap. Anthony was hunched at the reins, Kate cuddled up beside him, looking very sorry for herself. We met Tam on the road at the end of their lane. He had been waiting for us.

"Stop a minute," I told Anthony and I got back down to say my goodbyes to Tam.

"I hope you'll take more away with you than just a sad tune," he said.

"What else is there?" I said.

"The happy ones need the sad ones to dance on," he said.

"Maybe you are right," I said.

"What about the fiddle?"

"I left it to him," I said. "I have one at home."

I did not have the heart to tell him what I had done with it.

"You were right, I did bring them trouble," I said. He looked puzzled for a second. Then he remembered and smiled.

"Ah, the poem. I thought you must have found it."

"I did....and I took it. I didn't want *an máistir* finding it," I told him, more bitterness in my tone than I meant to show.
"Agh now girl, dinnae be o'er hard on him. It will only eat you up," he said.
Then he hugged me so tightly and stroked my hair.
"Ah, Sally Anne," he said, "if only I had been twenty years younger there would have been nae need for you to bother with Matthew Henderson."
"Twenty years younger?" I said. "Maybe thirty or forty, Tam; not twenty. Give me some credit!"
"Away wie ye," he said.
Away I went but I had the smell of him on me for miles.
Joe's father and Kate took me all the way to Lifford station. All three of us shed tears as we parted. I promised to keep in touch by letter. All three of us knew that I probably would not.
From the window of the train I watched Tyrone disappear behind the bushes alongside the track. I half hoped that was the last I would see of it.
I was making for home.

Epilogue

1945

Matthew Henderson

What am I to do about this letter?
I have done nothing but think about it since the postman rode into my yard with it this morning. It has me near demented. I must have read it ten times in the course of the day and I got no work redd up on account of it.
What an odd thing, a letter from her. I could not believe my eyes when I opened it. Even now as I sit here in the kitchen at the end of the day...it is the oddest thing ever.
Why, in the name of all that's sacred, would she write to me? Why now, after all this time? She wonders if I remember her? How in God's name could I forget? It's not as if I haven't tried.
Here she is back to haunt me again. I can see her with that wee, tempting half-smile; I can nearly smell her off these pages that seem stuck to my fingers. Since Millie went to bed tonight they haven't been out of my hands.
Sally Anne, from all that time ago! I can hardly believe it. Amazing! And what a letter to be getting!

Ranahuel
Kincasslagh
Co Donegal
22nd June 1945

Dear Matthew,
It is a strange thing to be writing to somebody that I used to know and who might no longer be alive, for all I know.

Believe me, it is even stranger to be sitting here reading it....and I am very much alive.

You likely have no memory of me and I could not blame you if that is the truth.

No memory of you? Are you daft altogether, woman? How could I ever forget? And, if I do forget, one look up at the corner of this kitchen reminds me, for hanging there beside the window is my father's fiddle with a wee dint in it and three of its strings still in place, just the one hanging loose. I well remember the last person to play it and I wonder what made her damage it the way she did before she upped and left us, half a life-time ago.

I was hired on your farm twenty three years ago, in the year that disaster struck your friend, Joe Kearney, God rest him. At the same time, I am thinking, how could any of us not remember that night?

How indeed? There's not a day passes when I don't remember. I am sitting looking over at the old grandfather clock here; its hands are stuck and haven't moved in years. If only we could turn them back to some time that autumn, some time before everything changed, and live again in those days of glory. How many times have I wished and prayed for the chance to do it all again...relive it and change everything that went wrong in those last couple of weeks of that season? I know it is a hopeless fantasy but whiles I let my imagination take me to how it might have been, and how I wish it had been. I can dream those dreams for hours on end during a lonely winter evening here by this hearth; it is one of the only pleasures I have left to me, those lovely, impossible dreams.

You are probably wondering why you are getting a letter from me after all this time. Well, I am sailing to America in a couple of weeks and I just felt the need to tell you. That and some other things.

'Sailing to America'? What would she want to be doing that for? What about her folks, her mother and all? Seems a very stupid thing to be doing, too drastic an action. We are just coming out of a war, America too. Everything is in chaos. Has she no sense? What will she do when she gets there? Like, it's not as if she has much education behind her or anything; no great skills or talents, apart from just the way she is in herself...sparky and friendly and ready for anything. She was always very confident, she knew her own mind and had her own way of seeing things. But America? A big place like that? And her a single girl still?

That was the first thing I noticed when my eyes fell to the bottom of this page and I read her signature; 'Sally Anne Sweeney'. So she never got round to marrying, did she? I wonder why that was, for in my opinion....ah, God what am I thinking? Catch yourself on Matthew Henderson; you're an oul done farmer!

But why does she feel she has to be telling me? 'I just felt the need to tell you'. What is that about? It's not as if a word has passed between us since...since that night she is talking about, not a word. Not even a 'Goodbye'.

I resented that for a long time. It wasn't as if I had abused her or been rough with her. Truth be told, my opinion of the matter was that I had acted honourably towards her for much of the time she was here. Aye, we were close, of-course we were... goodness, we were courting, weren't we, but I never forced myself on her. I never took advantage of her when there's manys another man in my position then that wouldn't have had a second thought about going in and having his way with her every night that she lay in our attic. I tried my best to be decent to her...as I understood it, and that came from how I felt about her as a person. She was the soul of goodness, so she was, right up until whatever soured our relationship towards the end.

You know, I would love the chance to try and explain that to her, just to see if...

I often wonder what became of you. It was a very tough time that you went through.

What became of me? If I started writing back to her now to answer that one I wouldn't be finished before Christmas. I suppose she means what happened about the shooting. Was I charged or anything? Nothing happened. That's not how things are done in our wee country. I talked to the police and they understood that it was a case of mistaken identity....which was nothing less than the truth. There were no charges; to be honest I had mixed feelings about that at the time. Of-course I felt guilty. Of-course it was a tragic mistake. Of-course I carried that around on my back for years, the feeling that I should be punished in some way for the killing of my best friend...for that is what Joe Kearney was, even if we had fallen out a bit at the time. But his folk wanted it no other way; when the RUC spoke to his father, that is what he said. I remember well what they told me; Anthony would not

hear tell of anything else. "Matthew has suffered enough. He meant no harm to our Joe. He thought he was defending himself."
That did not stop me feeling as if I would be punished by bad luck in my life; cursed or whatever you want to call it. That is why when Alice Porter ran away with her 'commercial traveller', six weeks before we were due to be married in Castlederg Methodist Church, I accepted it as part of my punishment...sort of like Divine justice on me.
John Sproule thought he was being a big help to me then. "She was never cut out to be a farmer's wife," he told me. "You'd have had nothing but bother with her. Can you imagine her milking the cows, or cleaning the pig-house or gathering spuds?"
He meant well. Of-course I couldn't imagine Alice doing such things...but I could imagine another girl milking, gathering spuds, carrying feed around the yard...and so I went looking for the newspaper photograph, the day we got the binder going for the first time, her standing beside my horses and me up on the back of the machine. She should have been the one, and the truth of it pained me more, I think, than the flight of the faithless Alice. I have that photo yet; Sally Anne standing there with a grin on her like a Halloween turnip, proud as punch. Now that I think about it, that picture had lain in the bottom of a drawer for ages, until Alice took off and left me, and I brought it back out, got it framed and set it on the windowsill where it stands yet. Millie lifts it and stares at it every time she dusts the place. "Poor Sawey Anne," she always says.

I feel bad now that I did not stay to help you in it. I cut myself off and would not even talk to you when you needed help, because of how I felt after what happened between us. I suppose I was carrying a big hurt but that is no excuse. So that is another reason for me writing to you now, to say sorry that I left you in the middle of it all, sorry that I never even came to bid you goodbye and thank you for the work and for the times you were kind to me.

I have to say that, when I read this bit the first time this morning, a tear welled up in my eye; that's no word of a lie. I just thought, 'What a lovely, decent human being she was! What a lovely person....and how did I ever come to hurt her the way I did?
What was that word she used to always say.... *'Galantá'* or something? Lord but I haven't thought of that in years....but it's still there.

What sort of a young fool was I that I let the greatest love of my life wither before my eyes and couldn't come up with a way of bringing her back?
Yet here she is asking for my forgiveness, like she was the one who had wronged me? Aye, I know she did shut me out and, as she says, she left me in the middle of it all when I needed her the most, but I can understand why she couldn't bear the sight of me after that night; especially after poor Joe...

Over the years I have often thought that, if the truth be told, it was as much my fault as yours that Joe died. If I had not persuaded him to go to your aid that night the tragedy would never have happened. You would not have had to be carrying such a terrible burden for the rest of your life. I am sorry for that; not for encouraging him to help his old friend but for letting all the blame of it fall on your shoulders.

Dear God in Heaven! What a girl she was. What happiness I have denied myself in this tight wee life of mine.

It would be great if we could only remember the good times. If there had only been the good times, who knows, I might be still around Lismore. But it seems to me now, looking back on it, that those terrible things that happened were somehow out of our control. We were just like characters in the play that was written for us and we could not change the course of those events.

Strangely I have often wondered that myself. I understand what she means...that things were in some way beyond us, that we had little say in how it all happened. We were just the pawns in a game that was being played at the time, pushed around by other people and turned away from doing what was in our instincts to be doing. If my sad, deluded cousin hadn't arrived into the middle of our relationship when she did how would things have turned out? Aye, Sally Anne, you are right...you might still be around Lismore, instead of me sitting here reading your letter with this strange lump in my throat and my heart fluttering in my chest like a bird against a window, oul fool that I am.
But I cannot believe that that was how it was meant to be. Joe could never have been meant to die like that, at the hands of his friend and neighbour...and him only coming to try to help. No God could be cruel enough to write that story for us and manipulate us into acting it out for his pleasure, surely not? And if it wasn't in the plan of God for us,

like I say, if there was some other plan that we missed and messed up through my stupidity...then what was that other plan supposed to have been? I have often wondered about that question.
I can't believe we are puppets. We made our decisions, or at least I made my decisions...of my own free will. I say my own free will but I know I am arguing against myself here. I felt pushed into things, things like that night at the ceili when I could have danced with Sally Anne but chose to stand on my dignity and please Victoria instead. Was that my own free will? Agh, I don't know what I think about that.
She has made the decision to go to America. Her own choice, a daft one to my mind. It will not be much like her beloved Donegal; she will not hear much Irish over there, will she? I can't imagine what has influenced her to want to do that. Has she anything to be going to, a job or a contact? She doesn't say. I would worry about her setting out to a place like America. I don't know much about it of-course, just what I've read in the papers, that and what I have seen of their servicemen that were stationed here during the past few years. And, if they are anything to be judging by, my opinion of it is that she would be far safer staying at home.
I wonder would she change her mind? What if this is another wrong choice and she only exchanges one sorry set of circumstances for another? What if I could stop her going and maybe save her life, for all either of us know? I ruined her happiness once...maybe it's time to try to make amends. Maybe that is what I am meant to do; maybe, whether I am 'meant' to do it or not, it is the right thing to do, or at least to try to do?

I often wonder if you had not met that Englishman might Joe still be alive today. If he had not taken his father's gun to carry for him that night, you might have seen the shape of him rather than the glint of the gun in his hands.

Ah, how right you are, girl. The 'shape of him rather than the glint of the gun'! I wish I had seen the shape of him, indeed I do. The gun was what killed him, both the one in my hands and the one in his. Would to God that Stanley had never entered my yard; would to God I had not listened to his advice about needing a weapon! I'm sure Victoria wishes manys a time that she had never set eyes on him either, her having to rear a handicapped boy on her own and him born out of wedlock. The boul Stanley wasn't long in hoofing it back to England when she told him she was in the family way. That was brave of him, the lousy bastard that he was. He left a trail of damage behind him.

I will never forget the details of that night. In particular I can still see you and Anthony walking, so slowly, inch by inch, across the street towards us, you in your suit and tie and the grief in you twisting your white face. It is an image that is stuck in my mind and I wish I could shift it. I have often wondered what made you change into your Sunday clothes to come down to look at poor Joe.

Goodness but she does have a great memory! I had forgotten that, the bit about the suit I was wearing. When I read this letter the first time this morning it took me a minute to straighten out in my head why I had a suit on....then I remembered and I shook my head in amazement at how close things might have been to a nice conclusion to everything that night, and how it all went wrong, so tragically wrong.

When I read that this morning I wanted to tell her; I wanted to shout it across the miles, over the Donegal bogs and mountains, all the way to wherever she lives in this Ranahuel place; 'I put on a suit to ask you to marry me, Sally Anne Sweeney! And I meant it; I would have married you and, my good Lord, how happy we could have made each other. If only, if only...if only I hadn't been such a buck eejit; if only you had made it back here before Joe did and warned me that he was coming up the back lane! A matter of minutes, seconds even, would have made the difference, a matter of a few yards; I would never have fired a shot; he would have been alright; him and me could have shook hands and let bygones be bygones; Anthony would have stood and looked at us and smiled over a cup of tea and, above all, I could have taken your hand and said sorry and told you that I loved you above anything in the world and I wanted you to stay and marry me and the devil take anybody who tried to stop us!'

That is what I wanted to do this morning and now, after a day's thinking about it, I still want to do it. This evening I feel like climbing the hill behind us here, up to the bog where it is so lovely and quiet... and shouting it to the west at the top of my voice and hope that the sense of it will somehow be carried to her soul on the pure night air.

But let me read on here.

And I have often wondered what became of you after that night? I wonder did you ever get married yourself. I wonder about the twins and your poor mother. How did

Anthony and Monica get over the death? And old Tam. Is he dead or alive? He thought a lot of you. I recall him telling me not to be too hard on you. I still sometimes wonder if he really had heard what he said he heard or if that tale was just a silly old drunken nightmare of his. Maybe there was no plot at all. If that was so it would make Joe's death all the more tragic. No, nothing could have made it any more tragic, I am thinking.
I hope this letter finds you and, if it does, that you are in good health.
Yours sincerely,
Your old hired hand,
Sally Anne Sweeney

I have to tell her.
I could find an old writing pad somewhere in this kitchen, I know I could, but what is the point of that? I could come up with a few words to spread over these wounded years like some kind of soothing ointment. I could tell her about my mother's death ten years ago, a pathetic sinking into nothingness with barely a word to any of us in her last year or two. I could tell her of Jane's happy match with a farmer in Drumquin and her wee flock of children, every one a picture of their mother, as if one twin wasn't enough. I could tell her of the Kearneys, and how our Millie cares for them every day as they stiffen up into the frailty of old age. No man alive could have asked for better neighbours than them and I am proud of Millie for looking after them. Even Joe's sister Mary came back into the fold after Joe's death; she visits them often and I recall that she was able to tell us from her connections that the 'B' Specials had been out that fateful night and Duggan had had to abandon the operation and make a run for it across the border. Poor Joe died for nothing. Of-course he died for nothing!
She asks about Tam Glenn; so typical of her nature to do that....they were great friends. I could tell her that her old pal continued to wander the roads and play his tunes until he had a stroke; I got word that he was in Lifford Hospital and I travelled up to see him several times before he died. I could tell her that one of the last things he said to me was, "Did you ever think, son, that you should take yourself away into Donegal and try and find that wee fiddle player and make your peace with her?" (And that would be the God's honest truth I would be telling her...those were his very words.)
I could write all these things in a letter;
I could maybe even post it;

Or I could put it in the fire;
Or I could do nothing; let the hare sit.
That is my dilemma...what to do?
This is a lonely house. Millie is a good girl but she has never been the best of company. No chat from her at all. I spend almost every evening in the same routine of reading the paper and lonely hearth-gazing. I seldom even play a game of draughts now with John Sproule, since he took to going to mission meetings with the Bonds. My farm is in good enough shape, I suppose, but I haven't the same joy in working it as I used to have.
Time has slipped away on me and the old ghosts of the past whisper to me from every corner of the place; especially when I sit at this table and look up at my father's sorry fiddle hanging there in its coat of soot and grease and dust. I wonder can I have a go at fixing it up tonight, maybe mend that broken string and give the wood a good clean and a bit of a polish. Aye, that is what I will do; I will have a go at it later.
First, though, I would need to go down and ask John if he would be fit to do the milking for me tomorrow night. He's turned out a right obliging sort, so he has, but I will not be telling him my plan...just in case.
And I would need to check the amount of petrol in the motor car. With this war-rationing still on I'll maybe call in with the Bonds and see if they could lend me a can with a few gallons in it. You wouldn't want to run out on some of those wee roads in the middle of a Donegal bog. That would be another twist of fate.
But even then, I could always walk the rest of the way, the fiddle under my arm, like oul Tam would have done.
I'll not be beat this time.

About the author

David Dunlop was born and raised in County Antrim, N Ireland. He spent many years in education, both as a teacher and as a school leader; in those roles he exercised his passion to bring together young people from across Ireland's various divides so as to encourage a shared understanding of history and culture. To that end he wrote and directed several stage musicals with historical and cross-cultural themes and which drew on his experience of various musical genre.

His first novel was published in 2014. "Oileán na Márbh - Island of the Dead", (also available on Amazon), was set in west Donegal in 1897. "The Broken Fiddle", whilst not exactly a sequel, is a connected historical novel; set in the troubled Irish border country of 1922, the story has strong Co. Donegal and Co. Tyrone connections. The text draws richly on the language and dialect differences of these areas.

David currently lives in west Donegal with his wife, Mary.